THE HYPNOTIST

Lars Kepler is a No.1 bestselling international sensation, whose Joona Linna thrillers have sold more than 10 million copies in 40 languages. The first book in the series, *The Hypnotist*, was selected for the 2012 Richard and Judy Book Club and the most recent, *Stalker*, went straight to No.1 in Sweden, Norway, Holland and Slovakia.

Lars Kepler is the pseudonym for writing duo, Alexander and Alexandra Ahndoril. They live with their family in Sweden.

Facebook.com/larskepler

www.larskepler.com

Also by Lars Kepler

The Hypnotist
The Nightmare
The Fire Witness
The Sandman
Stalker

Like fire, just like fire. Those were the first words the hypnotised teenage boy spoke. Even though he had life-threatening injuries – hundreds of cuts to his face, legs, torso, back, the soles of his feet, and on his neck and the back of his head – he had been put into a state of deep hypnosis in the hope that he would be able to describe what he had seen.

'I'm trying to blink,' he muttered. 'I'm going into the kitchen, but it's not right, there's lots of crackling between the chairs and bright red fire spreading across the floor.'

The policeman who found him among the other bodies in the terraced house thought he was dead. The boy had lost a lot of blood. He had gone into a state of shock and had not regained consciousness until seven hours later.

He was the only surviving witness, and Detective Joona Linna thought it likely that he could give them a good description. Whoever attacked the family had intended to kill them all, so he probably hadn't gone to any trouble to hide his face.

But if the circumstances hadn't been quite so extraordinary, no one would ever have considered calling in a hypnotist.

THE HYPNOTIST

LARS KEPLER

Translated from the Swedish by Neil Smith

HarperCollins*Publishers*

HarperCollins*Publishers*
1 London Bridge Street
London SE1 9GF

This paperback edition 2018
2

First published in Great Britain by HarperCollins*Publishers* 2011

Originally published in 2009 by Albert Bonniers Förlag, Sweden, as *Hypnotisören*

Lars Kepler assert the moral right to be identified as the author of this work

A catalogue record for this book is available from the British Library

ISBN: 978-0-00-824181-0

Typeset in Electra LT Std by Palimpsest Book Production Limited,
Falkirk, Stirlingshire

Printed and bound in Great Britain by
CPI Group (UK) Ltd, Croydon, CR0 4YY

MIX
Paper from
responsible sources
FSC™ C007454

This book is produced from independently certified FSC™ paper
to ensure responsible forest management.

For more information visit: www.harpercollins.co.uk/green

In Greek mythology, the god Hypnos is a boy with wings carrying poppy seed-heads in his hand. His name means sleep. He is the twin brother of death, and the son of night and darkness.

The term hypnosis was first coined in 1843 by the Scottish surgeon James Braid. He used it to describe a sleep-like state of both heightened awareness and extreme receptivity.

Today it has been scientifically proven that almost anyone can be hypnotised, but opinion still varies on the uses, reliability and safety of hypnosis. The lack of consensus probably stems from the fact that hypnosis has been misused by fraudsters, entertainers and secret services the world over.

In purely technical terms, it is easy to put someone in a hypnotic state. The hard part is controlling the process, guiding the patient and analysing the results. It takes great skill to manage deep hypnosis. There are only a handful of genuine expert hypnotists in the entire world who are medically competent.

1

Early morning, 8 December

Erik's phone is ringing. Before he is fully awake he says:

'Balloons and streamers.'

His heart is racing from being awakened so suddenly. Erik doesn't know why he said that. He has no idea what the dream was about.

In order not to wake Simone he creeps out of the bedroom and closes the door before he answers.

'Hello, this is Erik Maria Bark.'

A detective by the name of Joona Linna tells him that he needs his help. Erik's only half awake as he listens to the detective.

'I've heard you're good at dealing with trauma,' the detective says.

'Yes,' Erik replies simply.

He takes a paracetamol pill as he listens. The detective explains that he needs to question someone, a fifteen-year-old boy who has witnessed a double murder. The problem is that the teenager has been seriously injured. His condition is unstable. He's in a state of shock, and he hasn't yet regained consciousness.

'Who's treating him?' Erik asks.

'Daniella Richards.'

'She's highly competent, I'm sure she'll be able to . . .'

'It was her idea to call you,' the detective interrupts. 'We need your help, and we probably don't have much time.'

Erik goes back into the bedroom to get his clothes. A streetlight shines in between the blinds. Simone is lying on her back watching him with an oddly vacant expression.

'I was trying not to wake you,' he says softly.

'Who was that?' she asks.

'A police officer . . . a detective, I didn't catch his name.'

'What did he want?'

'I have to go to Karolinska,' he replies. 'They need help with a young boy.'

'What time is it, anyway?'

She looks at the alarm clock and closes her eyes. He can see the lines made by folds in the sheet across her freckled shoulders.

'Go back to sleep, Simone,' he whispers.

Erik carries his clothes out into the hallway, turns the light on and quickly gets dressed. A length of steel suddenly flashes behind him. Erik turns and sees that his son has hung his ice skates from the handle of the front door so that he won't forget them. Even though Erik is in a hurry, he goes over to the wardrobe and digs out the protective guards. He fastens them to the sharp blades, then puts them down on the hall carpet and leaves.

It's three o'clock in the morning on Tuesday, 8 December. Snow is falling slowly from the black sky. There's no wind at all, and the heavy flakes land sleepily on the deserted street. He turns the key in the ignition and a soft wave of music rolls through the car: Miles Davis, 'Kind of Blue'.

He drives the short distance through the sleeping city, down Luntmakar Street and along Sveavägen towards Norrtull. The water of Brunnsviken is a large, dark expanse beyond the snow. He drives slowly into the hospital campus, between the understaffed Astrid Lindgren Children's Hospital and the maternity ward, past the radiotherapy department and psychiatric unit, and parks in his usual spot in front of neurosurgery. The glow of the streetlights reflects off the windows of the large complex. There are hardly any cars in the car park. Blackbirds flit through the gloom around the trees, the flapping of their wings breaks the silence.

He swipes his card, taps in the six-digit code and enters the lobby, then takes the lift up to the fifth floor and walks down the hall. The fluorescent lights reflect off the blue linoleum floor, making it look like ice. Now that the initial adrenalin rush is fading, he starts to feel tired. He passes an operating room and walks past the doors to the huge hyperbaric chamber, and says hello to a nurse as he recalls what the detective told him over the phone: a teenage boy has knife-wounds all over his body. The police attempted to speak to him, but his condition deteriorated quickly.

Two uniformed police officers are standing outside the door to Ward 18. Erik can see a trace of anxiety cross their faces as he approaches. Maybe they're just tired, he thinks as he stops in front of them and shows them his ID. They glance at it and then one of them presses the button to make the door swing open.

Erik walks in and shakes hands with Daniella Richards, noting the tension in her face and stress in the way she moves.

'Grab some coffee,' she says.

'Do we have time?' Erik asks.

'I've managed to get the bleeding from his liver under control,' she replies.

A man in his mid-forties, dressed in jeans and a black jacket, is tapping the frame of the coffee machine. His blond hair is untidy, and his lips are clenched. Erik wonders if he might be Daniella's husband, Magnus. He's never met him, just seen a picture in her office.

'Is that Magnus?' Erik asks, gesturing towards the man.

'What?'

She looks both amused and surprised.

'I thought maybe Magnus had come with you.'

'No,' she laughs.

'Are you sure? Maybe I should ask him,' Erik jokes, and starts to walk towards the man.

Daniella's mobile phone rings and she's still laughing as she takes it out.

'Stop it, Erik,' she says as she answers and puts the phone to her ear. 'Yes, Daniella here.'

She listens, but can't hear anything.

'Hello?'

She waits a few seconds, then ends the call with a sarcastic 'Have a nice day,' slips the phone in her pocket and follows Erik.

He's already walked over to the blond man. The coffee machine is bubbling and wheezing.

'Have some coffee,' the man says, and tries to hand Erik a mug.

'No, thanks.'

The man tastes the coffee and smiles, revealing dimples in his cheeks.

'It's good,' he says, and tries to give Erik the mug again.

'I don't want any.'

The man drinks some more as he looks at Erik.

'Could I borrow your phone?' he suddenly asks. 'I left mine in my car.'

'You want to borrow my phone?' Erik asks.

The blond man nods and looks at him with pale eyes, grey as polished granite.

'You're welcome to borrow mine,' Daniella says.

'Thanks.'

'Don't mention it.'

The blond man takes her phone.

'I promise you'll get it back,' he says.

'You're the only person who ever calls me on it anyway,' she teases.

He laughs and moves away.

'He must be your husband,' Erik says.

'A girl can always dream,' she says, and glances at the tall man.

Daniella has been rubbing her eyes, and her silver-grey eyeliner is streaked across one cheek.

'Shall I take a look at the patient?' Erik asks.

'By all means,' she nods.

'Seeing as I'm here,' he quickly adds.

'Erik, I'd love to hear what you think. I'm not sure about this one.'

2

Tuesday, early morning, 8 December

Daniella Richards opens the heavy, silent door and he follows her into a very warm room next to the operating theatre. A thin boy is lying on the bed. Two nurses are tending to his wounds. He has stab-wounds all over his body. On the soles of his feet, on his chest and stomach, the back of his neck, on his scalp, his face and hands.

His pulse is shallow but very fast. His lips are pale grey, he's sweating and his eyes are tightly closed. His nose looks like it's broken, and he's suffering from subcutaneous bleeding, spreading in a dark cloud across his throat and chest.

Erik notes that the boy's face, despite his injuries, is beautiful.

Daniella is quietly giving an account of how the boy's readings have changed, when a sudden knock silences her. It's the blond man again. He waves at them through the window in the door.

Erik and Daniella exchange a glance and leave the treatment room. The blond man is standing beside the wheezing coffee machine again.

'A large cappuccino,' he says to Erik. 'You might need one before you meet the police officer who found the boy.'

Only now does Erik realise that the blond man is the detective, whose call awakened him. His Finnish accent hadn't been so pronounced over the phone, or Erik had just been too sleepy to register it. Erik recalls that his name is Joona Linna.

'Why would I want to meet the police officer who found him?' Erik asks.

'To understand why I need to question . . .'

Joona stops talking when Daniella's phone rings. He pulls it out from his jacket pocket, ignores her outstretched hand and looks at the screen.

'It's for me,' Joona says, and takes the call. 'Yes . . . No, I want him here. I don't give a damn about that.'

The detective smiles as he listens to his colleague's objections on the other end of the line.

'But I've found something,' Joona replies.

The other person shouts something.

'I'm going to do it my way,' Joona says calmly, and ends the call.

He hands the phone back to Daniella and thanks her.

'I need to question the patient,' he says seriously.

'I'm afraid not,' Erik says. 'I agree with Dr Richards.'

'When will he be able to speak to me?' Joona asks.

'Not while he's still in shock.'

'I knew you were going to say that,' Joona replies in a low voice.

'His condition is still critical,' Daniella explains. 'His pleural cavity has been injured, as well as his small intestine, liver, and . . .'

A man in a grimy police uniform comes in. He looks worried. Joona goes over and shakes his hand. The officer says something quietly to Joona, then wipes his mouth and looks at the doctors. The detective reassures the police officer that it's OK to talk, and that under the circumstances, it could be a great help to them.

'Well,' the police officer says, and clears his throat slightly. 'We heard over the radio that a cleaner had found a dead man in the bathroom at the football field in Tumba. And we were already in the car on Huddingevägen, we took the call. Janne, my partner, he went in while I was talking to the cleaner. At first we thought we were dealing with an overdose, but I soon realised something else was going on. Janne came out of the locker room, his face was really pale, and he didn't want to let me past. "A hell of a lot of blood" – he said that three times, and then he sat down on the steps and . . .'

The policeman trails off, sits down on a chair and stares ahead of him.

'Do you want to go on?' Joona asks.

'Yes . . . so the ambulance arrived and the dead man was identified, and I was charged with telling the family. We're a bit short-staffed, so I had to go on my own. My boss basically said she didn't want to send Janne while he was in that state. That was understandable.'

Erik looks at his watch.

'You've got to listen to this,' Joona tells him in his soothing Finnish accent.

'The deceased,' the policeman goes on, looking down at the floor. 'He was a teacher at Tumba High School, lived in those new houses up on the hill. I rang the doorbell a few times, but no one came to the door. I had a bad feeling, so I went around to the back and shone my torch through one of the windows.'

The policeman stops speaking. His mouth is trembling and he starts scratching the arm of the chair with his thumbnail.

'Please, go on,' Joona says.

'Do I have to? Because I . . . I . . .'

'You found the fifteen-year-old boy, his mother, and a five-year-old girl. The boy was the only one who was still alive.'

'Although I thought . . . I . . .'

He stops talking. His face has drained of all colour.

'Thanks for coming, Erland,' Joona says.

The officer nods quickly and stands up, rubs his hand nervously over his dirty jacket and leaves the room.

'They'd all been slashed, horribly injured,' Joona says to Erik and Daniella. 'It was a frenzied attack – they'd been kicked, beaten, stabbed, and the little girl . . . she was cut in two. Her legs and bottom half were lying on the sofa in front of the television, and . . .'

He stops and looks at Erik before going on.

'It looks as if the killer knew the father was going to be at the field,' Joona goes on. 'There was a football match. He was the referee. The killer waited until he was alone before murdering him, then started to dismember him, very aggressively, before going to the house and killing his family.'

'It happened in that order?' Erik asks.

'As I understand it, yes,' the detective says.

Erik feels his hand trembling as he wipes his mouth. Father, mother, son, daughter, he thinks slowly to himself, then looks Joona in the eye.

'The killer wanted to eradicate an entire family,' Erik concludes in a faltering voice.

Joona gives a non-committal shrug.

'The eldest daughter is still missing. Twenty-three years old. We can't find her. We're assuming it's highly likely that the killer is after her as well. That's why we want to talk to the witness as soon as we possibly can.'

'I'll conduct a more thorough examination,' Erik says.

'Thanks,' Joona nods.

'But we can't risk the patient's life.'

'I understand,' Joona says. 'But the more time that passes, the longer the killer has to look for the daughter.'

'You can investigate the crime scenes, can't you?' Daniella says.

'Already underway,' he replies, 'but we're not going to find anything useful there.'

'What do you mean?'

'We're going to find a mixture of DNA from hundreds of people at the crime scenes.'

'I'll go in and see the patient at once,' Erik says.

Joona looks him in the eye and nods:

'If I can just ask him a couple of questions, that might be all it takes to save his sister.'

3

Tuesday, early morning, 8 December

Erik goes back to the patient's room. He stands in front of the bed, looking at the victim's pale, scarred face. He's breathing very shallowly. His lips look frozen. Erik says his name, and his face seems to wince slightly in pain.

'Josef,' he repeats quietly. 'My name is Erik Maria Bark, I'm a doctor, and I'm going to examine you. Feel free to nod if you understand what I'm saying.'

The boy lies perfectly still, his stomach rising and falling shallowly with each breath, but Erik is certain that the boy understood what he said.

When Erik leaves the room a half hour later Daniella and the detective look at him.

'Is he going to be OK?' Joona asks.

'It's too early to say, but he . . .'

'That boy is our only witness,' he says again. 'Someone has killed his father, his mother and his little sister, and we can only assume that the murderer is going to try to kill his older sister as well.'

'We know that,' Daniella says. 'But shouldn't the police be looking for her instead of getting in our way?'

'We are looking, but we haven't found anything to go on. We

need to talk to the boy, because he can probably provide a description of the killer.'

'It could take weeks before the boy can be questioned,' Erik says. 'We can't just shake him until he wakes up.'

'But under hypnosis,' Joona says.

Silence settles on the room. Erik thinks about the snow that was falling over Brunnsviken when he was driving here. Drifting down between the trees over the dark water.

'No,' he whispers to himself.

'Wouldn't hypnosis work?'

'I don't know,' Erik replies.

'I've got a very good memory for faces,' Joona says. 'You're a famous hypnotist, you could . . .'

'I was a fraud,' Erik says, cutting him off.

'That's not what I think,' Joona says. 'And this is an emergency.'

Daniella's cheeks turn red and she looks down at the floor.

'I can't,' Erik says.

'I'm the one who's responsible for the patient's wellbeing,' Daniella says, raising her voice. 'And I'm not particularly inclined to permit hypnosis.'

'What if you came to the conclusion that it wouldn't harm your patient?' Joona asks.

Erik realises that the detective had been considering hypnosis as a possible solution right from the start. This isn't just a spur-of-the-moment suggestion. Joona asked him to come to the hospital with the sole intention of trying to persuade him to hypnotise the boy, and not for his expertise in the treatment of shock and trauma.

'I promised myself that I'd never get involved with hypnosis again,' Erik says.

'OK, I understand,' Joona says. 'I'd heard that you were the best, but what the hell, I have to respect your decision.'

'I'm sorry,' Erik says.

He looks at the patient through the window and then turns to Daniella.

'Has he been given desmopressin?'

'No, I've been holding back on that,' she replies.

'Why?'

'The risk of thromboembolic complications.'

'I've been following that debate, and I don't think that's a concern. I'm still giving my son desmopressin,' Erik says.

Joona gets slowly to his feet.

'I'd be grateful if you could recommend another hypnotist,' he says.

'We don't even know if the patient is going to regain consciousness,' Daniella replies.

'I'm assuming . . .'

'And surely he needs to be conscious in order to be hypnotised,' she concludes. The corners of her mouth twitch slightly.

'He was listening when Erik spoke to him,' Joona says.

'I don't think so,' she mutters.

'Yes, he heard me,' Erik says.

'We could still save his sister's life,' Joona goes on.

'I'm going home now,' Erik says quietly. 'Give the patient desmopressin, and consider using the hyperbaric chamber.'

He leaves the room and takes off his lab coat as he walks down the hallway and gets in the lift. There are more people in the lobby now. The doors are no longer locked, and the sky is a little brighter. As his car pulls out of the car park, Erik reaches for the little wooden box he keeps in the glove-compartment. Without taking his eyes off the road, he opens the lid with the colourful parrot on it, digs out three pills and quickly swallows them. He has to get at least a couple of hours' sleep this morning before he needs to wake Benjamin and give him his injection.

4

Monday evening, 7 December

Seven and a half hours earlier a cleaner by the name of Karim Muhammed arrives at the Rödstuhage gym. It is 8:50 in the evening, and cleaning the locker rooms is his last job of the day.

He leaves his Volkswagen van in the car park, not far from a red Toyota. The tall floodlights around the football field are switched off, but the lights are still on in the locker rooms.

When he reaches the low wooden building and tries to turn the key in the lock to the men's locker room, he discovers that it is already unlocked. He knocks but there is no answer, so he opens the door and sees the blood on the floor.

When police officers Jan Eriksson and Erland Björkander arrive at the scene, Eriksson goes straight to the locker room, leaving Björkander to question the cleaner.

At first, Eriksson thinks he hears a noise and rushes in, thinking the victim might still be alive. When he turns the man over he realises that's impossible. The body is mutilated, the right arm is missing and the chest is so severely damaged it looks like a bloody crater. The ambulance arrives and, shortly after it, so does Police Inspector Lillemor Blom. A wallet left at the scene identifies the victim as Anders Ek, a chemistry and physics teacher at Tumba High School. Records indicate he is married to a Katja Ek, who works at Huddinge Central Library. They live in a terraced house at 8 Gärdesvägen and have two children still living at home, Lisa and Josef.

Detective Blom instructs Officer Björkander to go and talk to the victim's family on his own while she takes care of Jan Eriksson's report and supervises the cordoning off of the crime scene.

Björkander arrives at the house in Tumba, and rings the doorbell. When there's no answer he walks around to the back of the building and shines his torch through a window. The first thing he sees is a large smear of blood on the carpet in the living room, and a child's pair of glasses in the doorway. It looks as though someone was dragged through the living room and out the front door. Björkander forces the back door open and goes in with his pistol drawn. He searches the house, finds the three victims, and radios for immediate assistance from police and paramedics. He doesn't realise that the boy is still alive.

'Oh God, they've been slaughtered, the children have been slaughtered . . . I don't know what to do, I'm on my own and they're all dead.'

5

Monday evening, 7 December

It's 10:10 pm, and Joona Linna is sitting in his car on Drottningholmsvägen when he hears the call. A police constable is yelling that the children have been killed, that he's alone in the house, that the mother is dead, that they're all dead. A little while later the man is radioing from outside the house, and, calmer now, he explains that Detective Blom sent him to the house on Gärdesvägen on his own. Björkander breaks off abruptly, mutters something about using the wrong channel, and then vanishes.

The windshield-wipers brush a few drops of rain from the glass. As Joona drives slowly past Kristineberg he finds himself thinking about how his father was killed in the line of duty when his back-up failed to show. Joona pulls over to the side of the road near Stefan School, annoyed at the lack of leadership out in Tumba. No police officer should have to go on a job like that alone. He sighs, picks up his phone and asks to be put through to Lillemor Blom.

Lillemor was at the Police Academy at the same time as Joona. After their training she married a colleague from Surveillance named Jerker Lundkvist. Two years later they had a son, Daniel. Jerker chose not to take his paid paternity leave, even though he was entitled to it. His choice cost the family money, and delayed Lillemor's career. Jerker left her for a younger officer who had just finished her training, and Joona has heard that he only sees his son once a fortnight.

Joona says his name when Lillemor answers, and hurries through the pleasantries before telling her what he heard over the radio.

'We're short of people, Joona,' she explains. 'And in my considered opinion, there was . . .'

'That doesn't matter,' he interrupts. 'Your considered opinion was wrong.'

'You don't want to listen,' she says.

'I do, but . . .'

'So listen, then!'

'You can't send him to a crime scene on his own,' Joona continues.

'Are you done?'

After a brief silence Lillemor Blom explains that Björkander was asked to inform the family of their loss, and he took it upon himself to break in through the back door. Joona tells her she did the right thing, and apologises several times. He then asks – mostly out of politeness – what actually happened out in Tumba.

Lillemor tells him what Officer Björkander said about the knives and cutlery lying in a pool of blood on the kitchen floor, the girl's glasses, the trail of blood, the handprints, and the positions of the bodies and body parts in the house. She then goes on to explain that Anders Ek is known to Social Services because of his gambling addiction. He's been borrowing money from loan sharks in the area. Now a debt collector had gone after his family. Lillemor describes how Anders Ek's body was found in the locker room, the attempted dismemberment, and how a hunting knife and the amputated arm were found in the shower. She tells Joona what she knows about the family in the house. She mentions the fact that they're short-staffed several times, which means that the examination of the crime scenes will have to wait.

'I'm coming over,' Joona says.

'What for?' she asks.

'I want to take a look at this.'

'Now?'

'Yes, please,' he replies.

'Great,' she says, in a way that makes him think she actually means it.

6

Monday evening, 7 December

Fourteen minutes later Joona turns into the field at Rödstuhage in Tumba and parks a short distance away from the cleaner's van. It's dark, and small snowflakes are flying around in the wind. Two police cars and a minibus are already at the scene, and the whole area has been cordoned off with blue and white plastic tape.

Joona leaves his car, walks a few steps, then stops in the car park and looks out across the deserted football field and the locker rooms.

There are no police officers in sight.

There's an electrical buzzing noise.

He hears shuffling sounds and quick footsteps off to the left, and turns around.

Two people are walking through the tall grass by the fence. He can just make out their black silhouettes against the distant streetlamps.

The flash of a camera lights up the locker rooms and Joona heads that way. He crosses the ditch with a long stride and continues across the grass.

The buzzing sound gets louder, and then suddenly it vanishes and the floodlights around the football field come on. The whole area is lit up as bright as day, but surrounded by dense winter darkness.

Joona now sees that the two people over by the fence are uniformed police officers. The first one is walking fast, but stops abruptly and throws up, leaning against the fence. His colleague catches up with him and lays a hand on his back.

Joona walks towards the locker room. The door is wedged open and the crime scene officers have laid out protective mats to stop the evidence from getting contaminated.

Cameras flash repeatedly.

An older police officer is posted outside the door. He greets Joona. There is a very tired look in his eyes.

'Don't go in if you're prone to nightmares,' he says seriously.

'I'm done with dreams,' Joona replies, and walks in.

A strong smell of stale sweat, urine and fresh blood lingers in the air. The crime scene officers are taking photographs in the showers, and their cameras' white lights light up the locker room.

Blood is dripping from the ceiling.

Joona stops, clenching his jaw, and looks at the badly mutilated body lying on the floor between the wooden bench and the dented metal lockers. The victim is a middle-aged man with thinning hair and a moustache flecked with grey.

There's blood everywhere, on the floor, doors and benches, as well as on the ceiling.

Joona walks into the showers and greets the crime scene team quietly. The glare of a flash hits the white tiles and glints off a hunting knife on the floor.

A wooden-handled squeegee is leaning against the wall, its rubber strip surrounded by a large pool of blood, water, dirt, strands of hair, old plasters and an empty shower-gel bottle.

Next to the drain in the floor lies an entire human arm. The exposed ball-joint is surrounded by gristle and cut muscle.

Joona stands still, registering every detail. He reads the splatter pattern of the blood, the direction and shape of the drops, and surmises that the dismembered arm had been thrown against the wall several times before it was left on the floor.

'Detective,' the police officer posted outside the door calls.

Joona walks out and notes the anxious look on the officer's face as he takes the radio.

'Yes?' he says.

'Lillemor Blom here, I want you to come to the terraced house as quickly as you can.'

'What's happened?' Joona asks.

'One of the children is alive. We thought he was dead, but he's not . . .'

7

Monday night, 7 December

Joona Linna's colleagues at the National Crime Unit nurture a mixture of admiration and envy towards him. Most of them like Joona and his odd sense of humour, but there are still plenty who find his aloof nature irritating.

He has helped to solve more homicide cases than any other detective in Scandinavia.

That's because he lacks the capacity to give up. This is the chief cause of his colleagues' envy. But there's nothing enviable about it. Joona's stubbornness has its roots in a feeling of deep personal guilt.

It's that guilt which drives him, which means that he can't bear to leave a case unsolved.

Joona never talks about what happened, but the memories of the day when his life was destroyed are always with him.

He wasn't driving particularly fast, he knows that, but it had been raining and the sun was shining in the pools of water on the road as if they were burning from below.

He was leaving. He thought he could get away.

If he's honest with himself, he thinks he deserves his punishments.

On his way to the terraced house he passes an ambulance that is racing towards Huddinge Hospital, blue light flashing.

The emergency vehicle disappears through the sleeping suburb, leaving it in ghostly silence.

Joona turns into Gärdesvägen, stops his car and gets out.

Lillemor Blom is smoking beneath a streetlight when Joona arrives. The streetlights illuminate small yards and dark windows. The wind has picked up. A few dry snowflakes land on their faces.

Lillemor raises her hand listlessly in greeting as Joona comes closer. Her face was lined with tiredness and she wears a lot of make-up. Joona has always thought she was beautiful, with her straight nose, high cheekbones and slanted eyes.

'Joona Linna,' she says softly.

'Is the boy going to make it?'

'Hard to say. It's terrible, I've never seen anything like this before, and I never want to again,' she says, staring at the burning end of her cigarette.

'Have you started the preliminary investigation?' he asks.

She shakes her head and breathes out a plume of smoke.

'I'll take it,' he says.

'In that case I'll go home and get some sleep.'

'Sounds nice,' he smiles.

'Come with me,' she jokes.

'I'll go in and take a look . . . then I need to see if it's possible to talk to the boy.'

'Do you want me to call the Lab and put them in touch with Huddinge Hospital?'

'That would be good,' Joona says.

Lillemor drops the butt of her cigarette on the ground and steps on it.

'So what exactly are you doing here?' she asks.

'You can request help from the National Homicide Commission, but I doubt they'll have time, and I don't think they'd find the answers to what happened here anyway.'

'So what are you going to do?'

'We'll have to see,' Joona murmurs.

He walks through the small yard. A bicycle with training wheels is leaning against the sandpit. The grill had been left inside the playhouse for the winter. Joona goes up the steps, switches his torch on, and steps through the door.

He steels himself, then begins to investigate the crime scene.

The dark rooms play host to a gruesome scene. After just a few steps adrenalin starts to course through his body, and his heart pounds.

Joona forces himself to concentrate. He observes every horrific detail until it feels like he can't take it any more. Then he stops for a moment, closes his eyes, remembers his guilt, and continues examining the house.

In the cool, confined beam of his torch Joona sees how bodies were dragged across the floor. Blood has sprayed up across the walls, the stove and the television. He sees the overturned furniture, the cutlery on the kitchen floor, the blood on the kitchen cupboards and the oven, the footprints and hand-marks.

When he stops in front of the little girl's mutilated body, tears begin to run down his cheeks, but he stands still and observes everything, imagining the screams and violence down to the last detail.

These murders weren't the result of an attempt to collect outstanding gambling debts. That doesn't make sense, because Joona is convinced that the father was murdered first.

First the father, then his family.

Joona breaths out heavily through his teeth.

He isn't sure why, but he's sure the father was the first victim. Someone wanted to wipe out an entire family, and probably thinks he's succeeded.

8

Monday night, 7 December

Joona Linna leaves the terraced house, emerging into the cold wind. He steps over the fluttering blue and white plastic tape and gets back in his car.

I need to talk to the surviving witness, he thinks.

From there, Joona calls the hospital at Huddinge. Josef Ek has been taken to the neuro-surgical unit at Karolinska University Hospital in Solna, where the forensic team from Linköping supervised the securing of evidence from the boy. Since then his condition has deteriorated.

Joona arrives at the intensive care unit of Karolinska just after 2:00 in the morning. After a fifteen-minute wait, the doctor in charge appears.

'You must be Detective Linna. Sorry to keep you waiting. I'm Doctor Daniella Richards.'

'How is the boy, Doctor?'

'He's in circulatory shock,' she says.

'What does that mean?'

'He's lost a lot of blood. His heart is attempting to compensate for it and is beating extremely fast . . .'

'Have you managed to stop the bleeding?'

'I think so. I *hope* so. And he's receiving more blood, but the lack of oxygen in his body means that waste-products aren't being removed. His blood is getting more acidic, and that could damage his organs.'

'Is he conscious?'

'No.'

'As soon as he is, I need to interview him.'

'Detective, my patient is hanging on by his fingernails. Even if he survives his injuries, you won't be able to interview him for several weeks.'

'He's the sole eyewitness to a multiple homicide,' says Joona. 'Is there anything you can do?'

'The only person who might possibly be able to speed up the boy's recovery is Erik Maria Bark.'

'The hypnotist?' Joona asks.

She smiles at him, blushing slightly.

'Don't call him that if you want his help. He's our leading expert in shock and trauma.'

'Do you have any objection to having him in to consult?'

'Not at all, I've been considering it myself,' she says.

Joona realises that he left his phone in the car, and asks if he can borrow Daniella's. After outlining the situation to Erik Maria Bark, he calls Susanne Granat at Social Services and explains that he is hoping to be able to talk to Josef Ek soon. Susanne tells him that the family is on the Social Services register because the father was a gambling addict, and that they had some dealings with the daughter three years ago.

'With the daughter?' asks Joona.

'The older daughter,' explains Susanne.

'So there's a third child?' Joona asks quickly.

'Yes, her name's Evelyn.'

Joona ends the call, then immediately calls his colleagues in Surveillance and asks them to locate Evelyn Ek. He stresses how urgent it is, and tells them there is a risk she might be killed. He adds that they can't rule out the possibility that she's dangerous, and might be involved in a triple murder.

9

Tuesday morning, 8 December

Joona orders a large sandwich with parmesan, salted beef and sun-dried tomatoes from Il Caffé on Bergs Street. It's early in the morning and the café has only just opened: the girl who takes his order hasn't had time to unpack the bread yet.

Last night, before he headed home to get a couple of hours of rest, he called Surveillance again:

'Have you found Evelyn?' he asked.

'No.'

'You realise we have to find her before the murderer does,' Joona said.

'We're trying, but . . .'

'Try harder,' Joona interrupted, then added in a gentler voice: 'We might be able to save a girl's life.'

As he waits for his breakfast and gazes out at the city courthouse through the foggy window, Joona thinks about the tunnel that runs beneath the park, between the huge police complex and the courthouse.

Sleet is falling hard as he hurries up Bergs Street clutching the bag containing his warm sandwich in one hand and his gym bag, with his hockey stick poking out of it, in the other.

'We're playing Surveillance tonight,' Joona said to Benny Rubin over the phone. 'And we're going to get our arses kicked, just like they promised.'

The National Crime team always loses – to the Neighbourhood Police Unit, the traffic cops, the marine police, the National Response Unit, the riot squad and the Security Police. But it gives them a good excuse to go for a drink afterwards.

The façade of the Police Headquarters building is dark copper, polished, but somehow it looks like it's underwater. There are no bikes parked in the long rack next to the section for custody hearings, and the flags are hanging damply from both flagpoles. Joona jogs between the two metal pillars and underneath the tall, frosted glass overhang, where he stomps the snow off of his shoes before going in through the entrance to the National Police Committee.

The National Crime Unit is responsible for combatting serious crime on a national and international level. And Joona has worked here for nine years.

He walks down the hallway, taking off his hat as he passes the noticeboard. He glances at the posters about yoga, an RV for sale, information about the union and a time change for the shooting club.

The floor, which was cleaned thoroughly on Friday, is already extremely dirty. The door of Benny Rubin's office is half open. The sixty-year-old, with his grey moustache and sun-damaged skin, was part of the team that investigated the murder of Prime Minister Olof Palme, but now he's involved in the central communications unit, working on the transition to a new police radio system named 'Rakel'. He's sitting at his computer with a cigarette behind his ear, typing with agonising slowness.

'I've got eyes in the back of my head,' he says.

'That might explain why you type so badly,' Joona jokes.

He sees that Benny's latest find is a poster advertising the airline SAS: a young, suitably exotic-looking woman in a tiny bikini is depicted drinking a fruit cocktail through a straw. Benny got so upset at the ban on calendars of scantily clad women that most people expected him to hand in his notice. Instead he's devoted years to his own form of silent, stubborn protest. On the first day of each month he changes the decor in his office. It's not against regulation to display ads for airlines, pictures of ice-skating champions with their legs apart, yoga posters or underwear ads from H&M. Joona remembers one particular poster of the sprinter Gail Devers in tight shorts, and a risqué print of one of Egon Schiele's paintings, of a red-headed woman wearing a pair of frilly pantaloons.

Joona stops to say hello to his assistant and colleague Anja Larsson, but she's sitting at her computer with her mouth half-open, and has a look of such concentration on her round face that he decides not to disturb her. He makes his way to his office, and hangs his wet coat on the back of the door. He looks through his post: a memo about the work environment, a proposal about low-energy lamps, a request from the Public Prosecutors' Office and an invitation to the staff Christmas dinner at Skansen open-air museum.

Joona leaves his office and heads into the conference room. He sits down in his usual seat, and unwraps his sandwich.

On the large whiteboard attached to the one wall are the words: clothes, protective clothing, weapons, tear-gas, communications devices, vehicles, technical support, channels, signal strength, radio silence, codes, connectivity.

Petter Näslund, Joona's immediate boss, is standing in the hall, chuckling to himself. He is a bald, muscular man in his mid-thirties. Everyone knows that Joona is far more qualified, but he has no interest in administrative work or fancy titles.

For several years, Petter has been flirting with Magdalena Ronander, apparently without noticing her discomfort and her constant attempts to steer conversations in a more professional direction. Magdalena has been an inspector with the Surveillance division for the past four years, and is hoping to finish law school before she turns thirty.

Petter lowers his voice and asks Magdalena about her choice of service weapon, and how often she changes the barrel because, he says, it looks like the grooves are worn. Pretending not to notice his clumsy double-entendres, she explains that she keeps a careful note of the number of shots fired.

'But you like things a bit rough, don't you?' Petter says.

'No, I stick with my Glock 17,' she replies. 'Partly because it can handle some of the army's 9mm ammunition.'

'You don't use Czech?'

'Yes, but I prefer m39B,' she says.

The two of them walk into the conference room and say hello to Joona.

'And the Glock has gas-vents next to the sights,' she goes on. 'That makes a hell of a difference to the recoil, so you can take your next shot much faster.'

'What does Moomintroll think?' Petter asks.

Joona smiles gently and his pale grey eyes become icily clear. He replies in his Finnish accent:

'The make of the gun isn't crucial. There are other, more important, factors to consider.'

'So you don't need to be able to shoot?' Petter grins.

'Joona's a good shot,' Magdalena says.

'Good at everything,' Petter sighs.

Magdalena ignores Petter and turns towards Joona.

'The biggest advantage with the Glock's compensator is that the percussive gases aren't visible in the barrel when it's dark.'

'Absolutely right,' Joona says quietly.

She looks happy as she opens her black leather folder and starts to leaf through her papers. Benny comes in and sits down. He looks at everyone, then slams the palm of his hand down hard on the table to quieten the room. He grins when Magdalena Ronander looks up at him irritably.

'I took the case out in Tumba,' Joona says.

'Which case is that?' Petter asks.

'An entire family's been stabbed to death,' he replies.

'That has nothing to do with us,' Petter says.

'I think we could be dealing with a serial killer, or at least . . .'

'Oh, for God's sake!' Benny interrupts. He looks Joona in the eye and slams his hand on the table again.

'A private matter that got out of hand,' Petter goes on. 'Debts, gambling problems . . . he was a familiar figure out at Solvalla racetrack, after all.'

'Addicted to gambling,' Benny confirms.

'He borrowed money from local criminal gangs, and paid the price,' Petter concludes.

Silence descends. Joona drinks some water. He picks up some crumbs from his sandwich and pops them in his mouth.

'I've just got a feeling about this case,' he says in a subdued voice.

'Well, you'd better ask for a transfer, then,' Petter says with a smile. 'This isn't a case for National Crime.'

'I think it is.'

'You might want to join the local police in Tumba if you want the case,' Petter says.

'I'm going to investigate these murders,' Joona persists.

'That's my decision,' Petter replies.

Yngve Svensson comes in and sits down. His gelled hair is combed back, and he has blue-grey circles under his eyes. He's wearing his usual crumpled black suit.

'*Yngwie*,' Benny says happily.

Yngve Svensson is one of the country's foremost experts in organised crime. He's responsible for the analysis unit, as well as being involved in liaison work with Interpol.

'Yngve, what do you say about Tumba?' Petter asks. 'You've just been looking at the report, haven't you?'

'Yes, it looks like a local thing,' he says. 'Debt collector goes to the house. The father would usually be there, but he has been asked to referee a football match at the last minute. The debt collector's probably high on speed and Rohypnol, and then something gets to him and he attacks the family with a swat-knife in order to find the guy. Presumably they tell him what he wants to know, but he loses control and kills them before heading off to the gym.'

Petter smiles smugly, drinks some water, burps into his hand, then looks at Joona and asks:

'What do you make of that explanation?'

'It would be pretty good if it wasn't completely wrong,' Joona replies.

'What's wrong with it?' Yngve asks defensively.

'The murderer killed the man at the field first,' Joona replies calmly. 'Then he went to the house and killed the rest of them.'

'Which means it can't have been about collecting a debt,' Magdalena Ronander says.

'We'll just have to see what the post-mortems show,' Yngve mutters.

'They'll show I'm right,' Joona replies.

'Idiot,' Yngve sighs, and tucks two pinches of chewing tobacco under his top lip.

'Joona, I'm not going to let you have this case,' Petter says.

'Yes, I realise that,' he sighs, and gets up from the table.

'Where are you going? We've got a meeting,' Petter says.

'I need to talk to Carlos.'

'Not about this.'

'Yes,' Joona replies, and leaves the room.

'Stop,' Petter calls. 'Otherwise I'll . . .'

Joona doesn't hear the threat, he just calmly closes the door behind him and walks away. He says hello to Anja as she glances up at him curiously over the screen of her computer.

'Don't you belong in the meeting?' she asks.

'Yes,' he replies, and walks towards the lift.

10

Tuesday morning, 8 December

Carlos Eliasson, head of the National Crime Unit, has his office on the fifth floor. The door is ajar, but as usual is more closed than open.

'Come in, come in,' Carlos says. 'I just need to feed my little ones.'

He smiles as the fish swim to the surface, then he crumbles some fish-food onto the water.

'And there's some for you,' he whispers.

Carlos leads the smallest paradise fish to the corner of the tank and drops in some food, then he turns and says in a friendly tone:

'The Homicide Unit asked if you could take a look at that murder up in Dalarna.'

'They can solve that themselves,' Joona says.

'They don't seem to think so – Tommy Kofoed has been here, asking for you by name.'

'I don't have time, anyway,' Joona says.

He sits down across from Carlos. The room smells pleasantly of leather and wood. The sunlight is refracted by the aquarium and dances across the desk.

'I want to take over the Tumba case,' Joona says.

Carlos gives Joona an irritated look.

'Petter Näslund called me a few moments ago, and he's right – that isn't a case for National Crime,' he says carefully.

'I think it is,' Joona persists.

'Only if these debt collectors are linked to broader organised crime, Joona.'

'It's not about debt collection.'

'No?'

'The killer attacked the man first,' Joona says. 'Then he went to the house to deal with the rest of the family. He wanted to wipe them all out. He's going to track down the adult daughter, and he'll find the boy if he survives.'

'Really,' Carlos says sceptically. 'And how do you know that?'

'Because the footsteps in the blood were closer together in the house.'

'What do you mean?'

Joona leans forward and says:

'Obviously there were footprints everywhere, and I haven't measured anything, but I read the prints in the locker room as more energetic, and the footsteps in the house showed fatigue.'

'Here we go,' Carlos says flatly. 'Now you're complicating things again.'

'But I'm right,' Joona replies.

Carlos shakes his head.

'I don't think you are, not this time.'

'Yes, I am.'

Carlos turns to the fish and says:

'That Joona Linna, he's the most stubborn person I've ever met.'

'But what happens if you back down when you know you're right?'

'I can't go over Petter's head and give you the case because you have a feeling,' Carlos explains.

'Yes, you can.'

'Everyone believes it was score-settling over gambling debts.'

'You too?' Joona asks.

'Yes, actually, I do.'

'The footprints in the house showed fatigue because the man was murdered first,' Joona insists.

'You never give up, do you?' Carlos asks.

Joona shrugs his shoulders and smiles.

'I might as well call the Pathology Department,' Carlos mutters, picking up the phone.

'They're going to confirm that I'm right,' Joona says, looking down at the floor.

Joona knows he's a very stubborn man, and he knows he's going to need to continue being stubborn if he wants to make any progress.

He can't give up.

Long before Joona lost his father.

Perhaps that was where it all started.

Yrjö Linna, Joona's father, was a beat officer in Märsta police district. He was out on the old Uppsala road, just north of Löwenströmska Hospital, when a call came in and he was sent to Hammarbyvägen in Upplands Väsby. A neighbour had called the police. Said the Olsson kids were being beaten again. Sweden was the first country in the world to ban the corporal punishment of children, and the police had been given orders from the National Police Committee to treat the new law seriously. Yrjö drove into the yard in his police car and stopped outside the door. He waited for his colleague, Jonny Andersen. After a few minutes he tried calling him. Jonny was standing in line at a hotdog stand. Yrjö was a soft-spoken man. He knew regulations dictated that there should be two of them on an intervention like this, but he let it go. He didn't say anything, even though he knew he had the right to request back-up. Yrjö walked up the stairs to the third floor and rang the doorbell. A scared-looking girl opened the door. He asked her to step out onto the landing, but she shook her head and ran back into the flat. Yrjö Linna followed her into the living room. The girl was banging on the door to the balcony. Yrjö discovered that there was a little boy standing out there, wearing nothing but his nappy. He looked to be about two years old. Yrjö hurried across the room to let the child in. The drunk man was sitting completely still on the sofa behind the door. Yrjö had to use both hands to undo the bolts and turn the handle. He only stopped when he heard the click of the shotgun. The shot went off, and thirty-six small balls of lead went into his back and killed him instantly.

Eleven-year-old Joona and his mother Ritva had to move out of their light, airy flat in the centre of Märsta to his aunt's three-room flat in Fredhäll in Stockholm. When he graduated from high school on Kungsholmen he applied to the Police Academy. He still thinks about the cadets in his class, the calm of those early months when they seemed to be forever crossing the huge grass lawns, and then his first years as a police officer. Joona has done his share of desk work, he's done his bit for equal-opportunities planning and union work, he's directed traffic during the Stockholm Marathon and at hundreds of road accidents, he's been embarrassed when football hooligans harassed female colleagues with raucous singing in underground carriages – 'What do you do with your truncheon, darling? In and out, in and out!' He's found dead heroin-addicts, has tried to reason with shoplifters, has helped paramedics with vomiting drunks. He's talked to terrified prostitutes shaking from drug-withdrawal, he's encountered hundreds of men who've abused their wives and children, always the same pattern, drunk but controlled, with the radio on loud and the blinds closed. He's stopped people speeding and driving drunk, he's seized weapons, drugs and moonshine. Once, when he was off sick with a bad back, he saw a skinhead grab a Muslim woman's breast outside Klastorp School. Despite the pain in his back, he chased the skinhead, down by the water, through the park, past Smedsudden, up onto the Western Bridge, across the water to Långholmen and Södermalm, before finally arresting him at the traffic light on Högalids Street.

Without any great desire to forge a career for himself, Joona gradually rose through the ranks. He likes challenging work, and he never gives up. He's completely uninterested in being anyone's boss, and has refused to be seconded to the National Murder Commission, even though he's extremely good at complex murder cases.

He became famous when, during his first year as a detective, he pursued and stopped serial killer Jurek Walter.

For Joona, every investigation is important. He never backs down, and he can't stand the tendency among the police to regard other people's pain and fear as routine.

Now Joona listens as Carlos Eliasson talks to Professor Nils 'The Needle' Åhlén, chief medical officer at the pathology lab in Stockholm.

'No, I just need to know which crime scene came first,' Carlos says, then listens for a while. 'I understand that, yes, of course I understand that . . . but based on your initial estimation, what would you say?'

Joona leans back in his chair, scratches his messy blond hair. He watches as his boss's face turns red. He listens to Nils Åhlén's monotonous voice, then instead of replying he hangs up without saying goodbye.

'They . . . they . . .'

'They've concluded that the father was killed first,' Joona says.

Carlos nods.

'What did I say?' Joona says with a smile.

Carlos looks down and clears his throat.

'OK, you're in charge of the preliminary investigation,' he says. 'The Tumba case is yours.'

'And . . .' Joona says seriously.

'And?'

'Who was right? Who was right, you or me?'

'You were,' Carlos exclaims. 'For God's sake, Joona, what is it with you? You were right, as usual!'

Joona hides his smile with his hand as he gets to his feet.

'Surveillance haven't been able to locate Evelyn Ek,' Joona says seriously. 'She could be anywhere. I honestly don't know what we're going to do if we don't get permission to speak with the boy. Without him it'll take too long. It's going to be too late.'

'You want to question the boy?' Carlos asks.

'I have to.'

'Have you spoken to the prosecutor?'

'I'm not going to hand over this investigation until I've got a suspect,' Joona says.

‘No, that wasn’t what I meant,’ Carlos says. ‘I just think it’s a good idea to have the prosecutor on your side if you’re going to talk to someone who’s been as badly injured as this boy.’

‘OK, good advice, as usual – I’ll give Jens a call,’ Joona says, and walks out.

11

Tuesday morning, 8 December

Erik Maria Bark has just returned home from meeting Joona Linna at Karolinska Hospital. Erik rather liked him, despite the fact that he had tried to persuade him to break his promise never to practise hypnotism again. Perhaps it was the detective's obvious and honest concern for the boy's older sister that had made him so appealing. The killer was probably hunting for her at that very moment.

Erik goes into the bedroom and looks at his wife Simone in bed. He's extremely tired now. The pills have started to work. His eyes are heavy and sore. Almost the entire night has passed since he left. Now Simone has taken over the bed. She's pushed the covers down, and her nightdress has bunched around her waist. She's lying on her stomach. Erik gently pulls the covers over her again. She mutters something and huddles up. He sits down and strokes her ankle, and sees her toes respond.

'I'm going to take a shower,' he says, leaning back.

'What was the policeman's name?' she asks hazily.

But before he can answer he suddenly finds himself in the park at Observatorielunden. He's digging in the sandpit and finds a yellow stone, round as an egg, as big as a pumpkin. He digs with his hands and discovers a raised image on one side, a jagged row of teeth. When he turns the heavy stone over he realises that it's a dinosaur's skull.

'Damn you!' Simone shrieks.

He startles awake and realises that he must have fallen asleep and started to dream. The pills knocked him out mid-conversation. He tries to smile and meet Simone's cold gaze.

'Simone? What's the matter?'

'Has it started again?'

'What?'

'*What?*' she mimics irritably. 'Who's Daniella?'

'Daniella?'

'You promised, you made a real promise, Erik,' she says, now very upset. 'I trusted you, I was so stupid that I actually trusted . . .'

'What are you talking about?' he asks. 'Daniella Richards is a doctor at Karolinska. Why are you asking about her?'

'Don't lie to me.'

'This is kind of absurd,' he says with a smile.

'You think this is funny?' she asks. 'Sometimes I think . . . sometimes I even *believe* that I might be able to forget what happened.'

Erik dozes off for a few seconds, but still hears her.

'Maybe it would be best if we separated,' Simone whispers.

'But nothing's going on between me and Daniella.'

'It doesn't really matter,' she says wearily.

'It doesn't matter? So you want to split up because of a thing I did ten years ago?'

'A thing?'

'I was drunk, and . . .'

'I don't want to hear it, I know it all by heart now, I . . . oh, damn it! I don't want to play this part! I'm not a jealous person, but I am loyal. And I need loyalty in return.'

'I've never cheated on you again, and I never will . . .'

'So why not prove it to me?' she interrupts. 'That's what would help.'

'You're just going to have to trust me,' he says.

'Right,' she sighs, and walks out of the bedroom, taking her pillow and the duvet with her.

He takes a deep breath and knows he should go after her. He should make her come back to bed, or he should lie down on the floor next to the sofa-bed in the guest bedroom, but right now sleep is stronger than anything else. He doesn't have the strength to resist. He sinks back onto the bed, feeling the dopamine float around his body. The delicious relaxation spreads across his face, and all the way out to his toes and fingertips. Heavy, chemical sleep embraces him like a cloud.

12

Tuesday morning, 8 December

Two hours later Erik slowly opens his eyes to the grey light pressing against the curtains. Images from last night flit past: Simone's accusations, and the boy lying with hundreds of knife cuts on his pale body. The deep wounds to his neck and chest.

Erik thinks about the detective who seems convinced that the killer is determined to eradicate an entire family. First the father, then the mother, son and daughter.

The phone rings on the bedside table.

Erik stands up, but instead of answering he pulls the curtains open and peers out at the building opposite and tries to gather his thoughts. Simone has already left for the gallery. He can't understand why she reacted the way she did, why she started ranting about Daniella. He wonders if it might be about something else altogether. The pills, maybe. He knows that he's taking too many. But he has to sleep. All those night shifts at the hospital have given him insomnia. He'd be lost without his sleeping pills. He reaches out for the alarm clock but only succeeds in knocking it to the floor.

The phone stops ringing, then starts again.

He considers going into Benjamin's room and lying down beside his son.

Erik answers the phone.

'Erik Maria Bark.'

'Hi, it's Daniella.'

'Are you still at the hospital? What time is it now, anyway?'

'Eight fifteen – I'm starting to get tired.'

'You should go home.'

'Other way around,' Daniella says matter-of-factly. 'You have to come back. That detective's on his way here. He seems more convinced than ever that the killer is after the older sister. He says he has to talk to the boy.'

Erik feels a sudden dark weight behind his eyes:

'That's really not a good idea.'

'But the sister,' she interrupts. 'I almost think he *should* talk to Josef.'

'If you think that the patient can handle it,' Erik says.

'Of course he can't handle it, it's far too early. He's going to have to find out what happened to his family without any preparation, without having time to build up any defences. He could have a complete breakdown, he . . .'

'It's your decision,' Erik cuts in.

'On the one hand I don't want to give the police access to him, but on the other I can't just sit and wait. There is no doubt that his sister is in danger,' she says.

'But that . . .'

'A murderer is looking for my patient's older sister,' Daniella interrupts, raising her voice.

'Probably.'

'Sorry, I don't know why this is affecting me so much,' she says. 'Maybe because there's still time to do something. This time we might be able to save a girl's life.'

'What exactly do you want?' Erik asks.

'You need to come back and do what you're good at.'

'I can talk to the boy about what's happened once he's a little better.'

'You could come and hypnotise him,' she says seriously.

'No, I can't,' he replies.

'It's the only solution.'

'I can't.'

'But there's no one who's as good as you.'

'I don't even have permission to practise hypnosis at Karolinska.'

'I can sort that out before you get here.'

'But I've sworn never to hypnotise anyone again.'

'Can't you just come up here?'

There's a brief pause, then Erik asks:

'Is he conscious?'

'Soon.'

He sighs into the phone.

'If you don't hypnotise him, I'm going to let the detective go in and see him.'

She hangs up.

Erik is left standing with the phone in his trembling hand. Pressure is building behind his eyes, and a headache is coming on. He opens the drawer of the bedside table. The wooden box with the parrot on isn't there. He must have left it in the car.

The flat is flooded with sunlight as he goes to wake Benjamin.

The boy is still asleep with his mouth open. His face is pale and he looks exhausted, despite having slept all night.

'Benni?'

Benjamin opens his sleep-drenched eyes and looks at his father as if he's a complete stranger before his face breaks into his familiar smile.

'It's Tuesday – time to wake up!'

Benjamin sits up with a yawn, scratches his hair and then looks at the phone hanging around his neck. That's the first thing he does every morning: check that he hasn't missed an important message during the night. Erik pulls out the yellow Puma bag that contains the desmopressin, aluminium acetotartrate, sterile needles, alcohol swabs, bandages, and paracetamol.

'Now or after breakfast?'

Benjamin shrugs.

'Doesn't matter.'

Erik quickly swabs his son's thin arm, turns it towards the light, feels the softness of the muscle, then taps the syringe and inserts the needle beneath the skin. While the syringe slowly empties Benjamin sits and taps at his phone with his other hand.

'Shit, my phone is almost dead,' he says, then lies back down as Erik presses gauze to his arm to stop the bleeding. Benjamin has to stay like that for a while before he applies a bandage.

Erik gently bends and straightens his son's legs, then he stretches his thin knee ligaments and finishes off by massaging his feet and toes.

'How does that feel?' he asks, looking at his son's face the whole time.

Benjamin grimaces.

'Same as usual,' he says.

'Do you want any paracetamol?'

His son shakes his head, and Erik thinks about the unconscious witness, the boy with all the knife-wounds. Perhaps the killer is looking for his adult sister at this very moment.

'Dad? What is it?' Benjamin asks gently.

Erik meets his gaze and says:

'I can drive you to school if you'd like.'

'What for?'

13

Tuesday morning, 8 December

The rush-hour traffic is moving slowly. Benjamin is sitting next to his father, allowing himself to be lulled by the stop and go motion of the car. He lets out a big yawn. He can tell his dad's in a hurry, but he's still taken the time to drive him to school. Benjamin smiles to himself. It's always been like this, he thinks. Whenever his dad has to deal with anything really bad at the hospital, he gets extra worried that something is going to happen to Benjamin.

'We forgot your skates,' Erik suddenly says.

'Oh, yeah.'

'We'll go back,' Erik says.

'No, there's no need,' Benjamin says.

Erik tries to change lanes, but another car blocks him. When he tries to get back into his original lane he almost hits a dustbin lorry.

'We've got time to go back and . . .'

'Forget the stupid skates, I don't care!' Benjamin says, raising his voice.

Erik shoots him a startled sideways glance.

'I thought you liked skating?'

Benjamin doesn't know what to say: he hates being interrogated, and doesn't want to start lying.

'Don't you?' Erik asks.

'What?'

'Don't you like skating?'

'Why would I like skating?' he mumbles.

'But we've just bought new . . .'

'How much fun can it really be?' Benjamin interrupts wearily.

'So you don't want me to go home and get them for you?'

Benjamin just sighs in response.

'So skating's boring,' Erik says. 'Chess is boring and computer games are boring. So what's fun?'

'I don't know,' he replies.

'Nothing?'

'Some things are.'

'Watching films?'

'Sometimes.'

'Sometimes?' Erik smiles.

'Yes,' Benjamin replies.

'Says the boy who can watch three or four films in one evening,' Erik says with a smile.

'So?'

'Oh, nothing,' Erik goes on, still smiling. 'Nothing at all. Some people might wonder how many films you could manage to watch in a day if you actually liked it. I mean, if you really loved films . . .'

'Stop it.'

'Maybe you'd have double screens, and would have to keep hitting fast forward to fit them all in.'

Benjamin can feel himself starting to smile, the way he always does when his dad teases him like this.

Suddenly there's a muffled bang and a pale blue star appears in the sky before its points fall away, smoking.

'Strange time of day for holiday fireworks,' Benjamin says.

'What?' his dad asks.

'Look,' Benjamin says, pointing.

A star made of smoke is hanging in the air. For some reason Benjamin sees Aida's face, and his stomach clenches and he feels hot.

As Erik parks the car outside the school grounds Benjamin spots Aida. She's standing on the other side of the fence waiting for him. On Friday they sat very quietly, and very close together, on the sofa in Aida's cramped living room out in Sundbyberg. They watched the film *Elephant* while her little brother played with his Pokémon cards on the floor and talked to himself. When she catches sight of him she waves. Benjamin picks up his bag and says quickly:

'Bye, Dad, thanks for the ride.'

'I love you,' Erik says quietly.

Benjamin nods and starts to walk away.

'Do you want to watch a film tonight?' Erik asks.

'I don't know,' he says, staring at the ground.

'Is that Aida?' his dad asks.

'Yes,' Benjamin replies almost inaudibly.

'I'd like to meet her,' Erik says, and gets out of the car.

'Why?'

They head towards Aida. Benjamin can barely look at her, he feels like a small child. He doesn't want her to think he needs his dad's approval. Aida looks nervous now that they're getting closer. Her eyes keep flitting between him and Erik. Before Benjamin manages to think of an explanation, Erik holds his hand out and says:

'Hi.'

Aida shakes his hand warily. Benjamin sees that his dad is taken aback by the swastika tattoed next to a small star of David on her neck. She's wearing black eye make-up, her hair is tied up in two childish braids and she has on a black leather jacket and a wide black tulle skirt.

'I'm Erik, Benjamin's dad,' Erik says.

'Aida.'

Her voice is high and thin. Benjamin blushes, and he looks nervously at Aida and then down at the ground.

'Are you a Nazi?' Erik asks.

'Are you?'

'No.'

'Neither am I,' she says, and looks him briefly in the eye.

'Why do you have . . .?'

'No reason,' she interrupts. 'I'm not anything, I'm just . . .'

Benjamin steps in, his heart thudding hard with embarrassment.

'She got in with the wrong crowd a few years ago,' he says loudly. 'But thought they were idiots and . . .'

'You don't have to explain it to him,' Aida cuts him off irritably.

He's silent for a moment.

'I . . . I just think it's brave to accept your mistakes,' he finally says.

'Yes, but the way I see it,' Erik says. 'The way I see it is that it shows a continuing lack of insight not to have it removed and . . .'

'Stop it!' Benjamin shouts. 'You don't know anything about her.'

Aida just turns and walks away. Benjamin hurries after her.

'Sorry,' he pants. 'My dad, he's so embarrassing . . .'

'You don't think he's right, then?' she asks.

'No,' Benjamin replies weakly.

'I think he might be, you know,' she says, then smiles briefly and takes his hand in hers.

14

Tuesday morning, 8 December

The Pathology Department is based in a red-brick building, in the middle of Karolinska Institute's large grounds. Joona drives to the visitors' car park and gets out of the car. He passes a patch of frosty grass and a metal ramp on his way to the main entrance.

The girl at reception lets him through to see Nils 'The Needle' Åhlén, Professor of Forensic Medicine.

The professor's office is furnished in a modern style, with clean expanses of white and pale grey. It looks expensive, like he hired a designer. The few chairs are brushed steel with white leather seats. The light above the desk comes from a large, hanging light fixture.

The Needle shakes Joona's hand without getting to his feet. He's wearing a white polo-neck shirt under his lab coat, and aviator glasses with white frames. His face is thin, he's clean-shaven, and he has a grey crew-cut. His lips are pale, and his nose is long and not particularly straight.

'Good morning,' he says.

On the wall hangs a faded colour photograph of him with some of his colleagues: pathologists, forensic chemists, geneticists and dental experts. They're all wearing lab coats, and they all look cheerful. They're standing around some dark fragments of bone on a table. The caption below the photograph says that it was taken during excavations at the ninth-century burial ground on the island of Björkö.

'Another new picture,' Joona says.

'I have to tape photographs to the wall,' The Needle says bitterly. 'In the old pathology lab they had a painting that measured eighteen square metres.'

'Wow,' Joona replies.

'Painted by Peter Weiss.'

'The author?'

The Needle nods, and the light above the desk reflects off his glasses.

'Yes, he painted the whole institution in the Forties. Six months' work, for the princely sum of six hundred kronor, apparently. My dad's in that painting with the other pathologists; he's at the end next to Bertil Falconer.'

The Needle tilts his head and looks back at his computer.

'I'm sitting here with the results of the post-mortems from the Tumba murders,' he says hesitantly.

'Oh?'

The pathologist grins at Joona.

'Carlos called and chased me about them this morning.'

Joona smiles. 'I know,' he says.

The Needle pushes his glasses further up his nose.

'Evidently the estimated times of death are important.'

'Yes, we needed to know the sequence of events . . .'

The Needle scans the screen as he purses his lips.

'It's only a preliminary estimate, but . . .'

'The man died first?'

'Exactly . . . based on body temperature,' he says, pointing at the screen. 'Erixon said the places where the bodies were found, the locker room and the terraced house, were the same temperature, so my conclusion was that the man died more than an hour before the other two.'

'And have you changed your opinion since then?'

The Needle shakes his head and stands up with a groan.

'Herniated disc,' he says, then leaves his office and starts to walk down the hall.

Joona follows him as he limps slowly towards the lab.

They pass through an unlit room containing a stainless-steel autopsy table. It looks a bit like a draining board, but with raised sides all the way around. They enter a cooler room where the bodies are stored in drawers. The Needle stops, double-checks the number, then pulls out a long tray. It's empty.

'Gone,' he smiles, and starts to walk down the hall. The floor is covered in scuff-marks from thousands of small black rubber wheels. He opens another door and holds it open for Joona.

They find themselves in a brightly lit, white-tiled room with a large sink attached to the wall. Water is dripping into a drain in the floor from a bright yellow hose. On the oblong, plastic-covered examination table lies a naked, colourless body, covered by hundreds of dark cuts.

'Katja Ek,' Joona says.

She looks remarkably peaceful. Her mouth is half open and her eyes are gazing out calmly. It looks like she's listening to a piece of beautiful music. The expression jars with the deep knife-wounds across her forehead and cheeks. Joona looks down at the body, where signs of marbling are already visible around her neck.

'We're hoping to have time to take a look inside this afternoon.'

'Fucking hell,' Joona sighs.

The other door opens and a young man walks in with an uncertain smile on his face. He has several eyebrow piercings, and his dyed black hair hangs down over the back of his lab coat in a ponytail. Smiling back, The Needle raises a fist with his index and little fingers sticking up, and the young man makes the same gesture back.

'This is Joona Linna from National Crime,' The Needle says. 'He visits us from time to time.'

'Frippe,' the young man says, shaking Joona's hand.

'He's chosen to specialise in forensic medicine,' The Needle explains.

Frippe pulls on a pair of latex gloves. Joona follows him over to the examination table and immediately notices the cloying smell emanating from the body.

'She's the one who suffered the least violence,' The Needle points out. 'Despite the multiple cuts and stab-wounds.'

They look at the dead woman.

'And, unlike the other two, she's hasn't been dismembered,' he goes on. 'The direct cause of death isn't one of the wounds to her neck, but this one, which went straight into her heart according to the CAT scan.'

'It's kind of hard to see the bleeding on the scans,' Frippe explains.

'Obviously we'll be able to confirm that when we open her up,' the professor says to Joona.

'She put up some resistance,' Joona says.

'My view is that initially she tried to fight back,' the Needle replies. 'Considering the wounds on the palms of her hands. But that later she just tried to get away, and defend herself as best she could.'

The young man glances at his older colleague.

'Look at the injuries on the sides of her arms,' The Needle says.

'Self-defence,' Joona murmurs.

'Exactly.'

Joona leans over and looks at the brownish yellow marks that are visible on the woman's open eyes.

'You're looking at the suns?'

'Yes . . .'

'You tend to see them first a few hours after death, although sometimes it can take several days,' The Needle says. 'They turn completely black eventually. It's related to the pressure inside the eye dropping.'

He picks up a reflex hammer from a shelf and asks Frippe to check if there are still signs of idiomuscular contraction. The young doctor taps the centre of the woman's bicep and feels the muscle for contractions.

'Minimal,' he says to Joona.

'That usually stops thirteen hours after death,' The Needle explains.

'The dead aren't completely dead,' Joona says. Frippe taps again and Joona shivers when he sees a ghostly movement in Katja Ek's limp arm.

'*Mortui vivos docent* – the dead teach the living,' The Needle says, and smiles to himself as he and Frippe turn the woman onto her stomach.

He points out the reddish brown marks on her buttocks and lower back, and across her shoulders and arms.

'Hypostasis is often less pronounced when the victim has lost a lot of blood.'

'Of course,' Joona says.

'Blood's heavy, and when you die there's no longer any internal pressure in the system,' the professor explains to Frippe. 'It's fairly obvious, but the blood settles in the lowest parts of the body and is most visible at the points where the body is in contact with the surface it's lying on.'

He presses on one of the marks on the woman's right calf until it almost disappears.

'There, see . . .? You can press them away during the first twenty-four hours after death.'

'But I thought I saw marks on her hips and chest?' Joona says tentatively.

'Bravo,' The Needle says, smiling at him in mild surprise. 'I didn't think you'd spot those.'

'So she was on her stomach when she died and was later turned over,' Joona says, with a hint of Finnish matter-of-factness.

'Two hours, I'd say.'

'So the killer stayed for two hours,' Joona says, thinking out loud. 'Unless he returned to the scene and turned her over.'

The Needle shrugs.

'I'm not finished with the examination yet.'

'Can I ask something? I noticed that one of the wounds to her stomach looks like an emergency C-section . . .'

'A C-section,' The Needle smiles. 'Why not? Shall we take a look?'

The two doctors turn the body again.

'This one, you mean?'

The Needle points at a fifteen-centimetre-long cut running down from her navel.

'Yes,' Joona says.

'We haven't had time to examine all of the injuries yet.'

'*Vulnera incisa s scissa*,' Frippe says.

'Yes, it certainly looks like a vertical cut,' Nils says.

'And not a stab-wound?' Joona says.

'Considering the neatness of the cut and the fact that the surrounding skin is intact . . .'

The Needle feels the wound with one finger, and Frippe leans forward to see.

'Yes . . .'

'The sides of the wound,' The Needle goes on. 'There's not much blood there, but . . .' He stops abruptly.

'What is it?' Joona asks.

The Needle looks at him with a surprised expression on his face.

'This incision was made after she died,' he says.

He pulls off his gloves.

'I need to look at the CAT scan,' he says, and goes over to the computer beside the door.

He taps his way through the three-dimensional images, stops, then changes the angle.

'The cut appears to penetrate her womb,' he whispers. 'And it seems to follow the line of an old scar.'

'Old scar? What do you mean?' Joona asks.

'You said it yourself,' The Needle smiles, and returns to the body. 'An emergency C-section.'

He points at the vertical incision. Joona looks closer and sees signs of the pale pink scarring left by a long healed C-section all the way along one edge of the wound.

'But she wasn't pregnant when she died?' Joona asks.

'No.'

'Are we dealing with a murderer with surgical skills?' Joona asks.

The professor shakes his head. Joona considers the facts. Someone killed Katja Ek with extreme brutality and in a great rage. Two hours later he went back, rolled her onto her back and sliced open her old C-section.

'Check if there's anything similar on the other bodies. Look for anything out of the ordinary.'

'You want us to prioritise everything, as usual,' The Needle says.

'Yes,' Joona says, and leaves the room.

When he gets back into his car, he notices how cold he feels. He starts the engine and phones Senior Prosecutor Jens Svanehjälm.

'Svanehjälm,' he answers.

'Joona Linna here.'

'Good morning . . . I've just spoken to Carlos – he said you'd be getting in touch.'

'It's a bit difficult to explain what we've got here,' Joona says.

'Are you driving?'

'I've just come out of the Pathology Department, and was thinking of stopping at the hospital. I really need to speak to the surviving witness.'

'Carlos explained the situation to me,' Jens says. 'We need to speed things up here. Do you have the profilers working on this yet?'

'A criminal profile isn't going to be helpful,' Joona replies.

'No, I know, I'm inclined to agree with you. If we're going to have any chance of saving the boy's sister, we need to talk to him. That's clear.'

Joona suddenly sees a firework go off – a bright blue star high above the rooftops of Stockholm.

'I've been in touch with . . .' Joona goes on, clearing his throat. 'I've been in touch with Susanne Granat at Social Services, and I was thinking of bringing in a psychiatrist, Erik Maria Bark. He's an expert in shock and trauma.'

'That's all fine,' Jens says reassuringly.

'OK, I'll get up to neurosurgery at once.'

'OK. Sounds good.'

15

Tuesday morning, 8 December

After dropping Benjamin off at school and arriving at the hospital, Erik thinks about how stupid it had been to comment on the tattoo on Aida's neck. All it had done was make him look arrogant and patronising.

The two uniformed police officers let him into the unit. Joona is already waiting outside Josef Ek's room. When he catches sight of Erik he smiles and waves, the way little children do, by opening and closing his hand.

Erik walks over and looks at the patient through the window in the door. A bag of almost black blood is hanging above him. His condition has stabilised, but he could start to bleed again at any time.

He's lying on his back with his mouth closed firmly. His stomach is rising and falling quickly, and occasionally his fingers splay.

A fresh cannula has been inserted into the crook of his arm. A nurse is preparing a morphine drip.

'I was right when I said the killer got to the father first,' Joona says. 'Then he went to the house and killed the little girl and thought he killed the son too. Then he killed the mother.'

'Did the pathologist confirm that?'

'Yes,' Joona replies.

'I see.'

'So if he intends to wipe out the entire family,' Joona goes on, 'there's only Evelyn left.'

'Assuming he hasn't found out that the boy is still alive,' Erik says.

'Yes, but at least we can protect him.'

'Yes.'

'We have to find the killer before it's too late,' Joona says. 'I need to find out what the boy knows.'

'But I have to consider the best interests of the patient.'

'Maybe the best thing for him would be keeping his sister alive.'

'That thought has occurred to me. Obviously I can take another look at him,' Erik says. 'But I'm still pretty sure it's far too early to interview him.'

'OK,' Joona says.

Daniella hurries in wearing a fitted red coat, says she has to run and hands over a set of half-written medical notes.

'I don't think it will be long, maybe only a couple of hours, before he's conscious,' Erik tells Joona. 'But beyond that, you have to understand, we've got a long treatment process ahead of us. A formal interview now could jeopardise the boy's mental condition so much that . . .'

'Erik, it doesn't matter what we think,' Daniella says, cutting him off. 'The prosecutor has already concluded that there are sufficiently strong reasons to go ahead.'

Erik turns and looks at Joona in surprise.

'So you don't need our permission?' he asks.

'No,' Joona replies.

'So what are you waiting for?'

'I think Josef has already suffered more than anyone should ever have to,' Joona replies. 'I don't want to subject him to anything that might harm him, but at the same time I have to find his sister before the murderer does. And the boy has probably seen the killer's face. If you won't help me question him, I'll have to do it the usual way, but naturally, I'd prefer the approach that works best for him.'

'And which approach is that?' Erik asks.

'Hypnosis,' Joona replies.

Erik looks at him, then says very slowly:

'I don't have authorisation to hypnotise . . .'

'I've spoken to Annika,' Daniella says.

'What did she say?' Erik asks.

'It was hardly a popular decision, permitting the hypnosis of an unstable patient who also happens to be a minor, but seeing as I'm responsible for the patient, she's leaving the final decision up to me.'

'I really don't want to do this,' Erik says.

'Why not?' Joona asks.

'I don't want to talk about it, but I promised never to hypnotise anyone again. And that still feels like the right decision.'

'Is it right in this instance?' Joona asks.

'I honestly don't know.'

'Make an exception,' Daniella says.

'Hypnosis,' Erik sighs.

'I want you to try it as soon as you think the patient is even remotely susceptible,' Daniella says.

'I'd like you to be there,' Erik says.

'I'll make the decision about hypnosis,' she says. 'But from then on you're responsible for the patient.'

'So I'm on my own with this?'

Daniella looks at him wearily and says:

'I've been working all night. I really have to go home and get some sleep. I'm no good to anyone in my current state.'

16

Tuesday morning, 8 December

Erik watches Daniella walk down the hall, her red coat flapping behind her, then goes into the bathroom and washes his face. He calls Simone but she doesn't answer. When it tells him to leave a message, he's suddenly at a loss for words:

'Simone, I . . . listen, I don't know what you're thinking, but nothing has happened. Maybe you don't care, but I swear I'm going to find a way to prove to you that I . . .'

Erik trails off, aware that his words are meaningless. He lied to her ten years ago, and he hasn't managed to win back her trust. He ends the call, walks over to Joona and looks into the patient's room.

'What exactly is hypnosis?' the detective asks after a while.

'It's really just an altered state of consciousness, related to suggestion and meditation,' Erik replies.

'Go on,' Joona says.

'When you say hypnosis, what you really mean is hetero-hypnosis, where one person hypnotises another for a specific purpose.'

'Such as?'

'Such as to temporarily remove negative emotions.'

'Like what?'

'The most common use is inhibiting the conscious registration of pain.'

'But the pain is still there.'

'That depends on how you define pain,' Erik replies. 'The patient obviously responds physically to painful stimuli, but experiences no actual pain as such. In fact it's possible to conduct surgery during clinical hypnosis.'

Joona writes something in his notebook.

'In purely neurophysiological terms,' Erik goes on, 'the brain works in a very particular way during hypnosis. Parts of the brain that we rarely use suddenly get activated. Someone who has been hypnotised appears to be extremely relaxed, almost asleep, but EEG scans show that their brain activity is both awake and alert.'

'The boy sometimes opens his eyes,' Joona says, looking in through the window.

'Yes, I've noticed that.'

'What's going to happen now?' he asks.

'With the patient?'

'Yes, when you hypnotise him.'

'During dynamic hypnosis the patient almost always splits into one observing, and one or more experiencing selves.'

'Like watching himself on stage?'

'Yes.'

'What are you going to say to him?'

'First and foremost, I need to get him to feel safe. He's experienced horrific trauma, so I'll start by explaining what my intentions are, and then move on to relaxation. I'll talk soothingly about his eyelids feeling heavier, and him wanting to close his eyes, about breathing deeply through his nose, then I'll move through his body, from the top down, before doing the same thing in reverse.'

Erik waits as Joona writes.

'After that we get to what's known as induction,' Erik says. 'Where I help the patient to imagine certain places and simple events, and then suggest wandering further into his thoughts until the need to control the situation practically disappears. It's like when you read a book that gets so exciting that you're no longer aware that you're sitting and reading.'

'I see.'

‘If you lift the patient’s hand like this, and then let go, the hand should remain raised, cataleptically, once the induction is complete,’ Erik explains. ‘After the induction I count backwards, deepening the hypnosis even further. I usually count, but other people ask their patients to imagine a grey scale, to loosen the boundaries in their thoughts. What takes place in purely practical terms is that the fear and critical thinking that block certain memories are removed.’

‘Will you be able to hypnotise him?’

‘If he doesn’t resist.’

‘What happens then?’ Joona asks. ‘What happens if he resists?’

Erik doesn’t answer at first. He looks at the boy through the glass, trying to read his face and evaluate his receptivity.

‘It’s hard to say what I’ll be able to bring out,’ he says. ‘There’s no way of predicting just how relevant it’s going to be.’

‘I’m not after a full witness statement. I just need something to go on, a description, anything.’

‘So all you really want me to look for is the person who did this to them?’

‘Ideally a name, or a place, some sort of connection.’

‘I have no idea if it’s going to be possible. We’ll see,’ Erik says, then takes a deep breath.

17

Tuesday morning, 8 December

Joona goes in with him, sits down on a chair in the corner, kicks his shoes off and leans back. Erik lowers the lighting, pulls up a metal stool and sits down beside the bed. Very carefully he begins to explain to the boy that he wants to hypnotise him in order to help him understand what happened yesterday.

'Josef, I'm going to be sitting here the whole time,' Erik says calmly. 'There's absolutely nothing to be scared of. You are completely safe. I'm here to help you. You don't have to say anything you don't want to, and you can end the hypnosis whenever you want.'

Only now does Erik realise just how much he's missed this.

It's easy to get the boy to feel very relaxed: his body is already in a resting state.

When Erik opens his mouth and starts the induction, it feels like he's never stopped hypnotising people: his voice is precise, calm and focused, the words come easily and obviously, they stream out, suffused with warmth and a soporific tone.

He can already sense that Josef is extremely receptive. It's as if the boy is intuitively clinging to the security Erik is conveying. His wounded face is getting heavier, his features settling and his mouth becoming slacker.

'Josef, if you like . . . imagine a summer's day,' Erik says. 'Everything is wonderful, lovely. You're lying on the deck of a little wooden boat that's rocking gently. The water is lapping softly at the sides, and when you look up you can see small clouds moving across the blue sky.'

The boy responds so well to the induction that Erik wonders if he ought to slow the process slightly. He knows that difficult experiences can often heighten sensitivity to hypnosis.

'I'm going to count backwards now, and with each number you're going to relax a little bit more. You're going to feel like you're filling up with calmness, and that everything around you is beautiful. Start feeling relaxed in your toes, your ankles and calves. Nothing is troubling you, everything is calm. The only thing you hear is my voice, and the numbers counting down. Now you're relaxing even more. You're feeling heavier. Your knees and your thighs are relaxed. You can feel yourself sinking slowly deeper, nice and gently. Everything is calm and quiet and relaxing.'

Erik puts one hand on the boy's shoulder. He's watching his stomach, and with each breath he counts down another number. Sometimes he breaks the logical rhythm, but keeps counting down the whole time. Erik is filled with a sense of dreamlike ease and physical strength. He counts, and simultaneously sees himself sinking in a blue sea, through clear water. He had almost forgotten this part. With a smile he slips down the side of a vast rock formation, a continental shelf that leads to great depths. The water is sparkling with tiny bubbles. Feeling very happy, he drifts weightlessly down beside the craggy rock-face.

The boy is showing clear signs of hypnotic relaxation. His cheeks and mouth look slack and calm. Erik has always thought that his patients' faces become wider and more open, more honest under hypnosis.

Erik sinks deeper, reaches out one arm to touch the rocks as they pass. The clear water gradually turns a pinkish colour.

'Now you're extremely relaxed,' Erik says softly. 'And everything is beautiful.'

The boy's eyes sparkle behind his half-closed eyelids.

'Josef . . . try to remember what happened yesterday. It starts off as a perfectly ordinary Monday, but in the evening someone comes to visit.'

The boy remains silent.

'Now you're going to tell me what's happening,' Erik says.

The boy nods almost imperceptibly.

'Are you sitting in your room? Is that what you're doing? Are you listening to music?'

He doesn't answer. His mouth is moving tentatively, uncertainly.

'Your mum was there when you got home from school,' Erik says.

He nods.

'Why? Do you know? Is it because Lisa isn't feeling well?'

The boy nods and licks his lips.

'What do you do when you get home from school, Josef?'

The boy whispers something.

'I can't hear,' Erik says. 'I want you to speak so I can hear you.'

The boy's lips move and Erik leans forward.

'Like fire, just like fire,' he murmurs. 'I'm trying to blink, I'm going into the kitchen, but it's not right, there's lots of crackling between the chairs and bright red fire spreading across the floor.'

'Where's the fire coming from?' Erik asks.

'I don't remember, something happened before . . .'

He falls silent again.

'Go back a bit, to before the fire was in the kitchen,' Erik says.

'There's someone there,' the boy says. 'I hear someone knock on the door.'

'The front door?'

'I don't know.'

The boy's face suddenly tenses. He starts to whimper anxiously, and bares his lower teeth in a peculiar grimace.

'You're not in any danger,' Erik says. 'There's no danger, Josef, you're safe here. You're calm, and you're not feeling worried at all. You're just watching what's happening. You're not part of it, you're just seeing it from a distance and it isn't remotely dangerous.'

'Pale blue feet,' he whispers.

'What did you say?'

'There's a knock on the door,' the boy slurs. 'I open it, but there's no one there, I can't see anyone. But the knocking continues. I realise someone's playing a trick on me.'

The patient is breathing faster, his stomach moving irregularly.

'What's happening now?' Erik asks.

'I go to the kitchen and make a sandwich.'

'You eat a sandwich?'

'But now the knocking has started again. It's coming from Lisa's room. Her door is slightly open, and I can see that her princess lamp is switched on. I gently push the door open with the knife and look in. Lisa's lying in bed. She's got her glasses on, but her eyes are closed and she's gasping for breath. Her face is white. Her arms and legs are really stiff. Then she leans her head back and her neck tenses. She starts kicking the end of the bed with her feet. She kicks faster and faster. I tell her to stop, but she keeps kicking harder. I shout at her, and the knife has already started stabbing. Mum runs in and grabs me and I turn round and the knife goes in. It just pours out of me. I get more knives, I'm scared of stopping. I have to keep going, I can't stop. Mum crawls through the kitchen, the floor is all red. I have to try the knives on everything, on myself, on the furniture, the walls, I hit and stab and then I feel really tired and lie down. I don't know what's happening, I hurt all over and I'm thirsty, but I can't move.'

Erik feels himself sinking with the boy in the bright ocean. He looks down. It's endless. The water gets blue-grey and then black.

'You went to see . . .' Erik asks, and hears how his voice is shaking. 'You went to see your dad earlier.'

'Yes, down at the football field,' Josef replies.

He looks confused, stares sleepily ahead of him.

Erik notices his pulse-rate increasing, which means that his blood pressure is falling.

'I want you to sink deeper,' Erik says gently. 'You're sinking, feeling calmer, more peaceful, and . . .'

'Not Mum?' the boy asks in a pathetic voice.

'Josef, tell me . . . did you go and see your big sister, Evelyn?'

Erik watches Josef's face intently, aware that his guess could cause problems, a crack in the hypnosis if it turns out he's wrong. But he had to change course abruptly, because time is running out. He's going to have to stop the hypnosis soon, the patient's condition is clearly deteriorating again.

'What happened when you went to see Evelyn?' he asks.

'I should never have gone to see her.'

'Was that yesterday?'

'She was hiding in the cottage,' the boy says with a smile.

'Which cottage?'

'Aunt Sonja's,' he says tiredly.

'Tell me what happens in the cottage.'

'I'm just standing there. Evelyn isn't happy, I know what she's thinking,' he mutters. 'I'm nothing but a dog to her, I'm worth nothing . . .'

Tears are running down Josef's cheeks, and his mouth is quivering.

'Does Evelyn say that to you?'

'I don't want to, I don't have to, I don't want to,' Josef whimpers.

'What don't you want to do?'

His eyelids starts to quiver.

'What's happening now, Josef?'

'She says I have to bite and bite to get my reward.'

'Who do you have to bite?'

'There's a picture in the cottage . . . a picture in a frame that looks like a toadstool . . . Dad, and Mum, and little Lisa, but . . .'

His body suddenly tenses, his legs twitch spasmodically, he's on the point of slipping out of hypnosis. Erik gradually guides him away, calms him and brings him up a few levels. He carefully closes the doors to all his memories of that day. Nothing can be left open when he starts the slow process of bringing him back.

By the time Erik leaves him, Josef is lying in the bed smiling. The detective gets up from his chair in the corner and goes out of the room with Erik.

'I'm impressed,' Joona says as he takes out his phone.

A desolate feeling settles over Erik, a suspicion that something has gone irrevocably wrong.

'Before you make any calls, I just want to stress one thing,' Erik says. 'Patients always tell the truth during hypnosis, but obviously that can only be their truth. So he's only saying what he believes is true. He's describing his own subjective memories, and not . . .'

'I understand that,' Joona says, cutting him off.

'I've hypnotised people with schizophrenia in the past,' Erik goes on.

'What are you trying to say?'

'Josef talked about his sister . . .'

'Yes, and her demanding he bite like a dog and everything,' Joona says.

He makes a phone call.

'We don't know if his sister told him to do that,' Erik explains.

'But she could have,' Joona says, then holds one hand up to stop Erik. 'Anja, light of my life . . .'

A gentle voice can be heard from the phone.

'Can you check something for me? Yes, exactly. Josef Ek has an aunt called Sonja, and apparently she has a house or summer cottage somewhere, and . . . Yes, that's . . . Great.'

Joona looks up at Erik.

'Sorry, you were about to say something.'

'Only that it's by no means certain that Josef murdered his family.'

'Could he have inflicted those injuries on himself? Could he have cut himself like that? In your opinion?'

'I suppose, purely theoretically, yes,' Erik replies.

'In that case, I think our killer is lying in that room over there,' Joona says.

'So do I.'

'Is he in a fit state to try to escape from the hospital?'

'No,' Erik replies.

Joona starts to leave.

'Are you going to the aunt's house?' Erik asks.

'Yes.'

'I'll come with you,' Erik says, hurrying after him. 'Evelyn could be injured or in a state of shock.'

18

Tuesday, early morning, 8 December

For some reason Simone is already awake when the phone on Erik's bedside table starts to ring.

Erik mutters something about balloons and streamers, picks up the phone and hurries out of the bedroom.

The voice she hears through the door strikes her as sensitive, tender, almost. After a while he creeps back into the bedroom and she asks who the call was from.

'A police officer . . . a detective, I didn't catch his name,' Erik replies, and says he has to go to Karolinska Hospital.

She looks at the alarm clock and closes her eyes.

'Go back to sleep, Simone,' he whispers, and leaves the room.

Her nightdress has twisted around her, and is pulling tightly over her left breast. She adjusts it, rolls onto her side and lies there quietly listening to Erik's movements.

He gets dressed, then leaves the flat, locking the door behind him. A short while later she hears the door down in the street swing shut.

She lies in bed trying to get back to sleep for a long time, but fails. She doesn't think it sounded like Erik was talking to a police officer, it sounded too relaxed. Maybe he was just tired.

She gets up and goes to the bathroom, pours herself a glass of water and then goes back to bed. Then she starts thinking about what happened ten years ago, and finds it impossible to sleep. She lies there for half an hour, then sits up and turns the light on. She picks up the phone and brings up the details of the last call. She knows she should get some sleep, but still finds herself calling the number. The phone rings three times. Then there's a click and she hears a woman laughing away from the phone.

'Stop it, Erik,' the woman says brightly, then she speaks into the phone: 'Yes, Daniella here.'

Simone hears the woman wait and then say 'Have a nice day' in a tired voice before she ends the call. Simone is left sitting there with the phone in her hand. She tries to understand why Erik said it was a detective, a male detective calling him. She tries to find a rational explanation, but can't stop her mind from going to when she found out that Erik was having an affair and had been lying to her face.

It happened to be the same day that Erik declared that he was never going to hypnotise anyone again.

Simone remembers that for once she wasn't at her gallery. Maybe Benjamin didn't go to school that day, maybe she'd taken the day off? Either way, she was sitting at the kitchen table in their airy house in Järfälla going through the post when she noticed a pale blue envelope addressed to her. The sender was identified only by a first name: Maja.

There are moments in your life when every atom in your body can tell something's wrong.

With trembling fingers, she opened the envelope from 'Maja'. Ten photographs fell out onto the kitchen table. They certainly hadn't been taken by a professional. Blurred close-ups of a woman's breast, a mouth, a bare neck, pale green panties and tightly curled black hair. Erik appeared in one picture. He looked surprised, and happy. Maja was a pretty, and very young, woman with pronounced eyebrows. She had a wide, serious mouth. She was lying in just her panties on a narrow bed, her black hair draped across her large white breasts. She looked excited, and was even blushing slightly.

It's hard to explain how it felt. But she can still remember that her initial reaction had been surprise. Gaping, stupid surprise, at having been betrayed so fundamentally by someone she had trusted completely. For a long time after that there was nothing but sadness and an odd, empty feeling in her stomach, a desperate urge to avoid painful thoughts. Then came the shame, followed by a sense of inadequacy, rage and loneliness.

Simone lies in bed as her thoughts swirl.

She remembers how Erik had looked her in the eye and promised that he had never had an affair with Maja – that he didn't even know anyone named Maja. She asked him two more times, and both times he swore that he didn't know a Maja. Then she took out the photographs and threw them at him, one after the other.

Since then she hasn't been able to trust him.

The sky above the city gets slowly brighter. She falls asleep just minutes before Erik gets back from the hospital. He tries to be quiet, but when he sits down on the bed she wakes up. He says he's going to take a shower, but she can tell just by looking at him that he's taken those sleeping pills again. She asks him the name of the policeman who had called earlier, but he doesn't answer. She realises he's fallen asleep in the middle of the conversation. So Simone explains that she called the number and it wasn't a policeman who answered, but a giggling woman named Daniella. Erik can't stay awake, and dozes off again. She shouts at him. She demands to know what's going on, and accuses him of having ruined everything, just when she's finally starting to trust him again.

She sits on the bed looking at him. He doesn't seem to understand why she's upset. She can't handle any more lies. She says the words she has thought so many times, but which still feel so distant, so painful, such obvious signs of failure.

'Maybe it would be best if we separated.'

Simone walks out of the bedroom, taking her pillow and the duvet with her. She hears the bed creak behind her and hopes he's going to follow her, comfort her, explain what happened. But he stays on the bed, and she shuts herself in the guest bedroom and cries for a long time. Then she blows her nose, lies down on the sofa and thinks about getting some sleep. She can't face seeing her family this morning, though, so she washes her face, brushes her teeth, gets dressed and puts her make-up on. She looks in on Benjamin as he sleeps, leaves a note for him on the table and heads out of the flat to grab breakfast somewhere before going to the gallery.

She sits and reads for a long time in a café in Kungsträdgården, trying to finish the sandwich she bought. Through the large window she watches a group of about a dozen people preparing for some sort of event. They've erected pink tents in front of an outdoor stage. Barriers have been set up around the area where they're evidently going to set off fireworks. Suddenly something goes wrong. There's a bang, and one firework shoots up into the sky. The men stumble backwards yelling at each other. The rocket explodes, scattering a transparent blue glow across the pale sky as the bang echoes off the buildings.

19

Tuesday morning, 8 December

Simone is sitting in her office at the gallery, looking at a large portrait of an artist dressed as a ninja, holding a sword above his head. Her phone begins to buzz in her bag.

'Simone Bark Gallery,' she answers, trying to conceal the fatigue in her voice.

'This is Siv Sturesson, from the school office,' an older woman says down the line.

'Oh,' Simone says warily. 'Hello.'

'I'm just calling to see how Benjamin is.'

'How he is?'

'He's not at school today,' the woman explains, 'and he hasn't been reported sick. We always contact the parents if that happens.'

'You know what?' Simone says. 'I'll call the house and check. Benjamin and Erik were both still there when I left this morning. I'll call you back.'

She ends the call, then phones home immediately. It's not like Benjamin to oversleep or just ignore the rules.

There's no answer at home. Erik should have the day off today. Anxiety grabs hold of her again before she realises that Erik is probably lying there snoring, knocked out by sleeping pills, while Benjamin listens to loud music. She tries Benjamin's phone. No answer. She leaves a short message, then tries Erik's mobile phone, but of course it's switched off.

'Ylva,' she calls. 'I just need to run home, I'll be back soon.'

Her assistant looks up, smiles and says:

'Missing you already!'

Simone is too stressed to say anything funny back. She grabs her bag, throws her coat over her shoulders and hurries to the underground.

There's a particular silence outside the doors of empty houses. Simone knows there's no one home as soon as she puts her key in the lock.

Benjamin's skates are still on the floor, but his rucksack, shoes and jacket are missing, as is Erik's winter coat. Benjamin's Puma bag with his medication in it is still in his room. She hopes that means Erik remembered to give him his dose this morning.

Simone looks around Benjamin's room, and thinks it's sad that he's taken down his Harry Potter poster and put almost all his toys away in boxes for storage. He's been in such a hurry to grow up since he met Aida. He's become moody and distant, like he doesn't want to be part of the family. She tries to write it off as typical adolescent behaviour, but it's grown worse in the last couple of months, and she can't help blaming the girl.

Simone stops and wonders if he could be with her now.

Benjamin is only fourteen, Aida seventeen. He says they're friends, but it's obvious that she's his girlfriend. Simone wonders if he's told her about his haemophilia. Does she know that, without regular doses of his medication, the slightest blow could cost him his life?

She sits down with her hands over her face, trying to fend off all the terrifying thoughts.

Simone can't help worrying. In her mind's eye she's always seeing Benjamin getting hit in the face by a basketball during PE, or suffering a spontaneous clot in his head: a dark pearl spreading out like a star and meandering through his brain.

She feels so ashamed when she thinks of how she lost patience with him when he didn't want to walk. He was two years old, but still crawling everywhere. They didn't know at the time that he was a haemophiliac and that the blood vessels in his joints burst every time he stood up. She shouted at him when he started to cry. Told him he looked like a baby, crawling around like that. Benjamin tried to walk, took a few steps, but the excruciating pain made him lie down again.

After Benjamin was diagnosed with Von Willebrand disease, Erik was the one who took charge of his treatment, not her. Erik was the one who carefully flexed Benjamin's joints each morning after he had been asleep to reduce the risk of internal bleeding. It was Erik who took care of the injections, where the needle must not penetrate the muscle, but only be slowly and carefully injected just beneath the skin. It's a technique that's far more painful than a normal injection. During the first few years Benjamin would bury his face against his father's stomach and sob quietly when the needle went in. These days he just keeps on eating his breakfast without looking, holding out his arm so that Erik can swab it, give him the injection and put the plaster on.

The factor concentrate that's supposed to help Benjamin's blood coagulate is called Haemate. Simone can't help thinking it sounds like some Greek goddess of vengeance. It's an unpleasant medicine that severely increases the risk of blood-clots, and they keep hoping that something better will come along. Still, thanks to a combination of Haemate, high doses of desmopressin and a Cyklokapron nasal spray that's supposed to stop his mucous membranes from bleeding, Benjamin is relatively safe.

She can still remember when they were given his laminated risk-card from the Coagulation Clinic in Malmö, with the photograph from Benjamin's birthday. His laughing four-year-old face, and the words: *I have Von Willebrand disease. If anything happens to me, please call the Coagulation Clinic immediately: 040-331010.*

Since he met Aida, Benjamin has also kept his mobile phone around his neck at all times, fixed to a black strap with skulls on it. They text each other long into the night, and Benjamin still has his phone around his neck when he wakes up the next morning.

Simone looks carefully through the papers and magazines on

Benjamin's desk, opens a drawer, moves a book about the Second World War and finds a note with a black lipstick print and a phone number. She hurries to the kitchen and calls the number.

She hears a thin, croaking voice and heavy breathing.

'Hello,' Simone says. 'I'm sorry if this is a bad time, but my name is Simone Bark, I'm Benjamin's mother. I was wondering if . . .'

The voice, which seems to belong to a woman, hisses that she doesn't know a Benjamin and that Simone must have the wrong number.

'Please, wait,' Simone says, doing her best to sound calm. 'Aida and my son have been spending time together and I was wondering if you know where they might be, because I need to get hold of Benjamin.'

'Ten . . . ten . . .'

'I can't hear. I'm really sorry, but I can't hear what you're saying.'

'Ten . . . sta.'

'Tensta? Is Aida in Tensta?'

'Yes, that stupid . . . tattoo.'

Simone thinks she can hear an oxygen mask in the background, a gentle, regular hissing sound.

'What are you trying to say?' she pleads.

The woman snarls something, then ends the call. Simone sits and stares at her phone. She considers calling back but she realises what she heard: something about tattoos in Tensta. She quickly calls directory assistance and gets the address of a tattoo parlour in the centre of Tensta. A cold shiver runs down Simone's spine as she imagines Benjamin being tricked into getting a tattoo, and the blood pouring out of him, unable to clot.

20

Tuesday, lunchtime, 8 December

Simone is sitting on the underground looking out of the window. She's still winded from hurrying out of the empty flat and running to the station.

The train has ground to a halt in Huvudsta.

She tells herself she should have taken a taxi instead. She tries to persuade herself that nothing has happened, that she always worries too much.

A man across from her is rustling some newspapers. From the reflection in the window she can see that he keeps glancing at her.

'Hello?' he says in an annoying voice.

She tries to ignore him. She looks out of the window and pretends to listen to her phone.

'Hello-o?' the man says.

She realises he's not going to give up until he has her attention.

'Can't you hear I'm talking to you?' the man says.

Simone turns towards him.

'I can hear you perfectly well,' she says calmly.

'Why don't you answer, then?' he asks.

'I'm answering now.'

He blinks a couple of times, and then says:

'You are a woman? Aren't you?'

'Is that all you want to know?' she asks curtly and turns back towards the window.

He changes seats to sit next to her.

'Listen to this . . . I had a woman, and my woman, my woman . . .'

Simone feels a few drops of saliva land on her cheek.

'She was like Elizabeth Taylor,' he goes on. 'You know who that is?'

'Yes,' Simone says impatiently. 'Of course I do.'

Satisfied with her answer, he leans back.

'She kept getting different men,' he complains. 'Always wanted more, diamond rings, presents, necklaces.'

The train starts to slow down, and Simone realises that this is her stop, they're pulling into Tensta. She stands up, but he blocks her exit.

'Give me a little hug, I just want a hug.'

She says excuse me through gritted teeth, moves past him and feels a hand on her backside. At that moment the train stops, the man loses his balance and sits back down heavily.

'Bitch,' he declares calmly as she gets off.

She runs out of the underground station, across the bridge, and down the steps. In the covered square she finds a large sign listing the shops in the mall. She looks down the list until she finds the one she wants: Tensta Tattoos. According to the map, the parlour is at one end of the top floor. She hurries towards the escalators. She can't help imagining Benjamin bleeding to death.

She takes the escalator up. Just as she reaches the top floor her eye is caught by something peculiar going on in a deserted part of the floor. It looks like someone's hanging over the railing. She starts to walk in that direction, and as she gets closer she realises what's happening: two teenagers are holding a girl over the railing. A larger figure is walking around behind them repeatedly wrapping his arms around himself, as if he were trying to warm himself in front of a fire.

The children's faces look perfectly calm as they hold the terrified girl over the edge.

'What are you doing?' Simone calls out as she gets closer.

She doesn't run. She's worried they might get scared and let the girl fall. There's a drop of at least ten metres to the floor of the square below.

The boys have seen her and hold the girl out further over the drop. Simone shouts, but they hold onto her, and then very slowly start to pull her back. One of them flips Simone off before they run away. Only the larger boy is left. The girl is sitting curled up next to the railing. Simone stops and crouches down beside her. Simone's pulse is racing.

'Are you all right?'

The girl just shakes her head without speaking.

'We need to find the security guards,' Simone says.

The girl shakes her head again. Her whole body is trembling and she curls into a little ball beside the railing. Simone looks up at the bigger boy, who is just standing there watching them. He's wearing a black down jacket and dark sunglasses.

'Who are you?' Simone asks him.

Instead of answering he pulls a pack of cards from his pocket, and starts to shuffle them.

'Who are you?' Simone repeats, louder this time. 'Are you friends with those boys?'

His expression doesn't change.

'Why didn't you do anything? They could have killed her!'

Simone can feel the adrenalin in her body. Her pulse is throbbing in her temples.

'I asked you a question. Why didn't you do anything?'

She stares angrily at him. He still doesn't answer.

'Idiot!' she shouts.

The boy slowly starts to walk away. She goes after him to stop him from leaving, and he stumbles and drops his cards on the floor. He mutters something to himself and slinks away down the escalator.

Simone turns around to take care of the little girl, but she's vanished. Simone runs back along the walkway, past dark, vacant shop-fronts, but she can't see any trace of the girl or any of the boys. She's standing outside the tattoo parlour. The window is covered by crumpled black plastic and a large illustration of a wolf. She opens the door and walks in. The shop looks empty.

The walls are covered by photographs of tattoos. She's about to leave when she hears a high-pitched, nervous voice:

'Nicke? Where are you? Say something.'

A black curtain opens and a girl comes out clutching a mobile phone to her ear. Her top half is naked. A few tiny drops of blood are running down her neck. There's a look of anxious concentration on her face.

'Nicke?' the girl says into the phone. 'What's happened?'

She has goose-bumps on her breasts, but doesn't seem at all concerned at being half-naked.

'Can I ask you something?' Simone says.

The girl grabs a jacket from off a peg, puts it on, leaves the shop and starts to run. Simone follows her to the door when she suddenly hears a voice behind her:

'Aida?' a boy calls in an anxious voice.

She turns around and sees Benjamin standing there.

'Mum? What are you doing here? Where's Nicke?' he asks.

'Who?'

'Aida's little brother, he's got learning difficulties. Did you see him outside?'

'No, I . . .'

'He's quite big, and is wearing dark sunglasses.'

Simone walks slowly back into the shop and sits down on a chair.

Aida comes back with her brother. He stops outside the door, nodding wide-eyed at everything she says, then wipes his nose. The jacket barely covers her breasts. She walks past Simone and Benjamin without even looking at them and disappears behind the curtain. Simone sees that her neck has swollen up because she's had a dark red rose tattooed next to a Star of David.

'What's going on?' Benjamin asks.

'I saw a group of boys. They were crazy, holding a girl over the railing. Aida's little brother was just standing there and . . .'

'Did you say anything to them?'

'They stopped when I got there, but they just seemed to think it was funny.'

Benjamin looks worried and starts to blush. His eyes dart away as if he feels like running.

'I don't like you hanging out here,' Simone says.

'I can do what I want,' he replies.

'You're too young to . . .'

'Stop it,' he interrupts in a quiet voice.

'So, what? Were you thinking of getting a tattoo, then?'

'No, I wasn't.'

'I just think tattoos on people's face and necks are horrible . . .'

'Mum!' he exclaims.

'They're ugly.'

'Aida can hear what you're saying.'

'But I think . . .'

'Can you leave, please?' Benjamin says sharply.

She looks at him, thinking that she's never heard him speak like that before. But she knows where he learned it. She's aware that she and Erik sound like that far too often.

'You're coming home with me,' she says calmly.

'I'll come if you go outside first,' he replies.

Simone leaves the shop and notices Nicke standing by the darkened window with his arms folded. She goes over to him, trying to look kind, and points at his Pokémon cards.

'Everyone likes Pikachu best,' she says.

He nods to himself.

'But I like Mew better,' she goes on.

'Mew learns things,' he says warily.

'I'm sorry I yelled at you.'

'No one can do anything about Wailord. No one can deal with him, he's the biggest,' he goes on.

'Is he the biggest of all?'

'Yes,' the boy replies seriously.

She picks up a card that he's dropped.

'Who's this?'

Benjamin comes out. His eyes look moist.

'Arceus,' Nicke replies, putting the card on top of the others.

'He looks kind,' Simone says.

Nicke's face breaks into a broad smile.

'Let's go,' Benjamin says in a subdued voice.

'Goodbye,' Simone smiles.

'Goodbye, take care,' Nicke replies automatically.

Benjamin walks along beside her in silence.

'We'll take a taxi,' she decides as they get closer to the underground station. 'I've had enough of the underground.'

'OK,' Benjamin says.

'Just wait a minute,' Simone says.

She's spotted one of the boys who was threatening the little girl. He's standing by the turnstiles inside the station and seems to be waiting for something. Benjamin tries to pull her away.

'What is it?' she asks.

'Come on, let's go, you said we were going to get a taxi.'

'I have to talk to him,' she says.

'Mum, leave it,' Benjamin pleads.

His face is pale and anxious, and he hangs back when she marches over to the boy.

Simone puts her hand on the boy's shoulder and turns him around. He's about thirteen years old or so, but instead of being surprised or scared he grins as if he'd laid a trap for her.

'You're coming with me to the security guard,' she says sternly.

'What did you say, you old bitch?'

'I saw you when you . . .'

'Shut up!' the boy snaps. 'Just shut up unless you want to get raped.'

Simone is so astonished that she freezes. The boy spits on the ground in front of her, then jumps over the turnstile and slowly walks away.

Simone is shaken when she goes back out to join Benjamin.

'What did he say?' he asks.

'Nothing,' she replies wearily.

They walk over to the taxi stand and get in the back seat of the first car. As they pull away from Tensta Simone tells him she got a phone call from his school.

'Aida wanted me to be there when she had her tattoo fixed,' Benjamin says quietly.

'That was kind of you.'

They drive along Hjulstavägen without speaking.

'Did you tell Nicke he was an idiot?' Benjamin asks.

'I was wrong . . . I'm the idiot.'

'How could you?'

'I don't always get it right, Benjamin,' she says quietly.

As they cross the Traneberg Bridge, Simone looks out across the water towards the island of Stora Essingen. The ice hasn't settled yet, but the water seems pale and sluggish.

'It looks like your dad and I are going to separate.'

'Oh . . . Why?'

'It has absolutely nothing to do with you.'

'I asked why.'

'There's no good answer,' she says tentatively. 'Your dad . . . how can I explain this? He's the love of my life, but . . . sometimes things just come to an end. You don't think that when you meet, when you have a child, but if there are too many lies and . . . Sorry, I shouldn't be talking about this.'

'I don't want to get involved.'

'Sorry, I . . .'

'So stop, then!' he snaps.

21

Tuesday afternoon, 8 December

Erik knew he wouldn't be able to sleep, but he still tried. He's been wide awake the whole time, even though Joona has been driving very calmly through Värmdö on highway 274 towards the cottage where they believe they'll find Evelyn Ek.

They pass the old sawmill.

Erik peers out through the windshield and hears Joona speaking quietly over the police radio with colleagues who are heading the same way.

'I've been thinking about something,' Erik says.

'Oh?'

'I said Josef Ek wouldn't be able to escape from the hospital, but now I'm not sure. If he was able to inflict those knife-wounds on himself, who knows what he's capable of.'

'I was thinking the same thing,' Joona replies.

'OK.'

'I've already got one of my men outside the room.'

'It's probably unnecessary,' Erik says.

Three cars are parked by the side of the road beneath the power lines. Four police officers are talking as they put on their bulletproof vests and point at a map. Sunlight glints off the glass of an old greenhouse.

Joona gets back in the car, bringing the cold air with him.

He waits for the others, drumming one hand thoughtfully on the wheel.

The police radio suddenly emits a series of rapid notes, then a loud crackling sound that stops abruptly. Joona checks that they're all ready, exchanging a few words with them before starting the car.

The cars head off, past a brown field, a cluster of birch-trees and a big, rusting silo.

'You're staying in the car when we get there,' Joona says quietly.

'OK,' Erik replies.

Some crows fly out of the way.

'What are the negative repercussions of hypnosis?' Joona asks.

'What do you mean?'

'You were one of the best in the world, and then you stopped.'

'People can have good reasons for wanting to keep things hidden,' Erik replies.

'Sure, but . . .'

'And those reasons are hard to judge using hypnosis.'

Joona casts a sceptical glance at him.

'Why don't I believe that's the reason you stopped?'

'I don't want to talk about it,' Erik says.

The forest gets denser and darker the further they go. Grit crunches beneath the car. They turn off onto a narrow forest track, pass a few summer cottages and stop. Through the trees up ahead Joona can see a brown wooden house standing in a dark clearing.

'Stay where you are,' he says to Erik, then gets out of the car.

As Joona walks towards the driveway where the other police officers are already waiting, he thinks again about Josef, and the words that came pouring from his mouth. A boy describing his own brutality as if he were observing it from a distance. The memory must have been very clear to him: his sister's cramps, his growing rage, his choice of knives, his euphoria at crossing the line. Towards the end of the session Josef's descriptions had become confused and it was harder to understand. Had his older sister Evelyn really encouraged him to carry out the murders?

Joona gathers the other officers around him.

'I want to emphasise the need for everyone to act very cautiously, so we don't frighten the girl,' Joona says. 'She could be scared. She could be injured. But at the same time I don't want you to forget for a moment that we could be dealing with a dangerous person.'

They all study the house for a moment. The chocolate-brown clapboard cottage has white windows and doorframes and a black front door. The windows are covered by pink curtains. There's no smoke coming from the chimney. On the porch there's a broom and a yellow plastic bucket full of dry pine cones.

Joona sends three officers to the back, asking them to stay clear of the yard and approach from well behind the house.

22

Tuesday afternoon, 8 December

Joona watches his men spread out around the house with their weapons drawn. A branch creaks, and in the distance he can hear a woodpecker. Joona follows the movement of the other officers as he slowly approaches the house, trying to see behind the curtains. He gestures to a police officer, a young woman with a pointed face, to stop on the path. She nods without taking her eyes off the house. She draws her pistol and takes a few steps off to one side.

The house is empty, Joona thinks as he approaches the front steps. The planks creak beneath his weight. He looks at the curtains to see if they sway as he knocks on the door. Nothing happens. He waits for a while and stiffens when he thinks he hears a noise. He looks into the forest, through the undergrowth and trees. He draws his pistol, a heavy Smith & Wesson, releases the safety, and makes sure a round is chambered. Suddenly there's a rustling sound at the edge of the forest and a deer darts between the trees. The officer smiles nervously when Joona looks at her. He walks slowly over to the window and tries to see into the cottage through the gap in the curtains.

In the gloom he can see a glass-topped wicker table and a pale brown corduroy sofa. Two pairs of white cotton pants are hanging to dry on the back of a red rib-backed chair. In the kitchenette he can see packets of instant macaroni, jars of pesto, some canned vegetables and a bag of apples. There's some cutlery glinting on the floor in front of the sink, and under the kitchen table. Joona moves back to the porch and indicates to the officer that he's going in. Then he opens the door and steps to one side. When his colleague gives him the go-ahead, he glances inside and steps through the doorway.

Erik is sitting in the car and can vaguely see what's going on in the distance. He sees Joona and another officer disappear inside the brown cottage.

The after-effects of his codeine tablets are making Erik's eyes dry and sensitive. He squints out at the brown house and the cautious movements of the police.

Everything is quiet.

The trees stand bare in the December cold. The light and colours make Erik think back to school field trips when he was a child. His mum worked part-time as a nurse at Sollentuna high school, and she was convinced of the benefits of fresh air. It had been her idea that he should be named Erik Maria. She had studied abroad in Vienna, and had been to the Burgtheater to see Strindberg's *The Father* with Klaus Maria Brandauer in the title role. She had been so impressed that she gave her only son the middle name Maria many years later.

Erik's father, who worked at the National Insurance Office, had one passion in life. He was an amateur magician, and used to dress up in a home-made cape, a second-hand tailcoat and a peculiar collapsible top hat on his head, which he called his *chapeau claque*. Erik and his friends would sit on chairs in the garage where he had built a little stage with secret trapdoors. He had found most of his tricks in the catalogue from Bernardo's Magic in Bromölla: magician's wands that would extend automatically, pool balls that would appear to multiply because they had thin plastic shells, a velvet bag with hidden compartments, and the glittering hand-guillotine. These days Erik looks back on his father with fondness. He thinks about the way he would use his foot to turn on the tape of Jean Michel Jarre while making magical gestures above a floating skull. With all his heart, Erik hopes his father never noticed how ashamed of him he was when he was younger, how he would roll his eyes behind his father's back.

There's no deep explanation for why Erik became a doctor. He had never really wanted any other job, or imagined any other life.

The moment Erik set foot in the medical school at Karolinska Hospital it felt like coming home. He chose psychiatry and, after working as a junior doctor for eighteen months to earn his medical certificate, he went to work for Doctors without Borders. He ended up in Chisimayu, south of Mogadishu in Somalia. It was a very intense posting, working in a field hospital. In Somalia he encountered severely traumatised people for the first time. Children who had forgotten how to play, teenagers who would describe in a monotone how they had been forced to commit atrocities, women who had been so badly abused that they could no longer speak.

Erik returned home to Stockholm and went back to studying, this time psychotherapy. When he started to specialise in psychological trauma and disaster psychiatry he came into contact with different theories about hypnosis. What attracted him to hypnosis was its speed, the fact that a psychologist could get to the root of the trauma so quickly. Erik recognised that this sort of speed was vital if you wanted to work with victims of war and natural disasters.

Three years later he was a member of the Society for Clinical and Experimental Hypnosis, the European Board of Medical Hypnosis and the Swedish Society of Clinical Hypnosis.

Then Erik worked for the Red Cross in Uganda, treating trauma victims. He spent most of that time meeting basic medical needs. He only used hypnosis a dozen or so times during the whole period, and only in fairly basic cases, in place of pain medication, or as a first means of tackling fixations. But during his last year in Uganda, he encountered a girl who had been locked in a room because she wouldn't stop screaming. The Catholic nuns told him that the girl had been found crawling along the road near a shanty town north of Mbale. They thought she was a member of the Bagisu tribe because she spoke Lugisu. She wouldn't sleep, just screamed non-stop that she was a terrible demon with fire in her eyes. Erik asked them to open the door to the girl's room. As soon as he saw her he knew that she was suffering from acute dehydration. When he tried to get her to drink, she howled. She rolled around on the floor screaming. He decided to try hypnosis. A nun, Sister Marion, translated what he said into Bukusu and when she finally started to listen it was fairly easy to hypnotise her. In just one hour the girl was able to come to grips with the trauma she suffered. A petrol lorry had driven off the road north of the shanty town on the Mbale-Soroti Road. The heavy vehicle had rolled over and petrol gushed out of a hole onto the ground. The girl rushed home and told her uncle about the petrol. The uncle ran back with two empty plastic tanks. By the time the girl caught up with him, a group of people had already gathered around the lorry. They filled buckets with petrol. The sun was shining and the smell was terrible in the sweltering heat. The girl's uncle waved her over and gave her a tank to take home. It was very heavy. She stopped to lift it onto her head and saw a woman in a blue shawl standing beside the tanker with petrol up to her knees, filling small glass bottles. Further along the road the girl saw a man in a yellow camouflage shirt. He was smoking a cigarette as he walked.

Erik remembers the way the girl looked as she talked. Her voice was thick and muffled, and tears streamed down her cheeks as she told him what happened. She believed that she caught the flame from the cigarette with her eyes because when she turned back to look at the woman in the blue shawl, she caught fire. It started with the shawl and then the rest of her went up in flames. There was a storm of fire around the lorry, and the girl ran, hearing nothing but screaming behind her.

After the hypnosis Erik and Sister Marion were able to explain to the girl that it was the fumes from the petrol which had started to burn. The man's cigarette had set fire to the tanker through the air, and that was absolutely nothing to do with her.

When Erik finally returned to Stockholm, he applied for a grant from the Medical Research Council to conduct an in-depth investigation into hypnosis at Karolinska Hospital. That was just after he met Simone. He ran into her at a big party at the university. She looked like an angel with her freckles and curly, strawberry-blonde hair. He can still remember what she was wearing that evening: a tailored green silk blouse, long black trousers and high-heels.

Erik blinks and leans closer to the windshield, but he can only make out faint movement through the windows of the brown cottage. He can't hear anything. Presumably Evelyn isn't there. The curtains sway, then the front door opens, and Joona walks onto the porch steps. Three police officers come around the house and stop in front of him. They look at a map, then point towards the road and the other houses. Joona seems to want to show one of them something inside the house. They all follow, and the last one closes the door.

Erik sees someone standing among the trees where the ground starts to slope towards the marsh. It's a thin woman with a shotgun in her hand. The double-barrel glints as she drags it along the ground towards the cottage. It bounces softly on the blueberry bushes and moss.

The police officers haven't seen the woman, and she hasn't spotted them. Erik dials Joona's mobile, but a phone starts to ring on the driver's seat beside him.

The woman walks slowly between the trees with the shotgun in her hand. Erik realises that this could be a dangerous situation if either she or the police are taken by surprise. He gets out of the car and runs over to the driveway, then approaches very slowly.

'Hello!' he calls.

The woman stops and looks at him.

'Pretty cold today,' he says in a low voice.

'What?'

'I said it's cold when you're not in the sun,' he says, louder.

'Yes,' she replies.

'Are you new here?' he asks, still walking towards her.

'No, I'm just borrowing my aunt's cottage.'

'Oh, is Sonja your aunt?'

'Yes,' she smiles.

Erik walks up to her.

'What are you hunting?'

'Hare,' she replies.

'Mind if I take a look at your gun?'

She unloads it and hands it to him. The tip of her nose is red. Some dry pine-needles are caught in her sand-coloured hair.

'Evelyn,' he says calmly. 'There are some police officers here who'd like to speak to you.'

She looks worried and takes a step back.

'If you've got time?' he says, smiling at her.

She nods weakly and Erik calls towards the house. Joona comes out with a look of irritation on his face. When he sees the woman he stiffens.

'This is Evelyn,' Erik says, handing him the shotgun.

'Hello,' Joona says.

Her face is pale, and she looks like she might faint.

'I'd like to talk to you,' Joona says seriously.

'No,' she whispers.

'Come inside.'

'I don't want to.'

Evelyn turns to Erik:

'Do I have to?' she asks, her mouth trembling.

'No,' he replies. 'It's up to you.'

'Please, come with me,' Joona says.

She shakes her head, but still follows him into the cottage.

'I'll wait outside,' Erik says.

He walks back along the driveway. The ground is covered with pine-needles and brown cones. He hears Evelyn's scream through the walls of the cottage. A single scream. It sounds so lonely and desperate. An expression of incomprehensible loss. He recognises that scream all too well from his time in Uganda.

Evelyn is sitting on the corduroy sofa, both hands clasped between her thighs, her face white as ash. She's been told what happened to her family. The photograph in a frame that looks like a toadstool is lying on the floor. In it, her mum and dad are sitting in what looks like a hammock. Her little sister is sitting between them. Her parents are squinting in the bright sunlight, but her little sister's eyes are sparkling.

'I'm so sorry,' Joona says gently.

Her chin trembles.

'Do you think you'd be able to help us try to understand what's happened?' he asks.

The chair creaks under Joona's weight. He waits a moment before going on:

'Where were you on Monday December 7th?'

She shakes her head.

'Yesterday,' he clarifies.

'I was here,' she says weakly.

'In this cottage?'

She looks him in the eye:

'Yes.'

'You didn't go outside all day?'

'No.'

'You just sat here?'

She gestures towards the bed and the political science textbooks.

'You were studying?'

'Yes.'

'So you didn't leave the house yesterday?'

'No.'

'Is there anyone who can confirm that?'

'What?'

'Was there anyone here with you?' Joona asks.

'No.'

'Do you have any idea who might have done this to your family?'

She shakes her head.

'Has anyone threatened any of you?'

She doesn't seem to hear him.

'Evelyn?'

'What? What did you say?'

Her fingers are squeezed tightly between her legs.

'Has anyone threatened your family? Did you have any enemies, anyone who didn't like you?'

'No.'

'Did you know your dad was deeply in debt?'

She shakes her head.

'He was,' Joona says. 'Your dad borrowed money on the black market.'

'Oh.'

'Could any of them . . .?'

'No,' she cuts him off.

'Why not?'

'You don't understand!' she says, raising her voice.

'What don't we understand?'

'You don't understand anything.'

'Tell us then.'

'I can't!' she shouts.

She's so upset that she starts to cry, loudly. A policewoman comes over and hugs her, and after a while she calms down. She sits motionless in the policewoman's arms as occasional sobs wrack her body.

The officer holds the young woman and strokes her hair. Suddenly she yelps and pushes Evelyn onto the floor.

'Damn, she bit me . . . she fucking bit me.'

She looks in astonishment at her bloody fingers. Blood is oozing from a wound in her neck.

Evelyn is sitting on the floor, breathing rapidly. Her eyes roll backwards and she collapses, unconscious.

23

Tuesday evening, 8 December

Benjamin has locked himself in his room. Simone is sitting at the kitchen table with her eyes closed, listening to a live broadcast of a concert from Berwald Hall. She tries to imagine what life as a single woman would be like. It wouldn't be all that different from my life now, she thinks sardonically. I could go to concerts, the theatre, galleries, like all single women do.

She finds a bottle of malt whisky in the cupboard and pours herself a drink. The front door opens just as the warm notes of one of Bach's cello suites fills the kitchen. The melody is gentle and melancholic. Erik stops in the doorway and looks at her, his face grey with fatigue.

'That looks good,' he says.

'It's called whisky,' she says, and hands him the glass.

She pours another drink for herself. They stand in front of each other and solemnly raise their glasses in a toast.

'Did you have a rough day?' she asks quietly.

'Pretty rough,' he replies, smiling weakly.

He looks shattered. His features seem oddly indistinct, as if they were covered by a thin layer of dust.

'What are you listening to?' he asks.

'Shall I turn it off?'

'Not on my account – it's lovely.'

Erik empties his glass, hands it back to her, and she refills it.

'So Benjamin didn't get a tattoo after all?' he says.

'You've been able to follow the drama on your voicemail.'

'I listened to them on the way home just now, I didn't have time before . . .'

'No,' she says, thinking of the woman who answered when she called last night.

'It was good that you went and got him,' Erik says.

She nods, and thinks about how feelings always get mixed up, nothing is ever distinct and isolated. Everything is affected by everything else.

They drink some more, and suddenly she notices that Erik is standing there smiling at her. His smile, with those crooked teeth of his, has always made her go weak at the knees. She can't help thinking how much she'd like to have sex with him right now, without any talking, without any complications.

'I feel like I don't know anything,' she says. 'Or rather . . . I know I don't trust you.'

'Why do you say . . .?'

'It feels like we've lost everything,' she interrupts. 'All you do is sleep, or else you're at work or wherever it is you go. I wanted us to do things, travel, spend time together.'

He puts his glass down and takes a step towards her.

'Can't we still do that?' he asks.

'Don't say that,' she whispers.

'Why not?'

He smiles, strokes her cheek, then becomes serious. Suddenly they're kissing. Simone's whole body has been yearning for this, to be kissed.

'Dad, do you know where . . .?'

Benjamin stops speaking when he comes into the kitchen and sees them.

'You're both crazy,' he sighs, and walks out again.

'Benjamin,' Simone calls after him.

He comes back.

'You said you would pick up the food,' she says.

'Did you order it?'

'It'll be ready in five minutes,' she says, giving him her wallet. 'You know where the Thai place is, don't you?'

'Duh,' he sighs.

'And come straight back,' she says.

'Stop it.'

'Listen to your mother,' Erik says.

'I'm just going to pick up takeout from down the road, nothing's going to happen,' he says, and walks out.

Simone and Erik smile at each other.

Erik gets three glasses out of the cabinet, stops, takes Simone's hand and holds it to his cheek.

'To the bedroom?' she asks.

He looks happy and awkward at the same time, then the phone suddenly rings.

'Don't answer,' he says.

'It could be Benjamin,' she says, picking up the receiver. 'Yes, Simone here.'

She can't hear anything, just a ticking sound.

'Hello?'

She puts the phone back in its cradle.

'No one there?' Erik asks.

Simone can't help thinking he looks worried. He goes over to the window and looks down the street. And again she hears the woman's voice answering the phone this morning. Stop it, Erik, she had laughed. Stop what? Stop pawing at her clothes, licking her breasts, pulling her skirt up?

'Call Benjamin,' Erik says urgently.

'Why should I . . .?'

She picks up the phone the moment it rings.

'Hello?' she says.

When no one says anything she hangs up and dials Benjamin's number.

'Busy.'

'I can't see him,' Erik says.

'Should I go after him?'

'Maybe.'

'He'll be mad,' she says.

'I'll go,' Erik says, and hurries out into the hall.

He grabs his jacket from the hanger just as the door opens and Benjamin walks in. Erik hangs his jacket back up and takes the steaming bag full of the cartons of Thai food.

They settle down in front of the television and watch a film. They eat straight out of the cartons. Benjamin laughs at a funny line. They look happily at each other the way they did when he was little and used to roar with laughter at the children's shows. Erik puts his hand on Simone's knee and she puts hers on top and squeezes his fingers.

Bruce Willis is lying on his back, wiping blood from his mouth. The phone rings again and Erik puts his food down and gets up from the sofa. He goes out into the hallway and answers as calmly as he can.

'Erik Maria Bark.'

Nothing, just a slight ticking.

'OK, that's enough now,' he says angrily.

'Erik?'

It's Daniella's voice.

'Is that you, Erik?' she asks.

'We're in the middle of dinner.'

He hears her rapid breathing.

'What did he want?' she asks.

'Who?'

'Josef,' she says.

'Josef Ek?' Erik asks.

'Didn't he say anything?' Daniella asks.

'When?'

'Just now . . . on the phone.'

Erik looks through the living-room doorway and sees Simone and Benjamin watching the film. He thinks about the family out in Tumba. The little girl, and her mum and dad. And the astonishing rage behind the attack.

'What makes you think he called me?' Erik asks.

Daniella clears her throat.

'He must have convinced the nurse to give him a phone. I spoke to the switchboard and they said they put him through to you.'

'Are you sure?' Erik asks.

'Josef was screaming when I went in, he'd pulled his drip out. I gave him some Alprazolam but he said terrible things about you before he fell asleep.'

'What did he say?'

Erik hears Daniella swallow hard, and her voice sounds exhausted when she replies:

'That you'd fucked with his head, and that you should leave his sister the hell alone unless you want to be wiped out – he said that several times, that you could count on being wiped out.'

24

Tuesday evening, 8 December

It's been three hours since Joona went to Kronoberg Prison with Evelyn. She was taken to a small cell with bare walls and horizontal bars over the misted-up window. The stainless-steel sink in the corner smelled like vomit. Evelyn just stood next to the fixed bunk with its green vinyl mattress looking at him in confusion.

The prosecutor has twelve hours from the time of her arrest in which to decide if she should be remanded into custody or released. If she's remanded, they have until noon of the third day to either charge her or seek an extension. If neither of those things happens, she will be released.

Joona is now back in the prison, walking down the white-floored hallway past rows of pea-green cell doors. He catches glimpses of his reflection in the metal plates surrounding the locks and handles. There are white Thermoses on the floor outside each door. Red signs indicate the location of the fire extinguishers. A cleaning cart has been left at reception, with a white bag for laundry and a green bag for rubbish.

Jens Svanehjälm, the new Senior Prosecutor for the Stockholm District, is waiting outside one of the five interview rooms. He looks barely twenty, but is actually forty years old. There's something boyish about his cheeks.

'Evelyn Ek,' Jens says slowly. 'So, did she force her younger brother to murder the rest of the family?'

'That's what Josef said when . . .'

'But nothing Josef Ek said under hypnosis can be used in court,' Jens interrupts. 'That would be a breach of his right to remain silent and his right not to incriminate himself.'

'I understand that, but it wasn't a formal interview, and he wasn't a suspect,' Joona replies.

Jens looks at his phone as he goes on:

'The conversation merely has to be about the subject of the preliminary investigation for it to count as a formal interview.'

'I'm aware of that, but I had other priorities at the time,' Joona says.

'That's what I suspected, but . . .'

He stops and looks at Joona, as if he's expecting him to say something.

'I'll soon know what happened,' Joona says.

'Sounds good,' Jens says. 'Anita Niedel gave me one piece of advice when I took over from her; if Joona Linna says he's going to find out the truth, he will.'

'We had a few run-ins.'

'So she implied,' he smiles.

'Shall I go in?' Joona asks.

'You're lead interviewer, but . . .' Jens scratches his ear, 'I don't want any more generalised reports. Nothing can be left unclear.'

'I write up my interviews whenever possible,' Joona replies.

'If you write up this interview, I don't think we need to worry about representation, not at this point,' Jens says.

'That's what I thought.'

'Evelyn Ek is merely helping us with our inquiries,' Jens says pointedly.

'Do you want me to inform her that she's formally regarded as a suspect?' Joona asks.

'That's up to you, but the clock is ticking.'

Joona knocks on the door and walks into the dreary interview room, where the barred window is hidden by a blind. Evelyn is sitting on a chair with her shoulders hunched forward. Her face is impassive, and her jaw is clenched. She's staring at the tabletop with her arms folded over her chest.

'Hello, Evelyn.'

She glances up at him with frightened eyes. He sits down across from her. Like her brother, she's very attractive: her features aren't particularly remarkable, but they're very symmetrical. She has light brown hair and intelligent eyes. Her face doesn't seem particularly striking at first glance, but becomes more beautiful the longer Joona looks at it.

'I thought we could have a little chat,' he says. 'What do you think?'

She shrugs.

'When did you last see Josef?'

'Don't remember.'

'Was it yesterday?'

'No,' she says, sounding surprised.

'How many days ago was it?'

'What?'

'I want to know when you last saw Josef,' Joona says.

'Oh, it's been a while.'

'Has he been to visit you at the cottage?'

'No.'

'Never? He's never been to see you in the cottage?'

She shrugs her shoulders weakly.

'No.'

'But he does know about the cottage, doesn't he?'

She nods.

'He went there as a child,' she replies, looking intently at him with her soft brown eyes.

'When was that?'

'I don't know . . . I think I was ten when we borrowed the cottage the summer Aunt Sonja was in Greece.'

'And Josef hasn't been out there since then?'

Evelyn shifts her gaze and looks at the wall behind Joona.

'I don't think so,' she says.

'How long have you been living in your aunt's cottage?'

'I moved in just after the semester started.'

'In August.'

‘Yes.’

‘So you’ve been living there for four months. In a little cottage out on Värmdö. Why?’

Her eyes dart away again, to a point behind Joona’s head.

‘So I could study in peace,’ she says.

‘For four months?’

She shifts in her seat, crosses her legs and scratches her forehead.

‘I just needed to be left alone,’ she sighs.

‘Who’s bothering you?’

‘No one.’

‘So why do you need to be left alone, then?’

She smiles weakly and unhappily.

‘I like the forest.’

‘What are you studying?’

‘Political science.’

‘And you get by on your student stipend?’

‘Yes.’

‘Where do you buy food?’

‘I bike to Saltarö.’

‘Isn’t that quite a long way?’

Evelyn shrugs again.

‘Suppose so.’

‘Do you ever meet people you know there?’

‘No.’

He looks at Evelyn’s smooth young forehead.

‘You’ve never met Josef there?’

‘No.’

‘Evelyn, listen to me,’ Joona says, in a different, more serious tone. ‘Your younger brother Josef told us he was the person who murdered your dad, your mum and your little sister.’

Evelyn stares at the table, her lip quivering. Her pale face flushes red.

‘He’s only fifteen years old,’ Joona goes on.

He looks at her thin hands and the shiny, neatly brushed hair hanging over her fragile shoulders.

‘Why do you think he said he murdered your family?’

‘What do you mean?’ she says, looking up.

'It looks like you think he's telling the truth,' he says.

'Does it?'

'You didn't seem surprised when I said he'd admitted to the murders,' Joona says. 'Were you surprised?'

'Yes.'

She sits perfectly still on the chair, frozen and exhausted. A small worry-line has appeared between her eyebrows. Her lips are moving, as if she's praying or whispering to herself.

'Is he locked up?' she asks out of the blue.

'Who?'

She doesn't look up at him when she answers, just addresses her words tonelessly to the table.

'Josef? Did you lock him up?'

'Are you afraid of him?'

'No.'

'I thought maybe you had a shotgun because you were afraid of him?'

'I go hunting,' she replies, meeting his gaze.

There's something odd about her, something he doesn't understand yet. It's not one of the usual things – guilt, fury, hatred. It's more like some sort of immense resistance. He can't make sense of it. A defence mechanism or protective barrier unlike anything he's come across before.

'Hares?' he asks.

'Yes.'

'Do they taste good?'

'Not especially.'

'How do they taste?'

'Sweet.'

Joona thinks of how she stood in the cold air in front of the cottage. He tries to remember the sequence of events.

Erik had taken her shotgun. He was holding it over his arm, and it was open. Evelyn was squinting at him in the sunlight. Tall and thin, with her sandy brown hair pulled up in a ponytail. A silvery down vest and low-cut jeans, damp trainers, and the pine trees behind her, the moss on the ground, the lingon twigs and decaying toadstools.

Suddenly Joona sees a contradiction in what Evelyn has said.

When he spoke to Evelyn out at her aunt's cottage she sat very still on the corduroy sofa with her hands clasped between her thighs. On the floor by her feet was a photograph in a toadstool frame. Evelyn's little sister was in the photograph. She was sitting between her parents and the sunlight was glinting off her big glasses.

The younger sister must have been four, maybe five years old in the photograph, Joona thinks. So it couldn't have been more than a year old.

Evelyn was claiming that Josef hadn't been to the cottage for many years, but Josef had described the photograph when he was hypnotised.

Naturally there could be other copies of the photograph in other toadstool frames, Joona thinks. This same photograph could even have been moved about. And Josef could have been in the cottage without Evelyn's knowledge.

But it could also be a crack in Evelyn's story.

'Evelyn,' Joona says. 'I'm wondering about something you said a little while ago.'

There's a knock on the door of the interview room. Evelyn starts and seems to tense up. Joona gets to his feet and goes and opens the door. Jens asks him to step outside.

'I'm letting her go,' Jens says. 'This is silly, we've got absolutely nothing, just one inadmissible interview with her fifteen-year-old brother in which he implies that she . . .'

Jens quietens down when he sees the way Joona is looking at him.

'You've found something, haven't you?' he says.

'It doesn't matter,' Joona replies.

'Is she lying?'

'I don't know, maybe . . .'

Jens rubs his chin, thinking.

'Give her a sandwich and a cup of tea,' he eventually says. 'Then you've got one more hour before I decide whether to hold her.'

'There's no guarantee it's going to lead anywhere.'

'But you'll give it a try?'

*

Four minutes later Joona puts a plastic mug of tea and a sandwich on a paper plate in front of Evelyn and sits back down on his chair.

'I thought you might be hungry,' he says.

'Thanks,' she says, perking up.

Her hand is shaking as she eats the sandwich and sweeps the crumbs off the table.

'Evelyn, in your aunt's cottage there's a photograph in a frame that looks like a toadstool.'

Evelyn nods.

'She bought it up in Mora, thought it would look good in the cottage, and . . .'

She trails off and blows on her tea.

'You don't have any other frames like that?'

'No,' she smiles.

'Has that picture always been in the cottage?'

'What are you trying to say?' she asks weakly.

'Nothing, it's just that Josef mentioned that picture, so he must have seen it, and I was wondering if you might have forgotten something.'

'No.'

'That was all,' Joona says, then stands up.

'Are you going?'

'Evelyn, I trust you,' Joona says seriously.

'Everyone seems to think I'm involved.'

'But you're not – are you?'

She shakes her head.

'Not like that, anyway,' Joona says.

She quickly brushes some tears from her cheeks.

'Josef came to the cottage once. He took a taxi, and he brought cake,' she says in a shaky voice.

'On your birthday?'

'No. It was his birthday.'

'When was this?' Joona asks.

'The 1st of November.'

'About a month ago,' Joona says. 'What happened?'

'Nothing,' she replies. 'I was surprised.'

'He didn't tell you he was coming?'

'We hadn't been in touch.'

'Why not?'

'I needed to be on my own.'

'Who knew you were living in the cottage?'

'No one, apart from Sorab, my boyfriend . . . well, he broke up with me, so we're just friends now, but he's been helping me, telling everyone I'm staying with him, answering when my mum calls and . . .'

'Why?'

'I need to be left alone.'

'Did Josef visit again?'

'No.'

'This is important, Evelyn.'

'He hasn't been there ever again,' she replies.

'Why did you lie about this?'

'I don't know,' she whispers.

'What else have you been lying about?'

25

Wednesday afternoon, 9 December

Erik is walking past the brightly lit counters in the jewellery department of the NK department store. A woman dressed in black is talking quietly to a customer. She opens a drawer and lays a couple of pieces of jewellery on a velvet tray. Erik stops in front of a display case and looks at an expensive necklace. Large, softly polished triangles have been linked together like petals to form a chain. The sterling silver gives off a subtle glow, almost like platinum. Erik thinks how beautiful the necklace would look around Simone's neck, and decides to buy it for her as a Christmas gift.

As the shop-assistant is wrapping the necklace in sparkly, dark red paper, Erik's phone starts to buzz loudly because it's vibrating against his little wooden pill box with the parrot on it. He pulls his phone out and answers without checking the number on the screen.

'Erik Maria Bark.'

The line crackles and he hears Christmas songs in the background.

'Hello?' he says.

Then he hears a weak voice.

'Is this Erik?'

'Yes, it's me,' he says.

'I was wondering . . .'

Erik hears faint giggling in the background.

'Who am I talking to?' he asks sharply.

'Wait a moment, Doctor. I just want to ask something,' the voice says, now sounding openly mocking.

Erik is about to hang up when the voice on the phone suddenly roars:

'Hypnotise me! I want to be . . .'

Erik jerks the phone away from his ear. He ends the call and tries to see who was calling, but the number was withheld. Another buzz tells him that he's received a text, also from a withheld number. *Try to hypnotise a corpse*

Thoroughly confused, Erik walks out of the jewellery department carrying the Christmas present. Just inside the main entrance on Hamn Street, he catches the eye of a woman in a loose black coat. She's standing under the suspended, three-storey-high Christmas tree, staring at Erik. He's never seen her before, but the look in her eyes is definitely hostile.

With one hand he opens the lid of the little wooden box in his pocket, slips a codeine pill into his hand, puts it in his mouth and swallows.

He walks outside into the chilly air. People are huddling in front of the Christmas displays in the shop windows. Little elves dance around a landscape made of sweets. Pre-school children wearing yellow reflective vests over their thick winter coats look on.

His phone rings again, but this time he checks the number. It's a Stockholm area code, and he answers warily:

'Erik Maria Bark.'

'Yes, hello, my name is Britt Sundström. I work for Amnesty International.'

'Hello,' he says, wondering what this is about.

'I'd like to know if your patient was in a position to refuse to be hypnotised?'

'What did you say?' Erik asks, as he watches a large snail pull a sleigh full of Christmas presents in the shop window.

His heart begins to beat faster and he can feel bile rising in his stomach.

'In KUBARK, the CIA's handbook about undetectable torture,

hypnosis is actually listed as one of the . . .'

'The physician in charge of the patient's treatment decided . . .'

'So you're saying you're not personally responsible?'

'I don't think I should comment on this,' he says.

'You've already been reported to the police,' she says curtly.

'Really,' he says, and ends the call.

He walks slowly towards the Stockholm City Theatre, with its glittering glass columns. As the Christmas market comes into view, he hears a trumpeter playing 'Silent Night'. He stops outside a 7-Eleven and reads the headlines for the evening papers:

CHILD TRICKED INTO CONFESSING
TO MURDERING HIS WHOLE FAMILY
UNDER HYPNOSIS

And:

SCANDALOUS HYPNOSIS!
Erik Maria Bark
RISKS BOY'S LIFE

Erik feels his pulse throbbing in his ears. He hurries on, trying not to catch anyone's eye. He passes the site where Prime Minister Olof Palme was murdered. Three red roses are lying on the dirty memorial stone. Erik hears someone call after him and slips into an electronics store. He feels feverish, and he's full of anxiety and despair. His hands are shaking as he pops another codeine. His stomach stings as the capsule takes effect.

On the radio they're discussing whether hypnosis should be banned as a form of treatment. One man says he was once hypnotised into believing he was Bob Dylan.

'I mean, I knew it wasn't true,' he says in a drawl. 'Even so, I felt I was being forced into saying the things I said. I knew I was hypnotised, but I still believed I was Dylan, I couldn't help it. I'd have confessed to absolutely anything.'

The Justice Minister says in his Småland accent:

'Using hypnosis as an interview technique is without a doubt an infringement of the subject's rights.'

'So Erik Maria Bark has broken the law?' the journalist asks sharply.

'The Public Prosecutors' Office will have to look into that . . .'

26

Wednesday afternoon, 9 December

Sweat is pouring down Erik's back as he stops outside the door to 73 Luntmakar Street, taps in the code and opens the door. He fumbles for his keys as the lift takes him up. Once he's inside, he locks the door. He stumbles into the living room, and tries to take his shoes and coat off, but he's unsteady on his feet.

He turns the television on and sees the Chair of the Swedish Society for Clinical Hypnosis. Erik knows him well, and he's seen plenty of colleagues suffer as a result of his arrogance and ambition.

'We expelled Bark ten years ago, and he's not welcome back,' the chairman says with a slight smile.

'Does this affect the reputation of serious hypnosis?'

'All our members adhere to strict ethical rules,' he replies pompously. 'Sweden has very strict laws against malpractice.'

Erik finally gets his coat off, and sits down on the sofa to rest. He opens his eyes again quickly, wondering what Benjamin will think when he sees the news.

Erik turns the television off, then goes into the bedroom, and sits down on the bed. He takes his trousers off and puts the wooden box with the parrot on it in the drawer of the bedside table.

He tries not to think about the longing that stirred inside him when he hypnotised Josef Ek, and was pulled down into that deep blue sea.

Erik lies down and reaches towards the glass of water on the bedside table but falls asleep before he can pick it up.

He wakes up, and in his drowsy state finds himself thinking about his own father performing at children's parties, dressed in his tails with sweat running down his cheeks. He would make balloon animals and pull colourful flowers from a hollow walking stick. When he got older and had moved into a nursing home, he heard about Erik's work on hypnotherapy and wanted them to work on an act together. He would play a gentleman thief and Erik would be the stage hypnotist who could make people sing like Elvis or Zarah Leander.

He snaps out of it, and sits up, his stomach aching badly. He grabs his phone from the bedside table and calls Simone.

'Simone Bark Gallery,' she answers.

'Hey, it's me,' Erik says.

'Hang on a minute.'

He hears her cross the wooden floor and close the office door behind her.

'What's going on? Benjamin called and . . .'

'There's a big media-storm, and . . .'

'What have you done?' she interrupts.

'The doctor in charge of the patient's care asked me to hypnotise him.'

'But confessing a crime under hypnosis is . . .'

'Listen to me,' he says. 'Please, just listen to me.'

'OK.'

'It wasn't a formal interview,' Erik says.

'Surely it doesn't matter what you . . .'

She stops speaking. He can hear her breathing.

'Sorry,' she says quietly.

'It wasn't a formal interview. The police needed a description, anything really, because they thought a girl's life was in danger. The doctor in charge of his treatment concluded that any potential health risk was low enough to allow it.'

'But . . .'

'We thought he was a victim, and we were trying to save his sister's life.'

He stops, and Simone takes a deep breath.

'What on earth have you done? You . . . you promised not to hypnotise anyone again,' she says in a trembling voice.

'It'll be OK. It's really nothing to worry about, Simone.'

'Nothing to worry about?' she says. 'You break a promise but don't think it's anything to worry about? You really can't be trusted, can you? You just keep on lying.'

Simone hangs up.

Erik stands completely still for a while. He goes into the kitchen, and dissolves an Alka-Seltzer in water, then swallows a Prilosec with the sweet, fizzy liquid.

27

Thursday afternoon, 10 December

Joona looks out at the dark, empty office. It's almost eight o'clock at night and he's the last person left in the entire department. Advent stars and electric candles are shining softly in all the windows, their glow doubled by their reflections in the dark glass. Anja has left a bowl of Christmas sweets on his desk, and he eats way too much as he types up notes from his interview with Evelyn.

After catching Evelyn in a lie, the prosecutor decided to hold her in custody. As a result, Joona now has three days to investigate before formal charges must be filed. If he doesn't find enough evidence for a reasonable chance of conviction, she will have to be released.

Joona is well aware that Evelyn's lies don't necessarily mean that she's guilty of a crime, but at least he has three days to find out what she's hiding, and why.

He prints out the report, and puts it in the pile of post for the prosecutor. He locks his pistol in the gun-cabinet, then walks out of Police Headquarters to his car.

As Joona is driving across Fridhemsplan his phone rings, but for some reason he can't seem to pull it out of his coat. It's slipped through a hole in his pocket into the lining. The light turns green and the cars behind him start to honk their horns. He pulls into a bus-stop outside an Indian restaurant. He shakes his phone out and returns the call.

'This is Joona Linna – you just called me.'

'Great, yes,' Officer Ronny Alfredsson says. 'We're not quite sure what we should be doing.'

'Have you talked to Evelyn's boyfriend, Sorab Ramadani?'

'That's not going so well.'

'Did you check his office?'

'It's not that,' Ronny says. 'He's here, in his flat, but he refuses to open the door. He doesn't want to talk to us. Keeps shouting at us to go away. He says we're disturbing the neighbours and we're harassing him because he's a Muslim.'

'What have you said to him?'

'Nothing, just that we'd like his help with something. We did exactly what you told us to do.'

'I see,' Joona says.

'Do we break the door down?'

'I'm coming over. Leave him alone until I get there.'

'Should we wait in the car outside?'

'Yes, please.'

Joona turns around and makes his way past the *Dagens Nyheter* skyscraper and out across the Western Bridge. In the darkness the lights of the city make the sky look like a misty grey dome above them.

He thinks back to the crime scene. There's something odd about the pattern that's emerging. Some of the circumstances appear to be irreconcilable. At a red light, Joona opens the folder on the passenger seat beside him. He leafs quickly through the photographs from the locker room. Three showerheads, with no screens between them. The glare from the camera flash reflects off the white tiles. One picture shows the wooden-handled squeegee leaning against the wall. The strip of rubber is surrounded by a large pool of blood, water and dirt, strands of hair, old plasters and an empty shower-gel bottle.

Next to the drain in the floor lies an entire human arm. The ball-joint is surrounded by gristle and cut muscle. The hunting knife with its broken blade is lying in the shower.

The Needle found the end of the blade embedded in Anders Ek's pelvis when he ran a CAT scan.

The mutilated body is lying on the floor between a wooden

bench and the dented metal lockers. A red windbreaker is hanging from a hook. There's blood everywhere, on the floor, doors, ceiling and benches.

Joona drums the steering-wheel while he waits for the light to change. The forensics team managed to secure plenty of evidence in the form of fingerprints, fibres and strands of hair. They found a huge amount of DNA, from hundreds of people, but nothing so far that can be linked to Josef Ek. A lot of the DNA that was secured was degraded and therefore useless.

He told the forensics experts that they should concentrate on looking for traces of the father's blood on Josef Ek. Blood from the other crime scene doesn't mean anything. Everyone in the terraced house was covered in each other's blood. The fact that Josef had traces of his little sister's blood on him was no more suspicious than the fact that she had his on her. But if they can find traces of the father's blood on Josef, or traces of Josef's in the locker room, that would tie him to both crime scenes. And if they can place him in the locker room, that would be enough to press charges.

While Josef was at Huddinge Hospital a doctor was instructed by forensics to secure all available biological evidence from his body.

Joona calls Erixon, an extremely fat man who is the forensics officer in charge of the crime scene investigation in Tumba.

'Go home,' a thick voice answers.

'Erixon?' Joona teases. 'Erixon? Give me some sign, anything to prove that you're still alive.'

'I'm asleep,' he replies tiredly.

'Sorry.'

'OK, I'm not, but I am on my way home.'

'Have you found anything that puts Josef in the locker room?' Joona asks.

'No.'

'You must have.'

'No,' Erixon replies.

'I don't think you're doing your job.'

'You're wrong,' Erixon replies calmly.

'Have you put pressure on our friends in Linköping?' Joona asks.

'I'm leaning on them with the whole of my considerable weight,' he replies.

'And?'

'They haven't found any of the father's DNA on Josef.'

'I don't believe them either,' Joona says. 'He was covered in . . .'

'Not one drop,' Erixon interrupts.

'That doesn't make sense.'

'They sounded pretty damn smug when they told me.'

'Anything?'

'No, not even the tiniest little drop. Nothing.'

'OK . . . we can't be that unlucky.'

'I'm afraid we can.'

'No.'

'You might have to back down on that point,' Erixon says.

'OK.'

They end the call and Joona thinks about how things that look like mysteries can sometimes be complete coincidences. The killer's modus operandi at both crime scenes appear to be identical: frenzied stabbing and aggressive attempts to dismember the bodies. So it's extremely odd that they haven't found any of the father's blood on Josef if he is the killer. He should have been so drenched in his father's blood when he left the locker room that someone would have noticed, Joona thinks, and calls Erixon again.

'Yes?'

'I've thought of something.'

'In twenty seconds?'

'Did you examine the women's locker room?'

'No one's been in there – the door was locked.'

'The victim would have had a set of keys on him.'

'But . . .'

'Check the drain in the women's shower,' Joona says.

28

Thursday evening, 10 December

Joona drives to Tantolunden and parks in front of the flats overlooking the park. He wonders where the police car is parked. He checks the address, and considers the possibility that Ronny and his partner have been knocking on the wrong door. He smiles. That would explain why 'Sorab' was so reluctant to let them in, seeing as that wasn't even his name.

The evening air is cold. He walks quickly towards the front door and thinks about how Josef described the sequence of events in the terraced house. Josef did nothing to conceal the crimes and made no attempt to protect himself. He wasn't thinking of any potential consequences and let himself get covered in blood.

Perhaps Josef Ek was describing his emotional state while he was hypnotised, a confused and tumultuous rage, but perhaps he was physically far more controlled at the time, at least at first, at the football field. Maybe he wore a full-body rain suit, and then showered in the women's locker room before he went home.

He needs to talk to Daniella Richards and find out when she thinks Josef will be healthy enough for an official interview.

Joona goes inside, and sees his own reflection in the black squares of the chequerboard tiles on the wall. In front of the lift he calls Ronny again, but gets no answer. Maybe Sorab finally let them in. Joona goes up to the sixth floor, then walks up to Sorab's door and rings the bell.

He waits for a while, then knocks. He waits a little longer, then opens the letterbox and says:

'Sorab? My name is Joona Linna. I'm a police officer.'

There's a noise from the door, as if someone leaning against it moved away.

'You were the only person who knew where Evelyn was,' he says.

'I didn't do anything,' a deep male voice says from inside the flat.

'But you said . . .'

'I don't know anything!' he yells.

'OK,' Joona says. 'But I want you to open the door, look me in the eye, and tell me you don't know anything.'

'Go away.'

'Open the door.'

'What the hell? Can't you just leave me alone? I've got nothing to do with this, I don't want to get involved.'

His voice sounds desperate. He quietens down, but Joona can hear him breathing, then hitting something with his hand.

'Evelyn's OK,' Joona says.

The letterbox rattles slightly.

'I thought . . .'

He stops talking again.

'We just want to talk to you?'

'Is that true, nothing's happened to Evelyn?'

'Open the door.'

'I don't want to, I already told you.'

'You should come with me.'

Neither of them says anything for a few moments.

'Has he been here more than once?' Joona asks.

'Who?'

'Josef.'

'Who's that?'

'Evelyn's brother.'

'He hasn't been here at all,' Sorab says.

'So who has been, then?'

'I never said anyone was here, you're just trying to trick me.'

'No, I'm not.'

Another silence. Then a long sob behind the door.

'Is she dead?' Sorab asks. 'Is Evelyn dead?'

'Why do you ask that?'

'I don't want to talk to you.'

Joona hears footsteps, moving away, then the sound of a door closing. Loud music starts to play inside the flat. Joona walks down the stairs, thinking that someone must have scared Sorab into saying where Evelyn was hiding.

Joona emerges into the cold night air and sees two men in Pro Gym jackets standing by his car. They turn around when they hear him coming. One of them sits down on the bonnet holding a phone to his ear. Joona quickly sizes them up. They're both in their thirties. The one sitting on the bonnet has a shaved head, while the other one has what looks like a bowl cut. Joona guesses that the man with the bowl cut weighs more than two hundred pounds, maybe does aikido, karate or kickboxing. He probably takes steroids, Joona thinks. The other one might be carrying a knife, but probably doesn't have a gun.

A thin dusting of snow has settled on the grass.

Joona turns as if he hasn't noticed the men and starts to walk towards the illuminated path.

'Hey, old man,' one of them calls.

Joona pretends not to hear, and walks towards the steps next to the lamppost.

'Aren't you taking your car?'

Joona stops and glances up at the building. He realises that the man on the bonnet is talking to Sorab on the phone, and that Sorab is watching them from his window.

The larger of the pair is walking slowly towards Joona, and Joona turns around to meet him.

'I'm a police officer,' he says.

'And I'm a little fucking monkey.'

Joona takes his phone out and calls Ronny again. 'Sweet Home Alabama' starts playing in the pocket of the larger man and he grins. He pulls out Ronny's phone and answers.

'Hello, this is the cops.'

'What's going on?' Joona says.

'You need to stay the fuck away from Sorab – he doesn't want to talk.'

'Do you really think you're helping him by . . .?'

'This is a warning,' the man interrupts. 'I don't give a shit who you are, you need to stay away from Sorab.'

'Where are my colleagues?' Joona asks calmly.

'Didn't you hear me? Leave Sorab the fuck alone.'

The man in front of him runs his hand through his hair, and starts to breathe faster. He moves closer and lifts the heel of his back foot a few centimetres off the ground.

'I used to train when I was younger,' Joona says. 'If you attack me, I'll defend myself and arrest you.'

'We're shaking with fear,' the man sitting on the car says.

Joona doesn't take his eyes off the other man.

'You're thinking of kicking me in the leg,' Joona says. 'Because you know you're too clumsy to kick any higher.'

'Idiot,' the man mutters.

Joona moves to his right to give himself more options.

'If you decide to kick,' Joona goes on, 'I won't back away, like you're used to. I'll come at you instead, aiming for the knee of your other leg, and as you fall backwards I'll hit you in the neck with this elbow.'

'Christ, he talks a lot of shit,' the man on the car says.

'Yeah,' the other man grins.

'If your tongue's sticking out when that happens, you'll bite it off,' Joona says.

The man with the bowl cut rocks slightly, and when the kick finally comes it's slower than expected. Joona has already taken his first step by the time the man's hips start to swivel. And before his leg straightens out and hits its target, Joona kicks out as hard as he can at the knee of his planted leg. He's already off balance, and falls backwards as Joona swings round and slams his elbow into his neck.

29

Friday morning, 11 December

It's five thirty in the morning, and there's a knocking sound somewhere in the flat. Simone hears the noise as part of a frustrating dream in which she is playing an elaborate version of the shell game. She understands the rules, but keeps getting it wrong. A boy is knocking on the table and pointing out how badly she's doing. Simone is suddenly wide awake.

Someone or something is knocking inside the flat. She tries to figure out where it's coming from in the darkness. She lies still and listens, but the knocking has stopped.

She hears Erik snoring gently beside her.

Simone is just thinking that the noise must have come from her dream when the knocking starts again. Someone's inside the flat. Erik has taken pills and is fast asleep. When she puts her hand on his arm, Erik's snoring gets quieter. With a long exhalation of air he rolls over in his sleep. As quietly as she can, Simone gets out of bed and slips out through the half-open bedroom door.

There's a light on in the kitchen. She walks in and sees that it's coming from the fridge. The fridge and freezer doors are open. Drops of water are falling from the thawing food, and making little tapping sounds as they land on the plastic.

It is cold in the kitchen and it smells like cigarette smoke.

She looks out into the hall.

And then she sees that the front door is wide open.

She hurries to Benjamin's room, but he's fast asleep. She just stands there for a few moments, listening to the regular sound of his breathing.

When she goes to close the front door her heart almost stops. There's someone standing in the doorway. He nods to her and hands her an object. It takes her a few seconds to realise that it's the newspaper man, holding out the morning paper. She thanks him, takes it, and when she finally closes and locks the door, her whole body is shaking.

She turns on all the lights and checks the whole flat. Nothing seems to be missing.

Simone kneels down and is wiping the water from the floor when Erik comes in. He tosses a towel on the floor and starts to wipe the water with his foot.

'It was probably me, sleepwalking,' he says.

'No,' she says tiredly.

'The fridge is a classic, though – I was probably hungry.'

'This isn't funny. Besides, I sleep so lightly that I wake up every time you roll over in bed or stop snoring. I wake up when Benjamin goes to the bathroom.'

'Then it must have been you sleepwalking.'

'Why would the front door be open then? Why . . .'

She trails off, unsure if she should mention it or not.

'And I definitely smelled cigarette smoke in the kitchen,' she eventually says.

Erik chuckles and Simone's cheeks flush angrily.

'Is it so hard to believe someone was here?' she asks irritably. 'After all the crap the papers have been printing about you? It would hardly be that much of a surprise if some lunatic broke in here and . . .'

'Just stop it,' he interrupts. 'This isn't logical, Simone. Who, who in all the world, would break into our flat, open the fridge, smoke a cigarette and then just leave?'

Simone throws the towel on the floor again:

'I don't know, Erik! I don't know, but that's exactly what someone just did!'

'Calm down,' Erik says.

'How can I calm down?'

'Can I tell you what I think? I mean, a bit of cigarette smoke isn't that strange. One of the neighbours probably had a cigarette under the vent fan. The whole building shares the same ventilation system. Or some arsehole dropped a cigarette in the stairwell without thinking about . . .'

'You don't have to sound so patronising,' Simone says curtly.

'For God's sake, Simone, this isn't worth fighting over. I just don't think it's anything to worry about – I'm sure there's a perfectly reasonable explanation.'

'I could tell someone was in the flat when I woke up,' she says quietly.

He sighs and walks out of the kitchen. Simone looks at the dirty towel they've been wiping the floor with.

Benjamin comes in and sits down at the kitchen table in his usual seat.

'Good morning,' she says.

He sighs and rests his head in his hands.

'Why do you and Dad always lie about everything?'

'We don't,' she replies.

'Yeah, right,' he says.

'Are you thinking about what I said in the taxi?'

'I'm thinking about lots of things,' he says loudly.

'There's no need to shout at me.'

'Forget I said anything,' he sighs.

'I don't know what's going to happen with your dad and me. It's not that easy. You're probably right, and we're just fooling ourselves, but that's not the same thing as lying.'

'OK, if you say so,' he says quietly.

'Are you thinking about something else?'

'There aren't any pictures of me when I was little.'

'Yes, there are,' she replies with a smile.

'As a new-born baby,' he says.

'You know I had several miscarriages before, and we were so happy when you were born that we forgot to take pictures. I know exactly what you looked like when you were born, with your wrinkly little ears and . . .'

'Stop it!' Benjamin yells and goes to his room.

Erik comes into the kitchen and dissolves an Alka-Seltzer in a glass of water.

'What's up with Benjamin?' he asks.

'I don't know,' she whispers.

Erik drains his glass standing at the sink.

'He thinks we lie about everything,' she says.

'All teenagers feel like that.'

Erik belches silently.

'I let slip that we might be splitting up,' she says.

'What? How could you do something so stupid?' he says harshly.

'I just said what I felt at the time.'

'Christ, you can't just think about yourself here!'

'I'm not the one who does that, I'm not the one who sleeps with students, I'm not . . .'

'Shut up!' he shouts.

'I'm not the one who takes pills every day.'

'You've got no idea!'

'I know you're taking painkillers.'

'What business is that of yours?'

'So where does it hurt, Erik? Tell me if . . .'

'I'm a doctor, and I think I'm a better judge of this than . . .'

'You're not fooling me,' she snaps.

'What's that supposed to mean?' he laughs.

'You're an addict, Erik. We don't have sex any more because you're taking pills that . . .'

'Maybe I don't want to have sex with you,' he interrupts. 'Why would I want to when you're so fucking miserable all the time?'

'OK, we're splitting up,' she says.

'Fine,' he replies.

She can't look at him. She walks very slowly out of the kitchen as she feels her throat tightening and tears well up in her eyes.

Benjamin has shut the door to his room and is playing music

so loudly that the walls and doors are shaking. Simone locks herself in the bathroom, turns the light out and cries.

'Fucking hell!' she hears Erik shout before the front door opens and slams shut.

30

Friday morning, 11 December

Dr Richards called Joona a little before seven in the morning. She told him she thought Josef was now strong enough to deal with a short interview.

Joona feels a dull pain in his elbow when he gets in the car to drive to the hospital. He thinks back to the previous evening, the way the blue lights of the patrol cars swept across the façade of the building at Tantolunden where Sorab Ramadani lives. The big man with the bowl cut was spitting blood and muttering indistinctly about his tongue as he was led away by the police. Ronny Alfredsson and his colleague Peter Jysk were found in the bomb shelter in the basement of the block. They had been threatened with knives and locked up, then the two men drove their patrol car to the next building and left it in the car park there.

Joona went to Sorab's flat, and told him his bodyguards had been arrested and that the door to the flat would be smashed in if he didn't open up immediately.

Sorab let him in, and asked him to sit down on the blue leather sofa. He offered Joona some camomile tea and apologised on behalf of his friends.

He was a pale man with his hair in a ponytail. He was clearly worried, and kept looking around the whole time. He apologised for what had happened, but went on to explain that he had been having an awful lot of problems recently.

'That's why I thought I ought to get some protection,' he said quietly.

'What sort of problems?' Joona asked as he sipped the hot tea.

'Someone's out to get me.'

Sorab stood up and looked out of the window.

'Who?' Joona asked.

With his back to him, Sorab said he didn't want to talk about it.

'Do I have to talk?' he asked. 'Don't I have the right to remain silent or something?'

'You've got the right to remain silent,' Joona conceded.

Sorab shrugged his shoulders.

'Well, then.'

'But I'd like you to talk to me,' Joona went on. 'I might be able to help you – have you considered that?'

'Thanks a lot,' Sorab said, still facing the window.

'Is it Evelyn's brother who . . .?'

'No,' he snapped.

'So Josef Ek hasn't been here?'

'He's not her brother.'

'Who is he, then?'

'How should I know, but he's not her brother, he's something else.'

And with those words, Sorab became nervous again. He changed the subject, and started talking about football, and the German league and wouldn't answer any more questions properly. Joona wondered what Josef had said to Sorab, what he had done, how he had managed to scare him into revealing where Evelyn was.

Joona turns in and parks in front of the Neurology Department. He says hello to the police officer outside Josef's door and then goes into the room. A woman gets up from the chair beside the bed and introduces herself:

'Lisbet Carlén,' she says. 'I'm a social worker. I'll be supporting Josef during any future interviews.'

'Good,' Joona says, shaking her hand.

She looks at him in a way that he finds oddly sympathetic.

'Are you the lead interviewer?' she asks, sounding genuinely interested.

'Yes, sorry, my name is Joona Linna, from National Crime. We've spoken on the phone.'

The chest drainage unit bubbles at regular intervals as it removes the fluid from Josef's punctured lung.

Lisbet Carlén says quietly that the doctor said Josef must lie absolutely flat to limit the risk of further bleeding from his liver.

'I'm not here to jeopardise his health,' Joona says as he places the recorder on the table close to Josef's head.

He makes a questioning gesture towards Lisbet, and she nods. He starts the recording, describes the circumstances of the interview. Josef Ek is being questioned in order to help the police with their inquiries. It's Friday, 11 December, 08.15 in the morning. Then he lists the people present in the room.

'Hello,' Joona says.

Josef looks at him with heavy eyes.

'My name is Joona . . . I'm a detective.'

Josef closes his eyes.

'How are you feeling?'

The social worker looks out of the window.

'Can you sleep OK with that machine bubbling away?' he asks.

Josef nods slowly.

'Do you know why I'm here?'

Josef opens his eyes and slowly shakes his head. Joona waits, watching his face.

'There's been an accident,' Josef says. 'My whole family was in an accident.'

'Has anyone told you what happened?' Joona asks.

'A bit, maybe,' he says weakly.

'He's been refusing to see any psychologists or counsellors,' the social worker says.

Joona is struck by how different Josef's voice sounded when he was hypnotised. Now it's fragile, almost inaudible, and full of uncertainty.

'I think you know what happened.'

'You don't have to answer,' Lisbet Carlén says quickly.

'You're fifteen years old?' Joona goes on.

'Yes.'

'What did you do on your birthday?'

'I don't remember,' Josef says.

'Did you get any presents?'

'I watched TV,' Josef replies.

'Did you go and see Evelyn?' Joona asks in a neutral voice.

'Yes.'

'To her flat?'

'Yes.'

'Was she there?'

'Yes.'

Silence.

'No, she wasn't there,' Josef says hesitantly, correcting himself.

'Where was she, then?'

'In the cottage,' he replies.

'Is it a fancy cottage?'

'Not fancy, quite cosy.'

'Was she pleased?'

'Who?'

'Evelyn.'

Silence.

'Did you take anything with you?'

'A cake.'

'A cake? Was it good?'

He nods.

'Did Evelyn like it?' Joona goes on.

'She said it was the best she'd ever tasted.'

'Did she give you a present?'

'No.'

'Did she maybe sing . . .?'

'She didn't want to give me my present,' he says in a hurt voice.

'Did she say that?'

'Yes, she did,' he replies quickly.

'Why not?'

Silence.

'Was she mad at you?' Joona asks.

He nods.

'Did she want you to do something you couldn't do?' Joona says calmly.

'No, she . . .'

Josef continues in a whisper.

'I can't hear, Josef.'

He continues to whisper. Joona leans forward, trying to hear what he's saying.

'That bastard!' Josef screams, right in his ear.

Joona jerks back and walks around the bed, rubbing his ear and trying to smile. Josef's face is ash-grey as he hisses:

'I'll sniff out that fucking hypnotist and rip his throat out with my teeth, I'll hunt him and his . . .'

The social worker hurries to the bed and tries to switch off the recording.

'Josef! You have the right to remain silent if . . .'

'Keep out of this,' Joona interrupts.

She looks at him angrily, then says:

'Before questioning him you should have informed . . .'

'No, you're wrong, there's no legislation that applies here,' Joona says loudly. 'He has the right to remain silent, that's very true, but I'm not required to inform him of that right.'

'Sorry.'

'Don't worry,' Joona mutters, then turns back towards Josef. 'Why are you angry with the hypnotist?'

'I don't have to answer your questions,' Josef says, and tries to point at the social worker.

31

Friday morning, 11 December

Erik runs down the stairs and out onto the street. He stops on Sveavägen, and feels the sweat on his back turn cold. He feels sick with regret and can't believe how he could be so stupid, to push Simone away just because he feels wounded. He sits down on a bench outside the library. There's a chill in the air, but a man is sleeping nearby under a thick pile of blankets.

Erik gets up and starts to walk home. He buys some bread from the bakery, and a latte macchiato for Simone. He hurries back, and climbs the stairs with long strides. The door's locked, so he takes out his keys, unlocks it and finds the flat empty. Erik tells himself that he's going to show Simone that she can trust him, no matter how long it takes to convince her again. He stands by the kitchen table and drinks the coffee, then feels sick and takes an Alka-Seltzer.

It's barely nine o'clock in the morning. His shift at the hospital doesn't start for another few hours. Taking a book with him, he goes and lies on the bed. But instead of reading he starts thinking about Josef Ek. He wonders if Joona can get him to talk.

The flat is silent, abandoned.

A soothing calm spreads out from his stomach as the medication takes effect.

Nothing that's said under hypnosis can be used as evidence, but Erik knows that Josef was telling the truth. He was the one who murdered his own family, even if his motive is unclear and they don't know how much his sister was controlling him.

Erik closes his eyes and tries to picture the family in their terraced house. Evelyn must have been aware that her brother was dangerous, he thinks. Over the years she's learned to live with his inability to control his temper. Always walking on eggshells trying to prevent his angry outbursts. Josef would have been a boy who got into fights, got yelled at, but kept getting into more fights. As his older sister, she wouldn't have had any direct protection, and as Josef grew bigger and stronger, things would've gotten even more dangerous for her. The family would have tried to handle Josef's outbursts day by day, trying to live with them, never quite realising how serious the situation was. Perhaps the parents thought his aggressive behaviour was simply part of being a boy. Maybe they blamed themselves for letting him play violent computer games and watch horror films.

Evelyn moved out as soon as she could and got a job and a flat of her own. But something made her realise the growing severity of the situation, and suddenly she got so scared that she went and hid in her aunt's cottage, taking a shotgun with her to defend herself.

Had Josef threatened her?

Erik tries to imagine how frightened Evelyn must have been at night in the cottage, in the darkness, with a loaded shotgun beside the bed.

He thinks back to Joona's phone call after his interview with her. What happened when Josef showed up with a cake? What did he say to her? Was that when she got a shotgun? Has she been terrified that he was going to kill her ever since?

Erik can picture the way she looked out at the cottage. A young woman in a padded silver down vest, knitted grey sweater, ratty jeans and trainers. She's walking slowly through the trees with her ponytail swaying. Her face is open and childlike. She's holding the shotgun loosely in her hand. It's dragging along the ground, bouncing off the blueberry bushes and moss. The sun is shining through the branches of the pine-trees.

Suddenly Erik realises something important: if Evelyn was

scared, if she had the gun to defend herself against Josef, she would have been carrying it differently, not dragging it behind her as she approached the cottage.

Erik remembers that her knees were wet; she had muddy patches on her jeans.

She went out into the forest with the gun to kill herself, he thinks.

She kneeled down on the moss and put the barrel of the gun in her mouth, then changed her mind, couldn't summon up the courage.

When he saw her at the edge of the forest with the gun trailing behind her, she was on her way back to the cottage, back to what she had been trying to escape.

Erik picks up his phone and calls Joona.

'Joona Linna.'

'Hi, this is Erik Maria Bark.'

'Erik? I've been meaning to call, but there's been so much . . .'

'Don't worry,' Erik says. 'I've . . .'

'Listen,' Joona interrupts, 'I'm really sorry about the whole media witch-hunt, I promise, I'm going to find out who the leak is once things have calmed down.'

'That doesn't matter.'

'I feel responsible, because I persuaded . . .'

'I made the decision to do it, I'm not going to blame anyone else.'

'Speaking personally, which I'm not supposed to do these days, I still think hypnotising Josef was the right thing to do. We still don't really know anything yet, and it could very well have saved Evelyn's life.'

'That's why I'm calling,' Erik says.

'Oh?'

'I had a thought. Do you have a few minutes?'

Erik hears Joona move something. It sounds like he's pulling up a chair and sitting down.

'Yes,' he says. 'I've got time.'

'It's about when we were at the aunt's cottage,' Erik says. 'I was sitting in the car, and I saw a woman through the trees. She was holding a shotgun in one hand. Somehow I realised it was

Evelyn and figured things could get dangerous if she was surprised by the police presence.'

'Yes, she could have fired through the window,' Joona says. 'If she thought it was Josef.'

'I've been sitting here at home thinking about Evelyn,' Erik goes on. 'I saw her through the trees. She was walking slowly back towards the cottage with the gun in one hand, letting the barrel drag on the ground.'

'OK?'

'Is that how someone who's afraid of being killed would carry a gun?'

'No,' Joona replies.

'I think she went into the forest to commit suicide,' Erik says. 'The knees of her jeans were wet. She'd probably been kneeling down on damp moss with the barrel aimed at her head or chest, but then changed her mind, lost her nerve. That's what I think.'

Erik falls silent. He can hear Joona breathing heavily down the phone. A car alarm goes off further down the street.

'Thanks,' Joona says. 'I'll go and talk to her.'

32

Friday afternoon, 11 December

Joona's interview with Evelyn is going to take place in one of the offices in the custody unit. To make the drab little room more pleasant someone has put a tin of ginger cookies on the table and some Christmas lights from Ikea in the window. Evelyn and her public defender are already waiting when Joona comes in and starts the recording.

'I know my questions are likely to be rather upsetting, Evelyn,' he says quietly, glancing at her quickly. 'But I'd be very grateful if you could try to answer them anyway, the best you can.'

Evelyn just stares down at her lap.

'I don't think it's going to help you if you choose to keep quiet,' he says gently.

She doesn't react, just keeps staring at her lap. The public defender, a middle-aged man with a short beard, looks at Joona without expression.

'Shall I get started, Evelyn?'

She shakes her head. He waits. After a few moments she raises her head and looks at him.

'You went out into the forest to commit suicide, didn't you?'

'Yes,' she whispers.

'I'm glad you didn't.'

'I'm not.'

'Have you tried to do it on other occasions?'

'Yes.'

'Before this time?'

She nods.

'But not before Josef came out to see you with the cake.'

'No.'

'What did he say?'

'I don't want to think about it.'

'About what? About what he said?'

Evelyn sits up in her chair and purses her lips.

'I don't remember,' she says, almost silently. 'It probably wasn't anything special.'

'You were planning to shoot yourself, Evelyn,' Joona reminds her.

She stands up and goes over to the window, switches the Christmas lights off and then on again, before returning to her chair and sitting with her arms folded.

'Why can't everyone just leave me alone?'

'Is that what you want? Is that what you really want?'

She nods, without looking at him.

'Do you need to take a break?' her counsel asks.

'I don't know what it is with Josef,' Evelyn says in a quiet voice. 'There's something wrong with his head. There always has been. When he was little he used to fight, too hard, too rough. He broke all my things, I wasn't allowed to have anything.'

Her mouth trembles.

'When he was eight he asked if he could be my boyfriend. That might not sound so bad, but I was horrified, and then he demanded that we kiss. I was scared of him. He used to do weird things. He'd creep up on me at night and bite me, hard enough to draw blood. I started to fight back. I was still stronger than him.'

She wipes tears from her cheeks.

'Then he started to hit my dog, Buster, if I didn't do what he said. It just got worse. He wanted to see my breasts, he wanted to get in the bathtub with me. He killed Buster and threw him off a bridge.'

She gets to her feet and walks restlessly over to the window.

'Josef was about twelve when he . . .'

Her voice breaks and she whimpers quietly to herself before going on.

'He asked if I wanted to put his dick in my mouth. I told him he was disgusting. So he went off and started to hit Lisa. She was only two years old . . .'

Evelyn manages to calm down, but her tears keep falling.

'I had to watch while he masturbated, several times a day. He used to hit Lisa if I refused, said he'd kill her. Then, maybe a few months later, he started to demand that I sleep with him, he threatened me every day. But I came up with an answer. I said he was underage, that it was against the law, that I couldn't do something that was illegal.'

She wipes her cheeks.

'I thought it would just go away when I moved out, and a whole year passed, but then he started calling me to tell me he'd be fifteen soon. That was when I went into hiding. I . . . I don't know how he found out I was in the cottage, I . . .'

She starts sobbing loudly, uncontrollably.

'Oh, God . . .'

'So he threatened you,' Joona says. 'He threatened to kill your whole family unless he . . .'

'He didn't say that!' she shouts. 'He said he'd start with Dad. It's all my fault, all of it. I just want to die . . .'

She slides down the wall to the floor and curls into a ball.

33

Friday afternoon, 11 December

Joona is sitting in his office, staring blankly down at his hands. He's still holding the phone. When he told Jens Svanehjälm about how Evelyn had suddenly changed her story, he had listened in silence. Then he sighed when Joona explained the grim motive behind the murders.

'To be honest,' he said when Joona had finished, 'I'm afraid this is still a bit too thin, bearing in mind the sister has in turn been accused by Josef Ek. What we really need is either a confession or some compelling forensic evidence.'

Joona looks around the room, rubs his face, then calls Josef's doctor, Daniella Richards, to schedule a time for another round of questioning, preferably when Josef doesn't have as many painkillers in his system.

'I need him to be clear-headed,' Joona says.

'You could come in at five o'clock,' Daniella says.

'This afternoon?'

'He doesn't get his dose of morphine until six. We let the level drop when he eats.'

Joona looks at the time. It's two thirty.

'That works for me,' he says.

He hangs up, then calls Lisbet Carlén, Josef's social worker, to tell her what they've arranged.

He goes out to the staffroom to grab an apple. When he

returns Erixon is sitting in his office, resting his considerable weight on Joona's desk. His face is red. He raises one hand in greeting and wheezes:

'Stuff that apple in my mouth and you've got your Christmas pig.'

'No chance,' Joona says, taking a bite.

'I deserve it,' Erixon says. 'Since that Thai place opened up on the corner I've put on eleven kilos.'

'They have good food.'

'I hate them.'

'How did it go in the women's locker room?' Joona asks.

Erixon holds his pudgy hand up to stop him:

'Don't say "I told you so", but . . .'

Joona grins broadly.

'We'll see,' he says diplomatically.

'OK,' Erixon sighs, and wipes the sweat from his cheeks. 'We found strands of hair belonging to Josef Ek in the drain, and there was blood from the father, Anders Ek, in the cracks on the floor.'

'I told you so,' Joona says, beaming at him.

Erixon laughs.

Joona calls Jens Svanehjälm again as he gets into the lift to leave the building.

'I'm glad you called,' Jens says. 'They've been on to me about this hypnosis business. They think we should drop the preliminary investigation against Josef. They reckon it's going to cost a whole lot of money and . . .'

'Give me a second,' Joona interrupts.

'I've decided . . .'

'Jens?'

'Yes?' he replies.

'We've got forensic evidence,' Joona says seriously. 'Josef Ek can be linked to the first crime scene.'

Jens takes a deep breath, then says calmly:

'Joona, you got this at the very last minute.'

'That's good enough,' he replies.

'Yes.'

Just as they're about to end the call Joona says:

'Didn't I say I was right?'

'What?'

'I was right, wasn't I?'

Silence on the line. Then Jens says, very slowly and clearly: 'Yes, Joona, you were.'

They hang up and the smile fades from Joona's face. He walks along the glass wall towards the exit and checks the time again. He needs to be at the Nordic Museum out on Djurgården in half an hour.

34

Friday afternoon, 11 December

Joona walks up the staircase inside the museum. He passes hundreds of illuminated display cases without so much as glancing at them. He doesn't notice the tools, treasures and handicrafts, he doesn't see the special exhibitions, the folk costumes, the big photographs.

The guard has already placed a chair in front of the dimly lit display case. Without saying anything, Joona sits down just as he usually does and looks at the Sami bridal crown. Fragile and delicate, it forms a perfect circle. The points resemble the petals of a flower, or a pair of hands held together with their fingers reaching up. Joona slowly moves his head, to look at it in slightly different light. The bridal crown was woven by hand from roots. The raw materials were dug from the ground, and shine like gold.

The moment is gone, but memory is merciless.

He's driving a car. The rain has passed, but the puddles flare like fire in the evening sun – all of it so incredibly beautiful, and gone forever.

This time Joona only sits in front of the display case for an hour before he gets up, nods to the guard, and walks slowly out of the museum. The slushy snow on the ground is specked with black, and the air smells like diesel from a boat beneath the bridge. As he's walking slowly back towards Strandvägen his phone rings. It's The Needle.

'I'm glad I caught you,' he says when Joona answers.

'Are the post-mortems finished?'

'Close enough.'

Joona watches a young father up ahead on the pavement, tilting a pushchair back again and again to make his child laugh. A woman is standing at a window, just staring out at the street. When he meets her eye she quickly steps back into her flat.

'Anything unusual?' Joona asks.

'Well, I don't know that . . .'

'But?'

'There's that incision on the stomach, of course.'

'OK?'

The Needle takes a deep breath and something clatters in the background.

'Dropped my pen,' he whispers, and the line crackles.

'These bodies have been subjected to extreme levels of violence,' The Needle goes on seriously when he comes back. 'Especially the little girl.'

'So I saw,' Joona says.

'Most of the injuries are completely unnecessary, they seem to have been inflicted just for the fun of it.'

'Yes,' Joona says, thinking of how the crime scene looked when he got there – the shocked police officers, the sense of chaos in the air. The bodies inside. He remembers Lillemor Blom's blanched cheeks as she stood and smoked, her hands shaking. He recalls the way the blood had sprayed across the windows, and had run down the glass in the patio door at the back of the house.

'So back to the cut on the woman's stomach?'

The Needle sighs.

'Well, it's as we suspected. That incision was made approximately two hours after she died. Someone rolled her over, then used a very sharp knife to cut open the scar of her C-section.'

He leafs through his papers.

'Our killer doesn't seem to know very much about C-sections, however. Katja Ek's was an emergency operation, which runs down vertically from the navel.'

'Oh?'

The Needle lets out another deep sigh.

'The womb is always opened horizontally, even if the cut on the skin is vertical.'

'But Josef didn't know that?' Joona asks.

'No,' The Needle says. 'He just opened the skin, without realising that a C-section consists of two separate procedures, one incision in the skin, and another in the womb.'

'Is there anything else I should know?'

'Perhaps the fact that he took an unusually long time. He never stopped, even though he was getting more and more tired. His rage seems to have been inexhaustible.'

They're both quiet. Joona walks along Strandvägen. He starts thinking about his most recent conversation with Evelyn.

'I just wanted to confirm what we were thinking,' The Needle says after a while. 'That the incision was made approximately two hours after death.'

'Thanks.'

'You'll have the full post-mortem report tomorrow.'

Joona clicks to end the call, and thinks how terrible it must have been to grow up with Josef Ek. Evelyn must have felt so exposed, and he can't even imagine how afraid Lisa, the younger sister, must have been.

Joona tries to remember what Evelyn said about her brother's birth.

Evelyn had sat curled up on the floor, leaning against the wall of the interview room, when she told him about Josef's almost pathological jealousy towards their little sister.

'There's something wrong with his head,' she whispered. 'There always has been. I remember when he was born, Mum was really ill. I don't know what it was, but they had to do an emergency C-section.'

Evelyn shook her head and bit her lip before she went on:

'Do you know what that means?'

'Yes, more or less,' Joona replied.

'Sometimes . . . sometimes there are complications when you give birth that way.'

Evelyn had glanced at him shyly.

'You mean a lack of oxygen, that sort of thing?' Joona asked.

She shook her head and brushed the tears from her cheeks.

'I mean psychological problems for Mum. A woman who suffers a difficult birth and is suddenly sedated so they can perform a C-section on her can have problems bonding with her child.'

'Did your mother suffer from post-partum depression?'

'Not exactly,' Evelyn said in a thick voice. 'Mum got a bit psychotic after she gave birth to Josef. They didn't pick up on it at the maternity clinic, so they let her take him home. I could tell right away. Everything was wrong. I ended up having to take care of Josef. I was only eight years old, but she didn't care about him at all. She wouldn't touch him. He just lay in his cot, crying and crying.'

Evelyn looked at Joona and whispered:

'Mum said he wasn't hers, that her baby had died. In the end she had to be taken into care.'

Evelyn paused.

'Mum came back to us a year or so later. She tried to pretend everything was normal, but she kept on avoiding him.'

'So you don't think your mum ever really got better?' Joona asked tentatively.

'Oh, she got better, because when she had Lisa everything was completely different. Mum was so happy.'

'And you had to look after Josef?'

'He started saying that Mum should have given birth to him properly. For him, the reason Lisa was being treated so much better than he had been was because she was born "through the cunt", and he wasn't. He kept saying that. That Mum should have given birth to him through her cunt, and not . . .'

Evelyn's voice trailed off. She turned her face away and Joona could only look at her tense, hunched shoulders.

35

Friday morning, 11 December

When Joona walks into the intensive care unit, for once it isn't completely silent. It smells like food, and a cart laden with stainless-steel trays, plates, glasses and cutlery is parked outside the cafeteria. Someone has turned the television on, and Joona can hear dishes rattling in the kitchen.

He's thinking about the fact that Josef cut open the old C-section scar on his mother's stomach, reopening the portal through which he was born, but simultaneously the portal that condemned him to motherlessness.

Josef felt from an early age that he wasn't like other children, that he was alone. The only person who gave him love and affection was Evelyn. He couldn't stand being rejected by her. The slightest hint that she was distancing herself from him left him desperate and furious, and that fury was increasingly directed at his younger sister, who was doted on by their mother.

Joona nods to Sunesson, who's standing outside the door of Josef Ek's room, then looks in to see the boy's face. The catheter bag is half full of urine, and a large drip beside the bed is supplying him with both fluids and blood plasma. The boy's feet are sticking out from under the blue blanket. The soles of his feet are dirty. Hair and dust has stuck to the surgical tape covering his stitches. The television is on but he doesn't seem to be watching it.

Lisbet Carlén is already in the room. She hasn't noticed Joona's arrival. She's standing by the window fastening a hairclip in her hair.

One of Josef's wounds has started to bleed again. It's running down his arm and dripping onto the floor. An older nurse leans over him, loosens the compress and tapes the edges of the wound together again, washes the blood off and then leaves the room.

'Excuse me,' Joona says, catching up with the nurse in the corridor.

'Yes?'

'How is he? How is Josef Ek doing?'

'You'll have to talk to his doctor,' the woman replies, and starts walking again.

'I will,' Joona smiles, and hurries after her. 'But . . . I'd like to show him something which . . . can I drive him there, I mean in a wheelchair . . .'

The nurse shakes her head and stops abruptly.

'The patient can't be moved under any circumstances,' she says sternly. 'He's in a lot of pain. He can't move. He could start bleeding again if he so much as tries to sit up.'

Joona returns to Josef's room. He walks in without knocking, picks up the remote and turns the television off. He switches on the tape-recorder, gives the date and time and the names of the people in the room, then sits down on the visitor's chair. Josef opens his heavy eyelids and looks at him with an expression of mild disinterest. The machine helping to restore the pressure in his punctured lung is making a gentle bubbling sound.

'You should be discharged soon,' Joona says.

'That'll be nice,' Josef says weakly.

'Although you'll only be transferred to prison.'

'Lisbet told me that the prosecutor won't allow that,' he says, glancing at the social worker.

'That was before we had a witness.'

Josef closes his eyes softly.

'Who?'

'We've talked quite a bit, you and me,' Joona says. 'I was wondering if you'd like to change anything you've told me, or add anything to what you've said.'

'Evelyn,' he whispers.

'You won't be getting out for a very long time.'

'You're lying.'

'No, Josef, I'm telling the truth. Believe me. You're going to be held in custody, so you now have the right to legal representation.'

Josef tries to raise his hand, but doesn't have the strength.

'You hypnotised her,' he says with a smile.

'No.'

'My word against hers,' he says.

'Not quite,' Joona says, looking at the boy's clean, pale face. 'We also have forensic evidence.'

Josef clenches his jaw.

'I don't have time to just sit here, but if you want to tell me anything I can stay longer,' Joona says amiably.

He lets thirty seconds pass, drums the arm of his chair, stands up, picks up the tape-recorder and then, with a curt nod to the social worker, leaves the room.

In his car outside the hospital Joona thinks that he should have confronted Josef with what Evelyn had said, just to see the boy's reaction. There's a furious arrogance to Josef Ek that might have prompted him to confess if he'd been provoked.

For a moment he considers going back in, but decides against it so he isn't late for dinner with Disa.

36

Friday evening, 11 December

It's dark and foggy by the time he parks outside the nice block of flats on Lützen Street. For once he actually feels cold as he walks over to the door, looking off towards the frosty grass and bare black branches of the trees at Karlaplan.

He tries to remember how Josef looked lying in his bed, but the only thing he can conjure up is the bubbling, wheezing drainage machine. He has a feeling he's seen something important without realising it.

The feeling nags at him as he heads up to Disa's flat and rings the doorbell. No answer. Joona can hear someone on the landing above him sighing and quietly crying.

Disa opens the door with a stressed look on her face. She's wearing nothing but her bra and tights.

'I was expecting you to be late,' she explains.

'So I came early instead,' Joona says, and kisses her lightly on the cheek.

'Come in and close the door before all the neighbours see me.'

The cosy flat smells like food. A pink tasselled lamp brushes Joona's head.

'I made sole with new potatoes,' Disa says.

'And melted butter?'

'And mushrooms, parsley and veal stock.'

'Great.'

The flat has only two rooms and a kitchen, but the ceilings are high. The big windows look out across Karlaplan. The windowsills are teak, the ceilings are decorated with wooden panels, and the floor has been neatly whitewashed.

He sits down in the armchair and waits while she finishes getting dressed. Without saying a word she stands with her back to him and lets him zip up her tight, simply cut dress.

Joona glances at an open book and sees a large black and white photograph of a graveyard. A group of archaeologists dressed in 1940s clothes are standing some distance away, peering at the camera. They seem to have just started their excavations, and have marked the ground with fifty or so little flags.

'They're graves,' she says quietly. 'The flags indicate burial sites. The man who excavated the site was called Hannes Müller. He died a few years ago, but he must have been a hundred years old by then. He was always at the institute. Looked like a kindly old turtle . . .'

She stands in front of the tall mirror, pulls her hair into two thin braids and then turns and looks at him.

'How do I look?'

'You look lovely,' Joona says.

'Thanks,' she says sadly. 'How's your mum?'

'OK,' he whispers. 'She sends her love.'

'That's nice. What did she say?'

'That you should stop caring about me.'

'Well,' Disa says unhappily, 'she's right, of course.'

She slowly runs her fingers through his thick, untidy hair. Then she smiles at him.

'Do you know that according to pre-Christian law, babies weren't considered real people until they started to nurse? Babies could legally be left out in the forest during the period between birth and suckling.'

'People only became people according to the choices of others,' Joona says slowly.

'Isn't that always the way?'

She opens her wardrobe, takes out a shoebox and pulls out

a pair of dark brown sandals with soft straps and striped wooden heels.

'New?' Joona asks.

'Sergio Rossi. I bought them as a treat for myself because I have such an unglamorous job,' she says. 'I spend all my days crawling around in a muddy field.'

'Are you still out in Sigtuna?'

'Yes.'

'What have you found?'

'I'll tell you while we eat.'

He points to the sandals.

'Very nice,' he says, and gets up from the armchair.

Disa turns round with a cheeky smile.

'Sorry, Joona,' she says over her shoulder. 'I don't think they come in your size.'

He freezes.

'Hang on,' he says, reaching out for the wall.

'It was only a joke,' she says.

'No, it was his feet . . .'

Joona goes past her into the hallway, takes his phone out of his jacket, calls dispatch and says very calmly that Sunesson needs immediate back-up at the hospital.

'What's happened?' Disa asks.

'His feet were filthy,' Joona tells her. 'They say he can't move, but he's been out of bed. He's been walking around.'

Joona dials Sunesson's number. When there's no answer he grabs his jacket, and whispers 'Sorry' as he leaves the flat and runs down the stairs.

37

Friday evening, 11 December

At around the same time that Joona rings Disa's doorbell, Josef Ek sits up in bed in his room at the hospital.

Last night he tried getting up: he slid his feet onto the floor, and had to hold on to the end of the bed for a long time. The pain from all his injuries washed over him like boiling oil, and the stabbing sensation from his damaged liver made his vision flare, but he could walk. Stretching the tubes to the drip and the chest drain as far as they would go, he checked what was in the medical equipment cupboards, then got back into bed.

It's been thirty minutes since the night staff came in and said hello. Josef very gently disconnects the tube from his wrist, and a little trickle of blood runs into his lap.

It doesn't hurt as much this time when he gets out of bed. He makes his way over to the cupboard, finds compresses, scalpels, disposable syringes and rolls of bandages. He slips some syringes into the wide, loose pocket of his hospital gown. With his hands trembling he removes the packaging from one of the scalpels and cuts the tube to the chest drain. Slimy blood dribbles out as his left lung slowly deflates. He feels pain beneath one of his shoulder-blades, coughs weakly, but doesn't really notice a significant change in his breathing.

He hears footsteps out in the hallway, rubber-soled shoes

on the linoleum floor. With the scalpel in his hand, Josef goes and stands by the door, glances out through the window and waits.

The nurse stops and talks to the policeman posted by the door. Josef hears them laugh at something.

'I've given up smoking,' she replies.

'If you've got a spare nicotine patch, I wouldn't say no,' the policeman says.

'I've stopped using them too,' she says. 'Slip out into the courtyard, I'm going to be here for a while anyway.'

'Five minutes,' the policeman says eagerly.

The policeman walks off with a jangle of keys, then the nurse looks through her notes and comes into the room. She really just looks surprised. The laughter lines at the corners of her eyes look more pronounced as the scalpel pushes into her neck. Josef is weaker than he had thought, he has to stab her several times. His body aches and burns from the sudden exertion and movement. The nurse doesn't collapse at once, and tries to cling onto him. They slip onto the floor together. Her body is hot and covered in sweat. He tries to stand up but slips on some of her hair that's come loose. As he pulls the scalpel from her neck she makes a squeaking sound. Her legs start to shake and Josef stands and watches her for a little while before leaving the room. Her dress has bunched up and he can clearly see the pink underwear inside her nylon tights.

He walks along the hallway. His liver is hurting badly now. He turns right and finds some clean clothes on a cart, and changes into them. A very short woman is mopping the floor and listening to music through headphones. Josef walks closer and stops behind her, and pulls out one of the disposable syringes. He stabs the air behind her back several times with the syringe, but stops each time before the needle makes contact. She doesn't notice a thing. He puts the syringe back in his pocket, pushes the woman out of the way with his hand and hurries past. She almost falls, and swears in Spanish. Josef stops abruptly and turns towards her.

'What did you say?' he asks.

She takes off her headphones and looks quizzically at him.

'Did you say something?' he asks.

She quickly shakes her head and goes on cleaning. He heads to the lift, presses the button and waits.

38

Friday evening, 11 December

Joona is driving fast along Valhallavägen. He changes lanes and passes a Mercedes on the driver's side as he sees the red-brick of Sophia Hospital flash past behind the trees. The tyres thunder over a large metal plate. He accelerates to get past a blue bus that's just pulling out from a bus-stop. The driver honks his horn angrily for a very long time.

Joona drives through a red light at Norrtull, passes Stallmästaregården and manages to hit 180 kilometres an hour on the short stretch of the Uppsala road before the exit ramp leads him under the motorway to Karolinska Hospital.

When he pulls up in front of the main entrance, there are several police cars with their blue lights still flashing across the brown bricks of the hospital building. A group of journalists has surrounded a number of nurses. They're shivering outside the entrance, and a couple of the nurses are weeping openly in front of the cameras.

Joona tries to go inside but is immediately stopped by a young police officer.

'Get lost,' the police officer says, giving him a shove.

Joona looks into his dull blue eyes. He removes the officer's hand and says calmly:

'National Crime.'

A look of suspicion flickers across the police officer's face.

'ID, please.'

'Joona, hurry up, we're over here.'

Carlos Eliasson is waving at him from the reception area. Through the window Joona sees Sunesson sitting on a bench crying. A younger officer is sitting beside him with his arm around his shoulders.

Joona holds up his ID and the policeman reluctantly stands aside. Large parts of the lobby have been cordoned off with blue and white tape. The reporters' cameras keep flashing outside the glass walls, and inside the hospital crime scene investigators are taking photographs.

Carlos is heading up the operation. He gives a few quick orders to dispatch, then turns towards Joona.

'Did you get him?' Joona asks.

'Witnesses say he made his way out through the lobby using a walker,' Carlos says, sounding very stressed. 'It's been found down at the bus-stop.'

He looks at his notes.

'Two buses have left the grounds, as well as seven taxis and medical transports, one ambulance and around a dozen private cars.'

'Did you block the exits?'

'It's too late for that.'

He waves over a uniformed officer waiting to speak to him.

'We traced the buses – nothing,' he says.

'And the taxis?' Carlos asks.

'We've checked Taxi Stockholm and Taxi Kurir, but . . .'

The police officer waves his hand in the air, as if he's forgotten what he was going to say.

'Have you contacted Erik Maria Bark?' Joona asks.

'We called him right away. He's not answering, but we're trying to get hold of him.'

'He needs protection.'

'Rolle!' Carlos calls. 'Have you reached Bark yet?'

'I just tried calling,' Roland Svensson replies.

'Call him again!' Joona says.

'I need to talk to Omar in dispatch,' Carlos says, looking around. 'We're going to issue a national alert.'

'What do you want me to do?'

'Stay here, see if I've missed anything,' Carlos says, then calls over one of the forensics officers from Homicide.

'Bring Detective Linna up to speed on what we've got so far,' Carlos orders.

Verner looks blankly at Joona and says in a nasal voice:

'One nurse dead . . . Several witnesses who saw the suspect leave using a walker.'

'Show me,' Joona says.

They take the stairs because the lift shafts haven't been searched yet.

Joona looks at the red footprints left by the barefoot Josef Ek on his way out. The air smells like electricity and death. A bloody handprint on the wall indicates that he stumbled or was forced to reach out for support. On the metal door of the lift Joona sees blood, and what looks like a greasy mark made by someone's forehead and the tip of nose.

They walk down the hallway and stop on the threshold of the room where he questioned Josef only an hour or so ago. An almost black pool of blood is spreading out from a body on the floor.

'She was a nurse,' Verner says in a firm voice. 'Ann-Katrin Eriksson.'

Joona looks at the dead woman's dark blonde hair and lifeless eyes. Her nurse's uniform has bunched up around her hips. It looks like the murderer tried to pull her dress off, he thinks.

'The murder weapon was probably a scalpel,' Verner says drily.

Joona pulls out his phone and calls Kronoberg Prison.

A sleepy male voice answers and says something Joona doesn't catch.

'This is Joona Linna,' he says quickly. 'I want to know if Evelyn Ek is still with you.'

'What?'

'Is Evelyn Ek still in custody?'

'You'll have to ask the duty officer,' the voice replies sourly.

'Can you get him, please?'

'Hold on,' the man says, and puts the phone down.

Joona hears talking, followed by some loud noises. He looks at the time. He's already been at the hospital ten minutes.

Joona heads back down to the main entrance with his phone to his ear.

'Jan Persson here,' a more amenable voice says.

'Joona Linna, National Crime. I want to know whether Evelyn Ek is still there,' he says quickly.

'Evelyn Ek,' Jan Persson repeats to himself. 'We've let her go. It wasn't easy. She refused to leave. She wanted to stay locked up.'

'You forced her to leave after she requested protection?'

'No, wait, the prosecutor was here, she's . . .'

Joona hears Jan Persson looking through a folder.

'She's in one of our protected flats.'

'Good,' he says. 'Put police officers outside the door. Got that?'

'We're not idiots,' Jan Persson says wearily.

Joona ends the call and goes over to Carlos, who's looking at a laptop. A woman is sitting next to him, pointing at the screen.

Omar from dispatch is repeating 'Echo,' the code used for dog units, into his radio. Joona guesses that they've managed to trace most of the vehicles that left the hospital by now, but haven't found Josef.

Joona waves at Carlos but fails to get his attention, so he gives up and walks out through one of the smaller glass doors. It's dark and the air is cold. The walker is standing at the empty bus-stop. Joona looks around past the people watching the scene from the other side of the cordon, past the flickering blue lights and anxious movements of the police, past the flashes of the reporters' cameras. He lets his eyes roam across the car park, the dark façades, and the buildings in the hospital complex.

Joona starts to walk, quickening his pace. He steps over the fluttering plastic tape cordoning off the area, pushes through a group of onlookers and looks out towards the Northern Cemetery. He moves on until he reaches Solna Kyrko road and walks along the fence, looking for anything unusual among the black silhouettes of trees and gravestones. A network of dimly illuminated paths spreads out across the sixty hectares containing 30,000 graves.

39

Friday evening, 11 December

Joona is surrounded by silence. He can no longer hear the noise around the hospital entrance. The branches of the trees sigh, and his own footsteps echo faintly between the gravestones. A large vehicle rumbles past on the highway. The dry leaves beneath one of the bushes rustle. Here and there memorial candles are burning in their clouded glass jars.

Joona walks towards the eastern edge of the cemetery, the part facing the highway, and suddenly sees someone moving in the darkness between the tall gravestones next to the office building, about four hundred metres away. He stops to focus his gaze. The figure is limping and seems to be leaning forward. Joona starts to run between the graves. He sees the thin figure hurry across the frosty grass between the trees. His white clothes are flapping around him.

'Josef!' Joona calls. 'Stop!'

The boy limps on, behind a large family grave surrounded by wrought-iron railings. Joona draws his pistol and runs sideways. He catches sight of the boy again, and shouts at him to stop, then takes aim at his right hip. Out of nowhere, an old woman pops up in the middle of Joona's line of fire. She was crouched down beside a grave, and stood up when she heard Joona shout. Joona feels a flash of anxiety as he loses Josef behind a conifer hedge. He lowers his pistol and runs after him. He hears the woman muttering that all she wanted was to light a candle on Ingrid Bergman's grave. He looks around in the darkness. Josef has disappeared between the trees and gravestones. The lampposts only illuminate small areas, a green park bench or a few metres of the path. Joona calls dispatch and asks for immediate backup: the situation is dangerous, he needs an entire unit, at least five teams and a helicopter. He runs up a slope, jumps over a low fence and stops. He can hear dogs barking in the distance. Something crunches on a gravel path a short distance away and Joona takes off in that direction. He sees someone crawling between the gravestones. He keeps his eyes on him and tries to get closer to find a line of fire. Some black birds fly up into the sky. A dustbin topples over. He sees Josef crouching in a run behind a brown, frost-covered hedge. Joona loses his footing and slides down a slope. When he gets to his feet again he can no longer see Josef. His pulse is racing in his ears. He can feel that he's scraped his back. His hands are cold and numb. He crosses the gravel path and looks around. He sees a car with the Stockholm City Council logo on its door in the distance, behind the office building. It pulls away slowly, and the glare from its headlights swings across the trees, illuminating Josef. He's standing on the narrow road, swaying. His head is lolling forward, and he takes a couple of faltering steps. Joona runs as fast as he can. The car has stopped, the front door opens, and a bearded man gets out.

'Police!' Joona shouts.

But they don't hear him.

He fires a shot in the air and the bearded man looks in his direction. Josef approaches the man with a scalpel in his hand. Joona only has a few seconds, there's no way he'll get there in time. He steadies his arm on a gravestone, but the distance is more than 300 metres, far longer than the firing ranges. The front sight drifts in front of Joona. It's hard to see, but he tries to focus his eye. The greyish white figure becomes thinner and darker. A tree branch keeps getting in the way of his line of fire. The bearded man has turned to face Josef again, and takes a step backwards. Joona tries to hold his line of fire and squeezes the trigger. The shot goes off and the recoil jolts his elbow and shoulder. The powder stings on his cold hand. The bullet vanishes among the trees. The echo from the shot fades away. Joona lines up the sights again and sees Josef stab the bearded man in the stomach with the scalpel. Joona fires again, and the bullet flies through Josef's clothes. He staggers and drops the scalpel. He reaches one hand around to feel his back as he gets in the car. Joona starts running towards the road, but Josef has already started the car. He drives straight over the bearded man's legs and accelerates. When Joona realises he's not going to make it in time, he stops and aims the pistol at the front tyre, shoots and hits it. The car lurches, but keeps moving, then speeds up and disappears towards the highway access ramp. Joona puts his pistol back in his holster and calls in a status report to dispatch, repeating that he needs a helicopter.

The bearded man is still alive, but a stream of dark blood is running through his fingers from the wound in his stomach, and both of his legs look like they're broken.

'He was only a boy,' he keeps repeating in shock. 'He was only a boy.'

'An ambulance is on its way,' Joona says, as he finally hears the sound of the helicopter above the cemetery.

It's late by the time Joona picks up the phone in his office to call Disa.

'Leave me alone,' she answers groggily.

'Were you asleep?' Joona asks.

'Of course I was.'

Neither of them says anything for a moment.

'Was the food good?'

'Yes, it was.'

'You do understand that I had to . . .?'

He trails off, hears her yawn and sit up in bed.

'Are you OK?' she asks.

Joona looks at his hands. Even though he's scrubbed them thoroughly, he imagines he can still smell blood on his fingers. He had knelt down beside the man in that car park and held the largest of his wounds together. The wounded man had been fully conscious the whole time, talking excitedly, almost deliriously, about his son, who had just graduated from high school and was going to visit his grandparents in Turkey on his own for the first time. The man had looked at Joona, then looked down at the hands on his stomach and declared that it didn't hurt at all. He sounded almost bemused.

'Isn't that funny?' he had said, looking at Joona with a clear, childlike gaze.

Joona tried to speak calmly, explaining to the man that his body was in a state of shock.

The man paused, then asked quietly:

'Is this what it's like to die?'

He tried to smile at Joona.

'Doesn't it hurt at all?'

Joona opened his mouth to answer, but at that moment the ambulance arrived and Joona felt someone carefully remove his hands from the man's stomach and lead him away.

'Joona?' Disa says again. 'Is everything OK?'

'I'm fine,' he says.

He hears her move. It sounds like she's drinking.

'Do you want another chance?' she asks.

'Yes, please.'

'Even though you don't give a damn about me?' she says coldly.

'You know that's not true,' he replies, and hears how tired his voice sounds.

'Sorry,' Disa says. 'I'm glad you're OK.'

They hang up.

Joona sits for a moment listening to the silence at Police Headquarters. Then he takes his pistol from the holster hanging on the back of the door, dismantles it and slowly cleans it, greasing each separate part. He puts it back together again, then locks it in the gun-cabinet. The smell of blood on his hands has been replaced by the smell of gun-grease. He sits down to write a report for Petter Näslund explaining why it was necessary to discharge his service pistol.

40

Friday evening, 11 December

Erik watches as the three pizzas are prepared, and asks for extra pepperoni on Simone's. His phone rings and he looks at the screen. He puts it back in his pocket when he doesn't recognise the number. Probably another journalist. He can't deal with any more questions right now. As he walks home with the big, warm boxes he thinks about what he plans to say to Simone. He got angry because he's innocent. He didn't do what she thinks he did, he didn't cheat on her. He loves her. He hesitates outside the florist's, then goes in. A heavy sweetness hangs in the air inside the shop. The window looking out onto the street is steamed up. He has just decided to buy a bouquet of roses when his phone rings again. It's Simone.

'Hello?'

'Where are you?' she asks.

'I'm on my way.'

'We're starving here.'

'Good.'

He hurries home, goes into the lobby and waits for the lift. Through the polished yellow glass in the door, the world outside looks enchanted. He wonders whether the roses were a mistake, a cheap attempt to make amends. He quickly puts the pizza-boxes on the floor and tosses the roses into the rubbish chute.

In the lift he second-guesses himself. Simone might have liked the roses after all.

He rings the doorbell. Benjamin opens the door and takes the pizzas from him. Erik hangs up his coat, then goes to the bathroom and washes his hands. He takes out a box of tiny, lemon-yellow pills, and swallows three before he goes to the kitchen.

'We've already started,' Simone says.

Erik gets out two wine glasses.

'Good,' Simone says as he uncorks a bottle.

'Simone,' he says. 'I know you're disappointed in me, but . . .'

Erik's mobile phone rings. They look at each other.

'Aren't you going to answer it?' Simone asks.

'I'm not talking to any more reporters tonight,' Erik says.

She slices her pizza, takes a bite, and says:

'Let it ring.'

Erik fills their wine glasses. Simone nods and smiles.

'Oh, yes,' she says. 'It's almost gone now, but it smelled like cigarette smoke again when I got home.'

'Do you have a friend who smokes?' Erik asks Benjamin.

'No,' he replies.

'Does Aida smoke?'

Benjamin doesn't answer. He's eating quickly, then suddenly stops, puts his knife and fork down and stares at the table.

'Hey, what's up?' Erik asks gently. 'What's on your mind?'

'Nothing.'

'You know you can tell us anything?'

'Do I?'

'Don't you think . . .'

'You don't get it,' he interrupts.

'So tell me,' Erik says.

'No.'

They eat in silence. Benjamin stares at the wall.

'Good pepperoni,' Simone says quietly.

She wipes the lipstick off her glass.

'It's a shame we've stopped cooking together,' she says to Erik.

'Where would we find the time for that?' he says, slightly defensively.

'Stop arguing!' Benjamin yells.

He drinks some water and looks out of the window at the dark city. Erik eats almost nothing, but refills his wine glass twice.

'Did you get your injection on Tuesday?' Simone asks.

'Has Dad ever missed one?'

Benjamin gets up and puts his plate in the sink.

'Thanks for dinner.'

'I looked at that leather jacket you've been saving up for,' Simone says. 'I thought I could make up the difference for you.'

Benjamin's face breaks into a smile. He goes over and hugs her. She holds him tight, but lets go when she feels him pulling away. He heads to his room.

Erik breaks off a piece of crust and pops it in his mouth. He has dark rings under his eyes, and the lines around his mouth are deeper. He looks tense.

His phone goes off again, vibrating its way slowly across the table.

Erik looks at the screen and shakes his head.

'No one I know,' he says.

'Are you sick of being a celebrity?' Simone asks gently.

'I've only spoken to two reporters today,' he smiles weakly. 'But that's more than enough for me.'

'What did they want?'

'It was that magazine, *Café*, or whatever it's called.'

'The one that has pin-ups on the cover?'

'Always some girl who looks astonished that she's being photographed in just a pair of Union Jack underwear.'

She smiles at him.

'What did they want?' she says again.

Erik clears his throat and says drily:

'They asked me if it was possible to hypnotise women into wanting sex, blah, blah, blah.'

'Seriously?'

'Yep.'

'What about the other one?' she asks. 'Who was that? *Ritz*, or *Slitz*?'

'*Dagens Eko*,' he replies. 'They wanted to know what I thought about being reported to the Judicial Ombudsman.'

'Boring,' she says sarcastically.

Erik rubs his eyes and sighs. He seems to have shrunk visibly.

'If I hadn't hypnotised him,' he says slowly, 'Josef Ek might have gone on to murder his sister the moment he was discharged from the hospital.'

'You still shouldn't have done it,' Simone says quietly.

'No, I know,' he replies, fingering his glass. 'I regret . . .'

He stops talking, and Simone feels a sudden urge to reach out to him and just give him a hug. But instead she just stays where she is, looks at him and says:

'What are we going to do?'

'Do?'

'About us. We've said things, about splitting up. I don't know what you want any more, Erik.'

He rubs his eyes hard.

'I realise that you don't trust me,' he says, then stops.

She looks into his tired, glassy eyes, sees his worn face, his untidy grey hair, and thinks back to a time when they almost always had fun together.

'I'm not the man you want me to be,' he goes on.

'Stop that,' she says.

'What?'

'You say I'm not happy with you, but you're the one having the affair. You're the one who thinks I'm not enough for you.'

'Simone, I . . .'

He touches her hand, but she pulls it away. There's a slightly glazed look in his eyes, and she knows he's taken pills.

'I need to go to bed,' Simone says, and stands up.

Erik follows her, his face as grey as ash. On her way to the bathroom she checks the front door carefully.

'You can sleep in the guest room,' she says.

He nods, apparently indifferent, and grabs his pillow and some covers. He seems almost sedated.

In the middle of the night Simone is woken by a sudden pricking sensation in her upper arm. She's lying on her stomach, and rolls onto her side to feel her arm. The muscle feels sore and tender. The bedroom is dark.

'Erik?' she whispers, then remembers that he's sleeping in the guest room.

She turns towards the door and sees a shadow disappear into the hallway. The parquet floor creaks as someone moves on it. She thinks Erik must have come into the room to get something, then remembers that he is probably sound asleep because of his pills. She turns the bedside lamp on, holds her arm towards the light and sees a bead of blood coming from a tiny pinprick in her skin. She must have caught her arm on something.

She hears muffled noises from the hall. Simone turns the lamp off again and gets out of bed on weak legs. She rubs her sore arm as she walks across the room. Her mouth is dry and her legs feel warm and numb. Someone is whispering in the hallway, laughing quietly. It doesn't sound like Erik at all. A shiver runs down Simone's spine. The front door is wide open. The stairwell is dark. Cool air is streaming in. She hears a noise from Benjamin's room, a gentle whimper:

'Mum?'

Benjamin sounds frightened.

'Ow!' she hears him say. He starts to cry, softly but insistently.

Through the mirror in the hall, Simone can see someone leaning over Benjamin's bed with a syringe in their hand. Thoughts swirl through her head. She tries to make sense of what's happening.

'Benjamin?' she calls anxiously. 'What are you doing? Can I come in?'

She clears her throat, takes a step closer, and suddenly her legs give out beneath her. She reaches out for the dresser with one hand, but can't catch herself. She collapses onto the floor and hits her head against the wall.

She tries to get up, but she can't move. She has no feeling in her lower body. Her chest is tingling, and her breathing is getting heavier. Her vision fades for a few seconds, then comes back, badly blurred.

Someone is pulling Benjamin across the floor by his legs. His pyjama top slides up, and his arms are moving slowly, like he's confused. His head bounces on the threshold of the door. Benjamin looks into Simone's eyes. He's terrified. His mouth is moving but he can't get a single word out. She reaches for his hand but misses it. She tries to crawl after him but doesn't have the strength. She can't see. She blinks and catches glimpses of Benjamin being dragged out into the stairwell. The door closes gently. Simone tries to call for help, but no sound comes out. Her eyes close, and her breathing slows down.

Everything goes black.

41

Saturday morning, 12 December

Simone's mouth feels like it's full of tiny pieces of glass. It hurts when she breathes. She tries to feel her gums with her tongue, but it's so swollen she can't move it. She opens her eyes. At first she can't make any sense of what she sees. Daylight, shiny metal and curtains slowly appear.

Erik is sitting on a chair beside her, holding her hand. His eyes are sunken and tired. Simone tries to talk, but her throat feels raw.

'Where's Benjamin?'

Erik startles.

'What did you say?' he asks.

'Benjamin,' she whispers. 'Where's Benjamin?'

Erik closes his eyes and clenches his jaw, then he swallows and meets her gaze.

'What have you done?' he asks quietly. 'I found you on the floor, Simone. You hardly had a pulse, and if I hadn't found you . . .'

He wipes his mouth and speaks through his fingers:

'What have you done?'

Breathing is hard. She swallows several times. She realises she's had her stomach pumped, but doesn't know what to say. She doesn't have time to explain that she didn't try to commit suicide. It doesn't matter what he thinks. Not right now. When she tries to shake her head she feels sick.

'What happened?' she whispers. 'Is he gone?'

'What do you mean?'

Tears run down her cheeks.

'Is he gone?' she repeats.

'I found you in the hall, darling. Benjamin had already left by the time I got up. Did you two have an argument?'

She tries to shake her head again, but doesn't have the strength.

'There was someone in the flat. They took him,' she says weakly.

'Who?'

She whimpers to herself through her sobs.

'Benjamin?' Erik asks. 'What about Benjamin?'

'Oh, God,' she mutters.

'What about Benjamin?' Erik practically shouts.

'Someone took him,' she replies.

Erik looks scared. He looks around, wipes his mouth and kneels down beside her.

'Tell me what happened,' he says as calmly as he can. 'Simone, just tell me what happened.'

'I saw someone drag Benjamin through the hall,' she says, almost inaudibly.

'What do you mean, drag?'

'I woke up in the middle of the night because I felt a prick in my arm, it was an injection, someone gave me . . .'

'Where? Where were you injected?'

She tries to roll up the sleeve of her hospital gown. He helps her and finds a small red mark on her upper arm. When he feels the swelling around the tiny hole with his fingertips all the colour drains from his face.

'Someone took Benjamin,' she says. 'I couldn't stop . . .'

'We need to find out what you were given,' he says, and presses the alarm button.

'Never mind that. I don't matter. You have to find Benjamin.'

'I will,' he says quickly.

A nurse comes in and Erik gives her concise instructions for blood tests. She hurries out and Erik turns back to Simone:

'You're sure you saw someone take Benjamin?'

'Yes,' she replies desperately.

'But you didn't see who it was?'

'He was dragging Benjamin through the hall by his legs, out through the door. I was lying on the floor. I couldn't move.'

She starts crying again, and he hugs her. She sobs against his chest, exhausted, wracking sobs that shake her whole body. When she calms down she pushes him away gently.

'Erik,' she says. 'You have to find Benjamin.'

'I will,' he says, and hurries out of the room.

The nurse knocks and walks in. Simone closes her eyes so she doesn't have to watch her blood fill four small tubes.

42

Saturday morning, 12 December

As Erik walks towards his office in the hospital he thinks about the trip in the ambulance that morning. The hurried drive through the city, rush-hour traffic slowly getting out of the way, pulling up onto the pavement to pass gridlocked cars. Then the stomach pump, the efficiency of the female doctor, her swift, calm actions. Then the dark screen showing the irregular rhythm of Simone's heart.

Erik switches his phone on and listens to his new messages. Yesterday a police officer named Roland Svensson had tried to reach him four times to offer police protection. There was no message from Benjamin or anyone claiming to be involved in his disappearance.

He calls Aida and feels an icy wave of panic when he hears her frightened, high voice say she has no idea where Benjamin might be.

'Could he have gone back to that place in Tensta?'

'No,' she replies.

Erik calls David, Benjamin's oldest friend. David's mother answers and says she hasn't seen Benjamin for a few days. He cuts her off while she's still speaking.

He calls the lab to find out what they've found in Simone's system, but they can't tell him anything yet.

'I'll stay on the line,' he says.

He hears them working, and after a while Dr Valdés picks up the receiver and says in a rasping voice:

'Right, hello Erik. It looks like Rapifen or something similar containing alfentanil.'

'Alfentanil? The sedative?'

'Probably stolen from a hospital or a vet. We don't use it here much, it's too addictive. Looks like your wife was extremely lucky.'

'How do you mean?' Erik asks.

'She's still alive.'

Erik goes back to Simone's room to ask more about the kidnapping, to go through everything one more time, but she's fallen asleep. Her lips are scabbed and cracked from the stomach pump.

His phone rings in his pocket.

'Yes?'

'This is Kajsa in reception – there's someone here to see you.'

It takes Erik a few seconds to realise that the woman is referring to the reception area here in the hospital, in the Neurology Department.

'Dr Bark?' she asks cautiously.

'Someone to see me? Who is it?'

'Joona Linna,' she replies.

'OK, ask him to come up to the cafeteria. I'll be waiting for him there.'

Erik stands in the hall, his thoughts racing. He thinks about those voicemails from Roland Svensson, calling over and over again to offer him police protection. What happened? Has someone threatened me? Erik asks himself, and a cold shiver runs through his body when he realises how out of the ordinary it is for someone like Joona Linna to pay a visit in person instead of just calling.

Erik walks to the cafeteria and stands in front of the plastic-covered salad bar. He smells the freshly sliced bread. A wave of nausea courses through him. His hands are shaking.

Joona is on his way here, he thinks, to tell me that they've found Benjamin's body. That's why he's here in person. He'll ask me to sit down, then tell me that Benjamin's dead. Erik doesn't want to continue the thought, but he can't help it. He refuses to believe it, but it keeps coming back, faster and faster. Horrifying images of Benjamin's body flash through his mind: in a ditch on the side of the road, in a black bin-bag in a patch of woodland, washed up on a muddy beach.

'Coffee?'

'What?'

'Shall I pour you a cup?'

A young woman with glossy fair hair is standing by the coffee machine, holding the pot up. She looks at him expectantly. He realises that he's standing there with an empty cup in his hand, and shakes his head. At that moment Joona comes into the room.

'Let's sit down,' Joona says.

His expression is troubled and evasive.

'OK,' Erik replies almost silently, after a brief pause.

They sit down at the furthest table. It's covered in a paper tablecloth and has salt and pepper shakers on it. Joona scratches one eyebrow and whispers something.

'Sorry?' Erik says.

Joona clears his throat quietly, then says:

'We've been trying to call you.'

'I wasn't answering my phone yesterday,' Erik says weakly.

'Erik, I'm sorry to have to tell you this, but . . .'

Joona pauses, looks at him with those granite grey eyes, and says:

'Josef Ek has escaped from the hospital.'

'What?'

'You're entitled to police protection.'

Erik's mouth starts to quiver and his eyes fill with tears.

'Is that what you wanted to tell me? That Josef has escaped?'

'Yes.'

Erik is so relieved that he feels faint. He quickly wipes the tears from his eyes.

'When?'

'Yesterday evening. He killed a nurse and seriously wounded another man,' Joona says heavily.

Erik nods several times. His thoughts reconfigure themselves into a new and frightening pattern.

'He came to our flat in the middle of the night and took Benjamin,' he says.

'What?'

'He took Benjamin.'

'Did you see him?'

'I didn't, but Simone . . .'

'What happened?'

'Simone was injected with something,' Erik says slowly. 'I just heard from the lab, it was a substance called alfentanil, a sedative used for serious surgery.'

'Is she OK?'

'She will be.'

Joona nods and writes down the name of the drug.

'Did Simone say that Josef took Benjamin?'

'She didn't see his face.'

'I see.'

'Will you be able to find Josef?' Erik asks.

'We will, trust me on that. A national alert has been issued,' Joona says. 'He's badly injured. He's not going anywhere.'

'But you don't have anything definite to go on?'

Joona looks him in the eye.

'I don't think it'll be long before we have him.'

'Good.'

'Where were you when he came to the flat?'

'I was sleeping in the guest bedroom,' Erik explains. 'I'd taken a sleeping pill, I didn't hear a thing.'

'So when he was there he only found Simone in the bedroom?'

'I suppose so.'

'But that doesn't make sense,' Joona says.

'It's easy to miss the guest room, it looks more like a wardrobe, and when the bathroom door is open it hides the door completely.'

'Not that,' Joona says. 'I mean the business with the injection. It doesn't seem like Josef, his behaviour is far more aggressive.'

'Maybe it just looks that way to us,' Erik says.

'What do you mean?'

'Maybe he knows exactly what he's doing the whole time. I mean, you haven't found any trace of his father's blood in the house.'

'No, but . . .'

'That indicates that he works systematically, coldly. What if he decided to get his revenge on me by taking Benjamin?'

Silence. From the corner of his eye Erik sees the woman at the coffee machine sip her drink as she gazes out across the hospital buildings.

Joona looks down at the table, then he meets Erik's gaze and says, very genuinely, in his Finnish accent:

'I'm so sorry, Erik.'

43

Saturday morning, 12 December

Erik goes back to his office and sits down at his battered desk. Everything around him is falling apart. He calls the same people over and over again, as if he could tell from the tiny changes in their tone of voice whether they've missed some detail, or if they're hiding something. He can feel himself getting hysterical when he calls Aida three times in succession. The first time he asks if she knows if Benjamin had any particular plans for the weekend. The second time he asks if she has the phone numbers of any of his other friends, because he doesn't know who Benjamin hangs out with. The third time he asks if she and Benjamin had an argument, then he gives her all the numbers she can reach him on, including his office at the hospital and Simone's mobile phone.

He calls David again and gets confirmation that no one's seen Benjamin since yesterday. Then he starts calling the police. He asks what's going on, if they're making any progress. Then he calls all the hospitals in the area. He calls Benjamin's switched-off mobile phone for the tenth time, and he calls Joona and demands that the police intensify the search, tells Joona to request more resources. Then he pleads with him to do everything he can.

Erik goes to Simone's room but stops outside. The walls seem to be spinning, and he feels like everything's closing in on him.

He repeats one single phrase over and over again in his head: 'I'm going to find Benjamin, I'm going to find Benjamin.'

Erik looks at his wife through the window in the hospital room door. She's awake, but her face looks tired and confused. Her lips are pale and there are dark rings around her eyes. Her strawberry-blonde hair is sweaty and tangled. She's twisting her wedding ring almost obsessively. Erik runs his hand through his hair, then feels his chin and notices how sharp his stubble has grown. Simone looks at him through the window but her expression doesn't change.

Erik goes in and sits down heavily at her side. She looks at him, then lowers her gaze. A few big tears well up in her eyes, and her nose looks red from crying.

'Benjamin tried to reach out to me. He tried to grab my hand,' she whispers. 'But I couldn't move.'

Erik's voice is weak when he replies:

'I've just been told that Josef Ek escaped last night.'

'I'm freezing,' she whispers.

He tries to pull the pale blue blanket over her, but she bats his hand away.

'It's your fault!' she says. 'You were so fucking desperate to hypnotise someone that you . . .'

'Stop it, Simone, it's not my fault. I was trying to save a girl's life, it's my job to . . .'

'What about your son, then?' she cries.

When Erik tries to touch her she pushes him away.

'I'm going to call Dad,' she says in a shaky voice. 'He'll help me find Benjamin.'

'Don't call him,' Erik says.

'I knew you'd say that, but I really don't give a damn what you think, I just want Benjamin back.'

'I'll find him, Simone.'

'Why don't I believe you?'

'The police are doing everything they can, and your father is . . .'

'The police? It was the police who let that madman escape!' she says angrily. 'They won't do a thing to find Benjamin.'

'Josef's a serial killer. The police will find him. They will but

I'm not stupid, I know Benjamin isn't that important to them. They don't care about him, not really, not like us, not like . . .'

'That's what I mean,' she snaps irritably.

'Joona Linna told me that . . .'

'This is his fault too. He was the one who made you hypnotise that boy.'

Erik shakes his head, then swallows hard.

'It was my choice.'

'Dad would do anything to get Benjamin back,' she whispers.

'I want the two of us to go through every little detail together. We need to think, we need peace and quiet in order . . .'

'What the hell can *we* do?' she shrieks.

They sit silently for a moment. Erik hears someone turn a television on in the next room.

Simone lies back on the bed with her face turned away from him.

'We need to think,' Erik says cautiously. 'I'm not convinced that Josef Ek . . .'

'You're so stupid!' she snaps.

Simone tries to get out of bed, but is too weak.

'Can I ask you just one thing?'

'I'm going to get a gun, and I'm going to find him,' she says.

'The front door was open two nights in a row, but . . .'

'That's what I said,' she interrupts. 'I said someone had been in the flat, but you wouldn't believe me. You never do. If only you'd believed me, none . . .'

'Listen,' Erik says, cutting her off. 'Josef Ek was in his bed here at the hospital that first night, so he couldn't have been in our flat.'

She's not listening to him. She just keeps trying to get up. She groans angrily and manages to make her way to the narrow wardrobe where her clothes are hanging up. Erik stands there without helping her. He watches her put her clothes on very shakily, all the while swearing quietly to herself.

44

Saturday evening, 12 December

It's already evening by the time Erik is allowed to discharge Simone from the hospital. The flat is a complete mess. The sheets are strewn along the hall, the lights are on, the tap in the bathroom is running, there are shoes littering the mat in the hallway, and the phone's halfway across the parquet floor with its batteries nearby.

Erik and Simone look around them. Their home has been ruined. All their possessions suddenly seem alien to them, utterly unimportant.

Simone picks one of the chairs up, sits down, and starts to pull off her boots. Erik turns the tap off, then goes into Benjamin's room. He looks at the red desk and at the schoolbooks beside the computer, wrapped in protective brown paper. On the corkboard there's a photograph of Erik from his time in Uganda, smiling and suntanned, with his hands in the pockets of his lab coat. Erik runs his hand over Benjamin's jeans and black sweater, which are hanging over the back of the chair.

He walks out and goes into the living room, where Simone is holding the phone in her hand. She puts the batteries back in and starts to dial a number.

'Who are you calling?'

'I'm going to call Dad,' she replies.

'Can't you wait a while?'

She lets him take the phone out of her hand.

'What is it?'

'I can't deal with Kennet, not now, not . . .'

He trails off, puts the phone on the table and rubs his face before trying again:

'Can't you respect the fact that I don't want to hand over everything I love to your dad?'

'Can't you respect the . . .?'

'Don't do that,' he interrupts.

She looks at him with a wounded expression.

'Simone, I'm having trouble thinking straight right now. To be honest, I just feel like screaming, and I really can't cope with having your father around.'

'Are you finished?' she says, and holds out her hand for the phone.

'This is about our child,' he says.

She nods.

'Can we let it stay that way? Can we just let it be about him?' he goes on. 'I want you and I to look for Benjamin, and work with the police. We should let them do their job.'

'I need my dad,' she says.

'And I need you.'

'I don't actually believe that,' she retorts.

'Why don't you think . . .?'

'Because you want to make my decisions for me,' she interrupts.

Erik paces around the room, then stops.

'Your dad's retired, he can't do anything.'

'He's got contacts,' she says.

'He thinks he has contacts. He thinks he's still a detective, but he's just a retiree.'

'You don't know . . .'

'He can't find Benjamin!' Erik interrupts.

'I don't care what you say.'

She looks at the phone.

'I can't stay here if he's coming.'

'Don't do this,' she says quietly.

'You just want him to show up here and tell you I've messed

up, that it's all my fault. Sure, I get that that's good for you, but for me it's . . .'

'You're behaving like a child,' she says.

'You're the one calling your dad for help! If he comes, I'm leaving.'

'I don't care what you do,' she says firmly.

His shoulders sink. She turns her back on him as she dials the number.

'Don't do it,' he pleads.

She doesn't turn around. There's no way he can stay if Kennet comes. He looks around him. There's nothing he wants to take with him. He hears the tinny sound of the phone ringing, and sees the shadow of Simone's eyelashes tremble on her cheek.

'Damn you,' he says, and walks out of the room.

Erik hears Simone talking to Kennet as he puts his shoes on. Sobbing quietly, she asks her father to come as soon as he can. Erik takes his jacket from its hanger and leaves the flat, shutting and locking the door behind him. He walks down the stairs, but stops. He thinks that he should go back and say something to her. This isn't fair. This is his home, his son, his life.

'Damn,' he says in a low voice, then walks down the rest of the stairs and out into the dark street.

45

Saturday evening, 12 December

Simone is standing at the window. Her reflection looks ghostly in the evening gloom. When she sees her father's old Nissan Primera double-park out front she has to make an effort not to burst into tears. She's waiting in the hallway when he knocks on the door. She opens it with the safety chain on, shuts it again, removes the chain and tries to smile.

'Dad,' she says, as the tears start to flow.

Kennet hugs her and when she smells the familiar leather and tobacco of his jacket she is transported momentarily back in time to when she was a child.

'I'm here now, sweetheart,' Kennet says. 'Is Erik here?' he asks.

'We split up,' she whispers.

'Oh . . .' Kennet says, clearly taken aback.

He fishes out a handkerchief, and she blows her nose several times. Then he hangs his jacket up, noting that Benjamin's winter coat is still there, his shoes are still on the rack and his rucksack is leaning against the wall next to the door.

Holding his daughter by her shoulder, he gently wipes the tears from under her eyes with his thumb, then leads her into the kitchen. He sits her down on a chair, and takes out the coffee and a fresh filter.

'Now, tell me everything,' he says calmly as he gets two mugs out. 'From the beginning.'

And Simone tells him in detail about the first night she woke up because she was sure someone was in the flat. About the smell of cigarette smoke in the kitchen, the open front door, and the blue light from the open fridge.

'What about Erik?' Kennet prompts. 'What did he do?'

She hesitates a moment, then meets her father's gaze and says:

'He didn't believe me. He said one of us must have been sleepwalking.'

'Christ,' Kennet says.

Simone feels her face crumple again. Kennet pours their coffee, jots something down on a piece of paper, and asks her to go on.

She tells him about the injection in her arm that woke her up the next night, and how she got up and heard disconcerting noises from Benjamin's room.

'What sort of noises?' Kennet asks.

'Whimpering,' she says hesitantly. 'Or muttering. I don't know.'

'Then what?'

'I asked if I could come in, and I saw there was someone there, someone bending over Benjamin, and . . .'

'Yes?'

'Then I just collapsed. I couldn't do anything, I just lay in the hallway and watched as Benjamin was dragged out. God, his face . . . he was so scared. He called out to me and tried to reach for me. And I couldn't move at all.'

She stares off ahead.

'Do you remember anything else?'

'Like what?'

'What did he look like? The man who took Benjamin?'

'I don't know.'

'Did you notice anything?'

'He moved in a strange way. His back was hunched over, like he was in pain.'

Kennet makes some more notes.

'Think really hard,' he prompts.

'It was dark, Dad.'

'And Erik?' Kennet asks.

'He was asleep.'

'Asleep?'

She nods.

'He's been taking a lot of sleeping pills lately,' she says. 'He was in the guest bedroom and didn't hear anything.'

Kennet's eyes are full of contempt and Simone suddenly feels a flash of understanding for Erik and his decision to walk out.

'What sort of pills?' Kennet says. 'Do you know what they're called?'

She takes her father's hands.

'Dad, Erik's not on trial here.'

He pulls his hands away.

'Violence towards children is almost always committed by someone in the family.'

'I know that, but . . .'

'Let's look at the facts,' Kennet interrupts calmly. 'The perpetrator clearly has a degree of medical knowledge and access to drugs.'

She nods.

'You didn't see Erik in the guest bedroom?'

'The door was closed.'

'But you didn't actually see him in there, did you? And you don't know if he took any sleeping pills that night.'

'No,' she has to admit.

'I'm just looking at what we know, Simone,' he says. 'And we know that you didn't see him asleep. Maybe he was sleeping in the guest bedroom, but we don't actually know that.'

Kennet stands up and gets out some bread and cheese. He makes Simone a sandwich and passes it to her.

After a while he clears his throat and asks:

'Why would Erik open the door for Josef?'

She stares at him.

'What do you mean?'

'If he did – what would his reasoning be?'

'I think this has turned into a ridiculous conversation.'

'Why?'

'Erik loves Benjamin.'

'Yes, but maybe something went wrong. Maybe Erik just wanted to talk to Josef, persuade him to contact the police, or . . .'

'Stop it, Dad,' Simone says.

'We need to be asking questions like this if we're going to find Benjamin.'

She nods. She feels tears in her eyes. She's cried so much that she can no longer recognise her own face. She says, in a barely audible voice:

'Maybe Erik thought it was someone else at the door?'

'Who?'

'I think he's been seeing a woman named Daniella,' she says, without meeting her father's gaze.

46

Sunday morning, 13 December, St Lucia's Day

Simone wakes up at five o'clock in the morning. Kennet must have carried her to bed and tucked her in. She goes straight to Benjamin's room but it's empty.

She doesn't cry, but the taste of tears and anguish seems to have seeped into everything, turned her whole world cloudy. She tries to keep her thoughts off Benjamin. She doesn't want to let the terror in.

The light is on in the kitchen.

Kennet has covered the table with pieces of paper. His police radio is on the counter, emitting a hum. He's standing very still, just staring out into space for a moment, then he rubs his chin a couple of times.

'It's good that you got some sleep,' he says.

She shakes her head.

'Simone?'

'Yes,' she murmurs. She goes over to the sink, where she fills her hands with cold water and rinses her face. As she dries her face she sees her reflection in the window. It's still dark outside, but soon dawn will arrive with its December gloom.

Kennet writes something on a piece of paper. She sits down on the chair across from her dad and tries to understand where Josef might have taken Benjamin, how he was able to get inside their flat, and why he took Benjamin and no one else.

'Son of happiness,' she whispers.

'What did you say?' Kennet asks.

'Oh, nothing . . .'

'"Son of happiness" is the Hebrew meaning of Benjamin. In the Old Testament, Rachel was Jacob's wife. He spent fourteen years wooing her. Rachel had two sons, Joseph, who went on to interpret the pharaoh's dreams, and Benjamin, the son of happiness.'

Simone's face tightens with withheld tears. Without a word, Kennet leans over the table and squeezes her shoulder.

'We're going to find him,' he says.

She nods.

'I received this folder just before you woke up,' he says, tapping a large file on the table.

'What is it?'

'You know that terraced house in Tumba, where Josef Ek . . . This is the report of the crime scene investigation.'

'Aren't you supposed to be retired?'

He smiles and pushes the folder towards her. She opens it and looks through the systematic overview of fingerprints, handprints, strands of hair, fragments of skin under fingernails, and damage to knife blades. There was blood and spinal fluid on a pair of slippers, and blood on the television, the rice-paper lampshade, the rag-rug, and the curtains. The photographs slip out of a plastic sleeve. Simone looks away quickly, but her brain still has time to register the horror of the room depicted. Everyday objects: bookcases, a stereo, are all covered in black blood. There are mutilated bodies and body parts on the floor.

She goes over to the sink and throws up.

'Sorry,' Kennet says. 'Sometimes I forget that not everyone is a police officer.'

She shuts her eyes and thinks about the look of terror on Benjamin's face and imagines a dark room, its floor smeared with blood. She leans forward and throws up again. Strands of slime and bile splatter the coffee cups and cutlery. As she rinses her mouth and listens to the shrill sound of her pulse in her ears she starts to worry that she's becoming hysterical.

She grips the sink tightly and composes herself.

'I just can't separate all of that from Benjamin,' she says weakly.

Kennet gets a blanket and wraps it around her, then gently helps her sit back down.

'If Josef Ek has abducted Benjamin, then he wants something – he must, because this is very different from the way he's behaved before . . .'

'I don't know if I can deal with this,' she whispers.

'Can I just say, I think Josef Ek was looking for Erik,' Kennet says. 'And when he didn't find him, he took Benjamin instead, so he could try to arrange a trade.'

'That means he must be alive – doesn't it?'

'Of course he is,' Kennet says. 'We just need to figure out where Josef's hidden him.'

'That could be anywhere.'

'On the contrary,' Kennet says.

She looks at him.

'It nearly always ends up being the kidnapper's home, or a summer cottage.'

'But that's his home,' she says, raising her voice and tapping the sleeve containing the photographs with her finger.

47

Sunday morning, 13 December, St Lucia's Day

Kennet repeats the words 'his home' to himself, then picks up the folder containing the photographs and preliminary report from the forensic examination of the terraced house and turns to his daughter.

'Dutroux,' he says.

'What?' Simone asks.

'Dutroux. Do you remember Dutroux?'

'I don't know . . .'

Kennet tells her about Marc Dutroux, a paedophile who kidnapped and tortured six girls in Belgium. Julie Lejeune and Melissa Russo starved to death while Dutroux was serving a short prison sentence for car theft. Eefje Lambrecks and An Marchal were buried alive in his yard.

'Dutroux had a house in Charleroi,' he goes on. 'In the basement he'd built a space with a false door weighing 200 kilos. It was so solid that you couldn't hear anything if you tapped on it. The only way to find the room was by measuring the house: the internal and external measurements were different. Sabine Dardenne and Laetitia Delhez were found alive.'

Simone tries to stand up. She can feel her heart beating oddly in her chest. She considers the fact there are men who are driven by a desire to wall people up, who find peace in the knowledge that their victims are down there, screaming for help behind impenetrable walls.

'Benjamin needs his medication,' she whispers.

Her dad goes over to the phone. He dials a number, waits a few seconds, then says quickly:

'Charley? Listen, there's something I need to know about Josef Ek . . . No, this is about the house, the terraced house in Tumba.'

There's a short silence, then Simone hears someone speaking in a gruff, deep voice.

'Yes,' Kennet says. 'I understand. I've had a chance to look at the report of the crime scene investigation.'

The other man speaks again. Simone closes her eyes and listens to the hum of the police radio, its sound merging with the muffled voice coming from the phone.

'But have you actually measured the house?' she hears her father ask. 'No, of course, but . . .'

She opens her eyes and suddenly feels a wave of adrenalin sweep her tiredness away.

'Yes, that would be great. Messenger the plans over,' Kennet says. 'And any applications for renovation. Yes, the same address. Thanks, thanks a lot.'

He ends the call and then stands there gazing out of the big window.

'Could Benjamin really be in that house?' she asks. 'Could he? Dad?'

'That's what we need to find out.'

'Let's go, then,' she says impatiently.

'Charley's sending the plans,' he says.

'What do you mean, plans? I don't give a damn about plans, Dad. What are you waiting for? Let's go, I'm ready to tear down . . .'

'That's not a good idea,' he interrupts. 'Of course we have to act quickly, but I don't think we'd gain anything by heading straight to the house and trying to pull it apart, brick by brick.'

'We have to do something, Dad!'

'That house has been crawling with police for the past few

days,' he says. 'If there's anything obvious they'd have found it already, even if they weren't looking for Benjamin.'

'But . . .'

'I need to examine the plans, see where it might be possible to build a hidden room, and get hold of the measurements so we can compare the plans to what we find at the site.'

'But what if there isn't a hidden room – where is he then?'

'The family used to share a summer house outside Bollnäs with the father's brothers. I've got a friend there, Svante, who's promised to take a look. He used to know the area well.'

Kennet looks at the time, then dials a number.

'Hi, Svante, it's Kennet here. I was just wondering . . .'

'I'm there now,' his friend says.

'Where?'

'Inside the house,' Svante says.

'You were only supposed to take a look.'

'The new owners let me in, a couple by the name of Sjölin, they . . .'

Someone says something in the background.

'Sjödin,' he corrects himself. 'They've owned the house for just over a year now.'

'Thanks for your help.'

Kennet ends the call. A sharp line furrows his brow.

'What about the other cottage?' Simone asks. 'The one where his sister was hiding?'

'The police have been out there, several times, but you and I could go and take a look anyway.'

They sit quietly, lost in thought. The letterbox rattles and the morning paper belatedly thuds onto the hall mat. Neither of them moves. They hear other letterboxes rattle on other floors, then the front door of the building opens.

Kennet turns up the volume of the police radio. An alert has been issued. Someone responds, requesting more information. Terse words are exchanged. Simone hears something about a woman hearing screams from the neighbouring flat. A car is dispatched. Someone starts laughing in the background, and embarks on a long explanation of why his grown-up younger brother still lives at home. Kennet lowers the volume again.

'I'll put some more coffee on,' Simone says.

Kennet pulls an atlas of Greater Stockholm from his khaki rucksack. He moves the candlesticks from the table to the windowsill before opening it. Simone stands behind him and looks at the tangled network of roads, trains and bus-lines curling across each other in different colours. She stares at the patches of forest and the geometric designs of the suburbs.

Kennet's finger follows a yellow road south and west of Stockholm, past Älvsjö, Huddinge, Tullinge and down to Tumba. Together they study the page covering Tumba and Salem, an old suburb built around a commuter railway station. The optimism of the post-war construction boom is evident in the proliferation of housing blocks and shops, the church and the bank. Around this core a network of terraces and detached houses spreads out. There are a few fields left on the map, a few kilometres to the north of the built-up area, before the fields in turn are replaced by forest and lakes.

Kennet studies the street names, then circles one of the narrow rectangles, lined up as neatly as ribs.

'Where the hell is that messenger?' Kennet mutters.

Simone fills two mugs with coffee and puts some sugar in front of her father.

'How could he have gotten in?' Simone asks.

'Josef Ek? Well, either he had a key, or someone unlocked the door for him.'

'Can this lock be picked?'

'Not this kind, it's too hard. It would be a lot easier just to smash the door in.'

'Maybe we should take a look at Benjamin's computer?'

'We should have done that before now. It did cross my mind, then I forgot. I must be getting tired,' Kennet says.

Simone realises how old he looks. She's never really thought about his age before. He looks at her sadly.

'Try to get some sleep while I check the computer,' she says.

'No, I'm fine.'

When Simone and Kennet walk into Benjamin's room it feels as if no one's ever lived there. Benjamin seems so horribly far away.

A wave of terror and nausea rises up from Simone's stomach. She swallows. Out in the kitchen the police radio burbles and whistles. But here in the darkness, death lies in wait like a black absence, a loss she will never be able to recover from.

She switches the computer on and the screen flickers. When the operating system's start-up sound rings out, it's as if part of Benjamin has come back.

They each pull up a chair and sit down. She clicks the tiny picture of Benjamin's face to log in.

'OK, sweetheart, we're going to do this nice and methodically,' Kennet says. 'We'll start with the emails, then . . .'

He trails off when the computer demands a password.

'Try his name,' Kennet says.

She types Benjamin, but that doesn't work. She tries Aida, then tries them backwards, and puts them together. She tries Bark, Benjamin Bark, blushes as she types Simone, then she tries Erik, and the names of bands Benjamin likes, Sexsmith, Ane Brun, Rory Gallagher, Lennon, Townes Van Zandt, Bob Dylan.

'It's not going to work,' Kennet says. 'We'll have to call someone who can get into it for us.'

She tries a few film titles and directors Benjamin has often talked about, but gives up after a while. It's impossible.

'We should have those plans by now,' Kennet says. 'I'll call Charley and see what's going on.'

They both startle when there's a knock on the door of the flat. Simone stops in the corridor with her heart pounding and watches as Kennet goes into the hall and turns the lock.

48

Sunday morning, 13 December, St Lucia's Day

The morning is as pale as sand, and it's a few degrees above freezing when Kennet and Simone drive into the part of Tumba where Josef Ek was born and raised, and where, at the age of fifteen, he slaughtered almost his entire family. The house looks like all the others in the street. Neat and unremarkable. If it wasn't for the blue and white police tape, no one would be able to tell that just a couple of days ago this house had been the scene of two of the most brutal murders in the country's history.

A bicycle with training wheels is leaning against the sandpit in the front yard. One end of the cordon tape has come loose and is caught on the letterbox. Kennet doesn't stop, he drives slowly past the house. Simone peers at the windows. The house looks completely deserted. The deck is strangely dark. They continue until they reach the roundabout, swing back and are just approaching the crime scene again when Simone's phone rings.

'Hello?' she says, then listens briefly. 'Has something happened?' she asks.

Kennet stops, letting the engine idle for a moment, then he turns off the car and gets out. He takes a crowbar, a measuring tape and a torch out of the boot. He hears Simone say she has to go before he closes the boot.

'What do you think?' Simone shouts at the phone.

She looks upset when she gets out of the car, clutching the plans in her hand. Without speaking, they walk towards the white gate in the low fence. Kennet takes the key out of the envelope he got with the plans, walks up to the door and unlocks it. Before he goes inside he turns to Simone and nods at her.

As soon as they enter the building they are met by the suffocating smell of rancid blood. For a moment Simone feels panic building in her chest: it's a rotten, cloying, almost faecal smell. She glances at Kennet. He doesn't appear to be scared, just focused. He walks with carefully measured movements. They go past the living room, and from the corner of her eye Simone catches a glimpse of utter chaos: the blood on the wall, the blood on the soapstone stove.

There's an odd tapping sound coming from somewhere inside the house. Kennet stops abruptly, slowly draws his old service pistol, releases the safety catch and checks that it's loaded.

Another noise. A heavy, brushing sound. Not like footsteps – more like someone slithering along the floor.

49

Sunday morning, 13 December, St Lucia's Day

Erik wakes up in the narrow bed in his office at the hospital. It's the middle of the night. He looks at the time on his phone. Almost three o'clock. He takes another pill, then lies shivering under the blanket until the tingling spreads through his body and darkness sweeps in.

When he wakes up three hours later he has a splitting headache. He takes a painkiller, then goes and stands by the window. His gaze slides up the hospital wing opposite, with its hundreds of windows. The sky is white, but the building appears dark. Erik leans forward, feels the cold glass against the tip of his nose.

He puts his phone down on the desk and gets undressed. The shower in his office bathroom smells like plastic and disinfectant. The hot water runs down his head and neck and noisily batters the plexiglass.

He dries himself and wipes the mirror, then wets his face and rubs on some shaving cream. The clear patch on the mirror shrinks as he shaves.

He thinks back to what Simone said about the door being open the night before Josef Ek escaped from hospital. So that first time, it can't have been Josef. Erik tries to figure out what could have happened. There are too many unanswered questions. How had the intruder managed to get in? Maybe he just knocked on the door until Benjamin went and opened it. Erik imagines the two boys, Benjamin and Josef, standing there staring at each other in the dim light from the landing. Benjamin barefoot, his hair sticking straight up, standing in his pyjamas and blinking wide-eyed at the older boy. Josef has murdered his parents and younger sister, he's just murdered a nurse at the hospital with a scalpel, and seriously injured a man in the North Cemetery.

'No,' Erik says to himself. 'I don't believe that. It doesn't make any sense.'

Who could have got in, why would Benjamin open the door? Who would Simone or Benjamin have entrusted with a key? Maybe Benjamin thought Aida might show up. Maybe it was her? He mustn't rule anything out. Maybe someone was working with Josef and helped him with the door. Maybe Josef really had been planning to get out that first night but wasn't able to escape. That was why the door was open, because that was what they had arranged.

Erik finishes shaving, brushes his teeth and calls Joona.

'Good morning, Erik,' a gruff voice says in a Finnish accent.

'Did I wake you?'

'No.'

'Sorry to call again, but . . .'

Erik coughs.

'Has something happened?' Joona asks.

'You haven't found Benjamin?'

'We need to talk to Simone, go through everything properly.'

'You don't think it was Josef who took Benjamin, do you?'

'No, I don't,' Joona replies. 'But I'm not sure, I want to take a look at your flat, and knock on some doors to see if we can't find someone who saw something.'

'Shall I ask Simone to call you?'

'No need.'

A drop of water falls from the tap and hits the sink.

'I still think you should agree to police protection,' Joona says.

'I'm here at Karolinska, and I hardly think Josef is going to come back here of his own volition.'

'What about Simone?'

'Ask her, she might have changed her mind,' Erik says. 'Even if she already has her own protection.'

'Ah, yes, I heard about that,' Joona says brightly. 'I have to admit, I'm having trouble imagining what it would be like to have Kennet Sträng as a father-in-law.'

'Me too,' Erik replies.

'I can sympathise with that,' Joona says.

'Did Josef try to escape the night before yesterday?' Erik asks.

'No, I don't think so. We haven't found anything to suggest that,' Joona replies. 'Why do you ask?'

'Someone opened the door to the flat that night, just like they did the following night.'

'I'm pretty sure Josef's escape was a reaction to the news that he was going to be arrested, and he only found out about that on Friday evening,' Joona says slowly.

Erik shakes his head and runs his thumb across his lips. He stares at the shower.

'This doesn't make sense,' he sighs.

'Did you see the door when it was open?' Joona asks.

'No, Simone did . . . She got up and looked.'

'Would she have any reason to lie?'

'I haven't considered that.'

'Think about it.'

Erik looks in the mirror. He no longer knows what to believe. Maybe Josef was working with someone else. What if he had an accomplice who did some preparatory work the night before the kidnapping, maybe just to see if the key worked? Maybe he reported back to Josef, the way the rooms were laid out, who slept where.

That would explain why Josef didn't find me, Erik thinks. I was sleeping next to Simone that first night.

'Was Evelyn still being held at Police Headquarters on Wednesday?' Erik asks.

'Yes.'

'All day and all night?'

'Yes.'

'Is she still there?'

'She's been moved to a safe location.'

'Has she been in contact with anyone?'

'You have to let the police do their job,' Joona says.

'And I'm doing mine,' Erik says in a low voice. 'I want to talk to Evelyn.'

'What do you want to talk to her about?'

'I want to ask if Josef has any friends, anyone who could be helping him.'

'I can ask her, but . . .' Joona sighs, then says:

'You know perfectly well that I can't let you conduct your own private investigation, Erik. Even if I might not disagree personally, it . . .'

'Can I be there when you talk to her?' Erik asks. 'I've spent years working with severely traumatised people.'

They both stop talking for a few seconds.

'Meet me at the entrance to Police Headquarters in an hour,' Joona says.

'I'll be there in twenty minutes,' Erik says.

'OK, twenty minutes,' Joona says, and ends the call.

His mind blank, Erik goes over to his desk and opens the top drawer. Among the pens, erasers and paperclips are various blister-packs of pills. He presses three different pills into his hand and swallows them.

He leaves his room and hurries to the cafeteria. He drinks a cup of coffee in front of the aquarium, watching a group of neon tetras as they make their way around a plastic shipwreck. He wraps a sandwich in some napkins and puts it in his pocket.

In the lift down to reception he stares at his reflection. His face looks sad, disconnected. As he stares at himself, he thinks about the lurching sensation you get in your stomach when you fall from a great height: it's almost sexual, yet you feel helpless. He barely has any energy left, but the pills are keeping him afloat and steady on a bright plane. He can go on a little longer, he tells himself. He's not going to fall apart. All he has to do is hold it together long enough to get his son back. Then everything can collapse.

As he heads out to his meeting with Joona and Evelyn, he tries to think through what he's done and where he's been during the past week. He realises that his keys could have been copied on numerous occasions. He always keeps them in his jacket pocket, and on Thursday he left his jacket hanging in a restaurant's coatroom. He'd also left it on the chair in his office, hanging on a hook in the staff cafeteria, and in plenty of other places too. The same probably applies to Benjamin and Simone.

As he's driving through the chaos of the rebuilding work at Fridhemsplan, he dials Simone's number.

'Hello?' she answers, sounding stressed.

'It's me.'

'Has something happened?' she asks.

'I just wanted to say that you should probably check Benjamin's computer – not just his email, but the whole thing: what he's downloaded, which sites he's visited, temporary internet folders, whether he's been chatting with anyone, and . . .'

'Obviously,' she interrupts.

'I won't bother you.'

'We haven't started with the computer yet,' she says.

'The password is Dumbledore.'

'I know.'

Erik turns into Polhems Street, and then Kungsholms Street, and drives past Police Headquarters, with its various guises: the smooth copper-coloured building, the concrete extension, and finally the original building with its yellow stucco.

'I need to go,' she says.

'Simone,' Erik says. 'Have you been telling me the truth?'

'What do you mean?'

'About what happened, the door being open the night before last, and seeing someone drag Benjamin out through . . .'

'What do you think?' she shouts, and ends the call.

Erik can't be bothered to look for a free parking space. Without really thinking about it, he pulls up right in front of the building. The tyres rumble as he stops beside the broad flight of steps leading to the courthouse. The lights of the car illuminate an attractive old wooden door that clearly hasn't been used for years. Ornate, old-fashioned letters announce that it leads to 'Homicide'.

He hurries around the building, up Kungsholms Street towards the park and the main entrance to the National Crime

Unit. He sees a father walking with three girls who are wearing St Lucia costumes over their winter clothes. The white gowns are stretched tight over their bulky winter clothes. The children have crowns of electric candles on top of their wool hats, and one of them is carrying a single electric candle in her gloved hand. Erik suddenly remembers how Benjamin loved to be carried when he was little, clinging to him with his arms and legs. 'Carry me, you're big and strong, Daddy.'

The entrance to National Crime is a large, illuminated glass cube. Erik is out of breath by the time he stops on the black rubber mat in the vestibule. Ahead of him in the spacious lobby are two large revolving doors in the glass wall, with coded locks. Erik crosses the white marble floor to the reception desk on the left and explains why he's there. The receptionist nods and taps at his computer, then picks up the phone.

'This is reception,' he says quietly. 'There's an Erik Maria Bark here to see you.'

The man listens, then turns towards Erik.

'He's on his way down,' he says.

'Thanks.'

Erik sits down on a low, backless bench with a big, creaking leather seat. He stares at a piece of art made of green glass, then looks over at the motionless revolving doors. Behind the large glass wall he can see another glass hallway. It leads across an internal courtyard to the next building. Erik sees Joona walking past the seating area to the right. He presses a button and walks out through one of the revolving doors. He tosses a banana peel in an aluminium rubbish bin, waves at the man in reception and walks over to Erik.

While they walk to Evelyn Ek's safe house on Hantverkar Street, Joona tries to summarise what they've found out from questioning her: she confirmed that she took the shotgun into the forest in order to commit suicide. Josef had been demanding sexual favours from her for years, and would beat their younger sister Lisa if she didn't do as he asked. Evelyn went into hiding at their aunt's summer cottage on Värmdö. Josef tried to find her. He went to see her former boyfriend, Sorab Ramadani, and somehow made him reveal where Evelyn was hiding. On his birthday Josef paid his sister a visit out at the cottage, and when she refused to have sex with him, he told her she knew what would happen, and that it was all her fault.

'The way it looks at the moment, Josef certainly planned his father's murder,' Joona says. 'We don't know why he picked that particular date, but that could just be down to opportunity, because his father was going to be on his own somewhere outside the home. On Monday Josef Ek packed a change of clothes, two pairs of shoe-covers, a towel, his father's hunting knife, a bottle of petrol and some matches in a gym bag, and biked off to Rödstuhage. Once he'd killed his father and dismembered part of the body, he took his father's keys from his pocket, went into the women's locker room, showered and changed clothes, locked up behind him, then set the bag containing his blood-stained clothes on fire in a playground and biked back home.'

'So what happened back at the house? Was it more or less the way he described it when he was hypnotised?' Erik asks.

'It was exactly like that, from the looks of it,' Joona says, and clears his throat. 'But we don't know what triggered it, we don't know why he suddenly attacked his little sister and his mother.'

He glances at Erik:

'Maybe he felt he wasn't finished, that Evelyn hadn't been punished enough.'

Just before they reach the church, Joona stops in front of a doorway, takes out his phone, dials a number and says that they've arrived. He taps in the code, and lets Erik into the plain stairwell.

50

Sunday morning, 13 December, St Lucia's Day

Two police officers are waiting outside the lift when they reach the third floor. Joona shakes their hands and then unlocks a reinforced door without a letterbox. Before he opens it completely he knocks.

'Can we come in?' Joona asks through the gap.

'You haven't found him, have you?'

Evelyn's face is backlit, and it's hard to read her expression. Erik and Joona can only see dark features surrounded by sunlit hair.

'No,' Joona replies.

Evelyn walks over to the door and lets them in. She closes the door behind them and double-checks the lock. When she turns around Erik can see that she's breathing very fast.

'This is a secure flat, and you've got police protection,' Joona says. 'No one's allowed to share, or even to look for, information about you. We've got a statement from the Prosecutors' Office to that effect. You're safe now, Evelyn.'

'Maybe as long as I stay in here,' she says. 'But I'm going to have to go out sometime, and Josef is very good at waiting.'

She goes over to the window and looks out, then sits down on the sofa.

'Where could Josef be hiding?' Joona asks.

'You think I know something.'

'Do you?' Erik asks.

'Are you going to hypnotise me?'

'No,' he smiles in surprise.

She's not wearing any make-up, and her eyes look vulnerable and defenceless as she studies him.

'You can if you want,' she says.

Erik looks around and follows her into the kitchen.

'Not bad,' he says.

Evelyn shrugs. She's wearing a red sweater and a pair of worn-out jeans. Her hair is pulled back in an untidy ponytail.

'I'm going to get a few more personal things today,' she says.

'Good,' Erik says. 'Things usually feel better when . . .'

'Better? Do you know what would make me feel better?'

'I've worked with many trauma victims.'

'Sorry, but I don't give a damn about that,' she interrupts. 'I keep saying I don't want to talk to any psychologists.'

'I'm not here in that capacity.'

'No?'

'I'm here to find Josef.'

She turns to him and says bluntly:

'Well he's not here.'

He doesn't know why, but Erik decides not to say anything about Benjamin.

'Listen, Evelyn,' he says quietly. 'I need your help understanding Josef's social circle.'

Her eyes look almost feverish now.

'OK,' she says, the corners of her mouth twitching.

'Does he have a girlfriend?'

Her eyes darken and she clenches her jaw.

'Apart from me, you mean?'

'Yes.'

She pauses, then shakes her head.

'What's his social life like?'

'He doesn't have a social life,' she says.

'Classmates?'

She shrugs again.

'He's never had any friends as far as I know.'

'If he ever needed help with something – who would he turn to?' Erik asks.

'I don't know. Sometimes he stops and talks to the drunks behind the shopping centre.'

'Do you know which ones, what their names are?'

'One of them has a tattoo on his hand.'

'What does it look like?'

'I don't really remember . . . a fish, I think.'

She stands up and goes over to the window. Erik looks at her. The daylight shines straight onto her young face, making her look very vulnerable. He can see the blue vein throbbing in her long, slender neck.

'Could he be staying with one of them, do you think?' Erik asks.

She does a sort of half-shrug.

'Well . . .'

'Do you think so?' Erik asks.

'No.' Evelyn responds.

'So what do you think?'

'I think he's going to find me before you find him.'

Erik wonders if it's worth trying to pressure her further. There's something about her toneless voice, her lack of hope, that tells him she knows something about her younger brother that no one else knows.

'Evelyn – what does Josef want?'

'I don't want to talk about it.'

'Does he want to kill me?'

'I don't know.'

'What do you think?'

She takes a deep breath, then answers in a hoarse, tired voice:

'If he thinks you're standing between him and me, if he's jealous, then he'll do it.'

'What?'

'Kill you.'

'He'll try, you mean.'

Evelyn licks her lips, turns towards him and looks down. Erik is about to repeat his question, but can't get the words out.

There's a knock on the door. Evelyn stares at Joona and Erik. She looks terrified and backs away into the kitchen.

Another knock. Joona goes over and looks through the peephole, then opens the door. Two police officers come into the hallway. One of them is carrying a cardboard box.

'I think we found everything on the list,' he says. 'Where do you want it?'

'Anywhere,' Evelyn says in a thin voice, coming out of the kitchen.

'Can I just get a signature?'

He holds out a receipt, and she signs it. Joona locks up after them when they leave. Evelyn hurries over and checks that the door is locked, then crouches down, pulls the brown tape from the box and folds back the top. She picks up a silver piggybank in the shape of a rabbit, and a framed picture of a guardian angel, then she freezes.

'My photograph album,' she says, and Erik sees that her mouth has started to tremble.

'Evelyn?'

'I didn't ask for it, I didn't say anything about it.'

She opens the first page to reveal a large school photograph of her. She looks about fourteen, and is smiling shyly, with braces on her teeth. Her skin is smooth and her hair cut short.

Evelyn turns the page and a folded piece of paper falls out onto the floor. She picks it up and opens it, and her face turns bright red as she reads it.

'He's at home,' she whispers, handing over the note.

Erik smooths it out and he and Joona read it together:

I own you, you're mine, I'll kill the others, it's your fault, I'll kill that cunt of a hypnotist, and you're going to help me, you will, you're going to show me where he lives, you're going to show me where you meet up and have fun, and I'll kill him while you watch me do it, and then you'll have to wash your cunt with loads of soap and then I'm going to fuck you a hundred times, and *then we'll be even and we can start again, just the two of us.*

Evelyn lowers the blinds and stands there with her arms wrapped tightly around herself. Erik puts the note down on the table and stands up. Josef is in the terraced house. He must be. If he was able to put the photo album in the box, he must be there.

'Josef's gone back home,' Erik says.

'Where else would he go?' she says quietly.

Joona has already gone out into the kitchen and is talking on the phone to the duty officer.

'Evelyn, do you have any idea how Josef could have hidden from the police?' Erik says. 'They've been conducting a crime scene investigation out there for almost a week now.'

'The basement,' Evelyn replies, and looks up.

'What about the basement?'

'There's a weird room down there.'

'He's in the basement,' Erik calls to the kitchen.

'The suspect is believed to be in the basement,' Joona says.

'Hang on a second,' the duty officer says on the phone. 'I need to . . .'

'This is urgent,' Joona snaps.

After a pause the duty officer says in a calm voice:

'We had an emergency call to the same address two minutes ago.'

'What? To Gärdesvägen 8 in Tumba?' Joona asks.

'Yes,' he replies. 'The neighbours called to say there was someone inside the house.'

51

Sunday morning, 13 December, St Lucia's Day

Kennet Sträng stops and listens before he walks slowly towards the stairs. He's aiming his pistol at the floor, close to his feet. Daylight is coming into the hallway from the kitchen. Simone follows her father, thinking about how the house looks like the one she and Erik lived in when Benjamin was little.

Something's making a creaking sound – either in the floor or deep inside the walls.

'Is it Josef?' Simone whispers.

The weight of the torch, plans and crowbar are making her hands feel numb. The crowbar alone is almost unbearable.

The house is completely silent now. The sounds they heard before, the creaking and the muffled thuds, have stopped.

Kennet gestures towards her with his head. He wants to go down into the basement. Simone nods back, even though every muscle in her body disagrees.

According to the plans, there could be a hidden room in the basement. Kennet had drawn on them, showing how the space where the old oil boiler had been could be extended to create a hidden room. The other area Kennet marked on the plans as a possibility was the attic storage space at the very back of the house.

Beside the pine staircase leading upstairs there's a narrow, doorless opening. There are still hooks in the wall from a childproof gate. The metal steps into the basement look almost homemade: the welding is clumsy and the stairs are covered with rough grey felt.

When Kennet presses the light-switch nothing happens. He tries again, but the bulb seems to be broken.

'Wait here,' he says in a low voice.

Simone feels a jolt of fear. A heavy, dusty smell is coming from the opening. It makes her think of a diesel lorry.

'Give me the torch,' he says, holding out his hand.

She slowly passes it to him. He switches it on, then starts to go down the steps very slowly.

'Hello?' Kennet shouts in an authoritative voice. 'Josef? I need to speak to you.'

There's no sound from the basement. No shuffling, no breathing.

Simone squeezes the crowbar and waits.

The light illuminates little more than the walls and the roof above the steps. The darkness of the basement remains undisturbed. Kennet keeps descending, and the light picks out individual objects: a white plastic bag, the reflector on an old pushchair, the glass of a framed film poster.

'I think I can help you,' Kennet says in a quieter voice.

He reaches the bottom and scans the room with the torch to make sure no one is going to charge him. The narrow beam slips across the floor and walls, jumping over objects and casting large, moving shadows. Kennet does the same thing again, calmly and systematically searching the room with the torch.

Simone starts to climb down the steps. The metal clangs dully beneath her feet.

'There's no one here,' Kennet says.

'So what did we hear, then? It must have been something,' she says.

A small patch of daylight is filtering in through a dirty basement window up by the ceiling. Slowly their eyes get used to the weak light. The basement is full of bicycles of various sizes, a pushchair, a bread machine, Christmas decorations and a stepladder with splashes of white paint on it. On one box someone has written 'Josef's comics' in thick marker.

A clicking sound starts to come from the ceiling and Simone looks over at the steps, then at her father. He doesn't seem to hear the sound, and walks slowly towards a door at the other end of the room. Simone knocks against a rocking horse. Kennet opens the door and looks into a laundry room containing a battered washing machine and tumble drier and an old-fashioned hand-wringer. A dirty curtain hangs in front of a large cupboard next to the geothermal pump.

'No one here,' he says, turning towards Simone.

She looks at him, and at the same time can see the curtain behind his back. It's hanging perfectly still, yet it's impossible to ignore.

'Simone?'

There's a patch of damp on the curtain, a small oval, like it's been made by a mouth.

'Let's get those plans out,' Kennet says.

As Simone stares, she thinks she sees the damp oval being sucked inwards.

'Dad,' she whispers.

'Yes,' he replies, leaning against the doorframe and tucking his pistol back in his shoulder holster, then scratching his head.

There's another creak. She turns around and sees that the rocking horse is still moving.

'What is it, Simone?'

Kennet comes over to her and takes the plans from her hand, then lays them out on a rolled-up mattress. He shines the torch at them and turns them around.

He looks up, then back at the plans again, and walks over to a brick wall where the pieces of a dismantled bunk-bed are leaning up against a cabinet containing bright orange life-vests. An assortment of chisels, saws and clamps hangs from a peg-board. The space beside the hammer is empty – the large axe is missing.

Kennet gauges the wall and ceiling with his eyes, then leans forward and knocks on the wall behind the bunk-bed.

'What is it?' Simone asks.

'This wall must be at least ten years old.'

'Is there anything behind it?'

'Yes, there is. A large room,' he replies.

'How do you get to it?'

Kennet shines the torch along the wall again, then at the floor next to the dismantled bed. Shadows slip around the basement.

'Shine it over there again,' Simone says.

She's pointing at the ground next to the wardrobe. Something's been repeatedly scraped in an arc across the cement floor.

'Hold the light,' he says, then draws his pistol again.

Suddenly they hear a noise from behind the wardrobe. It sounds like someone is moving very slowly and carefully in there.

Simone's pulse increases to a heavy thud. There's someone there, she thinks. Dear God. She feels like calling Benjamin's name, but doesn't dare.

Kennet gestures at her to keep back, and she's about to say something when the tense silence suddenly explodes. She hears a loud bang from the floor above, and the sound of splintering wood. Simone drops the torch and everything goes black. Quick steps thunder across the floor. The ceiling creaks, and blinding lights sweep around in lurching waves, down the steps and into the basement.

'Down on the floor!' a man yells hysterically. 'Get down on the floor!'

Simone stands there paralysed, dazzled like a rabbit in the headlights of a speeding car.

'Lie down!' Kennet calls.

'Shut up!' another man shouts.

'Down, down!'

Simone doesn't realise that the men mean her until someone hits her hard in the stomach, and she's pushed onto the cement floor.

'Down on the floor, I said!'

She gasps for air. Bright light fills the basement. Black shapes pull at them, dragging them up the narrow steps. Her hands are tied behind her back. She has trouble walking, and slips and hits her cheek against the sharp metal handrail.

She tries to turn her head but someone is holding her tight, breathing hard as they push her roughly up against the wall beside the basement door.

52

Sunday morning, 13 December, St Lucia's Day

Simone blinks against the daylight. She's having trouble seeing. She hears fragments of a nearby conversation, and she recognises her father's concise, clipped tones. It's a voice that makes her think of the smell of coffee on early school mornings, with talk radio on in the background.

Only now does she realise that it was the police who came storming into the terraced house. One of the neighbours probably saw the light from Kennet's torch and sounded the alarm.

A police officer in his mid-twenties, with a lined face and dark bags under his eyes, is staring at her. His head is shaved, revealing his uneven, lumpy scalp. He rubs his neck several times with one hand.

'What's your name?' he asks coldly.

'Simone Bark,' she says in a voice that's still shaky. 'I'm here with my dad.'

'I asked what your name was,' the man says, raising his voice.

'Take it easy, Ragnar,' one of his colleagues says.

'You're a fucking parasite,' he says, turning back towards Simone. 'That's my personal opinion of people who think it's fun to go and look at a bit of blood.' He scoffs and turns away.

She can still hear her father's voice. He sounds very tired.

One of the policemen walks past holding her dad's wallet.

'Excuse me,' Simone says to a policewoman. 'We heard someone down there.'

'Shut up,' the woman says.

'My son is . . .'

'Shut up, I said. Tape her mouth. Get some tape on her!'

Simone watches as the man who called her a parasite pulls out a wide roll of tape, but he stops when the front door opens. A tall blond man with sharp grey eyes comes in.

'Joona Linna, National Crime,' he says in a strong Finnish accent. 'What have you got?'

'Two suspects,' the policewoman says.

Joona looks at Kennet and Simone.

'I'll take over,' he says. 'This is a misunderstanding.'

Dimples appear in Joona's cheeks as he tells them to release the suspects. The policewoman goes over to Kennet and removes his handcuffs. She apologises and then stands there, her ears now flushing bright red, and exchanges a few words with him.

The police officer with the shaved head continues to stare at Simone.

'Release her,' Joona says.

'They resisted arrest, and I injured my thumb,' he replies.

'Are you going to arrest them?' Joona asks.

'Yes.'

'Kennet Sträng and his daughter?'

'I don't care who they are,' the policeman says.

'Ragnar,' the policewoman says. 'He's a colleague.'

'It's against the law to trespass on a crime scene.'

'Just calm down,' Joona says firmly.

'Am I wrong?' the man asks.

Kennet has walked over, but says nothing.

'Am I wrong?' Ragnar asks again.

'We'll deal with this later,' Joona replies.

'Why not now?'

Joona lowers his voice and says curtly:

'For your sake.'

The policewoman walks up to Kennet again, clears her throat and says:

'We're very sorry about this. We'll send you a cake tomorrow.'

'Don't worry,' Kennet says, helping Simone up from the floor.

'The basement,' she says, almost inaudibly.

'I'll take care of it,' Kennet says, and turns to Joona. 'There are one or more persons in a concealed room in the basement, behind the wardrobe containing the life-vests.'

'OK, listen,' Joona calls to the others. 'We have reason to believe that the suspect is in the basement. I'm in charge of this operation. Be very careful. This may turn into a hostage situation, and if it does, I'm the one who negotiates. The suspect is dangerous, but if you have to shoot, aim for his legs.'

Joona borrows a bulletproof vest and quickly pulls it on. Then he sends two police officers to the back of the house, and gathers his team around him. They listen to his concise instructions, then follow him into the basement. The metal staircase clatters beneath their weight.

Kennet stands with his arms around Simone. She's so frightened her whole body is shaking. He whispers that everything's going to be all right. The only thing Simone wants is to get her son back, and she prays that she'll hear his voice any second now.

In a few minutes, Joona comes back up, holding the bulletproof vest in his hand.

'He got away,' he says tersely.

'Benjamin, where's Benjamin?' Simone asks.

'Not here,' Joona replies.

'But the room . . .'

Simone walks over to the steps. Kennet tries to hold her back, but she pulls away and pushes past Joona to hurry down the metal steps. The basement is now as bright as a summer's day. Three arc-lights on tripods fill the room with light. The stepladder has been moved, and is now standing beneath the small, open basement window. The wardrobe with the life-vests has been pushed aside and a police officer is guarding the doorway to the hidden room. Simone walks slowly towards him. She hears her father say something behind her back, but doesn't understand the words.

'I have to,' she says weakly.

The policeman holds up his hand and shakes his head.

'I'm afraid I can't let you in,' he says.

'He's my son.'

She feels her father's arms around her, and pulls free again.

'He's not here, Simone.'

'Let go of me!'

She finds herself looking at a room containing a mattress, piles of old comics, empty bags of crisps, bright blue shoe-covers, cans of food, boxes of cereal and a large, gleaming axe.

53

Sunday morning, 13 December, St Lucia's Day

Simone is sitting in the car on the way back from Tumba, listening to Kennet complain about the police's lack of internal communication. She doesn't respond, just lets him vent as she stares out of the window at all the families out there. Mums on their way somewhere with little kids in winter coats. Children trying to push through the snow on scooters. They're all wearing the same rucksacks. A group of girls with tinselled St Lucia crowns in their hair are eating sweets out of a bag and laughing in delight.

A day has passed since Benjamin was taken from us, she thinks, looking down at her hands in her lap. The red marks left by the handcuffs are still visible.

There's nothing to indicate that Josef Ek is involved in his disappearance. There was no sign that Benjamin had ever been in the hidden room, though it seems likely that Josef had been in there when she and her father went down into the basement.

Simone thinks about how he must have huddled up and listened to them, realising that they were about to find his hiding place, and then reached out as quietly as he could for the axe. In the chaos that followed, when the police charged in and dragged her and Kennet upstairs, Josef pushed the wardrobe aside, moved the stepladder to the basement window and climbed out.

He got away. He eluded the police again, and is still on the run. A national alert has been issued, but Josef Ek couldn't have kidnapped Benjamin. They were just two things that happened at the same time, just like Erik has been trying to tell her.

'Are you coming?' Kennet asks.

She looks up. Kennet has to tell her to get out of the car and follow him several times before she realises that they're already parked in Luntmakar Street.

She unlocks the door to the flat and sees Benjamin's winter clothes in the hall. She thinks that he must be back before she remembers that he was dragged out wearing just his pyjamas.

Her dad's face is grey. He says he's going to take a shower.

Simone leans against the wall in the hall, shuts her eyes and thinks: if only I could have Benjamin back, I would forget everything that's happened. I would never talk about it, I wouldn't be angry at anyone. I would just be grateful.

She hears Kennet turn on the water.

With a sigh she kicks her shoes off, lets her jacket fall to the floor and sits down on the bed. She can't remember what she was going to do in her room – was she going to get something, or maybe just lie down? She feels the coolness of the sheet against her palm and sees Erik's crumpled pyjama bottoms sticking out from under his pillow.

Just as the shower turns off she remembers. She came in to get her dad a towel. Then she was going to log on to Benjamin's computer. She grabs a grey bath-towel from the wardrobe and goes back out into the hall. The bathroom door opens and Kennet emerges, fully dressed.

'Towel,' she says.

'I used the small one.'

His hair is damp and smells like lavender. She realises he must have used the cheap soap in the pump-bottle on the sink.

'Did you wash your hair with soap?' she asks.

'It smelled nice,' he replies.

'We've got shampoo, Dad.'

'Same thing.'

'OK,' she smiles, and decides not to tell him what the small towel is used for.

'I'll make coffee,' Kennet says, and goes into the kitchen.

Simone puts the bath-towel on the dresser and walks into Benjamin's room. She turns on the computer and sits down. Nothing in the room has changed: the sheets are still on the floor, the water glass is still on the bedside table.

The start-up sound plays, and she clicks the small icon with Benjamin's face on it to log in.

The computer wants a user name and password. Simone types in Benjamin, then takes a deep breath and writes Dumbledore.

54

Sunday midday, 13 December, St Lucia's Day

The screen flickers momentarily, like an eye opening and closing.

She's in.

The background picture is a photograph of a stag in a forest clearing. The image is suffused with a hazy, magical light. The creature seems perfectly calm.

Even though Simone knows she's invading Benjamin's personal space, it feels as if part of him is close to her again.

'You're a genius,' she hears her dad say behind her back.

'No, not really,' she replies.

Kennet puts his hand on her shoulder as she clicks to open Benjamin's emails.

'How far back do we want to look?' she asks.

'We'll go through all of them.'

She scrolls through the inbox, opening email after email.

A classmate asking about a charity donation.

Group homework.

An email claiming that Benjamin has won forty million euros in a Spanish lottery.

Kennet walks out and comes back with two mugs.

'Coffee really is the best drink in the world,' he says as he sits down. 'How the hell did you manage to crack the password?'

She shrugs her shoulders and sips her coffee.

'I need to call my friend and tell him we don't need his help after all.'

She opens an email from Aida. It's a funny description of a bad film.

Weekly newsletters from school.

His bank, warning against sharing his account details.

Facebook, Facebook, Facebook, Facebook, Facebook.

Simone opens Benjamin's Facebook account. There are hundreds of notifications from a group called 'hypno monkey'.

All the posts are about Erik, with various mocking suggestions that Benjamin has been hypnotised into being a nerd, proof that Erik has hypnotised the entire population of Sweden, and someone demanding compensation because Erik has hypnotised his dick.

There's a link to a YouTube clip. Simone opens it and watches a short film entitled 'Asshole'. It's a scientist explaining how serious hypnosis works, played over footage of Erik pushing his way past a group of people. He accidentally hits an old woman with a walker, who flips him off behind his back.

Simone goes back to Benjamin's inbox and finds a short email from Aida which makes the hairs on the back of her neck stand up. She turns towards Kennet.

'Read this one, Dad.'

She turns the screen towards him so he can read the message: *Nicke says Wailord is angry, that he's opened his mouth in your direction. I think this could be really dangerous, Benjamin.*

'Nicke is Aida's younger brother,' Simone says.

'And Wailord?' Kennet asks, taking a deep breath. 'Do you know anything about this?'

Simone shakes her head.

'I think it's the name of a Pokémon character,' she says. 'Aida's brother, Nicke, said something about Wailord.'

Simone looks at Benjamin's sent folder and finds his agitated reply: *Nicke needs to stay indoors. Don't let him go down to the sea. If Wailord really is angry, something bad is going to happen. We should have gone straight to the police. I think it's too dangerous to do that now.*

'Shit,' Kennet says.

'I don't know if this is real or if it's part of a game.'

'Doesn't sound like a game.'

'No.'

Kennet lets out a deep sigh and scratches his stomach.

'Aida and Nicke,' he says slowly. 'What sort of people are they?'

Simone looks at her father and wonders how to reply. He would never be able to get his head around someone like Aida. A pierced, tattooed girl who dresses all in black, wears lots of make-up and has an unusual home life.

'Aida's Benjamin's girlfriend,' Simone says. 'And Nicke is her brother. There's a picture of her and Benjamin somewhere.'

She picks up Benjamin's wallet and finds the picture of Aida. Benjamin has his arm around her shoulders. She looks a little annoyed, but he's laughing at the camera.

'Why on earth does she look like that?' Kennet declares, staring at Aida's heavily made-up face.

'I don't know much about her,' Simone replies carefully. 'I just know that Benjamin is very fond of her. And that she seems to look after her brother. I think he's got learning difficulties of some sort.'

'Aggressive?'

She shakes her head.

'I don't think so,' she says.

'Benjamin clearly feels threatened,' Kennet says. 'But who is this Wailord?'

55

Sunday midday, 13 December, St Lucia's Day

Kennet folds his arms over his chest, leans back, and looks up at the ceiling. Then he straightens up.

'Wailord is a cartoon character, yes?'

'A Pokémon,' she replies.

'Am I supposed to know what that is?'

'If you have kids of a certain age, you know about Pokémon whether you want to or not,' she replies.

Kennet looks at her blankly.

'Pokémon,' Simone repeats. 'It's a kind of game.'

'A game?'

'Don't you remember, Benjamin was into it for a while when he was younger? Collected the cards and kept going on about their different powers, and how they could transform themselves.'

Kennet shakes his head.

'He must have stuck with it for a couple of years at least,' she says.

'But not any more?'

'He's too old for that now,' she replies.

'I saw you playing with dolls when you got home from horse-riding camp.'

'Well, who knows, maybe he plays Pokémon in secret,' she says.

'So what's it all about, this Pokémon thing?'

'How can I describe it? It has to do with animals, but not

real ones. I don't know. Some of them are cute and others are just revolting. It started in Japan, and first appeared some time in the 1990s, late 1990s, I think, and a whole industry grew up around it. So these characters are called Pokémon, from "pocket monsters". It's all a bit silly. You can play against other people by letting different Pokémon fight. The goal is to win as many fights as you can, because then you get money . . . well, the player gets money, the Pokémon character gets points.'

'And the one with the most points wins,' Kennet says.

'I don't actually know. It never seems to reach any sort of conclusion.'

'So it's a computer game?'

'It's everything at once, which is presumably why it became so big. It exists as a television show, a card game, stuffed toys, sweets, video games, Nintendo, and so on.'

'I'm not sure I'm any the wiser, to be honest,' he says.

'No,' she says slowly.

He looks at her.

'What are you thinking?'

'I just realised that that's the whole point, that it's supposed to exclude adults,' she says. 'The children get left in peace, because we can't possibly understand the world of Pokémon, there's too much to it, it's too big.'

'Do you think Benjamin's started playing again?' Kennet asks.

'No, not like he used to, anyway. This must mean something else,' she replies, pointing at the screen.

'You think Wailord is a real person?' he wonders.

'Yes.'

'Someone who has nothing to do with Pokémon?'

'I don't know . . . Aida's brother, Nicke, he mentioned Wailord to me, and it sounded like he was referring to the Pokémon character. But maybe that's just his way of talking. I mean, it's very strange that Benjamin wrote "don't let Nicke go down to the sea".'

'What sea?' Kennet asks.

'Exactly. There's no sea here, only in the game.'

'But at the same time, it sounds like Benjamin's taking the threat seriously, doesn't it?' Kennet says.

She nods.

'The sea may be made up, but it seems like the threat is real.'

'We need to find this Wailord.'

'It could be an avatar, or something,' she says hesitantly.

He looks at her, and can't help smiling.

'I'm starting to understand why it was time for me to retire,' he says.

'It's an identity people use in chat rooms,' Simone explains, and moves closer to the computer. 'I'll try searching for Wailord.'

The search brings up 85,000 results. Kennet goes out into the kitchen and Simone hears him turn up the volume on the police radio. The crackling and buzzing are interspersed with human voices.

She skims through page after page of Japanese Pokémon sites: *Wailord is the largest of all identified Pokémon up to now. This giant Pokémon swims in the open sea, eating massive amounts of food at once with its enormous mouth.*

'Well, there's the sea,' Kennet says quietly, reading over her shoulder.

The text goes on to explain how Wailord hunts his prey by launching into a gigantic jump, landing in the middle of a shoal and swimming away with his mouth full of fish. Simone reads that Wailord swallowing his prey in a single gulp is a terrible sight.

She narrows the terms of the search to pages in Swedish, and goes onto a forum where there's an interesting thread:

'*Hi, how do you get a Wailord?*'

'*The easiest way to get a Wailord is to capture a Wailmer somewhere out at sea.*'

'*OK but where in the sea?*'

'*Almost anywhere, as long as you use a Super Rod.*'

'Anything?' Kennet asks.

'It could take a while.'

'Look through all the emails, check the trash.'

She looks up and sees that Kennet has put his leather jacket on.

'Where are you going?'

'I'm going out,' he replies bluntly.

'Where? Home?'

'I need to talk to Nicke and Aida.'

'Should I come with you?' she asks.

Kennet shakes his head.

'It makes more sense for you to keep going through the computer.'

Kennet tries to smile as she follows him into the hallway. He looks exhausted. She gives him a hug and locks the door behind him. She remembers the time she spent an entire day standing in the hallway, staring at the door, waiting for him to come home. She was about nine years old, and had figured out that her mum was thinking of leaving them. She didn't dare hope that her dad was going to stay.

When Simone walks into the kitchen she sees that Kennet has left a coffee cake out. The coffee machine is still on, and there's dark residue at the bottom of the jug.

The smell of scorched coffee merges with the panicked sense that her life has been split into two acts, and the first of them, the happy one, has just ended. She doesn't want to think about what lies ahead.

Simone goes over to her handbag and takes out her phone. Just as she expected, she sees that Ylva has called from the gallery several times. Shulman's name is also on the list of missed calls. Simone finds his number and presses 'call' but changes her mind before the call goes through. She goes back to the computer in Benjamin's room.

The December darkness lingers outside the window. The traffic lights are swaying in the strong winds as damp snowflakes fall through their light.

Simone finds a deleted email from Aida with the heading: *I feel sorry for you, living in a house of lies*. The message has a large file attached to it. Simone feels her pulse throbbing in her ears as she moves the cursor. Just as she is selecting a program to open it there's a soft knock at the flat door. It sounds almost like someone brushing against it. She holds her breath, hears a second knock and gets to her feet. Her legs feel weak as she walks to the front door.

56

Sunday afternoon, 13 December, St Lucia's Day

Kennet is sitting in the car outside Aida's block of flats, thinking about the bizarre threat they found in Benjamin's emails: *'Nicke says Wailord is angry, that he's opened his mouth in your direction.'* Then: *'Don't let him go down to the sea.'* He thinks about all the times in his life when he has seen and heard fear. He knows how it feels, because he's experienced it himself, no one lives without it.

The building where Aida lives is small, just three floors. It looks unexpectedly idyllic, old-fashioned and sturdy. He looks at the photograph Simone gave him. Piercings, and a lot of dark make-up around her eyes. He wonders why he's having such difficulty imagining her in this building, at a kitchen table, in a room where the horses posters have been replaced by ones of Marilyn Manson.

Kennet is about to sneak over to the balcony that he thinks belongs to Aida's family, but stops when he sees a large figure moving back and forth on the path behind the building.

Then the door opens, and Aida comes out. She seems to be in a hurry. She looks over her shoulder and, without slowing down, takes a packet of cigarettes from her bag, pulls one out with her lips, lights it and inhales. Kennet watches as she walks off towards the underground station. He decides not to speak to her until he knows where she's going. A bus rumbles past and somewhere a dog starts barking. Kennet sees the large figure behind the house rush towards Aida. She must have heard him because she turns around. She looks glad. Her whole face is smiling: her pale, powdered cheeks and heavily made-up eyes immediately look more childish. The figure is jumping up and down in front of her. They kiss each other on the tip of the nose, then Aida waves goodbye. Kennet walks closer, thinking that the large figure must be her brother. He's standing still, watching as Aida walks off, waving occasionally. Kennet sees the boy's face, gentle and unguarded. He has a very pronounced wandering eye. Kennet stops beneath a streetlight and waits. The boy walks towards him with heavy footsteps.

'Hello, Nicke,' Kennet says.

Nicke stops and looks at him fearfully. Beads of saliva are hanging from both sides of his mouth.

'Not allowed,' he says slowly and warily.

'My name is Kennet, and I'm a policeman. Or rather, I'm a bit old now, so I'm retired, but that doesn't really change anything, I'm still a policeman.'

The boy looks at him curiously.

'So you have a gun?'

Kennet shakes his head.

'No,' he lies. 'And I don't have a police car either.'

The boy becomes serious.

'Did they take them away when you got old?'

Kennet nods.

'Yep.'

'Are you here to catch the thieves?' Nicke asks.

'Which thieves?'

Nicke pulls at his coat zipper.

'Sometimes they take things from me,' he says, kicking the ground.

'Who does?'

Nicke shoots him an impatient glance.

'The thieves.'

'Yes, of course.'

'My hat, my watch, and a nice stone with a shiny edge.'

'Are you afraid of anyone?'

He shakes his head.

'So everyone around here is nice?' Kennet asks slowly.

The boy lets out a deep breath and looks off in the direction where Aida disappeared.

'My sister's trying to find the worst monster.'

Kennet nods towards the newsstand down by the station.

'Would you like a Coke?'

The boy goes with him, and says:

'I work at the library on Saturdays. I hang up people's coats for them, and they get pieces of paper with numbers on them, thousands of different numbers.'

'You must be very clever,' Kennet says, and asks for two bottles of Coke.

Nicke looks on happily and asks for an extra straw. Then he drinks, burps, drinks, and burps again.

'What did you mean by that thing you said about your sister?' Kennet asks casually.

Nicke frowns.

'That guy. Aida's guy. Benjamin. I haven't seen him today. But before he was so angry, so angry. Aida cried.'

'Was Benjamin angry?'

Nicke looks at Kennet in surprise.

'Benjamin isn't angry, he's nice. He makes Aida happy and she laughs.'

Kennet looks at the boy.

'So who was angry, Nicke? Who was angry?'

Nicke suddenly looks worried. He stares at the bottle, and starts to look for something.

'I'm not allowed to let people give me . . .'

'It's OK this time, I promise,' Kennet says. 'Who was angry?'

Nicke scratches his neck and wipes the saliva from the corners of his mouth.

'Wailord – his mouth is this big.'

Nicke holds his arms out.

'Wailord?'

'He's bad.'

'Where was Aida going, Nicke?'

The boy's cheeks tremble when he says:

'She can't find Benjamin. It's not good.'

'But where was she going now?'

Nicke looks like he's going to burst into tears when he shakes his head.

'No, no, no, mustn't talk to strange men I don't know . . .'

'Look at me, Nicke – I'm not a strange man,' Kennet says, taking out his wallet and finding a photograph of himself in his police uniform.

Nicke scrutinises the picture. Then he says in a serious voice:

'Aida's going to see Wailord now. She's worried he might have bitten Benjamin. Wailord's mouth opens this wide.'

Nicke holds his arms out again, and Kennet tries to keep his voice completely calm when he says:

'Do you know where Wailord lives?'

'I'm not allowed to go down to the sea, not even close.'

'How do you get to the sea?'

'On the bus.'

57

Sunday afternoon, 13 December, St Lucia's Day

Nicke feels for something in his pocket and whispers to himself, then looks up at Kennet:

'Wailord played a trick on me once when I was going to pay,' he says, and tries to smile. 'He was only joking. They tricked me into eating a thing you're not supposed to eat?'

Kennet waits. Nicke turns red and picks at his zipper. His fingernails are dirty.

'What did you eat?' Kennet asks.

The boy's cheeks tremble again.

'I don't want to,' he replies, and a few tears trickle down his wide face.

Kennet pats Nicke's shoulder and tries to keep his voice calm and steady when he says:

'It sounds like Wailord is really mean.'

'Mean.'

Kennet notices that Nicke has something in his pocket that he keeps touching.

'I'm a policeman, you know that, and I say no one's allowed to be mean to you.'

'You're too old.'

'But I'm strong.'

Nicke looks happier now.

'Can I have more Coke?'

'If you like.'

'Yes, please.'

'What's that you've got in your pocket?' Kennet asks, pretending not to be particularly interested.

Nicke smiles.

'It's a secret,' he says.

'Really?' Kennet says, but holds off asking more.

Nicke takes the bait.

'Don't you want to know?'

'You don't have to tell me if you don't want to, Nicke.'

'Oh, oh, oh,' he says. 'You'll never guess what it is!'

'I don't think it's anything special.'

Nicke takes his hand out of his pocket.

'I'll tell you what it is.'

He opens his fist.

'It's my powers.'

Nicke has some dirt in his hand. Kennet looks curiously at the boy, who's grinning now.

'I'm a ground Pokémon!' he says happily.

'A ground Pokémon,' Kennet repeats.

Nicke closes his fist around the dirt and puts it back in his pocket.

'Do you know what my powers are?'

Kennet shakes his head. He sees a man with a thin, pointed face walking along in front of the dark building on the other side of the road. He seems to be looking for something, and has a stick in his hand that he's using to poke the ground. Kennet realises that the man could be trying to look in through the ground-floor windows. He considers going over and asking him what he's doing. But Nicke puts his hand on his arm:

'Do you know what my powers are?' the boy repeats.

Kennet reluctantly takes his eyes off the man, and focuses on Nicke, who is counting on his fingers as he talks.

'I'm good against all the electric Pokémons, the fire Pokémons, the poison Pokémons, the rock Pokémons and the steel Pokémons. But I can't fight flying Pokémons, or grass Pokémons, or insect Pokémons.'

'Is that right?' Kennet says distractedly, watching as the man appears to stop at a window. He looks like he's pretending to search for something while he leans towards the window.

'Are you listening?' Nicke says anxiously.

Kennet tries to smile encouragingly at him. But when he turns back around the man has vanished. Kennet peers at the ground-floor window across the way, but can't tell if it's open.

'I can't handle water,' Nicke explains sadly. 'Water's the worst, I can't handle it. I'm really afraid of water.'

Kennet gently frees himself from Nicke's grasp.

'Just a minute,' he says, and takes a few steps towards the window.

'What time is it?' Nicke asks.

'What time? Five forty-five.'

'I have to go. He gets angry if I'm late.'

'Who gets angry? Is it your dad who gets angry?'

Nicke laughs.

'I haven't got a dad!'

'Your mum, I mean.'

'No, Ariados gets angry. He comes to collect things.'

Nicke looks hesitantly at Kennet, then lowers his gaze and asks:

'Can I have some money now? Because if I don't have enough, he has to punish me.'

'Wait a second,' Kennet says, listening intently now to what Nicke is saying. 'Is Wailord the one who wants money from you?'

They leave the store together and Kennet repeats his question:

'Is it Wailord?'

'Are you stupid? Wailord? He'd swallow me . . . but the others, they can swim to him.'

Nicke looks over his shoulder. Kennet asks again:

'Who wants money?'

'Ariados, I said that,' the boy replies impatiently. 'Do you have money? I can do something if I get money. I can give you some power . . .'

'There's no need for that,' Kennet says, taking out his wallet. 'Is twenty kronor enough?'

Nicke giggles delightedly, puts the note in his pocket and starts to run down the street without saying goodbye.

Kennet stands still for a moment, trying to absorb what the boy said. He can't make any coherent sense of it, but follows him anyway. When he goes around the corner he sees Nicke standing and waiting at a set of traffic lights. They turn green and he hurries across. He seems to be heading towards the library in the square. Kennet follows him across the street and stands at an ATM to wait. Nicke has stopped again. He's pacing impatiently next to the library fountain. The streetlights aren't bright, but Kennet can still see that Nicke is playing with the dirt in his pocket the whole time.

A younger boy comes out from the bushes in front of the dentist's office and heads across the square. As he gets close to Nicke he stops and says something. Nicke immediately lies down on the ground and holds out the money. The boy counts it, then pats Nicke on the head. Then he grabs the collar of Nicke's jacket, drags him to the edge of the fountain and pushes his face in the water. Kennet gets ready to run over, but forces himself to stand still. He's here to find Benjamin. He doesn't want to scare off the boy in case he's Wailord, or could lead him to Wailord. Kennet waits, counting the seconds, ready to rush over if need be. Nicke's legs are jerking and kicking, and Kennet can see an inexplicable look of calm on the other boy's face when he finally lets go. Nicke slumps onto the ground beside the fountain, coughing and spluttering. The boy gives Nicke a final pat on the shoulder and walks away.

Kennet hurries after the boy, through the bushes and down a muddy bank to a footpath. He follows him into a residential area, all the way to a block of flats. He speeds up and manages to get inside just in time to catch the lift, where he sees that the button for the sixth floor is pressed. He gets out on the same floor as the boy, stops and pretends to look in his pockets, and sees the boy go over to a door and take out a key.

'You, boy,' Kennet says.

The boy doesn't react, and Kennet walks over, grabs his jacket and turns him around.

'Let go, you old bastard,' the boy says, looking him in the eye.

'Don't you know it's against the law to make people give you money?'

Kennet looks into a pair of slippery, strangely calm eyes.

'Your surname's Johansson,' Kennet says, glancing at the door.

'Yes,' he smiles. 'What's yours?'

'Detective Kennet Sträng.'

The boy just stands there looking at him, showing no trace of fear.

'How much money have you taken from Nicke?'

'I don't take money. Sometimes he gives it to me, but I don't take anything. Everyone's happy.'

'I'm going to talk to your parents.'

'Oh.'

'Do you want me to?'

'Please, don't, mister!' the boy says sarcastically.

Kennet rings the doorbell and after a while an overweight, suntanned woman opens it.

'Hello,' Kennet says. 'I'm a detective and I'm afraid your son has got into some trouble.'

'My son? I don't have kids,' she says.

Kennet sees the boy grinning towards the floor.

'Do you recognise this boy?'

'Can I see your badge?' the fat woman says.

'This boy is . . .'

'He doesn't have a badge,' the boy interrupts.

'Yes, I do,' Kennet lies.

'He's not a policeman,' the boy grins, pulling out his wallet. 'Here's my bus-pass, I'm more of a policeman than he . . .'

Kennet snatches the wallet from him.

'Give that back!'

'I'm just going to take a look,' Kennet replies.

'He said he wanted to kiss my willy!' the boy says.

'I'm calling the police,' the woman says, sounding scared.

Kennet pushes the button for the lift. The woman looks around, then hurries out and starts banging on the other doors on the landing.

'He gave me money,' the boy says to her. 'But I didn't want to go with him.'

One of the neighbours opens the door and peers out past the security chain.

'You stay the hell away from Nicke from now on,' Kennet says in a low voice.

'He's mine,' the boy says.

The woman starts to call the police. Kennet gets into the lift and watches the door close. He realises that the boy must have seen him following and tricked him by going into the wrong building and picking a door at random. Kennet looks in the boy's wallet: almost a thousand kronor, a loyalty card for a video store, a bus-pass and a crumpled blue business card with the words: *The Sea, Louddsvägen 18.*

58

Sunday afternoon, 13 December, St Lucia's Day

On top of the fast-food stand is a huge smiling hotdog. It squirts ketchup on itself with one hand while the other gives a thumbs-up. Erik orders a burger with fries, sits down on one of the high stools by the window, and looks out through the fogged glass. On the other side of the street is a locksmith. The windows are decorated for Christmas, with knee-high elves posing beside an assortment of safes, locking mechanisms and keys.

Erik opens his water bottle, takes a swig, then calls home. He hears his own voice on the answering machine. He hangs up and calls Simone on her mobile phone instead. When the voicemail beeps at him, he says:

'Hi, Simone . . . I just wanted to say that you should accept police protection, because Josef Ek, well, he seems to be very angry with me . . . That's all.'

As he takes a bite of the hamburger he realises how hungry he is. He spears the fries with a plastic fork and thinks back to the look on Joona's face when he read Josef's note to Evelyn. It was as if the temperature had suddenly dropped. His grey eyes turned to ice, and took on an intense sharpness.

Joona had called four hours ago to say that they'd missed Josef again. He had been in the basement, but had escaped. There was nothing to suggest that Benjamin had ever been there. Quite the opposite, in fact: preliminary DNA results showed that Josef had been alone in the room.

Erik tries to remember Evelyn's face and her exact words when she realised that Josef had returned to the terraced house. Erik doesn't believe that Evelyn intentionally hid the existence of the secret room before. She'd just forgotten about it. She only remembered when she realised that Josef had gone back home and was hiding there.

Josef Ek wants to hurt me, Erik thinks. He's jealous. He's convinced himself that Evelyn and I are having a sexual relationship, and he's determined to hurt me as a result. But he doesn't know where I live. In the note he demanded that Evelyn tell him.

'He doesn't know where I live,' Erik whispers. 'So he couldn't have broken into our home and taken Benjamin.'

Erik eats more of the hamburger, then tries to call Simone again. She needs to know that Josef Ek didn't take Benjamin. He feels relieved, even though it means he's going to have to start all over again. He takes out a sheet of paper, writes Aida's name on it, then changes his mind. Simone must have seen something, he thinks. After all, she was the one who witnessed the kidnapping.

She's been questioned by Joona, but couldn't remember anything else. But so far, they've been far too focused on Josef, and the coincidence that he happened to escape just before Benjamin was abducted. It never really made sense. He's thought that all along. The first break-in happened before Josef escaped. He's a serial killer, and he's developed a taste for killing. Abducting someone doesn't fit Josef's pattern. The only person he wants to abduct is Evelyn. He's obsessed with her. She's his motivation.

His phone rings and he puts the hamburger down and answers without checking the screen.

'Hello, Erik Maria Bark.'

The line crackles and roars, but sounds muffled.

'Hello?' Erik says, raising his voice.

He hears a faint voice.

'Dad?'

'Benjamin?'

The phone-line is still full of static.

'Hang on, I can't hear you.'

Erik pushes past some customers and hurries out into the car park. Snow is swirling around the yellow streetlights.

'Benjamin?!'

'Can you hear me?' Benjamin asks, much clearer now.

'Where are you? Tell me where you are!'

'I don't know, Dad, I have no idea. I'm lying in a car that just keeps driving and driving . . .'

'Who's taken you?'

'I woke up here. I haven't seen anything, I'm really thirsty . . .'

'Are you hurt?'

'Dad,' he sobs.

'I'm here, Benjamin.'

'What's happening?'

He sounds very small, and very scared.

'I'm going to find you,' Erik says. 'Do you have any idea where you're heading?'

'I heard a voice, sort of muffled, when I first woke up. Something about . . . about a house, I think . . .'

'Tell me more! What house?'

'No, not just a house . . . a haunted house.'

'Where?'

'We're slowing down, Dad, the car's stopped! I can hear footsteps!' Benjamin says in a terrified voice. 'I can't talk any more.'

Erik hears a noise like someone rummaging for something, then a creak, and then a sudden cry from Benjamin. His voice is shrill and unsteady. He sounds terrified.

'Leave me alone. I don't want to, please, I promise . . .'

Then silence as the line goes dead.

Dry snowflakes drift across the car park. Erik stares at his phone but doesn't want to risk using it in case Benjamin calls again. He waits outside, hoping that Benjamin is going to call back. He thinks through the conversation, but keeps losing track of it. Benjamin's terror keeps pulsing through his head. He has to let Simone know.

59

Sunday afternoon, 13 December, St Lucia's Day

Erik gets into the car, his hands shaking so fiercely he can't get the key in the ignition. He left his hat and gloves in the restaurant beside his unfinished hamburger, but he doesn't care.

A stream of red tail-lights snakes off to the north and forks, right towards the university and the E18, left towards Karolinska Hospital and the E4. Thousands of cars in a slow stream of rush-hour traffic. The road ahead shimmers grey and wet from the damp snow as Erik turns onto Valhallavägen.

Erik parks and walks quickly down to Luntmakar Street. He feels an odd sense of no longer belonging there as he goes in through the front entrance and climbs the stairs. After knocking, he hears footsteps, then the little clicking sound as the cover of the peephole is pushed aside. The door is unlocked. Erik waits a few seconds, then pushes it open and walks into the dimly lit flat. Simone moves backwards, and stops in the hallway with her arms folded over her chest. She's wearing jeans and a blue knitted top, and looks unusually resolute.

'Benjamin called me half an hour ago.'

Her face cracks under the weight of all the fear and anguish she's been trying to hide. She slaps one hand over her mouth and stares at him.

'Dear God . . .'

She takes a step closer.

'Where is he?' she asks, her voice louder now.

'He didn't know. He doesn't really know what's going on.'

'So what did he say?'

'That he was lying in a car.'

'Is he hurt?'

'I don't think so.'

'But what . . .'

'Hold on,' Erik says, cutting her off. 'I need to borrow your phone. We may be able to trace his call, but I don't want to use mine in case Benjamin calls back.'

'Who are you going to call?'

'The police,' he replies. 'I've got a contact who . . .'

'I'll talk to Dad – it'll be quicker,' Simone interrupts.

She takes the phone and he sits down on the low bench in the hallway, and feels his face starting to warm up in the heat of the flat.

'Did I wake you?' Simone asks. 'Dad, Erik's here, he's spoken to Benjamin. We need you to trace the call. I don't know. No, I haven't. You'll have to talk to him.'

Erik stands up and waves her away when she comes towards him, but takes the phone anyway and puts it to his ear.

'Hello.'

'Tell me what happened, Erik,' Kennet says.

'I wanted to tell the police, but Simone said you could trace the call faster.'

'She may be right.'

'Benjamin called me half an hour ago. He didn't know where he was, or who took him. The only thing he knew was that he was lying in a car, and while we were talking the car stopped, Benjamin said he could hear footsteps, then he shouted something and the line went dead.'

Erik can hear Simone trying not to cry.

'Was he calling from his own phone?' Kennet asks.

'Yes.'

'I tried to have it traced the day before yesterday, but it'd been switched off.'

Erik listens in silence as Kennet quickly explains that network operators are obliged to help the police.

'How much can they find out?' Erik asks.

'The level of precision varies, it depends on the base-stations and exchanges, but with a bit of luck we should soon have a location, to a radius of a hundred metres.'

'Hurry up, you need to hurry up.'

Erik hangs up.

'What have you done to your cheek?' he asks.

'What? Oh, nothing,' she replies.

They look at each other, tired and vulnerable.

'Do you want to come in?' she asks.

He nods, then, after hesitating for a moment, takes his shoes off and goes inside. He sees that the computer is on in Benjamin's room and walks towards it.

'Have you found anything?'

Simone stops in the doorway.

'Some emails between Benjamin and Aida,' she says. 'It looks like they felt threatened.'

'By who?'

'We don't know. Dad's working on it.'

Erik sits down in front of the computer.

'Benjamin's alive,' he says slowly, then looks at her for a long time.

'Yes.'

'It doesn't look like it has anything to do with Josef Ek.'

'But he called here, didn't he, so surely he could . . .?'

'That's different,' he interrupts.

'Is it?'

'The operator forwarded his call,' he explains. 'I've told them to do that if they think it's important. He doesn't know our phone number, and he doesn't know our address.'

'But someone's taken Benjamin and put him in a car . . .'

She falls silent.

Erik reads the email from Aida where she laments the fact that Benjamin lives in a house of lies, then opens the image she attached to the message: a colour photograph taken at night with a flash. It's a yellowish green expanse of wild grass. It seems to bulge slightly towards a low hedge. Beyond the hedge he can just make out the back of a brown wooden fence. At the edge of the brightly lit area there's a green plastic basket and what might be a vegetable patch.

Erik's eyes roam across the screen, trying to understand what the subject of the picture is: a hedgehog or a shrew that he might have missed? He tries to peer into the darkness beyond the light of the flash, to see if there's anyone standing there, a face, maybe, but he can't see anything.

'What a weird photograph,' Simone whispers.

'Maybe Aida attached the wrong one,' Erik says.

'That would explain why Benjamin deleted it.'

'We'll have to talk to Aida about this . . .'

'His injection,' Simone suddenly whimpers.

'I know . . .'

'Did you give it to him on Tuesday?'

Before he can answer she leaves the room and goes into the kitchen. He follows her. When he gets there she's standing by the window, blowing her nose on a paper towel. Erik reaches out his hand towards her but she pulls away. He knows exactly why she's worried. The factor concentrate, the compound that helps his blood to coagulate, which prevents spontaneous bleeding in his brain, which stops him bleeding to death from something as simple as moving too fast.

'On Tuesday morning, at nine ten, I gave him his injection. He was supposed to be going skating, but went out to Tensta with Aida instead.'

She nods, then does the calculation, her face twitching:

'It's Sunday today. He should have another injection tomorrow or the day after,' she whispers.

'There's no real danger for a few days after that,' Erik says reassuringly.

He looks at her tired face, her beautiful features, her freckles. Her low-cut jeans, with the seam of her yellow underwear just showing. He wishes he could stay. He'd like to make love to her, but knows it's far too early for all that, too early even to try, or to start longing for it.

'I'll go,' he mumbles.

She nods.

They look at each other.

'Let me know as soon as Kennet has traced the call.'

'Where are you going?' she asks.

'I have to work.'

'Did you sleep in the office?'

'It's fairly practical.'

'You can sleep here,' she says.

He's taken by surprise, and doesn't know what to say. But that brief moment of hesitation is enough for her to interpret his reaction as reluctance.

'I didn't mean it as an invitation,' she says quickly. 'Don't get any ideas.'

'Same here,' he replies.

'Have you moved in with Daniella?'

'No.'

'We've already split up,' she says, raising her voice. 'So you don't have to lie to me.'

'So why are you asking?'

He walks out into the hall, puts his shoes on, and leaves the flat. He waits until he hears her lock the door behind him and put the safety chain on before he heads down the stairs.

60

Monday morning, 14 December

Simone wakes up when the phone rings. The curtains are open and the bedroom is full of dull wintery light. Her first thought is that it's Erik calling. Then she feels like crying when she realises that he won't be calling, that he'll be waking up next to Daniella this morning, that she's all alone now.

She picks up the phone from the bedside table and answers:

'Yes?'

'Simone? It's Ylva. I've been trying to reach you for the past few days.'

Ylva sounds stressed. It's already ten o'clock.

'I've had a lot on my mind,' Simone says tersely.

'They haven't found him?'

'No,' Simone replies.

Neither of them says anything. A few shadows flit past outside the window and Simone sees that flakes of colour are falling from the roof opposite: men in bright orange outfits are scraping off the peeled paint.

'Sorry,' Ylva says. 'I won't bother you.'

'What happened?'

'The accountant's coming again tomorrow.'

Simone looks up and sees her reflection in the smoke-tinted mirror on the wardrobe. She looks tired and skinny.

'What about Shulman?' Simone asks. 'How's everything going with his exhibition?'

Ylva sounds anxious.

'He says he has to talk to you.'

'I'll call him.'

'There's something about the light that he wants to show you.'

She lowers her voice:

'Look, I've got no idea what's going on with you and Erik, but . . .'

'We've split up,' Simone says bluntly.

'Because I really think . . .'

Ylva falls silent.

'What do you think?' Simone asks patiently.

'I think Shulman's in love with you.'

Simone looks at the mirror again and feels a sudden tingle in her stomach.

'I suppose I should come in,' she says.

'Could you?'

'I just need to make a call first.'

Simone hangs up and sits on the edge of the bed for a few minutes. Benjamin is alive, that's the most important thing. He's alive, even though several days have passed. That's a very good sign. It means that the person who took him isn't interested in killing him. He wants something else, maybe a ransom. She quickly totals up her assets. What does she actually own? The lease on the flat, her car, a bit of art. And the gallery, of course. She can borrow money. It'll be OK. She's not rich, but her dad can sell the summer house and his flat. They can move in together in a rental somewhere. It'll be fine, as long as she gets Benjamin back, as long she gets to see her boy again.

Simone calls her dad but he doesn't answer. She leaves a short message saying she has to go to the gallery, then she takes a quick shower, brushes her teeth, puts on some fresh clothes and leaves the flat without bothering to turn the lights off.

It's cold out, and windy. The atmosphere is funereal, and the wintery morning's darkness makes her feel lethargic.

As she approaches the gallery her eyes meet Ylva's through the glass door. She walks in and Ylva rushes over and gives her a hug. Simone notes that Ylva hasn't tinted her hair the way she usually does, and her grey roots are visible along her parting. But her face is smooth and made-up, her lips dark red, as always. She's wearing a grey trouser-suit over black and white striped stockings, with heavy brown shoes.

'It's starting to look good,' Simone says, looking around. A greenish light is glinting off a series of Shulman's paintings. Shimmering, sea-green oil-paintings. 'You've done a great job.'

'Thanks,' Ylva whispers.

Simone goes over to the paintings.

'I haven't seen these like this before, the way they were meant to be seen,' she says. 'I've only seen them individually.'

She takes another step closer.

'The paint looks like it's dripping sideways.'

She walks into the next room. The blocks of stone with Shulman's cave-paintings are on wooden platforms.

'He wants oil-lamps in here,' Ylva says. 'I've told him it's impossible. People want to see what they're buying.'

'No, they don't.'

Ylva laughs.

'So Shulman can have what he wants?'

'Yes,' Simone replies. 'He can have what he wants.'

'You can tell him yourself.'

'What?' Simone asks.

'He's in the office.'

'Shulman?'

'He said he needed to make some calls.'

Simone glances towards the office and Ylva clears her throat.

'I'm just going to go and grab a sandwich for lunch.'

'Already?'

'I just thought . . .' Ylva says, lowering her gaze.

'Go on, then,' Simone says.

She is so anxious and sad that she has to stop and wipe the tears that have started to trickle down her cheeks before she knocks on the office door and walks in. Shulman is sitting behind the desk with a pencil in his mouth.

'How are you?' he asks.

'Not great.'

'So I gather.'

They stand in silence. She looks down. She feels suddenly exposed, as if she's been whittled down to her fragile core. Her lips part and she blurts out:

'Benjamin's alive. We don't know where he is or who has him, but he's alive.'

'That's great news,' Shulman says in a subdued voice.

'Damn,' she whispers, then turns away and wipes the tears from her face with trembling hands.

Shulman very gently touches her hair. She pulls away, without really knowing why. She'd like him to keep on doing it. His hand drops. They look at each other. He's wearing his soft, black outfit. His hood sticks up from the collar of the jacket.

'You've got your ninja costume on,' she says, and smiles in spite of herself.

'Shinobi, the real word for ninja, has two meanings,' he says. 'It means "hidden person", but also "one who endures".'

'Endures?'

'That might be the hardest challenge of all.'

'You can't do it alone – well, I can't, anyway.'

'No one's alone.'

'I can't do this,' Simone whispers. 'I feel like I'm falling apart, I have to stop replaying it in my head, but my mind doesn't have anywhere else to go. I keep thinking I just want something to happen. I could hit myself in the head or jump into bed with you, just to get this horrible panicky feeling to . . .'

She cuts herself off abruptly.

'That . . .' she tries to say. 'That sounded completely . . . I'm sorry, Sim.'

'So which one would you choose? Jump into bed with me or hit yourself in the head?' he asks with a smile.

'Neither,' she replies quickly.

Then she realises how that sounds, and tries to smooth over it:

'I didn't mean it like that, I'd love to . . .'

She stops again, and feels her heart beating hard in her chest.

'What?' he asks.

She looks into his eyes.

‘I’m not myself right now. That’s why I’m behaving like this,’ she says simply. ‘I feel so stupid.’

She blushes and looks down, then clears her throat.

‘Simone . . .’ he says, then leans forward and very briefly kisses her on the mouth.

Her legs feel weak, her knees are trembling. His gentle voice, the warmth of his body, the smell of that jacket, the smell of sleep and sheets, of herbs. It feels as if she’s forgotten the wonderful gentleness of a caress as his hand slips across her cheek to the nape of her neck. Shulman looks at her with a smile in his eyes. She’s no longer thinking of running away from the gallery. She knows this is probably just a way to escape, for a short while, the anguish, but so be it, she tells herself. She just wants it for a bit longer, so she can forget all the bad stuff. His lips approach hers again and this time she returns the kiss. She starts to breathe faster. She feels his hands over her back, the base of her spine, her hips. A wave of feeling washes over her, and her crotch feels like it’s burning: a sudden, blind lust overpowers her. The urgency of her desire scares her, and she backs away, hoping he hasn’t seen how turned on she is. She wipes her mouth and clears her throat while he turns away and hastily tries to adjust his clothes.

‘Someone might come in,’ she says tentatively.

‘What are we going to do?’ Shulman asks, and she hears the tremble in his voice.

61

Monday morning, 14 December

Without answering, Simone takes a step towards Shulman and kisses him again. She can't think any more. She reaches for his skin under his clothes, and feels his warm hands on her body. He caresses the base of her spine, and his hands make their way inside her clothes, pushing her underwear down, and when he feels how wet she is he groans and presses his hard penis against her pubic bone. She wants them to make love here, standing up against the wall, on top of the desk, on the floor – nothing else matters as long as she can distract herself from the panic for a few minutes. Her heart is beating hard and her legs are shaking. She pulls him towards the wall, and when he lifts her legs to push into her she whispers at him to do it, to do it now. At that moment they hear the bell attached to the front door ring. Someone has come into the gallery. The floor creaks and they let go of each other.

'Let's go back to my place,' he whispers.

She nods, and can feel herself blushing. He wipes his mouth and leaves the office. She waits for a while, leaning against the desk. Her whole body is trembling. She adjusts her clothes, and when she steps into the gallery Shulman is already standing over by the door.

'Have a nice lunch,' Ylva says.

Simone regrets her decision when they're sitting silently in the taxi taking them to Mariagränd. I'll give Dad a call, she thinks, and then say I've got to go. The thought of what she's about to do makes her feel sick with guilt, panic and excitement.

They walk up the narrow staircase to the fifth floor, and as he's unlocking the door she feels in her bag for her phone.

'I just need to call my dad,' she says.

Shulman doesn't answer, just walks down the hallway.

She's left standing there in her coat, and looks around the dimly lit, terracotta-coloured hall. The walls are covered with photographs, and up by the ceiling there's a ledge full of stuffed birds. Shulman returns before she has time to call Kennet.

'Simone,' he whispers. 'Don't you want to come in?'

She shakes her head.

'Just for a little while?' he asks.

'OK.'

Keeping her coat on, she goes with him into the living room.

'We're adults,' he says, picking up two glasses of cognac.

They drink a toast, and sip the strong liquor.

'That's good,' she says quietly.

One wall consists of nothing but windows. She walks over and looks out across the copper roofs of Södermalm. The unlit back of a neon sign shaped like a tube of toothpaste is directly in her vision.

Shulman walks up behind her and wraps his arms around her.

'Haven't you realised I'm crazy about you?' he whispers. 'I have been from the start.'

'Sim, I just don't know . . . I don't know what I'm doing,' Simone says hoarsely.

'Do you have to know?' Shulman asks with a smile, and starts to lead her towards the bedroom.

She goes with him as if she has always known that she would go. She has known it, and the only thing holding her back has been the thought that she doesn't want to be like her mother, like Erik. She has always thought that she would never cheat, that she had some kind of internal barrier guarding against it, but this isn't about betrayal. Shulman's bedroom is dark. The walls seem to be covered with what looks like dark-blue silk, the same fabric that's hanging in front of the windows. The fragile midwinter sun slants through the fabric. It doesn't cast light, just a slightly weaker darkness.

She unbuttons her coat with trembling hands and tosses it on the floor. Shulman removes all his clothes, and Simone sees the muscular curve of his shoulders, and the dark hair that covers his body. A line of thicker, tightly curled hair leads from his navel to his crotch.

He looks at her calmly with his soft dark eyes. She starts to undress, but is struck by an overwhelming feeling of utter loneliness as she stands there with him looking at her. He notices her hesitation and comes closer, then kneels down. She sees his long hair settle over his shoulders. He traces a line from her navel down across her hipbone with his finger. She tries to smile, but doesn't quite succeed.

Very gently, he nudges her back onto the edge of the bed, then starts to pull down her underwear. She lifts her buttocks and keeps her legs together, and feels her panties slip down and then catch on one of her feet. She leans back, closes her eyes, lets him part her thighs, feels his warm kisses on her stomach, over her hips and thighs. She gasps and runs her fingers through his long, thick hair. She wants Shulman inside her, wants it so much that her desire is pulsing through her. Blood courses through her veins, pulses of heat gather in her crotch, tickling. He lies on top of her, and she spreads her legs and sighs as he slides into her. He whispers something she doesn't hear. She pulls him to her, and when she feels the full weight of his body on her, it's almost like slipping into a warm, rippling ocean of forgetfulness.

She feels the physical release, but the possibility for forgetfulness is fleeting. She knows it's impossible. She can't stop thinking. She needs to go home, needs to look for Benjamin, needs to find him.

62

Monday afternoon, 14 December

It's an ice-cold day, and the sky is clear and blue. People are huddled together as they walk outside. Tired children are making their way home from school. Kennet stops outside the 7-Eleven on the corner. They've got a special offer on coffee and a saffron muffin for the holiday. He goes in and has just joined the line when his phone rings. It's Simone.

'Have you been out, Simone?'

'I had to go to the gallery. Then there was something I had to . . .'

She stops abruptly.

'I just got your message, Dad.'

'Have you been asleep? You sound . . .'

'Yes. I took a quick nap.'

'Good,' Kennet says.

He looks up at the cashier and points at the offer.

'Have they managed to trace Benjamin's call?' Simone asks.

'I haven't heard from them yet. This evening at the earliest, they said. I thought I might give them a call now.'

The cashier indicates Kennet should pick which muffin he wants, and he points at the one he thinks looks biggest. She puts it in a bag, takes his crumpled twenty-kronor note and gestures towards the coffee machine and cups. He nods and pulls a paper cup from the stack as he's talking to Simone.

'So you spoke to Nicke yesterday?' she says.

'He's a great kid.'

Kennet presses the symbol for black coffee.

'Did you find out anything about Wailord?'

'Quite a bit.'

'Like what?'

'Hang on a second,' Kennet says.

He removes the steaming cup from the machine, puts a lid on it, then takes his coffee and the bag containing the muffin over to one of the small round tables.

'Are you still there?' he asks as he sits down on a wobbly chair.

'Yes.'

'I think some kids are saying they're Pokémon characters and tricking Nicke out of money.'

Kennet watches a man with mussed hair push a modern-looking pushchair. A chubby little girl in pink overalls is lying in it, sucking on a lollipop with a tired smile on her face.

'Does it have anything to do with Benjamin?'

'The Pokémon boys? I don't know. Maybe he tried to stop them,' Kennet says.

'We need to talk to Aida,' Simone says firmly.

'After school, I was thinking.'

'What do we do now?'

'I've got an address, actually,' Kennet says.

'What for?'

'The sea.'

'The sea?' Simone asks.

'That's all I know.'

Pursing his lips, Kennet takes a sip of coffee. He pulls off a piece of the muffin and pops it in his mouth.

'So where's the sea?'

'Near Frihamnen,' Kennet says as he chews. 'The harbour out at Loudden.'

'Can I come?'

'Are you ready to go?'

'Give me ten minutes.'

'I need to get the car, it's parked up at the hospital.'

'Call me when you get here and I'll come down.'

'OK, see you soon.'

He picks up his cup and the rest of the muffin and walks out of the shop. Some schoolchildren walk past holding hands. A cyclist slips across the intersection between the cars. Kennet stops at the pedestrian crossing and presses the button. It feels like he's forgotten something important, like he's witnessed something vital but missed it. The traffic rushes past. He hears a siren in the distance. He sips his coffee and looks at a woman on the other side of the road holding a shivering dog on a leash. A lorry passes by right in front of Kennet, making the ground shake. He hears giggling and just has time to think that it sounds fake when someone shoves him hard in the back. He takes several steps out into the street so he doesn't lose his balance, and turns around to see a ten-year-old girl staring at him, wide-eyed. She must have pushed me, he thinks, because there's no one else there. At that moment he hears the shriek of brakes, then an indescribable force slams into his body. His legs are knocked out from under him. His neck cracks and his body is instantly limp. He's plunged into sudden darkness.

63

Monday afternoon, 14 December

Erik is sitting at the desk in his office. Pale light seeps through the windows overlooking the hospital's empty internal courtyard. A plastic container with the remains of a salad, and a two-litre bottle of Coke sit beside the pink desk lamp. He's staring at a printout of the photograph Aida sent Benjamin: the strong light from the flash forms a brightly lit space in the darkness made up of wild grass, the hedge and the back of the fence. Even though he's looking as closely as he can, it's impossible to tell what the picture is of. He holds it close to his face and tries to see if there's anything inside the plastic basket.

Erik thinks about calling Simone and asking her to read the email to him, so he knows exactly what Aida wrote to Benjamin, and how Benjamin replied, but tells himself that he can hardly expect Simone to talk to him. He has no idea why he was so cold to her.

He hears Benjamin's voice in his head again, when he called from the boot of the car, trying to be brave and not sound scared. Erik takes a pink codeine from the wooden box and swallows it with some cold coffee. His hand starts to shake so badly that he has difficulty putting the cup back on the saucer.

Benjamin must have been so scared, Erik thinks, locked inside a car in the darkness. He wanted to hear my voice. He didn't know who had taken him, or where he was being driven.

How long is it going to take Kennet to trace the call? Erik can't help feeling annoyed that he surrendered the task, but he reminds himself that if his father-in-law can find Benjamin, nothing else matters.

Erik picks up his phone. He needs to call the police, get them to hurry up, he thinks. He has to find out if they've made any progress. When he calls and explains what he wants, he gets transferred to the wrong number and has to call again. He's hoping to talk to Joona, but gets put through to a police officer named Fredrik Stensund. He confirms that he is in charge of the investigation into the disappearance of Benjamin Bark. The constable tries to be very understanding, and says that he too has teenage children:

'You spend all night worrying when they're out. I mean, you know you have to let go, but . . .'

'Benjamin isn't out having fun,' Erik says very pointedly.

'No, we've received information that contradicts . . .'

'He's been kidnapped,' Erik interrupts.

'I understand how it must feel, but . . .'

'But you're not going to prioritise Benjamin's disappearance,' Erik says, finishing the sentence off for him.

The line is silent. The police constable takes a few deep breaths before he goes on:

'I take what you're saying very seriously, and I can promise that we're doing our best.'

'Just get that call traced,' Erik says.

'We're working on it,' Stensund says in a sterner tone of voice.

'Please,' Erik concludes weakly.

He's left holding the phone in his hand. They have to find out where Benjamin is calling from, he thinks. We need a location, a circle on the map, a direction: it's the only thing we've got to go on. And the only thing Benjamin had been able to say was that he had heard a voice.

Like under a blanket, Erik thinks he said, but isn't sure he's remembering correctly. Did Benjamin really say that he had heard a voice, a muffled voice? Maybe it was just a murmur, something that sounded like a voice, no words, no actual meaning. Erik looks at the photograph and asks himself if there's

anything lying in the long grass, but can't see anything. When he leans back and shuts his eyes, the image lingers: the hedge and the brown fence flash pink, the yellow-green slope is dark blue, slowly slipping away. The last remnants of sunset, Erik thinks, then remembers that Benjamin said something about a house, a haunted house.

He opens his eyes and stands up. The muffled voice had said something about a haunted house. Erik can't understand how he could have forgotten that. That was what Benjamin was saying when the car stopped.

As he pulls on his coat he tries to remember where he's seen buildings that look like haunted houses. There aren't many. He remembers one he saw somewhere, north of Stockholm, somewhere near Rosersberg. Before you get to the stone ship at Runsa borg, on the left, not far from the water, there is a miniature wooden castle with towers.

Erik tries to think back to when he was there and remembers that Benjamin was in the car with him and Simone. They had been to see the stone ship, one of the largest Viking graves in Sweden. They had stood in the middle of the oval of large grey stones set in an expanse of green grass. It was late summer, and very warm. Erik remembers the still air, and the butterflies floating across the car park when they got back into the hot car.

As he takes the lift to the garage Erik remembers pulling over onto the shoulder after a few kilometres, pointing at the old house and jokily asking Benjamin if he'd like to live there.

'Where?'

'In the haunted house,' he had said, but he can't remember what Benjamin replied.

The sun is going down now. The low light is glinting off the ice in the visitors' car park. The grit crunches beneath his tyres as he pulls out and drives towards the main exit.

Erik knows that it's extremely unlikely that Benjamin would be at that particular 'haunted house', but it's not impossible. As he heads north along the E4, the dwindling light makes the world hazy and indistinct. He squints in an attempt to see better. It isn't until everything begins to take on a bluish tint that his brain actually registers that dusk is falling.

Half an hour later he's approaching the old house. He's tried calling Kennet four times to find out if he traced Benjamin's call, but he hasn't answered, and Erik hasn't left any messages.

The sky above the large lake has retained a faint glow, but the forest is now completely black. He drives slowly along the narrow road through the little hamlet that has grown up around the water. The headlights sweep across newly built villas, houses from the turn-of-the-century, small summer cottages. They reflect back off some of the windows, and light up a driveway where someone's left a child's tricycle. He slows down and sees the haunted house looming up beyond a tall hedge. Erik drives past a few more houses and parks at the side of the road. He gets out of the car and starts to walk back, then opens a gate leading to a dark brick villa, crosses the lawn and walks around the house. A cable slaps rhythmically against a flag-pole. Erik climbs over the fence into the next yard and hurries past a swimming pool that's been covered for the season. The plate-glass windows look black, and the deck is covered with dark leaves. Erik speeds up when he realises the old house is on the other side of the next hedge, and pushes his way through.

It's more secluded than the other houses, he thinks.

A car drives past on the road. Its headlights illuminate the trees and Erik finds himself thinking about Aida's peculiar photograph again. The yellow grass and bushes. As he gets closer to the big wooden house, he sees what looks like a blue fire burning in one of the rooms.

64

Monday afternoon, 14 December

The house has tall, heavily leaded windows with ornate awnings. A tall, hexagonal tower at one end and two protruding bay windows with pointed roofs at the other make it look like a miniature wooden castle.

As Erik approaches the window he realises that the blue light flickering across the walls of the room is coming from a television. A fat man in grey tracksuit trousers is sitting on the sofa, watching figure-skating. The cameras follow the loops, spins and arcs of the skaters. The man adjusts his glasses and leans back again. He seems to be alone, there's only one cup on the table. Erik tries to see into the next room. Something rustles quietly behind the glass. Erik peers into a bedroom containing an unmade bed, and a closed door. There are crumpled handkerchiefs and a glass of water on the bedside table. A map of Australia has been hung on the wall. Erik moves along the wall to the next window. The curtains are closed. He can't see between them at all, but he can hear that odd rustling again, together with a sort of clicking sound.

He moves on, around the hexagonal tower, and finds himself looking into a dining room. A dark table and chairs sit in the middle of a highly polished wooden floor. Something tells Erik that it's hardly used. There's a black object on the floor beside a glass-fronted cabinet. A guitar case. He hears the rustling sound again. He leans closer to the window, shielding the reflection of the grey sky with his hands, and sees a large dog running across the floor towards him. It thuds against the window, then stands up on its back legs and starts barking. Erik stumbles back, trips over a flowerpot and runs around the house, where he stops and waits, his heart pounding.

The dog stops after a while. The outside lights come on, then go off again.

Erik doesn't understand what he's doing here. He feels horribly alone. He realises he might as well go back to the hospital and heads to the front of the house towards the driveway.

When he turns the corner he sees a figure by the entrance. The fat man is standing at the top of the steps wearing a down jacket. He looks worried when he catches sight of Erik. Perhaps he was expecting kids horsing around, or a deer.

'Hello,' Erik says.

'This is private property,' the man calls out in a shrill voice.

The dog starts barking behind the closed door. Erik walks closer, and sees a yellow sports car parked in the driveway. It only has two seats and the boot is far too small to fit a person inside.

'Is that your Porsche?' Erik asks.

'Yes, it is.'

'Do you have any other cars?'

'Why do you want to know?'

'My son is missing,' Erik replies seriously.

'I don't have any other cars,' the man says. 'OK?'

Erik makes a note of the registration number.

'Can you go now?'

'Yes,' Erik says, and walks towards the gates.

He stands in the darkness out on the road for a while, just looking at the old house before he gets back into his car. He takes out the little wooden box with the parrot on it, and shakes some pills into his hand, counts them with his thumb, then tips them into his mouth.

He decides to call Simone. She's probably at Kennet's, eating a sandwich. Erik imagines the flat on Luntmakar Street in darkness, the hall with its coats, the post lying on the doormat, a pile of newspapers, ads, plastic-wrapped brochures. When he hears the beep he doesn't bother leaving a message, just ends the call and starts to drive back towards Stockholm.

He can't think of anyone he could talk to, and he's aware of the irony of this. He's spent so many years researching group dynamics and collective psychotherapy, yet he's isolated and alone. The power of the collective has propelled his career. He has tried to understand how people who have survived war together find it easier to process the trauma they've been through than those who have been through similar trauma alone. What, he wondered, is it about the shared experience that helps us to heal?

When he reaches the highway he dials Joona's office number. After five rings he gives up and tries his mobile phone instead.

'Yes, Joona here,' he says nonchalantly when he answers.

'Hello, this is Erik. Have you found Josef Ek?'

'No,' Joona sighs.

'He seems very hard to pin down.'

'I've said it before and I'm going to go on saying it, Erik: you ought to accept police protection.'

'I've got other priorities.'

'I know.'

Silence.

'Benjamin hasn't been in touch again?' Joona asks, his Finnish accent making the question sound even more forlorn.

'No.'

Erik can hear a voice in the background, possibly from a television.

'Kennet was going to get the call traced, but he . . .'

'So I heard, but it can take time,' Joona says. 'You have to send a technician out to focus on those specific exchanges, and that particular base-station.'

'But by then at least they know what station we're dealing with.'

'I think the operators can identify that pretty much immediately,' Joona says.

'What? They can identify the base-station?'

Neither of them speaks for a few seconds. Then Erik hears Joona's neutral voice:

'Why don't you talk to Kennet?'

'I can't reach him.'

Joona sighs gently.

'I'll look into it, but don't get your hopes up.'

'What do you mean?'

'Just that we're probably talking about a base-station in Stockholm, and that won't tell us anything until a technician can narrow it down for us.'

Erik holds his breath for a moment. He knows that Joona has to focus on catching Josef Ek. He knows that Benjamin's case isn't a high priority for the police, a teenage boy disappearing from his home is a hell of a long way from the work National Crime usually does. But he still has to ask. He can't let it go.

'Joona,' Erik says. 'I want you to take charge of the investigation into Benjamin's disappearance, can you do that?' he pleads. 'It would feel . . .'

He trails off. His jaw muscles ache – he's been clenching them harder than he realised.

'You and I both know,' Erik goes on, 'that this isn't an ordinary missing person case. Someone injected Simone and Benjamin with a knock-out drug. I know you're in charge of the search for Josef Ek, and I understand that Benjamin is no longer connected, but something even worse could have happened . . .'

He stops talking, too upset to continue.

'I've told you about Benjamin's illness,' he forces himself to say. 'In just two days his blood will stop clotting. And in a week's time his blood vessels will be under so much pressure that he could end up paralysed, or have a stroke, or suffer bleeding in his lungs if he coughs.'

'He needs to be found,' Joona says.

'Can you help me?'

Erik sits there with his plea hanging helplessly in the air. He doesn't care. He'd get down on his knees and beg if it worked.

'I can't just take over a preliminary investigation from the Stockholm Police,' Joona says.

'The officer's name is Fredrik Stensund. He seems pleasant enough, but he's not going to leave his nice warm office.'

'I'm sure they know what they're doing.'

'Don't lie to me,' Erik says quietly.

'I don't think I can take the case,' Joona says heavily. 'There's nothing that can be done about that. But I will try to help you. You need to sit down and think about who might have taken Benjamin. It could just be someone who saw your face in the paper. But it could also be someone you know. If there's no suspect, then there's no case, nothing. You need to think very carefully, go through your whole life, everyone you know, everyone Simone knows, everyone Benjamin knows. Go through your neighbours, relatives, colleagues, patients, competitors, friends. Is there anyone who has ever threatened you? Who's threatened Benjamin? Try to remember. It could be an impulsive act, or it could be the result of years of planning. Think very, very carefully, Erik. Then get back to me.'

Erik opens his mouth to ask Joona to take the case once more, but doesn't have enough time. He hears a click. He sits in his car, watching the traffic through eyes pricked with tears.

65

Late night, 14 December

It's cold and dark in the office. Erik kicks off his shoes. He can smell how mouldy his coat is when he hangs it up. Shivering, he boils some water on the hotplate to make a cup of tea. He takes two strong painkillers and sits down at his desk. The desk-lamp is the only one switched on in the room. He looks out at the dense black darkness through the window. He can just make himself out as a shadow next to the reflection of the lamp. Who hates me? he wonders. Who's jealous of me, who wants to punish me? Who wants to take everything I have away from me, my life, my loved ones – who wants to crush me?

Erik stands up from the desk and turns the ceiling light on. He paces back and forth, then stops and reaches for the phone. He knocks over a glass of water on the desk. The little puddle slowly spreads towards the *Doctors' Journal*. Without really thinking about it, he calls Simone and leaves a short message saying that he'd like to look at Benjamin's computer again.

'Sorry,' he says quietly. He hangs up, then tosses the phone on his desk.

The lift rumbles out in the hallway. He hears the doors ping and slide open, then the squeaking sound of someone pushing a hospital bed past his door.

The cocktail of pills starts to take effect, and he feels tranquillity rising through his body.

'OK, come on now,' he tells himself.

Someone took Benjamin, someone's doing this to me.

'I'm going to find you,' he whispers.

Erik looks at the damp pages of the *Doctors' Journal*. One picture shows the new head of Karolinska Institute leaning over a desk. The water has made her face fuzzy and dark. When Erik tries to move the paper he realises it's stuck to the desk. Half of the ad on the back for the Global Health Conference tears off. He sits down on his chair and starts to pick at it with his thumbnail, but suddenly stops and stares at a haphazard group of letters: e v A.

A slow wave is building in his memory, culminating in a clear image of a woman. She refuses to return what she's stolen. He knows her name is Eva. Her mouth is tight, and froth bubbles on her thin lips. She's shrieking at him: 'You're the one who's always taking! You take and take and take! How the hell would you like it if I started taking things from you? How do you think that would feel?' She hides her face in her hands and tells him she hates him. She repeats it over and over again, maybe a hundred times before she calms down. Her cheeks are pale, her eyes red, and she stares at him uncomprehendingly, exhausted. He remembers her. He realises that he remembers her all too well. He can't believe he blocked her out of his memory for so long.

Eva Blau, he thinks. He knew he'd made a mistake accepting her as his patient, right from the start.

It was many years ago, back when he was still using hypnosis as part of his patients' treatment. Eva Blau. The name hails from another life. Before he stopped practising hypnosis. Before he promised never to hypnotise anyone again.

He had believed in hypnosis so passionately. He had seen that if patients were hypnotised in front of each other, the taboos surrounding their abuse, their crimes, their sense of violation, became less personalised. Guilt could be shared, the distinctions between abusers and victims dissolved. No one could blame themselves for what happened if they were in a room where everyone else had been through the same thing.

Why had Eva Blau become his patient? He can't remember

what her specific problem was. He encountered so many unimaginable forms of suffering. People whose pasts had been painful came to him. They were often aggressive, always scared, obsessive, paranoid, occasionally maimed, and with a history of suicide attempts. A lot of them came to him very close to full-blown psychosis or schizophrenia. They had been systematically abused and tortured, and had either witnessed or been forced to take part in horrific atrocities.

What did she steal? Erik asks himself. I accused her of theft, but what had she stolen?

He can't pin down the memory. He stands up, walks a few steps, stops and closes his eyes. Something else happened, but what? Did it have anything to do with Benjamin? On one occasion he had explained to Eva Blau that he could find a different therapy group for her. So why can't he remember what had happened? Had she threatened him?

The only thing he can recall is one of their early meetings, in this very office. Eva Blau had shaved off all her hair and was wearing heavy eye make-up. As she sat on the sofa, she very casually unbuttoned her blouse and showed him her pale breasts.

'You've been in my home,' Erik said.

'You've been in my home,' she replied.

'Eva, you've told me about your home,' he went on. 'Breaking in is an entirely different matter.'

'I didn't break in.'

'You broke a window.'

'The stone broke the window,' she said.

66

Monday night, 14 December

The key is already in the lock of the cabinet, and the wooden ribs of the lid slide back smoothly as Erik pushes it open and starts to search. Somewhere here, he tells himself. I know there's something about Eva Blau.

Whenever his patients, for whatever reason, act differently than he anticipates, he keeps his notes on them until he figures out what's going on.

It could be a note, an observation, or even an object. He searches through the papers, notebooks, scraps of paper and receipts with notes scribbled on them. Faded photographs in a plastic folder, an external hard drive, some diaries from back when he believed in complete transparency between patient and doctor, a picture drawn by a traumatised patient one night. Several cassettes and video recordings of his lectures. A book by Hermann Broch full of Post-it notes. Erik's hands stop. His fingertips are tingling. There's a sheet of paper wrapped around a VHS tape, held by a brown rubber band. The label on the cartridge says just *Erik Maria Bark, tape 14*. He removes the paper, adjusts the desk-lamp and recognises his own handwriting: *HAUNTED HOUSE*.

A shiver runs up his spine and down his arms. The hair on the back of his neck stands up and he can hear the ticking of his wristwatch. His head is thudding, his heart racing. He sits back down on his chair and stares at the tape. With his hands shaking, he calls the janitors' office and asks to have a VHS player sent to his room. He walks over to the window, and adjusts the angle of the blinds, then stands and stares at the layer of damp snow in the courtyard. Heavy flakes are drifting through the air. Some of them hit his window and melt. He tells himself that it's probably just a coincidence, an odd coincidence, but at the same time he can't deny the feeling that the pieces of the puzzle seem to fit.

The haunted house. Those words, written on a sheet of paper, transport him back to another time. He is going to try and see what lies hidden in his memory, even though he doesn't want to.

The janitor knocks softly on the door. Erik wheels in the stand holding the television and the absurdly obsolete-looking video player.

He inserts the tape, turns off the light and sits down.

The picture flickers and the sound crackles for a while, then he hears his own voice through the television. He sounds like he has a cold as he runs through the time, place and date, and concludes with:

'We've had a short break but are still in a post-hypnotic state.'

More than ten years have passed, he thinks as the camera angle changes. The picture shakes and then settles. The lens is pointing at a semi-circle of chairs. Then he steps in front of the camera. There's a lightness to his body ten years ago, a spring in his step that he doesn't have any more. His hair isn't grey and there are no lines on his forehead and cheeks.

The patients come in, moving slowly, and sit down on the chairs. Some of them talk quietly among themselves. One of them laughs. The quality of the recording is poor. All of their faces look grainy and blurred.

Erik swallows hard and hears himself explain in a tinny voice that it's time to continue the session. Some of them go on talking, others sit there in silence. A chair creaks. He sees himself standing by the wall, taking notes on a pad. There's a knock at the door and Eva Blau comes in. She's wound up, her neck and cheeks are flushed. He takes her coat and hangs it up, then introduces her briefly to the group. The others nod warily, a few whisper hello, a couple of them pretend not to have seen her and just stare down at the floor instead.

Erik remembers the atmosphere in the room that day: the members of the group were still affected by the session before the break and were disturbed by the arrival of a new member. The others had already got to know each other and had started to bond.

The group consisted of at most eight members at any one time, and the therapy was based on using hypnosis to explore their pasts. They would gradually approach their trauma together. The theory was that this method would make them more than mere witnesses to each other's experiences, that the openness offered by hypnosis would allow them to share pain and grieve together, the way people did after communal catastrophes.

Eva Blau sits down on the empty chair. She looks directly into the camera for a moment, and something about her face becomes sharp and hostile.

This is the woman who broke into his home ten years ago. But what had she stolen?

Erik watches himself initiate the second part of the session by recapping what happened before the break and following up with light-hearted associations. It was a way to get them to feel more comfortable, feel that a degree of levity was possible despite the deep trauma they were exploring. He moves to stand in front of the group.

'We're going to start with thoughts and associations raised by the first part of the session,' he says. 'Does anyone have any comments?'

'Confusing,' says a sturdy young woman wearing a lot of make-up.

Sibel, Erik thinks to himself. Her name is Sibel.

'Frustrating,' Jussi adds in a strong Norrland accent. 'I mean, I only had time to open my eyes and scratch my head before it was over.'

'What did you feel?' Erik asks him.

'Hair,' he replies with a smile.

'Hair?' Sibel asks, then giggles.

'When I scratched my head,' Jussi explains.

Some of them laugh at the joke. A glimmer of joy is visible on Jussi's gloomy face.

'Give me some associations around hair,' Erik says. 'Charlotte?'

'I don't know,' she says. 'Hair? Beards, maybe . . . no.'

'A hippie, a hippie on a motorbike,' Pierre says with a smile. 'Sitting like this, chewing Juicy Fruit and riding . . .'

Eva gets to her feet with a clatter.

'This is childish,' she says.

'Why do you think that?' Erik asks.

Eva doesn't answer, but stays standing up.

'Pierre, would you like to go on?' Erik asks.

Pierre shakes his head, crosses his index fingers, holds them up towards Eva, and pretends to be taking cover from her.

Jussi raises his hand towards Eva and says something in Norrland dialect.

Erik isn't sure he's heard what Jussi says, and reaches for the remote, but knocks it onto the floor and the batteries fall out.

'Christ,' he mutters to himself as he gets down on his knees.

He shakily presses the rewind button, then turns the volume up when the tape starts to play again.

'This is childish,' Eva Blau says.

'Why do you think that?' Erik asks, and when she doesn't answer he turns to Pierre and asks if he'd like to go on.

He shakes his head, crosses his fingers, then holds them up towards Eva.

'They shot Dennis Hopper because he was a hippie,' he whispers.

Sibel giggles and looks at Erik. Jussi clears his throat and raises his hand towards Eva.

'You won't have to put up with our childishness in the haunted house,' he says in his thick Norrland accent.

They quieten down. Eva turns towards him and looks like she's going to react aggressively, but something stops her, possibly his sombre voice and the calmness in his eyes.

67

Monday night, 14 December

The phrase *haunted house* is echoing through Erik's head. As he watches the old tape, he remembers how the group always started with the shared relaxation exercises before he moved on to hypnotising them.

'I try to get the whole group in a state of deep hypnosis,' Erik says, looking at Eva.

Erik is struck by how familiar the situation is, yet also how incredibly distant, from a different time. He watches himself pull up a chair, sit down in front of the semi-circle of people and talk to them, getting them to close their eyes and lean back. After a while he prompts them to sit up, but keep their eyes closed. He walks behind them, evaluating how relaxed each one of them is in turn. Their faces grow softer and slacker, less conscious, detached from pretence and artifice.

Erik watches as he stops behind Eva Blau and places a heavy hand on her shoulder. His stomach tingles as he hears himself start the process of hypnosis, confident in his own abilities, pleasurably aware of his own special talent.

'You're ten years old, Eva,' he says. 'You're ten years old. This is a good day. You're happy. Why are you happy?'

'Because the man is dancing and jumping in the puddles,' she says, her face barely moving.

'Who's dancing?'

'Who?' she repeats. 'Mum says it's Gene Kelly.'

'So you're watching *Singin' in the Rain*?'

'Mum is.'

'Not you?'

'I am too.'

'And you're happy?'

She nods slowly.

'What's happening?'

Eva closes her mouth and her face sinks.

'Eva?'

'My tummy's big,' she says almost inaudibly.

'Your tummy?'

'I think it's really big,' she says, and tears start to trickle down her cheeks.

'The haunted house,' Jussi whispers. 'The haunted house.'

'Eva, listen to me,' Erik goes on. 'You can hear everyone else in the room, but my voice is the only one you should listen to. Don't worry about what anyone else says, my voice is the only one you need to pay attention to.'

'OK.'

'Why is your tummy big?' Erik asks.

'I want to go into the haunted house,' she whispers.

Erik pauses the tape and sits down on the bunk in his room at the hospital, aware that he is approaching his own hidden rooms, things he's forgotten, things that are long gone.

He rubs his eyes, watches the flickering television screen and mutters:

'Open the door.'

He presses play. He hears himself counting out loud, sinking her deeper into hypnosis, explaining that she'll soon do what he tells her without thinking first. She'll just accept that his voice is leading her the right way. She shakes her head gently, and he keeps counting down, letting his voice get heavy.

The image quality deteriorates. Eva looks up with hazy eyes, licks her lips and whispers:

'I see them take someone, they just go up and take someone . . .'

'Who is it that's taking someone?' he asks.

Her breathing becomes irregular.

'A man with a ponytail,' she moans. 'He's hanging the little . . .'

The tape crackles and the image vanishes.

Erik fast-forwards to the end, but the picture doesn't come back. Half the tape has been erased.

He sits in front of the television screen. He sees himself stare back out from the deep, dark reflection, and simultaneously sees his face as it was ten years ago. He looks at the video cassette, tape 14, and then at the rubber-band and the sheet of paper with the words *HAUNTED HOUSE* on it.

68

Tuesday morning, 15 December

Erik must have pressed the button more than ten times before the lift doors finally close. He knows it doesn't make them close any quicker but he can't help it. What Benjamin said to him from the boot of the car is now merging with odd fragments of memory. He hears Eva Blau's weak voice saying that a man with a ponytail had taken someone. But there was something dishonest about the set of her mouth.

There's a rumble from the machinery high above, and the lift starts to descend.

'The haunted house,' he says, hoping that it was all just a coincidence, that Benjamin's disappearance has nothing to do with his past.

He hurries through the garage and into the cramped stairwell. Two floors down he unlocks a steel door and heads down a white-washed tunnel to an alarmed door. He presses the intercom button for a long time, and eventually gets a reluctant response. He leans closer to the microphone and explains what he wants. The hospital doesn't really want anyone down here, he thinks. The archive contains all the medical records, all the research, results of experiments and monitored tests, but also the background to the thalidomide scandal and numerous other dubious public health programmes. Its shelves contain thousands of files filled with the results of tests conducted on people suspected of having HIV, files documenting the enforced sterilisation programme, as well as the so-called Vipeholm experiments, where the inmates of a mental hospital were fed large amounts of sweets as part of research which eventually led to the provision of free dental treatment in Sweden. Orphans, psychiatric patients and old people had their mouths stuffed with sugar until their teeth rotted.

The door whirrs and Erik steps into unexpectedly warm light. Something about the lighting makes the archive feel cosy, a long way from a windowless dungeon deep underground.

He can hear operatic music from the security station, playful coloratura from a mezzosoprano. Erik composes himself before he walks over to the office.

A short man wearing a straw hat is standing with his back to him, watering some plants.

'Hi, Kurt.'

The man turns around, looking pleasantly surprised.

'Erik Maria Bark! It's been a while. How are you?'

Erik doesn't know what to say.

'I'm not really sure,' he says honestly. 'Lots of family stuff going on right now.'

'Oh dear, that's . . .'

'Nice plants,' Erik says, to avoid further questions.

'Pansies. I love them. Conny kept saying nothing would grow down here. So I said, just you watch me!'

'Amazing,' Erik says.

'I've installed halogen lamps everywhere.'

'Wow.'

'A proper solarium!' he jokes, showing Erik a tube of sunscreen.

'I'm afraid I can't stay long.'

'Put a bit on your nose,' Kurt says, squeezing some out and holding it towards Erik's nose.

'Thanks, but . . .'

Kurt lowers his voice and whispers playfully:

'Sometimes I go around in nothing but my underwear. But don't tell anyone!'

Erik smiles at him, and can feel the strain in his face. Kurt looks at him.

'Many years ago,' Erik says, 'I used to record my hypnosis sessions.'

'How long ago?'

'Ten years, roughly. There was a series of VHS tapes . . .'

'VHS?'

'Yes, it was already pretty obsolete, even then,' Erik says.

'All the videotapes have been digitised.'

'Good.'

'They'll be in the archive.'

'How do I get to that, then?'

Kurt smiles and Erik notices the contrast between his white teeth and suntanned face.

'Well, I can help you there.'

They walk over to four computers tucked in an alcove next to the racks of shelving.

Kurt quickly taps in the password, then scrolls through the folders of digitised recordings.

'Would they have been filed under your name?' he asks.

'Yes, they should have been,' Erik says.

'Well, they're not,' Kurt says slowly. 'I'll try "hypnosis".'

He types the word into the search box.

'There are some there, you can see for yourself.'

None of the results matches Erik's therapy sessions. The only files that relate to him concern grant applications and funding. He types in the words 'haunted house', then tries the name Eva Blau, even though the members of his group were never registered as patients by the hospital.

'There's nothing,' he says tiredly.

'Well, there was a lot of trouble with the transfer,' Kurt says. 'A lot of material was ruined, all the Betamax tapes, and . . .'

'Who was responsible for the digitisation?'

Kurt turns to face him and shrugs his shoulders apologetically: 'Me and Conny.'

'But the original tapes should still be here somewhere?' Erik says tentatively.

'I'm sorry, but I honestly couldn't tell you.'

'Do you think Conny would know?'

'No.'

'Call him and ask.'

'He's down in Simrishamn.'

Erik turns away and tries to think logically.

'I know that a lot of material was accidentally discarded,' Kurt says.

Erik stares at him.

'But this is unique research,' he says flatly.

'Like I said, I'm sorry.'

'I know, I didn't mean . . .'

Kurt pinches a brown leaf off one of the plants.

'You gave up the hypnosis, didn't you?' he says. 'I was sure you had.'

'Yes, but I need to take a look at . . .'

Erik stops talking. He can't bring himself to finish the sentence. All he wants is to go back to his room, take a pill and get some sleep.

'We've always had technical problems down here,' Kurt goes on. 'But every time we mention it, they just tell us to do the best we can. They just told us not to worry when we accidentally erased a whole decade's worth of lobotomy research. They were old recordings, sixteen-millimetre film that were transferred to video in the Eighties, but they're lost now.'

69

Tuesday morning, 15 December

The large shadow of the courthouse falls across the front of Police Headquarters. Only the central tower is bathed in sunlight.

Carlos Eliasson is standing by his aquarium looking out of the window when Joona knocks and then opens the door without waiting for an answer.

Carlos is startled and turns around. Reluctantly, he gestures towards the visitor's chair and realises he's still holding the jar of fish-food.

'I just noticed it's been snowing,' he says vaguely and puts the jar down next to the aquarium.

Joona sits down and looks out of the window. A very thin, dry layer of snow has settled on Kronoberg Park.

'We might get a white Christmas yet, you never know,' Carlos smiles cautiously, taking his place on the other side of the desk. 'Back where I grew up, down in Skåne, there was never any proper weather at Christmas. It just looked the same the whole time. Heavy grey mist over the fields . . .'

Carlos stops talking abruptly.

'But you haven't come to talk about the weather,' he says tersely.

'Not really.'

Joona looks at him calmly and leans back.

'I want to take over the investigation into the disappearance of Erik Maria Bark's son.'

'No,' Carlos replies succinctly.

'I was the one who started . . .'

'No, Joona, you were permitted to look into it as long as there was a link to Josef Ek.'

'There still is,' Joona persists.

Carlos stands up, takes a couple of impatient steps, then turns to face Joona:

'Our directives are crystal clear, and our resources aren't . . .'

'I believe the kidnapping is directly connected to the hypnosis of Josef Ek.'

'What are you talking about?' Carlos asks irritably.

'It is no coincidence that Erik Maria Bark's son vanished just a week after Josef Ek was hypnotised.'

Carlos sits down again, and sounds suddenly less sure of himself.

'A boy who's run away from home isn't a case for National Crime. It's out of the question.'

'He hasn't run away from home,' Joona says bluntly.

Carlos glances at his fish, then leans forward and lowers his voice:

'The fact that you're feeling a bit guilty, Joona, is no reason for me to . . .'

'Then I'd like to request a transfer,' Joona says, getting to his feet.

'Where to?'

'To the unit that's handling the case.'

'Now you're just being stubborn again,' Carlos says, scratching his head in annoyance.

'But I'll be proved right,' Joona smiles.

'Dear God, not that again,' Carlos sighs, then looks at his fish again and shakes his head.

Joona starts to walk towards the door.

'Wait,' Carlos says.

Joona stops and turns round. He raises his eyebrows.

'How about this – you're not getting the case, but you can have a week to investigate the boy's disappearance.'

'That'll do.'

'So now you won't have to do that whole "what did I tell you?" routine.'

'We'll see.'

Joona heads to his wing of the building, and says hello to Anja, who waves at him without looking up from her computer screen. He walks past Petter Näslund's office, where the radio is on. A sports reporter is commentating on the women's biathlon with feigned enthusiasm in his voice. Joona retraces his steps and goes back to see Anja.

'I don't have time,' she says without looking at him.

'Yes, you do,' he says calmly.

'I'm in the middle of something very important.'

Joona tries to look over her shoulder.

'What are you working on?' he asks.

'Nothing.'

'What is it?'

She sighs.

'An auction. I'm the highest bidder right now, but another idiot keeps pushing the price up.'

'An auction?'

'I collect Lisa Larsson figurines,' she replies.

'Those fat little ceramic children?'

'They're art, but you wouldn't understand that.'

She looks at the screen.

'It's almost over. As long as no one else bids more, then . . .'

'I need your help,' Joona persists. 'Something connected to your profession. It's actually quite important.'

'Hang on, hang on . . .'

She holds one hand up towards him.

'Yes, I got them! I got them! I got Amalia and Emma!'

She quickly closes the page.

'OK, Joona, you old Finn. What is it you want help with?'

'I want you to put pressure on the mobile phone operators and get me a location for the call that Benjamin Bark made on Sunday. I want concrete information about where he was calling from. Within the next five minutes.'

'Jesus, you're in a bad mood,' Anja sighs.

'Three minutes,' Joona says, changing his mind. 'Your online shopping cost you two minutes.'

'Get lost,' she says as he leaves the room.

He goes into his office, closes the door and looks through his post. He stops to read a postcard from Disa. She's in London, and writes that she misses him. Disa knows he hates those ridiculous pictures of animals like chimpanzees playing golf or getting tangled in toilet paper, and therefore always manages to find one for him. Joona isn't sure whether he should turn the card over or just throw it away, but curiosity gets the better of him. He turns the postcard over and shudders. A bulldog with a beard, a sailor's hat and a pipe in its mouth. He smiles at the care she clearly put into selecting it, and is pinning it to his corkboard when his phone rings.

'Yes?' he says.

'I've got an answer,' Anja says.

'That was quick.'

'They said they'd had some technical problems, but that they called Superintendent Kennet Sträng an hour ago to tell him that the base-station was in Gävle.'

'Gävle,' he repeats.

'They're not quite finished, they said. In a day or two, definitely this week, they'll be able to say exactly where Benjamin was when he called.'

'You could have come to my room to tell me that, it's only four metres . . .'

'Why, do you miss me?'

70

Tuesday morning, 15 December

Joona writes the name Gävle on an empty page of the notepad in front of him, then picks up the phone again.

'Erik Maria Bark,' Erik says, answering immediately.

'It's me, Joona.'

'Have you found out anything?'

'I've got a rough location for the call.'

'Where is he?'

'All we've got so far is that the base-station is in Gävle.'

'Gävle?'

'Just north of Dalälven, and . . .'

'I know where Gävle is, I just don't understand, I mean . . .'

Joona hears Erik moving around.

'We'll get a more precise location later this week,' Joona says.

'When?'

'Hopefully tomorrow.'

He hears Erik sit down.

'So are you taking the case?' he asks anxiously.

'I'm taking the case,' Joona says tersely. 'I'm going to find Benjamin.'

Erik clears his throat, and when his voice feels steady again, he says quickly:

'I've done a lot of thinking about who could have done this, and I've got a name I'd like you to check out, a former patient of mine, Eva Blau.'

'Blau? As in the German for blue?'

'Yes.'

'Has she threatened you?'

'It's hard to explain.'

'I'll get her checked out right away.'

They pause.

'I'd like to meet up with you and Simone as soon as possible,' Joona says.

'OK.'

'There was never any attempt made to reconstruct the crime scene, was there?'

'Reconstruct?'

'We're going to figure out who could've seen Benjamin's kidnapper. Will you both be home in half an hour?'

'I'll call Simone,' Erik says. 'We'll be waiting for you there.'

'Good.'

'Joona,' Erik says.

'Yes?'

'I know it's the first twenty-four hours that really count in a case like this,' Erik says slowly. 'And now . . .'

'You don't think we're going to find him?'

'It's . . . I don't know,' Erik whispers.

'I'm not usually wrong,' Joona replies quietly but firmly. 'And I think we're going to find your boy.'

Joona hangs up. Then he picks up the note with Eva Blau's name on it and goes to see Anja again. Her room smells like oranges. There's a bowl of assorted citrus fruits next to the computer and its pink keyboard, and there's a large glossy poster on one wall showing a very muscular Anja swimming the butterfly in the Olympic Games.

'I was a lifesaver when I did national service,' Joona says, 'I had to be able to swim ten kilometres with a flag. But I've never been able to swim the butterfly.'

'It's a waste of energy, that's what the butterfly is.'

'I think it's a beautiful stroke – you look like a mermaid,' Joona says, gesturing at the poster.

Anja tries to hide the pride in her voice when she replies.

'The coordination is pretty demanding, it's all about counter-rhythm and . . . oh, who cares?'

Anja stretches her arms happily and her large bust almost hits Joona.

'OK,' he says, holding up the note. 'Now I'd like you to find someone for me.'

Anja's smile stiffens.

'I had a feeling you wanted something, Joona Linna. It was all a bit too nice, a bit too friendly. I helped you with that base-station, and then you came in here with that lovely smile of yours. I almost thought you were going to ask me out for dinner or something, but then . . .'

'I will, Anja. All in good time.'

She shakes her head and takes the note from his hand.

'So, trying to find someone. Urgent?'

'Very.'

'Why are you standing here distracting me, then?'

'I thought you liked it . . .'

'Eva Blau,' Anja says thoughtfully.

'It's not clear that's her real name.'

Anja bites her lip anxiously.

'A fictitious name,' she says. 'Not much to go on. Do you have anything else? No address, nothing like that?'

'No, no address. All I know is that she was a patient of Erik Maria Bark's at Karolinska ten years ago, probably only for a few months. You'll have to check the databases, not just the usual ones but all of them. Was there an Eva Blau enrolled at the university? If she ever bought a car, she'll be in the vehicle registry. Or if she's ever applied for a visa, or joined a library . . . clubs, AA, anything . . . And I'd like you to check people with protected identities too, victims of crime, and . . .'

'Yeah, yeah, yeah! Go on, get lost, so I can get some work done!' Anja says.

71

Tuesday morning, 15 December

Joona switches off the audiobook of Per Myrberg reading Dostoyevsky's *Crime and Punishment*. He parks the car outside Lao Wai, the vegetarian Asian restaurant that Disa has been nagging him about going to.

When he gets to the flat, he says hello to Erik and Simone, then gives them a quick outline of what he's planning to do.

'We're going to reconstruct the kidnapping as best we can. The only one of us who was here when it happened is you, Simone.'

She nods tensely.

'So you can play yourself. I'll be the kidnapper, and you, Erik, you can be Benjamin.'

'OK,' Erik says.

Joona looks at the time.

'Simone, what time do you think it was when the break-in happened?'

She clears her throat:

'I'm not sure, but the newspaper hadn't arrived, so it was before five. And I'd been up earlier to get a glass of water, and that was two o'clock. Then I lay awake for a bit, so some time between two thirty and five o'clock.'

'Good, I'll set my watch to three thirty, to give us a time roughly in the middle,' Joona says. 'I'm going to unlock the door and creep up on Simone in bed, pretend to give her an injection, then go in to Benjamin's room and inject you and drag you out of bed. I'll pull you through the hall and out onto the landing. You're heavier than your son, so we'll have to adjust the timing slightly. Simone, try to act exactly like you did at the time. Lie down in exactly the same position you were in at that moment. I want to know exactly what you could see, and what you thought was happening.'

Simone nods, her face pale.

'Thank you,' she whispers. 'Thank you for doing this.'

Joona looks at her with his ice-grey eyes.

'We're going to find Benjamin.'

Simone rubs her forehead quickly.

'I'll go into the bedroom,' she says in a hoarse voice, and Joona leaves the flat with a set of keys.

She's lying under the covers when Joona walks in. He moves purposefully towards her but doesn't actually run. It tickles as he pulls her arm out and pretends to inject her. She's looking Joona in the eye as he stands over her, and she remembers feeling a distinct prick in her arm, then seeing a figure slip quickly out of the room. Even the memory is enough to make the arm where she was injected tingle unpleasantly. When Joona disappears, she sits up, rubs her elbow and slowly gets out of bed. She goes out into the hall, looks into Benjamin's room and sees Joona leaning over his bed. And she just says the words, as if they had been echoing in her memory:

'What are you doing? Can I come in?'

She walks hesitantly towards the dresser. Her body seems to remember the way it lost all energy and fell. Her legs give way as she recollects the feeling of losing consciousness. She slumps against the wall and sees Joona dragging Erik by his feet. Her memory replays the way Benjamin tried to cling onto the door-frame, the way his head bounced on the threshold of the door, and how he reached out to her weakly with his arms.

As Erik is dragged past Simone and their eyes meet, it's as if a figure made out of fog or mist becomes visible for a fraction of a second. She can see Joona's face from below. Suddenly it fades away and is replaced in her consciousness by a fleeting glimpse of the kidnapper. Simone's heart is thudding hard as she hears Joona drag Erik out into the stairwell and close the door behind them.

An uneasy feeling lingers in the flat. Simone can't escape the idea that she's been drugged again, and her arms and legs feel stiff and numb as she gets to her feet to wait for them to come back in.

Joona drags Erik across the worn marble floor of the landing, all the while looking around and judging angles and heights, looking for anywhere a potential witness could have been watching. He tries to figure out how far down the stairs he can see, and thinks that someone could actually be standing just five steps down, right next to the banister, watching him right now. He goes over to the lift. He's already prepared, and has wedged the door open. As he leans over he sees his face in the shiny surface of the door, then he sees the wall behind him. Joona drags the prone Erik into the lift. Through the cage he can see the door to the right, the letterbox and brass name plate, but on the left nothing but the wall. The ceiling light on the landing is shaded by the doorpost. Joona looks at the large mirror at the back of the lift, but he can't see anything. The window in the stairwell remains hidden from view the whole time. But all of a sudden he sees something unexpected. He can see, in the smaller, angled mirror in the corner, right into the glinting peephole of the flat that has been out of sight the whole time. He shuts the lift door and notes that the angled mirror still gives him a clear view of the door. If someone was standing behind the door looking through the peephole right now, they'd be able to get a very clear look at his face. But if he moves his head just five centimetres in any direction, he disappears from sight.

Erik gets to his feet and Joona looks at his watch.

'Eight minutes,' he says.

They walk back to the flat. Simone is standing in the hallway, and has clearly been crying.

'He was wearing rubber gloves,' she says. 'Yellow rubber gloves.'

'Are you sure?' Erik asks.

'Yes.'

'So there's no point looking for fingerprints,' Joona says.

'What are we going to do?' she asks.

'The police have already knocked on doors,' Erik says gloomily as Simone brushes the dirt and dust from his back.

Joona pulls out a sheet of paper.

'This is the list of people they've spoken to. Obviously they concentrated on this floor and the flats below. There are five they haven't yet spoken to, and one which . . .'

He stares at the list, and sees that the flat behind the lift has been crossed off. That's the door he saw via the mirrors.

'One which has been crossed off altogether,' Joona says. 'The one on the other side of the lift.'

'They were away,' Simone says. 'They still are. Six weeks in Thailand.'

Joona looks at them intently.

'Time to knock on doors,' he says abruptly.

The name Rosenlund is written on the door that had a view of the lift through the mirrors. The police officers conducting door-to-door inquiries had ignored it altogether because it was empty, and hidden from sight anyway.

Joona leans over and looks through the letterbox. He can't see any letters or ads on the mat. He hears a faint sound from inside the flat. A cat comes trotting into the hall from the next room. The cat stops abruptly and looks warily at Joona, who's still holding the letterbox open.

'No one leaves a cat on its own for six weeks,' Joona says slowly to himself.

The cat adopts a watchful pose.

'Well, you don't look starving,' Joona says to the animal.

The cat lets out a big yawn, jumps onto a chair in the hall and curls up into a ball.

The first person Joona wants to talk to is the husband of Alice Franzén. She was at home on her own the last time the police tried. The Franzéns live on the same floor as Simone and Erik, in the flat opposite the lift.

Joona rings the doorbell and waits. He thinks back to when he was a child and went around knocking on people's doors selling felt flowers for charity: the feeling of alienation he had looking inside other people's homes, the caginess in the eyes of the people who came to the door.

He rings again. A woman in her thirties opens the door. She looks at him with a wary expression that makes him think of the cat in the empty flat.

'Yes?'

'My name is Joona Linna,' he says, holding up his ID. 'I'd like to talk to your husband.'

She looks back quickly over her shoulder, then says:

'I want to know what this is about first. He's very busy.'

'It's about the early hours of Saturday morning, December 12th.'

'But you already asked about that,' the woman says irritably.

Joona looks down at the list in his hand.

'It says here that the police spoke to you, but not your husband.'

The woman sighs unhappily.

'I don't know if he has time,' she says.

Joona smiles.

'It'll only take a minute, I promise.'

The woman shrugs her shoulders, then calls into the flat:

'Tobias! It's the police!'

After a while a man with a towel wrapped around his waist appears. His skin looks hot, and he has a pronounced suntan.

'Hello,' he says to Joona. 'I was on the tanning bed . . .'

'Nice,' Joona says.

'Not really,' Tobias Franzén says. 'My liver's missing an enzyme. I'm doomed to spend two hours on a tanning bed every day.'

'Well, in that case . . .' Joona says drily.

'You wanted to ask something?'

'I want to know if you saw or heard anything unusual in the early hours of Saturday morning, December 12th.'

Tobias scratches his chest, leaving white marks on his tanned skin.

'Let's see. I'm sorry, but I can't remember anything unusual. I really don't know.'

'OK, thanks very much,' Joona says, and bows his head.

Tobias reaches for the door handle.

'One more thing . . .'

Joona nods towards the empty flat.

'That family, the Rosenlunds,' he says.

'They're very nice,' Tobias smiles, and starts to shiver. 'I haven't seen them for a while.'

'No, they're away. Do you know if they have a cleaner, anything like that?'

Tobias shakes his head. The redness is starting to fade, and he's clearly shivering now.

'Sorry, I have no idea.'

72

Tuesday morning, 15 December

Joona moves on to the next name on the list: Jarl Hammar lives on the floor below Erik and Simone. He wasn't home the last time the police knocked.

Jarl Hammar is a thin man who is obviously suffering from Parkinson's disease. He's neatly dressed in a cardigan, with a cravat round his neck.

'National Crime?' Hammar says in a hoarse voice. He looks at Joona with eyes made cloudy by cataracts. 'What would National Crime want with me?'

'I just want to ask a question,' Joona says. 'Did you by any chance see anything unusual in the building or out on the street in the early hours of Saturday morning, December 12th?'

Jarl Hammar tilts his head and closes his eyes. He opens them a few seconds later and shakes his head at Joona.

'I'm on medication,' he says. 'It makes me sleep very heavily.'

Joona catches sight of a woman behind Jarl Hammar.

'And your wife?' he asks. 'Could I have a word with her?'

Jarl Hammar gives a wry smile.

'My wife, Solveig, was a wonderful woman. But I'm sorry to say that she's been in the ground for the past thirty years.'

The thin man turns and raises a shaky arm towards a dark figure further inside the flat.

'This is Anabella. She helps me with cleaning and so on.

Sadly she doesn't speak Swedish, but other than that she's beyond reproach.'

The shadowy figure steps into the light when she hears her name mentioned. Anabella looks Peruvian. She's in her twenties and has bad acne scars on her cheeks. Her hair is pulled up into a loose ponytail, and she's extremely short.

'Anabella,' Joona says gently. '*Soy comisario de policía*, Joona Linna.'

'*Buenos días*,' she replies with a lisp, looking at him with black eyes.

'*Tu limpias más departamentos aquí? En este edificio?*'

She nods: yes, she does clean other flats in the same building.

'*Qué otros?*' Joona asks: which ones?

'*Espera un momento*,' Anabella says, and thinks for a while before starting to count on her fingers. '*El piso de Lagerberg, Franzén, Gerdman, Rosenlund, el piso de Johansson también.*'

'Rosenlund,' Joona says. '*Rosenlund es la familia con un gato, no es verdad?*'

Anabella smiles and nods. Yes, she cleans the flat with the cat.

'*Y muchos flores*,' she adds.

'Lots of plants,' Joona says, and she nods.

Joona asks if she noticed anything unusual four nights ago, when Benjamin disappeared.

'*Notabas alguna cosa especial hace cuatros días? De noche . . .*'

Anabella's face stiffens.

'*No*,' she says instantly, and tries to retreat back inside Jarl Hammar's flat again.

'*De verdad*,' Joona says quickly. '*Espero que digas la verdad, Anabella.*' You need to tell the truth.

He repeats that it's very important, that it's about the disappearance of a child.

Jarl Hammar, who has been standing next to them the whole time, listening, holds up his badly shaking hands as he says in a hoarse voice:

'Now be nice to Anabella, she's a very good girl.'

'She needs to tell me what she's seen,' Joona explains sternly, then turns back to Anabella again.

'La verdad, por favor.'

Jarl Hammar looks on helplessly as large tears trickle from Anabella's dark, shining eyes.

'Perdón,' she whispers. *'Perdón, señor.'*

'Don't be upset, Anabella,' Jarl Hammar says, gesturing to Joona. 'Come in, I can't have her standing out in the stairwell crying.'

They go inside and sit down at Jarl Hammar's immaculately polished dining table, and he gets out a tin of Christmas gingerbread cookies. Anabella tells them quietly that she doesn't have anywhere to live. She's been homeless for the past three months but has managed to hide in the stairwell and in the storage compartments of the people she cleans for. When she was given the keys to the Rosenlunds' flat to water the plants and feed the cat, she finally had access to a bathroom again and could sleep soundly. She keeps repeating that she hasn't taken anything, that she isn't a thief, she hasn't taken food, she hasn't touched anything. She hasn't even been sleeping on the Rosenlunds' beds, but on the rug in the kitchen.

Then Anabella looks seriously at Joona and says that she's a very light sleeper, always has been since she was a girl and had to look after her younger brothers and sisters. In the early hours of Saturday morning she heard a sound in the stairwell and got frightened. She gathered her things together and crept into the hallway, and looked out through the peephole.

'The lift door was wedged open,' she says, but she didn't see anything. Then suddenly she heard noises, sighing, and slow footsteps. It was like an old, heavy person moving very slowly.

'But no voices?'

She shakes her head.

'Sombras.'

Anabella tries to describe how she saw shadows moving across the floor. Joona nods and asks:

'What did you see in the mirror? *Qué viste en el espejo?*'

'In the mirror?'

'You could see into the lift, Anabella,' Joona says.

Anabella thinks for a moment, then says slowly that she could see a yellow hand.

'And then,' she adds, 'after a little while I saw her face.'

'It was a woman?'

'*Sí, una mujer.*' Yes, it was a woman.

Anabella explains that the woman was wearing a wool hat that cast a shadow over her face, but for a few seconds she saw her cheek and mouth.

'*Sin duda era una mujer,*' Anabella repeats. There was no doubt that it was a woman.

'How old?'

She shakes her head. She doesn't know.

'The same age as you?'

'*Tal vez.*' Maybe.

'A bit older?' Joona asks.

She nods, then says that she doesn't know, she only saw the woman for a couple of seconds, and her face was mostly covered.

'*Y la boca de la señora?*' Joona says, illustrating what he means. How did the woman's mouth look?

'Happy.'

'She looked happy?'

'*Sí. Contenta.*'

Joona doesn't manage to get any sort of description. He asks about details, he tries rephrasing his questions, but Anabella has obviously said all she knows. He thanks her and Jarl Hammar for their help.

On his way back upstairs Joona calls Anja. She answers at once.

'Anja Larsson, National Crime.'

'Anja, have you found anything about Eva Blau?'

'I'm working on it, but you keep calling and interrupting me.'

'Sorry, but it really is urgent.'

'I know, I know. But I haven't got anything for you yet.'

'OK, call me as soon . . .'

'Stop nagging,' she says, and hangs up.

73

Wednesday morning, 16 December

Erik is sitting in the car next to Joona, blowing on the coffee in his paper cup. They drive past the university and the Natural History Museum. On the other side of the road, down towards the water of Brunnsviken, the greenhouses glint in the dim light.

'You're sure about the name? Eva Blau?' Joona asks.

'Yes.'

'There's nothing in any telephone directory, no criminal record, nothing in any police database, nothing with the Tax Office, the national population register, or even vehicle registrations. I've had all the regional and district records checked too, as well as the church, National Insurance, and the Immigration Office. There's no Eva Blau in Sweden, and there never has been.'

'She was a patient of mine,' Erik says insistently.

'Then she must have had another name.'

'I know perfectly well what my damn . . .'

He trails off and feels a fleeting suspicion that she could have had another name, but it vanishes.

'What were you going to say?' Joona asks.

'I'll go through my files. Maybe Eva Blau is just what she wanted to be called.'

The white winter sky is low and dense. It looks like it could start to snow at any moment.

Erik drinks some coffee and tastes sweetness, followed by a lingering bitterness. The car turns off towards a residential area in Täby. They drive slowly through the houses, past frosted yards with bare trees and small covered pools, glass greenhouses with wicker furniture, trampolines covered in snow, strings of coloured lights in fir trees, blue sleds and parked cars.

'Where are we going?' Erik asks.

Small, round flakes of snow start to swirl through the air, gathering next to the wiper blades.

'We're nearly there.'

'Nearly where?'

'I found a few other people with the last name Blau,' Joona replies with a smile.

He pulls in and stops by a garage, but leaves the engine running. In the middle of a lawn stands a two-metre-tall plastic Winnie-the-Pooh, with some of the paint missing from his red sweater. Apart from that there's no sign of any toys in the yard. A path of irregular slate tiles leads up to a large yellow wooden house.

'This is where Liselott Blau lives,' Joona says.

'Who's she?'

'No idea, but there's a chance she might know something about Eva.'

Joona sees the sceptical look on Erik's face and says:

'It's all we've got to go on right now.'

Erik shakes his head.

'It was such a long time ago, and I never think about those days.'

Erik looks straight at Joona's ice-grey eyes.

'Maybe this doesn't have anything to do with Eva Blau,' he says.

'Are you sure you remember everything?'

'I think so,' Erik says slowly, looking at his coffee.

'Really?'

'I don't know.'

'Do you know if she's dangerous, then, this Eva Blau?' Joona asks.

Erik looks out of the car window and sees that someone has

drawn sharp teeth and angry eyebrows on Winnie-the-Pooh. He drinks some more coffee and suddenly remembers the day he first heard the name Eva Blau.

It was eight thirty in the morning. The sun was shining through the windows. He had been on call all night and had slept in his office.

Ten years earlier, spring

The sun was shining in through the dusty windows. I had been on call all night. I felt tired, but still packed my sports bag. Lasse Ohlson had postponed our badminton match several times in recent weeks. He'd had too much to do, shuttling between hospitals, lecturing in London, and preparing to join the board, but the day before yesterday he had called and asked if I was ready.

'God, yes,' I had replied.

'So you're ready to get your arse kicked?' he said, but not in his usual lively tone.

Lasse Ohlson was already in the locker room when I got there. He looked up with a nervous expression.

'You're going to get beaten so badly you won't be able to sit down for a week,' he said, looking at me.

His hand was shaking as he closed his locker.

'You've had a lot on your plate,' I said.

'What? Yes, I have, it's been . . .'

He trailed off and sat down heavily on the bench.

'Are you OK?' I asked.

'Absolutely,' he replied. 'How about you?'

'I'm seeing the board on Friday.'

'Oh yes, your funding's up for renewal. It's always the same, isn't it?'

'I'm not really that worried,' I said. 'I mean, I think it's going well, my research is moving forward and I'm getting good results.'

'Frank Paulsson and I did our national service together, up in Boden. He's smart, and pretty open-minded, and he's on the board,' he said, standing up.

'Good,' I said quietly.

We left the changing room and Lasse took hold of my arm.

'Shall I give him a call and tell him that they simply have to support you?'

'Are we allowed to do that?' I asked.

'Definitely not, but what the hell?'

'Probably best to leave it alone,' I smiled.

'But you have to continue with your research.'

'It'll work out.'

'No one would know.'

I looked at him.

'Well, if you don't think it would do any harm . . .'

'I'll call Frank this evening.'

I nodded, and he gave me a pat on the back.

We walked out into the large hall.

'Would you be willing to take on one of my patients?' Lasse asked over the sound of squeaking shoes.

'What for?'

'I don't really have time for her,' he replied.

'I've already got a full list, I'm afraid,' I said.

'OK.'

I started to do warm-up exercises while we waited for a court to free up. Lasse was pacing up and down, then he ran a hand through his hair and cleared his throat.

'Eva Blau would probably suit your group,' he said. 'She's clinging onto an old trauma like you wouldn't believe.'

'I'd be only too happy to offer suggestions.'

'Suggestions?' he interrupted, and lowered his voice. 'To be honest, I'm at my wits' end.'

'Has something happened?' I asked.

'No, no, it's just . . . . I can't break through her defences.'

'Let me think about it,' I replied.

'Can't you just say you'll take her?'

Lasse jogged on the spot, then stopped and looked over towards the entrance to the hall, staring at the people coming in. He leaned back against the wall.

'I don't know, Erik, but it would be a hell of a relief if you'd take a look at Eva.'

He looked over at the court, where two young women were playing badminton. When one of them stumbled and missed a simple shot he scoffed and said:

'Women.'

I looked at my watch and rolled my shoulders. Lasse stood there biting his nails. His face looked older, thinner. Someone shouted outside the hall, and it startled him.

The women gathered their things and left the court, chatting as they walked off.

'Let's play,' I said.

'Erik, have I ever asked you to take on one of my patients?'

'No, it's just that I'm already full.'

'How about if I agree to be on call for you?' he said quickly, looking at me intently.

'That's a lot of work,' I replied. 'Is she dangerous?'

'What do you mean?' he asked with an uncertain smile, and started to pick at his racquet.

'Do you consider Eva Blau dangerous?'

He glanced over at the doors again.

'I don't know how to answer that,' he said quietly.

'Has she threatened you?'

'I mean, all patients of this sort have the potential to be dangerous. It can be hard to tell, but I'm sure you'd be able to handle her.'

'Probably,' I said.

'You'll take her?'

'Yes,' I replied.

Two days later there was a knock on the door. When I opened it Lasse Ohlson was standing in the hallway, several metres away from a woman in a white raincoat. Her face was thin and pointed, and she was wearing heavy pink and blue eye-shadow. She had a worried look in her eyes and her nose was red, as if she had a cold.

'This is Erik Maria Bark,' Lasse said. 'He's a very good doctor, much better than I'll ever be.'

'You're early,' I said.

'Is that OK?' he asked anxiously.

I nodded and asked them to come in.

'Erik, I'm afraid I don't have time,' he said quietly.

'It would be a good idea if you were here, though.'

'I know, but I've got to run. Call me any time, middle of the night, whenever. I'll always answer.'

He hurried away and Eva Blau followed me into my office, closed the door and then looked me in the eye.

'Is this yours?' she asked out of nowhere, holding out a porcelain elephant in her trembling hand.

'No, it's not mine,' I replied.

'But I saw the way you looked at it,' she said. 'You want it, don't you?'

I took a deep breath and asked:

'Why do you think I want it?'

'Don't you want it?'

'No.'

'Do you want this, then?' she asked, and pulled her dress up.

She wasn't wearing any underwear, and her pubic hair had been shaved off.

'Eva, don't do that,' I said.

'OK,' she said, her lips trembling nervously.

She was standing very close to me. Her clothes smelled strongly of vanilla.

'Shall we sit down?' I asked.

'On your lap?'

'You can sit on the sofa,' I said.

'On the sofa?'

'Yes.'

'You'd like that, wouldn't you?' she said, tossing her raincoat on the floor, then going over to the desk and sitting down on my chair.

'Would you like to tell me a bit about yourself?' I asked.

'What are you interested in?'

I wondered if she would allow herself to be hypnotised, or if she would resist.

'I'm not your enemy,' I explained calmly.

'No?'

She opened one of the desk-drawers.

'Don't do that,' I said.

She ignored me and rifled carelessly through my papers. I went over to her, removed her hand and closed the drawer, and said firmly:

'I asked you to stop.'

She looked at me defiantly and opened the drawer again. Without taking her eyes off me, she pulled out a bundle of papers and threw them on the floor.

'Stop it,' I said sternly.

Her lips started to tremble, and her eyes filled with tears.

'You hate me,' she whispered. 'I knew it, I knew you'd hate me, everyone hates me.'

She sounded frightened now.

'Eva,' I said gently. 'Don't worry, just sit down, you can borrow my chair if you like, or you can sit on the sofa.'

She nodded, stood up from the chair and walked over to the sofa. Then she quickly turned and said in a low voice:

'Can I touch your tongue?'

'No, you can't. Now sit down,' I said.

She sat down at last, but immediately started to fidget.

I noticed she was holding something in her hand.

'What have you got there?' I asked.

She quickly hid her hand behind her back.

'Come and have a look, if you dare,' she said, in a tone of frightened hostility.

I was feeling impatient, but forced myself to remain calm when I asked:

'Do you want to tell me why you've come to see me?'

She shook her head.

'What do you think?' I asked.

Her face twitched.

'Because I said I had cancer,' she whispered.

'Were you worried that you had cancer?'

'I thought he wanted me to have it,' she said.

'Lasse Ohlson?'

'They operated on my brain a couple of times. They sedated me and raped me while I was asleep.'

Her eyes met mine and she smiled briefly.

'So now I'm pregnant *and* lobotomised.'

'What do you mean?'

'That it's all good, because I really want kids, a son, a boy who can suckle my breast.'

She brought her hand round from behind her back and opened her clenched fist. Her hand was empty, and she turned it over several times.

'Do you want to examine my cunt?' she whispered.

I stood and walked towards the door, feeling like I needed an impartial observer. Eva got quickly to her feet.

'Sorry,' she said. 'Sorry. I'm just frightened you'll hate me. Please, don't hate me. I want to stay, I need help.'

'OK, calm down. I'm just trying to have a conversation with you. I'd like you to join my hypnosis group. Lasse explained that to you, right? He said you thought it was a good idea, that it was what you wanted.'

She nodded, then reached out her hand and knocked my coffee cup onto the floor.

'Sorry,' she said again.

Once Eva had left I picked up my papers from the floor and sat down at the desk. A gentle rain was falling outside the window, and I thought about Benjamin, who was on a field trip that day, and how Simone and I had both forgotten to pack his waterproof trousers.

I wondered if I should call his pre-school and ask them to let Benjamin stay inside. Every outing terrified me. I didn't even like the fact that he had to walk along several hallways and down two flights of steps to get to the cafeteria. In my mind's eye I saw him being shoved by boisterous children, someone opening a heavy door on him, or him tripping over the muddy shoes gathered around the hallway. Told myself I was doing all I could to protect him. I gave him his injections. The medicine would keep him from bleeding to death from a cut, but he was still so much more fragile than other children.

I remember the sunlight the following morning, the way it shone through the dark-grey curtains. Simone was lying asleep beside me, naked. Her mouth was half-open, her hair tangled, her shoulders and breasts covered with tiny pale freckles. Her arm had goose-bumps, so I pulled the covers over her. Benjamin coughed gently. I hadn't noticed he was there. He sometimes crept in at night and lay down on the mattress on the floor if he'd had a bad dream. I used to lie next to him, holding his hand until he went back to sleep.

I saw that it was six o'clock, rolled onto my side, closed my eyes and thought about how nice it would be if I could catch up on sleep.

'Daddy?' Benjamin whispered.

'Sleep a little longer,' I said quietly.

He sat up on the mattress, looked at me and said in his clear, high voice:

'Daddy, you were lying on top of Mummy last night.'

'Really?' I said, and felt Simone wake up beside me.

'Yes, you were under the covers and rocking on top of her,' he went on.

'That sounds silly,' I tried to say breezily.

'Hmm.'

Simone giggled and hid her head under the pillow.

'Maybe I was dreaming,' I said evasively.

Simone was shaking with laughter now.

'Were you dreaming that you were on a swing?'

'Well . . .'

Simone looked up with a wide smile.

'Go on, answer him,' she said seriously. 'Were you dreaming that you were on a swing?'

'Daddy?'

'I suppose I must have been.'

'But,' Simone went on, laughing again, 'why were you doing that, why were you lying on top of me when you . . .?'

'OK, time for breakfast,' I declared.

I saw Benjamin grimace when he stood up. Mornings were always the hardest. His joints had been inactive for several hours, and that could lead to spontaneous bleeding.

'How's it feel?'

Benjamin reached out to the wall to support himself.

'Hold on, little man, and I'll give you a massage,' I said.

Benjamin sighed and lay down on the bed, and let me carefully bend and stretch his joints.

'I don't want my injection,' he said in a sad voice.

'Not today, Benjamin, the day after tomorrow.'

'I don't want it, Daddy.'

'Think about poor Lasse who's got diabetes,' I said. 'He has injections every day.'

I finished massaging his arms and legs.

'Thank you, Daddy,' Benjamin said, and carefully stood up.

'Good boy.'

I hugged his thin body, but as usual held back from squeezing him too tightly.

'Can I watch *Pokémon*?' he asked.

'Ask Mummy,' I replied, and heard Simone call out 'Coward!' from the kitchen.

After breakfast I went and sat at Simone's desk in the study and called Lasse Ohlson. His secretary, Jennie Lagercrantz, answered. I made small-talk, then asked if I could have a word with Lasse.

'Just a moment,' she said.

If it wasn't already too late, I was going to ask him not to say anything about me to Frank Paulsson on the board.

There was a click, then I heard Jennie's voice again:

'I'm afraid Lasse can't take any calls right now.'

'Tell him it's me.'

'I already have,' she said tersely.

I hung up without another word and closed my eyes. I realised something wasn't right, that I had been tricked, and that Eva Blau was more trouble – and more dangerous – than Lasse Ohlson had let on.

'I can handle it,' I whispered to myself.

But then I started to worry that the delicate balance of my hypnotherapy group might be disturbed. I had put together a relatively small group of people whose backgrounds were extremely varied. I hadn't considered whether or not they would be easy to hypnotise. I wanted to allow them to develop their relationships not only with themselves, but also with each other. Many of them carried a lot of guilt that stopped them from functioning socially. They blamed themselves for the fact that they had been raped or abused. They had basically lost control of their lives.

During the most recent session the group had progressed to a new level. It took almost half an hour to put Marek Semiovic into a deep state of hypnosis. It was never easy with him. He was distracted and always put up resistance. And even when hypnotised, I felt I hadn't yet found the right way into his memories.

'A house? A field? A patch of forest?' I suggested.

'I don't know,' Marek replied, as usual.

'Because we need to start somewhere,' I said.

'Where, though?'

'Try to think of a place that you're going to have to go back to in order to understand the person you are now,' I said.

'The countryside around Zenica,' Marek said in a neutral voice. 'Zeničko-dobojski.'

'OK, good,' I said, writing it down. 'Do you know what happened there?'

'Everything happened there, in a large, dark wooden house, almost like a castle, a manor-house, with steep roofs and little towers and verandas . . .'

The group was concentrating now. They were all listening, they all understood that Marek had begun to open up.

'I was sitting in an armchair,' Marek says slowly. 'Or on some cushions. I was smoking Marlboros. There must have been hundreds of girls and women from my hometown who passed through.'

'Passed through?'

'Over the course of several weeks. They came in through

the main doors and were led up the big staircase to the bedrooms.'

'Is it a brothel?' Jussi asked in his thick Norrland accent.

'I don't know what happened there, I barely know anything,' Marek replied quietly.

'You never saw the rooms upstairs?' I asked.

He rubbed his face with his hands, then took a deep breath.

'There is one memory,' he said. 'I enter a small room, and see one of my teachers from high school. She's lying tied to a bed, naked, with bruises on her hips and thighs.'

'What happens?'

'I'm standing just inside the door with some sort of wooden stick in my hand, and . . . I don't remember more than that.'

'Try,' I said.

'It's vanished.'

'Are you sure?'

'I can't do any more now.'

'OK, you don't have to, that's enough,' I said.

'Hang on,' he said, then sat for a long time without saying anything.

He sighed, rubbed his face and stood up.

'Marek?'

'I don't remember anything,' he said in a shrill voice.

I took some notes and could feel Marek watching me.

'I don't remember, but everything happened in that damn house,' he said.

I looked at him and nodded.

'Everything I said – it's all in that wooden house.'

'The haunted house,' Lydia said from her seat next to him.

'Exactly, it was a haunted house,' he said.

I looked at the time. I would soon be presenting my work to the hospital's management team. I went over to the sink and rinsed my face, then I looked at myself in the mirror for a while, trying to smile, before I left the bathroom. As I locked the door of my office, a young woman stopped in the hallway just a few steps away from me.

'Erik Maria Bark?'

She had thick, dark hair pulled into a bun at the base of her neck, and when she smiled at me she had deep dimples in her cheeks. She was wearing a white lab coat and the name badge on her chest indicated that she was an intern.

'Maja Swartling,' she said, holding out her hand. 'I'm one of your greatest admirers.'

'Whatever for?' I asked with a smile.

She looked happy, and smelled of hyacinth and violets.

'I want to help you in your work,' she said without any preamble.

'In my work?'

She nodded and blushed heavily.

'Yes,' she said. 'It's incredibly exciting.'

'Sorry if I can't quite match your enthusiasm, but I'm not even sure there's going to be any more research,' I said.

'What do you mean?'

'My funding only runs until the end of the year.'

I thought about my upcoming meeting:

'It's great that you're interested in my work, and I'd love to discuss it with you. But right now I have an important meeting that I need to get to.'

Maja stepped out of the way.

'Oh God, sorry,' she said. 'I'm really sorry.'

'We can talk on the way to the lift,' I said, smiling at her.

She seemed nervous, and blushed again as she walked along beside me.

'Do you think you'll have any trouble getting more funding?' she asked anxiously.

Talking about my research was a fairly regular requirement, but I always found it difficult because I knew I would have to deal with the prejudice surrounding hypnosis.

'It's just that most people still think hypnosis is kind of flaky, and that makes it harder to present incomplete results.'

'But if you read all your reports, there's evidence of excellent progress even if it's too soon to publish anything.'

'You've read my reports?' I asked sceptically.

'There was quite a lot to read,' she replied drily.

We stopped in front of the lift doors.

'What do you think about engrams?' I probed.

'You mean the part about the patient with brain damage?'

'Yes,' I said, and tried to hide my surprise.

'Interesting,' she said. 'The way you challenge theories of how memory is spread through the brain.'

'Any thoughts?'

'Yes – you ought to do more research into the synapses and concentrate on the amygdala.'

'I'm impressed,' I said.

'You have to get more funding.'

'I know,' I said.

'What happens if they say no?'

'I'll have to wind down the programme and help the patients find other forms of treatment.'

'And the research?'

I shrugged.

'I might apply to other universities, if anyone would have me.'

'Do you have any enemies on the board?' she asked.

'I don't think so.'

She raised her hand and laid it gently on my arm as she smiled. Her blush deepened.

'You'll get the money, because your work is ground-breaking. They can't ignore that,' she said, and looked me in the eyes. 'If they can't see that, I'll come with you to whichever university you end up at.'

Suddenly I wondered if she was flirting with me. There was something about her soft, hoarse intonation. I glanced quickly at her name badge to make sure of her name: Maja Swartling, intern.

'Maja . . .'

'Don't just brush me off,' she whispered playfully. 'Erik Maria Bark.'

'We'll have to discuss this another time,' I said as the lift doors slid open.

Maja Swartling smiled, showing her dimples, put her hands together beneath her chin, and gave a deep, jokey bow.

'*Sawadee*,' she said softly.

I found myself smiling at the Thai greeting on the way up to the director's office. Annika Lorentzon was sitting, looking out of the window at the view across the Northern Cemetery and Haga Park.

'Nice,' I said.

Annika smiled calmly at me. She was suntanned and thin and smelled of expensive soap.

'Do you want any?' she asked, gesturing towards some bottles of water.

I shook my head and began to wonder where the board members were.

Annika stood up and said, as if she could read my mind:

'They're on their way, Erik. It's their sauna day.'

She gave a wry smile.

'One way to avoid having me at meetings. Smart, don't you think?'

At that moment five men with bright red faces came in the door. The collars of their suits were damp, their hair was wet, and they radiated heat and aftershave.

The conversation petered out as they made their way in.

I stood perfectly still for a moment and watched them. These people held the future of my research in their hands. It was remarkable.

The board members shuffled in their seats. Annika looked up, smiled, and said:

'All yours, Erik.'

I took a breath and thought about my patients. I wanted to unlock their memories and help them move on, and I needed this funding.

'My method,' I began, 'concerns the treatment of mental trauma with group-based hypnotherapy.'

'We'd figured that out for ourselves,' Ronny said.

I tried to give a summary of what I'd done so far. My audience listened distractedly.

'I'm afraid I have an appointment,' Rainer said after a while, and stood up.

He shook hands with a couple of the men, then left the room.

'You've already had the material in advance,' I went on. 'I appreciate that it's fairly comprehensive, but it seemed important not to omit anything.'

'Why not?' Mälarstedt asked.

'Because it's a little too early to draw any conclusions,' I explained.

'So, if we look ahead two years,' he said.

'It's hard to say, but I can see patterns emerging,' I replied, even though I knew I shouldn't get into this.

'Patterns? What sort of patterns?'

'Would you like to tell us what you're hoping to achieve?' Annika asked with a smile.

'I'm hoping to identify the mental barriers that linger even during hypnosis, the way the brain will find new ways to protect the individual from buried trauma even in a state of deep relaxation. I also believe – and this is the really exciting thing – that when a patient approaches the core of a trauma . . . When the suppressed memory finally starts to surface during hypnosis, the patient tries to preserve the secret, and then – I have begun to suspect – starts to draw material from dreams into their memories, in order to avoid confrontation.'

'To avoid having to confront the situation itself?' Ronny asked with sudden curiosity.

'Yes, in part, but mainly to avoid the perpetrator,' I replied. 'The perpetrator can be replaced by anything, but I've found animals to be the most common substitutes.'

Silence descended on the room.

I could see how Annika, who thus far had mostly looked embarrassed on my behalf, was smiling quietly to herself.

'How clear is this pattern?' Mälarstedt asked.

'Clear, but not definite,' I replied.

'Is there any other similar research being conducted internationally?' He wanted to know.

'No,' Ronny replied curtly.

'What I'd like to know,' Holstein said, 'is, if that is the case, then what's your considered opinion? Will the patient always find something else to hide behind in hypnosis?'

'Is it possible to get past this?' Mälarstedt asked.

I could feel my cheeks starting to flush as I cleared my throat slightly and replied:

'I think it's possible to get behind those images with deeper hypnosis.'

'What about the patients?'

'Yes, I was wondering about them too,' Mälarstedt said to Annika.

'All of this is obviously pretty damn appealing,' Holstein said. 'But I want guarantees . . . There can be no psychosis, no suicides.'

'Yes, but . . .'

'Can you promise that?' he interrupted.

'My priority is to help my patients,' I said.

'And the research?'

'That's . . .'

I cleared my throat.

'That's still a by-product,' I said quietly. 'That's how I have to look at it.'

Some of the men round the table exchanged glances.

'Good answer,' Paulson said, out of nowhere. 'I give Erik Maria Bark my full backing.'

'I'm still concerned about the patients,' Holstein said.

'It's all in here,' Paulson said, pointing at the folder. 'He's written about this, patient development, and it looks more than merely promising.'

'It's just that it's such an unorthodox form of therapy, so audacious, that we have to be sure we can defend it if anything were to go wrong.'

'I'm confident that I can avoid any serious negative consequences,' I said, and felt a shiver run down my spine.

'Erik, it's Friday and everyone wants to go home,' Annika said. 'I think you can count on continued funding.'

The others nodded in agreement, and Ronny leaned back and clapped his hands together.

Simone was standing in the kitchen when I got home. She was emptying four bags of groceries onto the table: bundles of asparagus, fresh marjoram, chicken, lemon, jasmine rice. When she saw me she laughed.

'What is it?' I asked.

She shook her head, then said with a wide smile:

'You should see yourself.'

'What?'

'You look like a little kid on Christmas Eve.'

'That obvious?'

'Benjamin,' she called.

Benjamin came into the kitchen with a box of medication in his hand. Simone did her best to look serious and pointed at me.

'Look,' she said. 'How does Daddy look?'

Benjamin looked me in the eye and started to smile.

'You look happy, Daddy.'

'I am, little man, I am.'

'Have they found the medicine?' he asked.

'What?'

'To make me better, so I don't have to have any more injections,' he said.

I picked him up and hugged him and explained that they hadn't found that medicine yet, but that I hoped they soon would, more than anything.

'OK,' he said.

I put him back down on the floor and saw the thoughtful look on Simone's face.

Benjamin tugged at my trouser leg.

'So what is it, then?' he asked.

'What?' I said.

'Why are you so happy, Daddy?'

'It's just work,' I said. 'I've been given money for my research.'

'David says you're a magician.'

'I'm not a magician. I hypnotise people who are sad and afraid to make them feel better.'

Simone let Benjamin run his hand through the sprigs of marjoram and sniff them before she turned to me:

'I'm signing the contract tomorrow.'

'Wow! Why didn't you say anything? Congratulations!'

She laughed.

'And I know just who I want for the first exhibition,' she said. 'A girl who went to Art College in Bergen, she's brilliant, does these big . . .'

Simone stopped talking when the doorbell rang. She tried to see who it was through the kitchen window before she went and opened the door.

'Who was it?' I asked.

'No one. There's no one here,' she said.

I looked out at the bushes over by the road.

'What's this?' she suddenly said.

On the doorstep lay a stick with a handle at one end and a small wooden plate at the other.

'That's odd,' I said, picking up the old implement.

'What on earth is it?'

'I think it's a rod. People used to use them to discipline children.'

The window of the therapy room was open, and I felt the fresh, mild spring breeze on my face. It was time for a session with the hypnotherapy group. They'd be there in ten minutes. The six usual members and Eva.

I grabbed my pad and read through my notes from the previous session a week before, when Marek had talked about the big wooden house in the countryside outside Zenica-Doboj.

It was Charlotte's turn to start, and then I thought I might have a try with Eva.

I arranged the chairs in a semi-circle, and positioned the video-camera stand as far away as possible.

Charlotte Cederskiöld came in. She was wearing a dark-blue trenchcoat with a wide belt pulled tight around her narrow waist. When she pulled off her hat her curly chestnut hair fell around her face. As always, she looked very sad.

When I turned round Jussi Persson had also arrived.

'Doctor,' he said in his soothing Norrland accent.

We shook hands and then he went and said hello to Sibel. He patted his beer belly and said something that made her blush and giggle. They talked quietly while the rest of the group arrived: Lydia, Pierre, and Marek, who was slightly late as usual.

I stood and waited for them to settle down. They were all different, but they had one common denominator: traumatic abuse. None of them was entirely aware of what had happened to them, they just knew that whatever the terrible thing that had happened in the past was, it was wrecking their lives.As Faulkner said: 'The past is never dead. It's not even past.' Every little thing that a human being has experienced comes with them into the present. Every experience influences every choice – and when it comes to traumatic experiences, the past takes up almost all of the available space.

They were ready to start, but Eva Blau had not yet arrived. I glanced at the clock and decided to begin without her.

Charlotte always sat at the end. She had taken her coat off and was, as usual, very elegantly dressed. When our eyes met she smiled cautiously. By the time I brought Charlotte into the group, she had already made fifteen attempts on her own life. The last time she tried, she shot herself in the head with her husband's elk-hunting rifle, in the middle of their villa out in Djursholm. The rifle slipped and the bullet grazed one ear and part of her cheek instead. There was no sign of it now: she'd been through a couple of operations, and had changed her hairstyle to hide her false ear and hearing aid.

Whenever I saw Charlotte tilt her head and listen politely to the others' stories, I was reminded of how beautiful she was, and how badly broken.

'Are you sitting comfortably, Charlotte?' I asked.

She nodded and replied in her soft, articulate voice:

'I'm fine, just fine.'

'Today we're going to explore Charlotte's inner rooms,' I explained.

'My haunted house,' she smiled.

'Exactly.'

Marek grinned mirthlessly and impatiently at me when our eyes met.

'I suggest we begin,' I said.

The initial relaxation was followed by induction, where their desires and boundaries were dissolved. Slowly I guided them into a trance, conjuring up images of a wet wooden staircase that I was leading them down.

A familiar, special energy began to flow between us, bringing a unique warmth. My voice was focused and precise at first, then became slowly more relaxed. Jussi seemed anxious, he was humming and wiped his mouth hard from time to time. I watched their bodies settle on their chairs, their faces relax and take on that vacant look that people have under hypnosis.

I walked behind them, rested my hand gently on each shoulder, all the while counting backwards, guiding them step by step.

Marek Semiovic's mouth was open, and a dribble of saliva hung from one corner.

Pierre looked thinner and weaker than ever.

Lydia's arms were hanging outside the armrests of her chair.

'Keep going down the steps,' I said in a low voice.

I hadn't told the hospital board that the hypnotist also entered a trance-like state. I wasn't sure they'd understand.

I had never completely understood why my own trance, the one which ran in parallel with the patients', always played out underwater. But I liked the aquatic imagery, it was pleasant and I had learned to read the situation quite effectively.

While I sank into the ocean, my patients were seeing completely different things as they drifted into their own memories, ending up wherever their trauma had occurred. They didn't know that to me they were all deep underwater, slowly falling beside some vast coral formation or the edge of a continental shelf.

This time I wanted to try taking them with me into a fairly deep state of hypnosis. My voice was counting down, talking about the pleasures of relaxation.

'I want you to sink just a little further,' I said. 'Keep going down, but more slowly now. Soon you'll come to a halt, very gently . . . a little bit deeper, and now we're going to stop.'

In my mind's eye, the whole group were standing in a semicircle in front of me on a sandy seabed. Flat and even, like a vast floor. The water was bright, with a greenish tint. The sand beneath our feet lay in gentle, regular waves. Some jellyfish sparkled as they drifted past above us. Every now and then fish would stir the sand up, then dart away.

'We're all deep down now,' I said.

They opened their eyes and looked at me.

'Charlotte, today it's your turn to begin,' I went on. 'What can you see? Where are you?'

Her mouth moved soundlessly.

'There's nothing here that can hurt you,' I said. 'We're all here with you.'

'I know,' she said in a monotone.

Her eyes were neither open nor closed. They looked like a sleepwalker's, blank and distant.

'You're standing outside the door,' I said. 'Do you want to go in?'

She nodded and her hair swirled above her head with the current of the water.

'Do it now,' I said.

'Yes.'

'What can you see?' I went on.

'I don't know.'

'Have you gone inside?' I asked, even though I had the sense I was going too fast.

'Yes.'

'But you can't see anything?'

'I can.'

'Is it anything unusual?'

'I don't know, I don't think . . .'

'Describe it,' I said quickly.

She shook her head and tiny, sparkling bubbles of air came free from her hair and rose up towards the surface. I was aware that I was doing it wrong. I wasn't listening properly. I wasn't guiding her – I was trying to nudge her forward, but I still couldn't help saying:

'You're back in your grandfather's house.'

'Yes,' she replied in a muted voice.

'You're already standing inside the door, and you keep walking forward.'

'I don't want to.'

'Just one step.'

'Maybe not right now,' she whispered.

'You take a look around.'

'I don't want to.'

Her bottom lip was trembling.

'Can you see anything unusual?' I asked. 'Anything that shouldn't be there?'

A frown appeared on her face, and I realised that she was about to emerge suddenly from her hypnotic state. That could be dangerous. She could end up in a deep depression if it happened too fast.

'You don't have to do it, Charlotte, you don't have to look,' I said soothingly. 'You can open the glass doors and go out into the garden if you like.'

Her body was shaking, and I realised it was too late.

'Stay nice and relaxed,' I whispered, and reached one hand out towards her.

Her lips were white, her eyes wide-open.

'Charlotte, we're going to go back up to the surface together, nice and slowly,' I said.

Her feet kicked up a little cloud of sand as she floated upwards.

'Wait,' I said gently.

Marek was looking at me, trying to shout something.

'We're already on our way up, and I'm going to count to ten,' I went on as we rose quickly towards the surface. 'And when I finish counting to ten, you'll open your eyes and you'll feel absolutely fine, and . . .'

Charlotte gasped for breath and stood up unsteadily.

'Let's take a short break,' I said.

The re-emergence had been far too rapid. I remained on my chair, rubbed my face and was making a few notes when Marek came over.

'Nice work,' he said with a wry smile.

'It wasn't quite what I had in mind,' I replied.

'I thought it was funny,' he said.

Lydia came over, her jewellery rattling. Her reddish hair shone like copper when she walked through a ray of sunlight.

'What?' I asked. 'Which part did you think was funny?'

'You putting that upper-class whore in her place.'

'What did you say?' Lydia asked, before I could comment.

'I'm not talking about you, I meant . . .'

'You can't say Charlotte's a whore, because it isn't true,' Lydia said gently. 'Is it, Marek?'

'OK, what the hell.'

I moved away, looked down at my notes, but went on listening to their conversation.

'Do you have a problem with women?' she went on.

'You can't understand if you weren't there . . . Things happened in the haunted house.'

'There's really nothing wrong now, Marek,' she said, taking his hand in hers.

Sibel and Pierre came back in. Everyone was quiet and subdued. Charlotte looked very fragile. Her thin arms were folded across her chest, with her hands on her shoulders.

I changed the cassette in the video-camera, quickly stated the date and time, then explained that everyone was still in a post-hypnotic state.

'Come and sit down, now. Let's continue,' I said.

There was a knock on the door and Eva Blau walked in. She looked stressed, so I went over to her.

'Welcome,' I said.

'Am I?' she asked.

'Yes,' I replied.

Eva sat down on the empty chair and squeezed her hands between her thighs. I went back to my place and cautiously began the second part of the session.

'Make sure you're sitting comfortably with your feet on the ground and your hands in your lap. The first part didn't quite turn out the way I'd imagined.'

'I'm sorry,' Charlotte said.

'No one needs to apologise, least of all you – I hope you know that.'

Eva was staring intently at me.

'We're going to start with thoughts and associations raised by the first part of the session,' I said. 'Does anyone have any comments?'

'Confusing,' Sibel said.

'Frustrating,' Jussi said. 'I mean, I only had time to open my eyes and scratch my head before it was over.'

'What did you feel?' I asked him.

'Hair,' he replied.

'Hair?' Sibel asked, then giggled.

'When I scratched my head,' Jussi explained.

Some of them laughed at the joke.

'Give me some associations around hair,' I said with a smile. 'Charlotte?'

'I don't know,' she said. 'Hair? Beards, maybe . . . no.'

'A hippie, a hippie on a motorbike,' Pierre goes on, smiling. 'Sitting like this, chewing Juicy Fruit and riding . . .'

Eva got to her feet so abruptly that her chair scraped the floor behind her.

'This is childish,' she said.

Pierre's smile faded.

'Why do you think that?' I asked.

Eva didn't answer, and just stared at me before sullenly sitting back down.

'Pierre, would you like to go on?' I asked calmly.

He shook his head, crossed his index fingers and held them up towards Eva, and pretended to be taking cover from her.

'They shot Dennis Hopper because he was a hippie,' he whispered conspiratorially.

Sibel giggled even louder and glanced at me expectantly. Jussi raised his hand and turned towards Eva.

'You won't have to put up with our childishness in the haunted house,' he said in his thick accent.

I realised that Eva had no idea what the haunted house meant to the group, but let it pass.

Eva turned towards Jussi and looked like she was about to yell at him, but he just looked back at her with such a calm, serious face that she stopped herself and changed position on her chair.

‘Eva, we’re going to start with some breathing and relaxation exercises, then I’ll hypnotise the group, one or two of you at a time,’ I explained.

‘Your feet should be flat on the floor, your hands on your lap.’

As I gently led them into hypnosis, it occurred to me that I should start by exploring Eva Blau’s secret room. It was important that she contribute something early on, to be accepted into the group. I started to count down, and listened to the group’s breathing, guiding them into a state of mild hypnosis, then leaving them floating just below the silvery surface of the water.

‘Eva, now I’m only talking to you,’ I said gently. ‘You can feel safe and relaxed, and listen to my voice and follow my instructions. Keep doing what I say, without questioning anything – you’ll find yourself inside the stream of words, not before or after, but always right in the middle . . .’

We sank through the grey water. I glimpsed the rest of the group floating with the tops of their heads just below the rippling mirror. We drifted down into the dark depths along a thick rope festooned with billowing strands of seaweed.

Simultaneously, in the real world I was standing behind Eva Blau’s chair with one hand resting on her shoulder as I went on talking, calmly and soothingly. Her hair smelled like smoke. She was sitting back in her chair, and her face was relaxed.

In my mind’s eye the water in front of her was shifting between brown and grey. Her face was in shadow, there was a sharp frown between her eyebrows, and her eyes were completely dark. I wondered how to begin. I really didn’t know much about her at all. Lasse Ohlson’s notes included very little about her background. I would have to explore it for myself, and I decided to try the gentle approach first. It often seemed that happy, calm memories were the shortest route to the very worst experiences.

‘You’re ten years old, Eva,’ I said, walking round the chairs so I could see her from the front.

Her chest was barely moving, she was breathing softly from deep in her stomach.

'You're ten years old. This is a good day. You're happy. Why are you happy?'

Eva pouted her lips, smiled to herself and said:

'Because the man is dancing and jumping in the puddles.'

'Who's dancing?'

She doesn't speak for a moment.

'Mum says it's Gene Kelly.'

'So you're watching *Singin' in the Rain*?' I said.

'Mum is.'

'Not you?' I asked.

'I am too,' she smiled, screwing her eyes up.

'And you're happy?'

Eva nodded her head slowly.

'What's happening?'

I saw her face slowly sink towards her chest. Suddenly she made a very odd face.

'My tummy's big,' she said very quietly.

'Your tummy?'

'I think it's really big,' she said, her voice catching in her throat.

Jussi let out a deep sigh beside her. From the corner of my eye I saw his lips moving.

'The haunted house,' he whispered in his state of mild hypnosis. 'The haunted house.'

'Eva, listen to me,' I said. 'You can hear everyone else in the room, but my voice is the only one you should listen to. Don't worry about what anyone else says, my voice is the only one you need to pay attention to.'

'OK.'

'Why is your tummy big?' I asked.

'I want to go into the haunted house,' she whispered.

Something didn't seem right as I counted backwards and talked about the flight of steps leading further down. I was surrounded by warm water as I slowly drifted down the side of the rock-face, deeper and deeper.

Eva raised her head, licked her lips, sucked her cheeks in, and then whispered:

'I see them take someone, they just go up and take someone . . .'

'Who is it that's taking someone?' I asked.

Her breathing became irregular, her face darker. Brown water swirled hazily in front of her.

'A man with a ponytail,' she moans. 'He's hanging the little person from the ceiling . . .' she moaned.

In my hypnotic state, I could see she was clutching onto the seaweed-covered rope with one hand, and her legs were kicking slowly.

With a lurch I was dragged out of the hypnosis. I knew Eva was bluffing, she wasn't really hypnotised. I didn't understand how I could know that, but I was absolutely certain. She had fended off my words and blocked my suggestions. I saw her rocking anxiously back and forth on her chair.

'The man is pulling and pulling at the little person, he's pulling too hard . . .'

Suddenly Eva looked me straight in the eye and stopped. A grin slowly spread across her face.

'Was I good?' she asked me.

I didn't answer, just stood there and watched as she got up, took her coat from the hook and walked calmly out of the room.

I wrote *HAUNTED HOUSE* on a sheet of paper, wrapped it around videotape number 14 and fastened it with a rubber-band. Instead of archiving the cassette as usual, I took it back to my room. I still wanted to analyse Eva Blau's lies, and my own reaction, but I had realised what had clued me in before I reached the hallway: Eva had been aware of her face, she had tried to look cute. She didn't have the slack, unaffected expression that hypnotised people always get. Someone in a hypnotic state can smile – but not their usual smile. They have a sleepy, loose smile instead.

When I reached my office the young medical student was waiting outside my door. I was surprised that I remembered her name: Maja Swartling.

We said hello and before I'd had time to unlock the door she said quickly:

'Sorry to bother you. But I'm basing part of my dissertation on your research, and my supervisor has suggested that I talk to you since you're the subject of the chapter. Is it OK if I ask you some questions?' she asked. 'Would you mind?'

She looked at me.

She had very dark eyes, emphasised by her unusually pale skin. Her braided hair shone. The old-fashioned style suited her.

'Would that be OK?' she asked quietly. 'I should warn you, I can be very persistent.'

I realised I was standing there smiling at her. There was something so fresh and bright about her that without really thinking about it I held my hands out and told her to fire away. She laughed. I unlocked the door and she followed me in, and sat down on the visitor's chair. She took out a notepad and a pen.

'So, what do you want to ask me?'

Maja blushed.

'I've read your reports,' she said. 'And your group doesn't only contain victims, people who have been subjected to abuse, but also perpetrators, people who have subjected other people to terrible things.'

'Their subconscious is actually affected in a similar way, and in a group therapy situation, it's actually an advantage.'

'Interesting,' she said, taking notes. 'I'd like to come back to that, but I'm wondering how perpetrators see themselves when under hypnosis – I mean, you advance the theory that victims often replace perpetrators with something else, in most instances an animal.'

'I haven't yet had time to fully examine how a perpetrator sees himself in those circumstances, and I wouldn't like to speculate.'

Maja leaned forward, pursed her lips and asked:

'But you have an idea?'

'I have one patient . . .'

I fell silent and started to think about Jussi Persson, the Norrlander who carried his loneliness as a terrible, self-imposed burden.

'What were you going to say?'

'Under hypnosis, this patient goes back to a hunting tower,

it's as if his rifle is in control of him, he shoots deer and just leaves them lying where they fall.'

We both stopped talking and looked at each other.

'Well, it's getting late,' I said.

'I've still got a lot of questions.'

I held my hand up.

'We'll have to meet up again.'

She looked at me. I felt a sudden warmth in my body. The atmosphere between us was oddly playful.

'Can I get you a drink as a way of thanking you? There's a good Lebanese place . . .'

The phone started to ring. I apologised and picked it up.

'Erik?'

It was Simone. She sounded stressed.

'What is it?' I asked.

'I . . . I'm around the back of the house, on the bike path. It looks like someone's broken into our house.'

A shiver ran through me. I thought about the rod that had been left outside the front door.

'What's happened?'

I heard Simone swallow hard. Some children were playing in the background, possibly over on the football field. I could hear a whistle, and shouting.

'What was that?' I asked.

'Nothing, just some schoolkids,' she said quickly. 'Erik, the door to Benjamin's balcony is open, and the window's been smashed.'

From the corner of my eye I saw Maja Swartling stand up and mime that she was leaving.

I nodded to her with an apologetic shrug. She bumped into her chair, which scraped on the floor.

'Are you with someone?' Simone asked.

'No,' I said, without knowing why I was lying.

Maja waved and closed the door quietly behind her. I could still smell her perfume, a simple, fresh fragrance.

'It's good that you haven't gone inside,' I said. 'Have you called the police?'

'Erik, you sound funny, did something happen?'

'Apart from the fact that there might be a burglar in our house? Have you called the police?'

'Yes, I called Dad.'

'Good.'

'He said he'd come over right away.'

'You need to move further away, Simone.'

'I'm standing on the bike path.'

'Can you see the house?'

'Yes.'

'If you can see the house, then anyone inside the house can see you.'

'Stop it,' she said.

'Please, just go up to the football field – I'm on my way.'

I parked behind Kennet's dirty Opel. Kennet came running towards me. His face looked stern.

'Where the hell is Simone?' he shouted.

'I told her to wait over at the football field.'

'Good, I was worried . . .'

'She'd have gone inside otherwise. I know her, she takes after you.'

He laughed and gave me a hug.

'It's good to see you!'

We walked around to the back of the house. Simone was close to the yard. She had probably been keeping an eye on the broken balcony door the whole time. She looked up, let go of her bicycle, came over and hugged me tight, then looked over my shoulder and said:

'Hi, Dad.'

'I'm going in,' he said.

'I'll come with you,' I said.

'Women and children have to wait outside,' Simone sighed.

The three of us climbed over the low hedge and walked across the grass to the deck with its white plastic table and chairs.

The step, the windowsill, and Benjamin's room were all covered with broken glass. There was a large stone lying on the carpet. We continued inside, and I realised I'd forgotten to tell Kennet about the rod we'd found.

Simone followed us, and switched on the Astrid Lindgren lamp hanging from the ceiling. Her face was flushed, and her strawberry-blonde hair lay curled across her shoulders.

Kennet went out into the hallway and looked into the bedroom on the right and then the bathroom. The reading light in the television room was on. One of the chairs in the kitchen was lying on the floor. Nothing was missing, but something seemed off. Someone had used the downstairs toilet, the toilet paper had been pulled out across the floor. Kennet looked at me with a confused expression.

'Can you think of anyone who would do this?' he asked.

'Not that I know of,' I said. 'Mind you, I do meet a lot of unstable people, just like you.'

He nodded.

'They haven't taken anything,' I said.

'Dad, is that common?' Simone asked.

Kennet shook his head.

'No, it's not common, not if you've smashed a window. Someone wanted you to know that he or she has been here.'

Simone was standing in the doorway to Benjamin's room.

'It looks like someone's been lying on his bed,' she said in a low voice. 'Like that fairytale, which one is it? Goldilocks.'

We hurried into our bedroom and saw that someone had been lying on our bed too. The bedspread had been pulled back and the sheet crumpled.

'This is weird,' Kennet said.

None of us spoke for a while.

'That thing we found,' Simone exclaimed.

'Of course,' I said, and went into the hall to get the rod from the coat rack.

'What the hell is that?' Kennet asked.

'It was lying outside the front door yesterday,' Simone said.

'Let me see,' Kennet said.

'I think it's a rod,' I said. 'The sort of thing people used to beat children back in the day.'

'Good for discipline,' Kennet said, weighing it in his hand.

'I don't like this at all, it feels really unsettling,' Simone said.
'Has anyone threatened you in any other way?'
'No,' she replied.
'Maybe that's how we should look at this,' I said. 'Someone thinks we need to be punished. I thought it was a bad joke about us babying Benjamin. I mean, if you don't know about Benjamin's illness, we probably look a bit neurotic.'

That evening we put Benjamin to bed early. I lay next to him, as usual, telling him the story of a film about an African boy, called *Kirikou*. Benjamin had seen it many times, but that was the story he almost always wanted me to tell him when he went to bed. If I forgot any of the details he would remind me, and if he was still awake at the end, Simone would come and sing lullabies.

After he'd fallen asleep, Simone and I made a pot of tea and sat on the sofa talking about the break-in.

'Maybe they were teenagers who wanted somewhere to have sex,' Simone said.

'No, they'd have made more of a mess.'

'Isn't it weird that none of the neighbours noticed anything? Adolfsson doesn't miss much.'

'Maybe it was him?' I suggested.

'Having sex on our bed?'

I laughed and pulled her closer. I loved how good she smelled. She was wearing my favourite scent, Aromatics Elixir, strange and heavy, but not cloying or sweet. She cuddled up against me, and I felt her slender body against mine. I let my hands slip inside her loose blouse, across her soft skin. Her breasts were warm, hard. She moaned when I kissed her neck, and I felt her breath in my ear.

We got undressed by the light of the television, helping each other with urgent, searching hands, fumbling and laughing. She led me to the bedroom and pushed me back onto the bed with playful sternness.

'Is it time for the rod now?' I asked.

She nodded and came closer, then bent her neck and let her hair brush across my legs, smiling as she made her way up my body. Her curly hair tumbled forward over her thin, freckled arms. Her muscles tensed as she sat astride my hips. Her cheeks turned bright red when I entered her.

A memory flitted briefly through my mind, of some photographs I had once taken on a beach in Greece. It was a couple of years before Benjamin was born. We had taken a bus along the coast and got off somewhere we liked the look of. Once we realised that the beach was deserted we didn't bother with bathing suits. We ate warm watermelon in the sun and lay naked in the clear, shallow water, caressing and kissing each other. We made love something like four times that day on the beach, getting hotter and more relaxed each time. Simone's hair was tangled from the salt water, the look on her face sultry, with a secretive smile. Her small, pert breasts, her freckles, her pale pink nipples. Her flat stomach, navel, her reddish-brown pubic hair.

Simone leaned forward across me, and started to chase her orgasm. She thrust back, kissed my chest, my neck. She began to breathe faster, closed her eyes, held my shoulders tight and whispered to me.

'Please, Erik, keep going, don't stop . . .'

Simone moved faster, heavier, her back and buttocks wet with perspiration. She was moaning loudly, still thrusting backwards, again and again, then she stopped, her thighs trembling, before carrying on, whimpering as she slowed to a halt, gasped for breath, licked her lips, and rested one hand on my chest.

I parked my bicycle outside the Neurology Department, then stood for a moment listening to the birds in the trees and looking at the spring colour among the branches. It hadn't been long since I'd woken up next to Simone.

My office looked exactly as I had left it the day before. The chair that Maja Swartling had sat on when she interviewed me was still pulled out, and the lamp on the desk was on. It was only eight thirty, so I had plenty of time to go through my notes from the previous day's failed hypnotherapy session with Charlotte. I knew it had ended badly because I had forced the pace and had been aiming for a particular target. It was a classic mistake, and I should have known better. It didn't work if you tried to force a patient to see something he or she absolutely didn't want to see. Charlotte had gone into the room, but hadn't wanted to look up. And that should have been enough for that session.

I changed into my lab coat, disinfected my hands and thought about my group. I wasn't entirely happy with Pierre's role in the group, which felt a little unfocused. He often followed Sibel or Lydia's lead. He was talkative and amusing, but he remained very passive during the hypnosis itself. He was a hairdresser, gay, and wanted to be an actor. Superficially, he seemed to lead a highly functional life – apart from one detail. Every Easter he would go on a vacation with his mother. There they would shut themselves away in their hotel room, get drunk, and have sex. Pierre ended up in a severe depression after each trip, and had tried to commit suicide a number of times.

There was a knock on the door. Before I had time to answer, it swung open and Eva Blau walked in. She made a strange face at me, as if she was trying to smile without moving any facial muscles.

'No, thanks,' she said out of nowhere. 'You don't have to ask me to dinner, I've already eaten. Charlotte's a lovely person, she cooks for me, portions for a whole week. I keep them in the freezer.'

'That's nice of her,' I said.

'She's buying my silence, obviously,' Eva said cryptically, standing behind the chair where Maja had been sitting the day before.

'Eva, do you want to tell me why you're here?'

'Not to suck your cock, just so you know.'

'You don't have to keep coming to the hypnotherapy group if you don't want to,' I said calmly.

She lowered her eyes.

'I knew you hated me,' she mumbled.

'No, Eva, I'm just saying that you don't have to be part of the group. Some people aren't particularly receptive to hypnosis, and some . . .'

'You hate me,' she interrupted.

'I'm just saying that I can't have you in the group if you really don't want to be hypnotised.'

'I didn't mean it,' she said. 'But you mustn't stick your cock in my mouth.'

'Stop that,' I said.

'Sorry,' she whispered, and pulled something from her bag. 'Look, you can have this as a gift from me.'

She handed me a photograph of Benjamin from the day he was christened.

'Sweet, isn't it?' she said proudly.

I felt my heart start to beat fast and hard.

'Where did you get this?' I asked.

'That's my little secret.'

'Answer me, Eva. Where did you get . . .'

She cut me off in a teasing tone of voice:

'Mind your own business and don't cause strife – then you'll have a happy life.'

I looked at the photograph again. It was taken from Benjamin's photo album. I recognised it. On the back were the remains of the glue we had used to stick it in the book. I forced myself to stay calm.

'I want you to tell me how you got this picture.'

She sat down on the sofa, slowly unbuttoned her blouse and showed me her breasts.

'Stick your cock in, then, if it'll make you happy.'

'You've been in my home,' I said.

'You've been in my home,' she replied defiantly. 'You made me open the door . . .'

'Eva, I was trying to hypnotise you. That's not the same thing as breaking into someone's house.'

'I didn't break in,' she retorted quickly.

'You broke a window . . .'

'The stone broke the window.'

I felt drained, and realised I was on the point of losing my temper and reacting angrily towards a sick and confused person.

'Why did you take this picture from me?'

'You're the one who's always taking! You take and take and

take! How the hell would you like it if I started taking things from you? How do you think that would feel?'

She hid her face in her hands and said she hated me. She repeated it over and over again, maybe a hundred times before she calmed down.

'You have to understand that you make me angry,' she said in a composed voice. 'When you say I take things. And when I've just given you such a nice picture, too.'

Her face broke into a wide smile and she licked her lips.

'You got something from me,' she went on. 'Now I want something from you.'

'What do you want?' I asked calmly.

'Don't try anything,' she said.

'Just tell me . . .'

'I want you to hypnotise me,' she replied.

'Why did you leave a rod outside my front door?' I asked.

She just stared at me.

'What's a rod?'

'You use them to beat children,' I said tersely.

'I didn't leave anything outside your door.'

'You left an old . . .'

'Don't lie!' she yelled.

She got up and walked to the door.

'Eva, I will tell the police if you can't understand where the boundaries are, if you don't realise that you have to leave me and my family alone.'

'What about my family?' she asked.

'Listen to me!'

'Fascist pig!' she shouted, and walked out.

My patients were sitting in a semi-circle in front of me. It had been easy to hypnotise them this time. I watched us descend through the lapping water, and then I continued working on Charlotte. Her face looked so sad in its relaxed state, the dark rings under her eyes, the little wrinkles on the tip of her chin.

I waited. It was clear that Charlotte was in a state of deep hypnosis now. She was breathing heavily but calmly.

'You know you're safe with us, Charlotte,' I said. 'Nothing can hurt you, you're fine, and you're feeling nice and relaxed.'

She nodded and I knew she could hear me, that she was following my instructions without being able to differentiate the hypnosis from the outside world.

'Don't be angry,' she whispered. 'Sorry. Please, I'm sorry. I'll make it better, I promise. I'll make it better.'

I heard the group breathing around me, and realised that we were in her haunted house, that we had reached Charlotte's dangerous room. I wanted her to stay, I wanted her to be strong enough to look up from the floor and see something, catch a glimpse of what she'd been so frightened of. I wanted to help her, but I wasn't going to force the pace this time. I wasn't going to repeat the previous week's mistake.

'It's cold in Granddad's gym,' Charlotte said.

'Can you see anything?'

'Long planks, a bucket, a cable,' she said almost inaudibly.

I saw her eyelids flutter, and tears seep through her eyelashes. She was holding her hands limply in her lap.

'You're holding onto the door handle, and you know you can leave the room whenever you want to,' I said.

'Can I?'

'You just have to push the handle and walk out.'

'That would probably be best, if I just leave . . .'

She trailed off, raised her chin, then turned her head slowly with her mouth hanging half-open, like a child.

'I'll stay a bit longer,' she said in a quiet voice.

'Are you alone in there?'

She shook her head.

'I can hear him,' she murmured, 'but I can't see him.'

She frowned, as if she was trying to see something that wasn't clear.

'There's an animal here,' she suddenly said.

'What sort of animal?' I asked.

'Daddy's got a big dog . . .'

'Is your daddy there?'

'Yes, he's here, standing in the corner by the chairs. He's sad. I can see his eyes. I've hurt Daddy, he says. Daddy's sad.'

'What about the dog?'

'The dog is sniffing around in front of his feet. It keeps coming closer, then stops. Now it's standing quietly beside him, panting. Daddy says the dog's going to look after me . . . I don't want that. It shouldn't be allowed to do that, it's not . . .'

Charlotte gasped for breath. A terrible shadow crossed her face, and I thought it would be best to bring her out of the trance, up out of the dark water. We had found the dog – she had stayed long enough to look at it. We would solve the riddle of who the dog actually was in due time.

As we floated up through the water I saw Marek bare his teeth to taunt Charlotte. Lydia was holding her hand out through a dark-green cloud of seaweed. She was trying to stroke Pierre's cheek. Sibel and Jussi had their eyes closed as we drifted upwards, to find Eva floating just below the surface.

We were almost awake, but the boundary between the hypnotic state and reality was always unclear, and the transition back to consciousness could be unsettling.

'We're going to take a break now,' I said, then turned towards Charlotte. 'Do you feel OK?'

'Thanks,' she said, and lowered her gaze.

Marek stood up, bummed a cigarette from Sibel and they walked outside together.

I picked up my notebook to make a few quick notes, but stopped when Lydia came up to me. Her jewellery was rattling gently, and I could smell her perfume as she stopped next to me and asked:

'Isn't it my turn soon?'

'Next time,' I replied without looking up from my notes.

'Why not today?'

'Because I thought we'd go a bit further with Charlotte, and then Eva.'

'But if she doesn't come back?' Lydia persisted.

'Lydia, I'm trying to help all my patients,' I said.

She tilted her head.

'But you're not going to succeed, are you?'

'What makes you think that?' I asked.

She shrugged.

'Statistically, one of us is going to commit suicide, one will end up in an institution, and . . .'

'But we can't think like that,' I tried to explain.

'I can,' she interrupted. 'Because I want to be one of the ones who survive.'

She took another step closer to me, and her eyes looked unexpectedly cruel as she lowered her voice:

'I think Charlotte's going to be the one who commits suicide.'

Before I had a chance to respond, she sighed and went on:

'At least she doesn't have kids.'

I watched Lydia go and sit down on her chair. I looked at the time and realised that more than fifteen minutes had passed. Pierre, Lydia, Jussi and Eva were back in their places. I called Marek back in from the corridor, where he was pacing up and down, talking to himself. Sibel was standing in the doorway smoking, and giggled sleepily when I asked her to come back in.

Lydia looked at me happily when I finally had to accept that Charlotte wasn't coming back.

'OK,' I said, putting my hands together. 'Let's continue.'

I looked at their faces in front of me. They were ready. The sessions were actually always better after the break. It was as if everyone wanted to immerse themselves again, as if the light and sound down there were beckoning us back.

The effects of the induction were immediate – Lydia slipped into deep hypnosis after just ten minutes.

We drifted down, and I felt the mild water on my skin. The big grey rocks were covered in coral. Their little fronds swayed in the current. I could see every detail, every luminous, vibrant colour.

'Lydia,' I said. 'Where are you?'

She licked her dry lips and leaned her head back. Her eyes were closed, but she looked irritated, and there was a frown line on her brow.

'I'm picking up the knife.'

Her voice was dry and rasping.

'What sort of knife?' I asked.

'The serrated knife on the draining board,' she said, then sat quietly with her mouth half-open.

'A bread-knife?'

'Yes,' she smiled.

'Go on.'

'I cut the pack of ice-cream in two and take one half back to the sofa in front of the television, with a spoon. Oprah Winfrey turns to Dr Phil. He's sitting in the audience, holding one finger up. He's tied some red string round his finger, and he's about to explain why, but then Kasper starts shouting. I know he doesn't want anything; he's just trying to annoy me. He's shouting because he knows it upsets me, because I can't handle bad behaviour in my house.'

'What's he shouting?'

'He knows I want to hear what Dr Phil says. He knows Oprah cheers me up. That's why he's shouting.'

'What's he shouting now?'

'There are two closed doors between us,' she said. 'But I can hear him shouting cunt, cunt, cunt . . .'

Lydia's cheeks were red and beads of sweat were breaking out on her forehead.

'What are you doing now?' I asked.

She licked her lips again, breathing heavily.

'I turn the sound up on the television,' she said quietly. 'It's blaring out, the applause makes the speakers crackle, but it feels wrong, it's not good. It's not fun any more. He's spoiled the moment. There's nothing I can do about that now, but I ought to explain it to him.'

She smiled with her lips pressed tightly together. Her face was almost white, and the water shimmered in waves across her forehead.

'So do you?' I asked.

'What?'

'What are you doing, Lydia?'

'I go past the utility room and down into the rec room. I can hear beeps and odd whirring sounds from Kasper's room. I don't know what he's come up with now. I just want to go back up and watch television, but I walk over to the door, open it and go in . . .'

She paused.

'You go in,' I repeated. 'Where are you, Lydia?'

Her lips moved gently. Bubbles of air shimmered as they rose through the water.

'What can you see?' I asked cautiously.

'Kasper's pretending to be asleep when I come in,' she said slowly. 'He's smashed the photograph of Grandma. He promised to look after it if I let him borrow it, and it's the only one I have. Now he's ruined it, and he's just lying there pretending to be asleep. I tell myself I'm going to talk to him about it on Sunday, that's when we talk through how we've been acting. I don't want to have to discipline him. I wonder what advice Dr Phil would give me. I realise I'm still holding the spoon in my hand, and when I look at it I can't see myself reflected in it. I can see a teddy-bear, it must be somewhere up in the ceiling . . .'

Lydia smiled, but looked pained. She tried to laugh, but all that came out were odd hiccoughing sounds. She tried again, but it still didn't sound like a laugh.

'What are you doing?' I asked.

'I look,' she said, and stared up at the ceiling.

Then Lydia slid off her chair and hit the back of her head on the seat. I rushed over. She was sitting on the floor, still hypnotised, but not deeply now. She stared at me with frightened eyes as I spoke to her gently and tried to calm her down.

I left the therapy room and walked back towards my office. The hospital entrance was unusually deserted, just a few older women waiting for hospital shuttle. It was lovely outside, bright and breezy, with dazzling sunshine. I told myself I should go for a run that evening.

By the time I reached my office Maja Swartling was already waiting for me. Her full, red lips parted in a broad smile, and the clasp in her jet-black hair sparkled as she bowed her head and said playfully:

'I hope you're not regretting your kindness in volunteering for a second interview, Doctor.'

'Of course not,' I said, and felt a tingling sensation as I stood beside her to unlock the door. Our eyes met, and I saw an unexpected seriousness in her face as she passed me and went into the room.

I felt suddenly very aware of my own body, my feet, my mouth. She blushed as she took out her folder, pen, and notepad.

'So what's been happening since we last met?' she asked.

I offered Maja a cup of coffee, then started to tell her about that morning's session.

'I think we've found Charlotte's abuser,' I said. 'The person who hurt her so badly.'

'Who is it?'

'A dog,' I said seriously.

Maja didn't laugh. She'd done her homework and knew my theory about animal transference.

Talking to Maja Swartling was easy, almost dangerously so. She was well-read, she asked intelligent questions, and she was an extremely good listener.

'What about the Bosnian War veteran, Marek Semiovic? How's he coming along?' she asked, sucking the end of her pen.

'Well, the hospital has only really treated his physical injuries. This is the first time anyone's tried to address his psychologicial scars.'

'Yes.'

'He's interesting in terms of my research. Every time he's under deep hypnosis he finds himself in the same place, the same memory, where he's forced to torture people he knows, boys he went to school with, but then something always happens.'

'Within the hypnotic state?'

'Yes – he refuses to go any further.'

Time passed, and evening came. The hallway outside the office had grown quiet.

Maja gathered her things in her briefcase, pulled her shawl round her neck and stood up.

'Time really does fly,' she said apologetically.

'Thanks for coming,' I said, holding out my hand.

She hesitated, then asked:

'Can I offer you a glass of wine this evening?'

I thought for a moment. Simone and her friends were at *Tosca* and she wouldn't be home until late. Benjamin was spending the night at his grandfather's, and I had been planning to work all evening.

'That would be good,' I said. I had the sense, however, that I had crossed a line.

'I know a little place on Roslags Street,' Maja said. 'Called Peterson-Berger. It's pretty simple, but nice.'

'Great,' I said. I picked up my jacket, turned the lights off and locked the door behind us.

We rode our bikes past Haga Park, along the banks of Brunnsviken and down towards Norrtull. There was hardly any traffic at all, even though it was only seven thirty. The birds in the trees were singing in the light spring evening.

We parked our bikes across from a little park by the old inn, Claes på Hörnet. As we walked through the door and the maître d' smiled at us, I felt hesitant. Should I really be there? What would I say if Simone called and asked what I was doing? I shook it off. Maja was a colleague, and we were just going to continue our conversation. Anyway, Simone was out with her friends. She was probably having a glass of wine in the Opera Bar right now.

Maja looked expectant. I couldn't really understand what she was doing there with me. She was young and extremely beautiful. I had to be at least fifteen years older than her, and I was a married man.

'The chicken kebab with cumin is really good,' she said, walking ahead of me to a table towards the back of the restaurant.

We sat down and a woman immediately appeared with a jug of water for us. Maja leaned her head on her hand, looked at the glass and said calmly:

'And if we get tired of it here, we can always go back to my place.'

'Maja, are you flirting with me?'

She smiled, making her dimples more pronounced.

'My dad always said I was born that way. An incorrigible flirt, he used to say.'

I realised I didn't know anything about her, while she had evidently immersed herself in my work.

'Was your dad a doctor too?' I asked.

She nodded.

'Professor Jan E. Swartling.'

'The neuro surgeon?' I asked, impressed.

'Well, whatever it's called when you poke around in people's heads for a living,' she said bitterly.

For the first time, the smile disappeared from her face.

As we ate, I began to feel more uncomfortable. I knew I was drinking too quickly, and yet I ordered more wine. The staff assumed that we were a couple. I was drunk. I didn't even look at the bill before signing for it. Out in the street, in the mild, airy spring evening, Maja pointed to a doorway and asked if I'd like to come up, just to see her flat and have a cup of tea.

'Maja,' I said, 'you really are incorrigible. Your dad was right.'

She giggled and tucked her arm under mine.

We stood close together in the lift. I couldn't help looking at her full, smiling lips, her pearl-white teeth, her high brow and glossy black hair.

She saw me looking and stroked my cheek softly. I leaned over and was about to kiss her when the lift stopped with a jolt.

'Come on,' she whispered, and unlocked the door.

Her flat was very small, but lovely. The walls were painted a gentle shade of Mediterranean blue, and a white linen curtain hung in front of the only window. The tiny kitchen was neat, with a tiled floor and a small, modern gas-stove. Maja went in and I heard her open a bottle of wine.

'I thought we were having tea?' I said when she emerged with the bottle and two wine glasses in her hands.

'This is better for the heart,' she said.

'Well, in that case,' I said. I took one of the glasses and managed to spill wine on my hand.

She dried it with a tea-towel, then sat down on the narrow bed and leaned back.

'Nice flat,' I said.

'It feels funny having you here,' she smiled. 'I've been an admirer of yours for so long, and . . .'

Suddenly she leapt up.

'I've got to take your picture!' she cried with a giggle. 'The great man himself in my little flat!'

She fetched her camera and tried to concentrate.

'Look serious,' she said, looking at me through the lens.

She giggled as she photographed me, telling me to pose, then jokily saying I looked really hot, and telling me to pout my lips.

'Really sexy,' she joked.

'The next *Vogue* cover, then?'

'If they don't pick me,' she said, handing me the camera.

I stood up and noticed how unsteady I was, and aimed the camera at her. She had thrown herself backwards across the bed.

'You win,' I said, and took her picture.

'My brother always used to call me Miss Piggy,' she said. 'Do you think I'm fat?'

'I think you're extremely beautiful,' I whispered. I watched her sit up and pull her sweater over her head. She was wearing a pale green silk bra over her full chest.

'Take my picture now,' she whispered, unfastening her bra.

She blushed and smiled. I adjusted the focus, looked into her eyes, then at her smiling mouth, her pert young breasts and pink nipples.

I photographed her as she posed, then she beckoned me closer.

'I'm going to take a close-up,' I mumbled, and kneeled down, feeling my lust starting to get the better of me.

She cupped one heavy breast in her hand. The camera flashed. She whispered to me to come closer. I had a raging erection straining against my trousers. I put the camera down, leaned forward and put my lips on one of her breasts as she pressed it towards my face and I licked and sucked her stiff nipple.

'God,' she moaned. 'God, that's wonderful.'

Her skin was hot, steaming. She unbuttoned her jeans, pulled them down and kicked them off. I stood up, telling myself that

I needed to leave, but I picked up the camera and took her photograph again. All she was wearing was a pair of thin, pale green panties.

'Come here,' she whispered.

I looked at her through the camera again, and she smiled and opened her legs. I could see a hint of her dark pubic hair at the edges of the sheer fabric.

'It's OK,' she said.

'I can't,' I replied.

'I think you probably can,' she smiled.

'Maja, you're dangerous, you're so dangerous,' I said, putting the camera down.

'I know I'm naughty.'

'I'm a married man.'

'Don't you find me attractive?'

'You're incredibly beautiful, Maja.'

'More beautiful than your wife?'

'Don't.'

'But I do turn you on?' she whispered, then giggled before suddenly becoming serious.

I nodded, took a step back and saw her smile happily.

'Can I still interview you again?'

'Of course,' I said, and moved towards the door.

She blew me a kiss, then I left the flat, hurried downstairs and went to get my bicycle.

That night I dreamed I was looking at a stone relief of three nymphs. I woke myself up saying something, so loudly that I could hear the echo of my own voice in the dark, silent bedroom. Simone had come home while I was asleep, and shifted in her sleep beside me. I was wet with sweat and still drunk. The house was quiet. I took a sleeping pill and tried not to think, then remembered what had happened that evening. What was wrong with me? How on earth had I let myself photograph Maja naked? She was beautiful, seductive. I had felt flattered by her. Was that all it took? I realised to my surprise that I had found a genuine weak spot in my character: I was vain.

I rolled over in bed and pulled the covers over my face, and after a while I was asleep again.

Marek was sitting slumped over in a state of deep hypnotic relaxation. His shirt stretched tightly across his bulging arms and chest. His hair was closely cropped, exposing a scalp covered with scars. He was chewing slowly and raised his head to look blankly at me.

'I can't stop laughing,' he said loudly. 'Because the electric shocks are making this guy from Mostar jump about like a cartoon character.'

Marek looked happy and was rocking his head up and down.

'The guy's lying on the cement floor, bleeding, and he's breathing fast, very fast. And then he huddles up and starts to cry. Fuck it, I yell at him to stand up, say I'll kill him if he doesn't stand up. I lean forward and give him another shock, but his body just jumps like a dead pig. I call to the door that the fun is over, but they come in with the guy's big brother. I've met him before. We spent a year or so working together at Aluminij, the factory that used to be . . .'

Marek trailed off, and his chin started to tremble.

'What's happening now?' I asked.

He sat without speaking for a while before he went on:

'The floor's covered with green grass. I can't see the guy from Mostar any more, there's just a little grass hill.'

'What's on the hill?' I asked.

'I don't know, but I can't see the room now. I'm outside, walking across a summer meadow. The grass is damp and cold beneath my feet.'

Very gently, I brought them all out of the hypnosis, and made sure that they were all OK before I kicked off the conversation. Marek wiped tears from his cheeks. He had large sweat-stains under his arms.

'They forced me to do it. That was their thing . . . They forced me to torture my friend,' he said.

'We know,' I said.

He looked around at all of us anxiously.

'I was laughing because I was scared. I'm not like that. I'm not evil,' he whispered.

'You liked hurting other people,' Lydia said with a gentle smile. 'Why can't you admit that to . . .?'

'Shut the fuck up!' Marek shouted, and walked over to her with his hand raised.

'Sit down,' I said in a loud voice.

'Marek, you don't shout at me,' Lydia said calmly.

He looked her in the eye and stopped.

'Sorry,' he said with an uncertain smile, then rubbed his head a couple of times and sat back down.

It was a gloomy day. There was rain in the air. The breeze that blew in was cool and brought with it a faint smell of leaves. They all started to take their seats again.

Eva was dressed entirely in blue. She was wearing blue lipstick and blue mascara. As usual, she seemed nervous. She kept putting her cardigan on, then taking it off, over and over again.

Lydia was talking to Pierre, and as he listened to her his eyes and mouth kept twitching in painful, repeated tics.

Marek had his back to me. His muscular frame rippled as he looked for something in his rucksack.

I stood up and beckoned Sibel back inside, and she put her cigarette out on her shoe and put the butt back in the pack.

'Let's continue,' I said, thinking that I'd try again with Eva.

Eva's face was tense, and there was a teasing smile on her blue lips. I was wary of her. She didn't want to feel she was being forced, but I had an idea of how I would help her.

When I told the group to let their chins sink onto their chests, Eva reacted immediately with a wide smile. I counted backwards and could feel the rope behind me as I sank into the water, but I made sure to remain attentive. Eva kept glancing over at Pierre and was trying to breathe with the same rhythm as him.

'You're slowly sinking,' I said. 'Deeper into relaxation, into rest, into heavy stillness.'

I walked behind my patients, saw their pale necks and rounded backs, then stopped behind Eva and put one hand on her shoulder. Without opening her eyes she tilted her face upwards and pouted her lips slightly.

'Now I'm talking to you, Eva,' I said. 'I want you to remain awake, but relaxed at all times. I want you to listen to my voice when I talk to the group, but you won't be hypnotised. You'll feel the same calm, the same lovely sensation of slowly falling, but you'll remain awake the whole time.'

I felt her shoulders relax.

'Now I'm talking to all of you again. Listen to me. I'm going to count backwards, and with each number, we are going to sink deeper, getting more and more relaxed, but Eva, you will only accompany us in your thoughts. You will remain awake and conscious the whole time.'

As I went back to my chair I counted backwards, and when I sat down in front of them I could see that Eva's face was slack. She looked different. It was almost hard to believe it was the same person. Her bottom lip was drooping, the pinkness inside contrasting with the blue lipstick, and she was breathing very heavily. I turned inwards, let go and drifted down through the water. In my mind, we were inside a wrecked ship, or a submerged building. A stream of cooler water rose to meet me from below. Air bubbles and small pieces of seaweed floated past.

'Keep going down, deeper, calmer,' I encouraged them gently.

After twenty minutes or so we were all standing deep underwater on a perfectly flat steel floor.

Eva's face looked naked when she was in such a deep state of relaxation. A bubble of saliva formed at one corner of her sagging mouth.

'Eva, I want you to talk very gently, and take your time over what you're seeing.'

'OK,' she murmured.

'Tell the rest of us,' I said. 'Where are you?'

She suddenly looked very strange. It was as if she was taken by surprise by something.

'I've wandered off. I'm walking along the soft path with pine-needles and long pine cones,' she whispered. 'I might go to the canoe club and look through the window at the back.'

'Are you doing that now?'

Eva nodded and puffed out her cheeks like a moody child.

'What can you see?'

'Nothing,' she said quickly and tersely.

'Nothing?'

'Just one little thing . . . which I'm writing in chalk on the road outside the post office.'

'What are you writing?'

'Just a silly thing.'

'You can't see anything through the window?'

'No . . . just a boy, I'm looking at a boy,' she slurred. 'Nice, really sweet. He's lying in a narrow bed, a sofa-bed. A man in a white towel is lying on top of him. It looks nice. I like looking at them. I like boys, I want to take care of them, kiss them.'

Afterwards Eva sat with her mouth twitching as her eyes swept across the rest of the group.

'I wasn't hypnotised,' she said.

'You were relaxed, which works just as well,' I replied.

'No, it didn't work well. It worked badly, because I wasn't thinking about what I said. I just said different things, it doesn't mean anything. It was just made up.'

'Doesn't the canoe club really exist?'

'No,' she said bluntly.

'The soft path?'

'I just made it up,' she said with a shrug.

It was obvious that she felt uncomfortable about being hypnotised, and describing things she had actually experienced. Eva was the sort of person who never said anything about herself that was anchored in reality.

'I've never done anything stupid to boys,' Eva went on in a louder voice. 'I'm nice. I'm a nice person, and children always like me. I'd be happy to babysit. Lydia, I went to your house last night, but I was too scared to ring the doorbell.'

'Don't do that again.'

'What?'

'Don't come to my house,' she said.

'You can trust me,' Eva went on. 'Charlotte and I are already best friends. She makes food for me, and I pick flowers for her to put on the table.'

Eva's lips twitched as she looked at Lydia again.

'I've bought a toy for your boy, Kasper. It's only a little thing, a fan in the shape of a helicopter. You can fan yourself with the propellers.'

'Eva,' Lydia said darkly.

'It's not dangerous. You couldn't possibly hurt yourself with it, I promise.'

'Don't come to my house,' Lydia said. 'Do you hear?'

'Not today, I can't, I'm going to Marek's, because I think he needs company.'

'Eva, you must respect Lydia's privacy,' I said.

'Maybe tomorrow then,' Eva smiled.

Lydia stood up, her face looked pale and drawn.

'Eva is just trying to be friendly,' I said, but Lydia left the room without a word. Eva remained in her chair and watched her go.

Simone hadn't arrived when I was shown in. Our table was empty, except for a note with our names perched in a glass. I sat down and thought about ordering a drink before she got there. It was seven ten. I had booked the table myself, at the KB restaurant down on Smålands Street. It was my birthday, and I was feeling happy. We didn't often have time to go out these days. She was so busy with her gallery project, and I was busy with my research. When we did get to spend an evening together we usually ended up spending it on the sofa with Benjamin, watching a film or playing video games.

At 7:20 I was sitting there with a martini glass containing Absolut vodka, a dash of Noilly Prat and a twist of lime. I decided to wait before calling Simone, and tried not to feel too irritated.

I sipped the cocktail, starting to get worried. Reluctantly I called Simone.

'Simone Bark.'

She sounded distracted, and there was an echo behind her voice.

'Simone, it's me. Where are you?'

'Erik? I'm at the gallery, we're busy painting and . . .'

She broke off. Then I heard her groan loudly.

'Oh, no. No! I'm so sorry, Erik. I completely forgot. Everything's been so crazy today, what with the plumber and the electrician and . . .'

'So you're still at the gallery?'

I couldn't hide the disappointment from my voice.

'Yes, I'm covered in paint and plaster . . .'

'We were supposed to have dinner,' I said flatly.

'I know, Erik. I'm sorry, it slipped my mind completely . . .'

'Oh, well. At least we got a good table,' I said sarcastically.

'There's no point you waiting for me,' she sighed, and although I could hear how sorry she was, I couldn't help feeling angry.

'Erik,' she whispered. 'Forgive me.'

'It's fine,' I said, and hung up.

It wasn't worth going anywhere else. I was hungry, and I was in a restaurant. I quickly beckoned the waiter over and ordered the herring platter and beer for a starter, the crispy duck breast with bacon lardons and orange sauce for my main course, with a glass of Bordeaux, and the Gruyère Alpage with honey to finish.

'You can take the other place setting away,' I said, and the waiter gave me a sympathetic glance as he poured my Czech beer and served the herring and crispbread.

I wished I'd had my notebook with me, so I could at least be doing something useful while I ate.

Then my mobile phone rang, and I had a fleeting fantasy that Simone had been teasing me and was about to walk through the door.

'Erik Maria Bark,' I said, and heard how hollow my voice sounded.

'Hi, this is Maja.'

'Maja, yes, hi,' I said quickly.

'I was thinking of asking . . . wow, it sounds very noisy wherever you are, is this a bad time to call?'

'I'm sitting in KB,' I said. 'It's my birthday,' I added, without really knowing why.

'In that case, happy birthday! Sounds like there's quite a crowd.'

'No, I'm by myself,' I said bluntly.

'Erik . . . I'm sorry about last night. I'm so embarrassed,' she said quietly.

I heard her clear her throat.

'I wanted to ask if you'd be interested in reading the transcript of my first interview with you. I've finished writing it up, and I'm about to send it to my supervisor, but if you'd like to read it first, I . . .'

'Just leave a printout in my letterbox, please,' I said.

We ended the call and I poured the last of the beer into my glass and drank it. The waiter cleared the table, then returned almost immediately with the duck breast and red wine.

I was unpleasantly conscious of the mechanics of chewing and swallowing, and the annoying scrape of the cutlery on the plate. I drank my wine and let the figures depicted in the mural on the wall of the restaurant become the patients in my hypnotherapy group.

I don't know how long I'd been sitting there staring at the mural when I heard a breathless voice behind me:

'Thank goodness you're still here!'

It was Maja.

She smiled and gave me a big hug, which I returned rather stiffly.

'Happy birthday, Erik!'

I could smell how clean her thick black hair was, and her neck smelled faintly of jasmine.

She gestured to the chair across from me.

'May I?'

I knew I should send her away. I had promised myself that I wouldn't see her again. But I hesitated. I admitted to myself that I was pleased to have some company.

She stood by the chair waiting for me to answer.

'I find it very hard to say no to you,' I said, then realised how ambiguous that sounded. 'I mean . . .'

She sat down, beckoned the waiter and ordered a glass of wine. Then she put a box down on the table in front of my plate.

'Just a little something,' she said, and blushed.

'A present?'

She shrugged her shoulders.

'A token gesture . . . I didn't even know it was your birthday until twenty minutes ago.'

I opened the box and found, to my surprise, what looked like a pair of miniature binoculars.

'They're anatomical binoculars,' Maja explained. 'My great-grandfather invented them. I think he got a Nobel Prize – not for these, admittedly. Mind you, that was in the days when most of the prizes went to Swedes and Norwegians,' she said nonchalantly.

'Anatomical binoculars,' I repeated, taken aback.

'Well, they're cute, and very old. I know it's a silly present . . .'

'Stop it, they're . . .'

I met her gaze, and saw how beautiful she was.

'It's extremely kind of you, Maja. Thank you, thank you very much.'

I carefully put the binoculars back in the box and tucked it in my pocket.

'My glass is empty already,' she said in surprise. 'Shall we get a bottle?'

It was late by the time we decided to move on to Riche, round the corner from the Royal Dramatic Theatre. We almost fell over when we were checking our coats – Maja leaned against me, and I misjudged the distance to the wall. Once we'd regained our balance, Maja started to laugh and I had to lead her over to a corner of the club.

It was very crowded. We each had a gin and tonic, stood close together, tried to talk, and suddenly were kissing. I felt the back of her head hit the wall as I pressed myself against her. The music was pounding as she spoke into my ear, saying that we should go back to her place.

We hurried out and got in a taxi.

'Roslags Street, please,' she slurred. 'Number 17.'

It was early in the morning and the sky was starting to get lighter. The buildings were flickering past. Maja leaned against me and I thought she was falling asleep until I felt her hand caressing my crotch. I immediately got an erection and she whispered 'Goodness!' and laughed against my neck.

I wasn't sure how we got up to her flat. I remember standing in the lift and licking her face, tasting salt and lipstick and powder.

In her flat, Maja dropped her coat on the floor and kicked off her shoes. She pulled me down onto the bed, helped me get undressed, then pulled off her dress and white underwear.

'Come here,' she whispered. 'I want to feel you inside me.'

I lay down heavily between her thighs and felt that she was very wet, and just sank into the warmth and tightness. She groaned into my ear, held onto my back and gently moved her hips.

We had messy, drunk sex. I felt more and more alone. As I got close to orgasm, I thought about pulling out, then just gave in to the sudden convulsions. She was gasping for breath. I lay on top of her as I softened and slid out. My heart was still beating hard. I saw Maja smile in a peculiar way that made me feel uneasy.

I felt sick. I didn't really understand what had happened, what I was doing there.

I sat up in bed beside her.

'What is it?' she asked, stroking my back.

I shrugged her hand off.

'Stop it,' I said brusquely.

My heart was thudding with regret.

'Erik? I thought . . .'

She sounded upset. I felt I couldn't look at her, I was angry with myself and with her. It never would have happened if she hadn't pursued me.

'We're just tired and drunk,' she whispered.

'I have to go,' I said in a stifled voice, then grabbed my clothes and stumbled into the bathroom. It was tiny, and full of creams, brushes, towels. A fluffy dressing-gown hung from a hook next to a pink razor on a thick, soft rope. I couldn't look at my reflection as I rinsed my face above the sink, then washed myself with pale blue soap shaped like a rose. I was shaking as I got dressed.

When I emerged she was standing there waiting for me. She'd wrapped the sheet around her and looked very young, and very worried.

'Are you angry with me?' she asked, and I saw her lips tremble like she was about to cry.

'I'm angry with myself, Maja. I should never, never . . .'

'But I wanted to, Erik. I'm in love with you, or haven't you noticed?'

She tried to smile at me, but her eyes filled with tears.

'You can't just treat me like shit now,' she whispered, reaching her hand out towards me.

I stepped back and said it had been a mistake. My tone was more dismissive than I intended.

She nodded and lowered her gaze. I didn't say goodbye, just left the flat and shut the door behind me.

I walked all the way to Karolinska Hospital. Maybe I could convince Simone that I'd wanted to be alone and had spent the night in my office.

The next morning I took a taxi home to Järfälla from Karolinska Hospital. My skin was crawling with disgust at the amount of alcohol I had drunk, and revulsion at all the stupid things I'd said and done. I couldn't believe I'd cheated on Simone. It simply couldn't be true. I had no interest in Maja. So how on earth had I allowed myself to jump into bed with her?

I didn't know how I was going to manage to tell Simone about this, but I knew I had to: I'd made a mistake, but people make mistakes. It's possible to forgive each other if you talk about things, explain them.

I was thinking that I could never let Simone go. I'd be hurt if she had an affair, but I'd forgive her. I wouldn't ever leave her.

*

Simone was standing in the kitchen pouring herself some coffee when I got in. She was wearing her worn, pale pink silk dressing-gown. We bought it in China when Benjamin was one year old and the two of them came with me to a conference.

'Do you want any?' she asked.

'Yes, please.'

'Erik, I'm so sorry that I forgot your birthday.'

'I slept in the office,' I said, and the deceptive tone in my voice sounded obvious, even to me.

Her strawberry-blonde hair hung across her face, and her pale freckles shimmered softly. Without a word she went into the bedroom and came back with a present. I tore the paper off with jokey eagerness.

It was a box of CDs of all the recordings made of saxophonist Charlie Parker's only visit to Sweden.

'Thanks,' I said.

'How does your day look?' she asked.

'I have to get back to work,' I said.

'I was thinking, maybe we could have a really nice meal together tonight, here at home?' she said.

'Sounds good,' I said.

'It can't be too late, though. The painters are coming at seven tomorrow. God knows why. Why do they always have to start so early?'

I realised she was waiting for a response.

'You always end up having to wait for them anyway,' I mumbled.

'Exactly,' she smiled, and drank some coffee. 'So what should we have? Maybe that dish with tournedos of beef in port and currant sauce, do you remember that?'

'That was a while back,' I said, struggling not to sound like I was about to burst into tears.

'Don't be angry with me.'

'I'm not, Simone.'

I tried to smile at her.

When I was putting my shoes on in the hallway, about to leave, Simone came out from the bathroom. She was holding something in her hand.

'Erik?' she asked.

'Yes?'

'What's this?'

She was holding Maja's anatomical binoculars.

'Oh, that. It was a present,' I said, hearing how unnatural my voice sounded.

'Very nice. Looks like an antique. Who did you get it from?'

I turned away so I didn't have to look at her.

'Just a patient,' I said, trying to sound vague as I pretended to look for my keys.

She laughed in surprise.

'I didn't think doctors were allowed to accept presents from patients. Isn't that unethical?'

'Maybe I should return it,' I said, and opened the door.

I could feel Simone's stare scorching my back. I should have told her, but I was too afraid I would lose her. I didn't dare. I had no idea where to start.

Marek stopped me just as I was about to go into the therapy room. He blocked the door and flashed a blank, distant smile at me.

'We're having some fun in here,' he said.

'What are you doing?' I asked.

'It's a private party.'

I heard someone cry out behind the door.

'Let me in, Marek,' I said.

He grinned.

'Sorry, Doctor, that's not possible at the . . .'

I pushed past him, and the door flew open. Marek lost his footing. He clung onto the door handle but still ended up on the floor, sitting there with one leg stretched out.

'I was only joking,' he said. 'For fuck's sake, it was just a joke.'

All the other patients were staring at us, their movements frozen. Pierre and Charlotte looked worried. Sibel and Jussi were standing in front of Lydia. Sibel's mouth was open, and it looked like she had tears in her eyes. Lydia looked at us and then turned her back on me again. There was an odd atmosphere emanating from the group.

Marek stood up and brushed his trousers off with his hand.

I noted that Eva hadn't arrived yet, and went over to set up the camera before the start of the session. Through the lens I saw Lydia smile at Charlotte, and heard her say cheerily:

'Exactly! That's always the way with kids! My Kasper, he can't talk about anything else, it's all Spiderman right now.'

'I hear everyone's crazy about him at the moment,' Charlotte smiled.

'Kasper hasn't got a dad, so maybe Spiderman acts as a male role model,' Lydia said, then laughed so loudly that the headphones crackled. 'But we do pretty well,' she went on. 'We laugh a lot, even if things have been a bit tricky recently, Kasper gets so jealous of everything I do. He tries to ruin my things, he won't let me talk on the phone, he threw my book in the toilet, shouts things.'

Jussi started to talk about his haunted house: his parents' house up in Dorotea, in southern Lapland, near Sutme. 'I live near a lake, Djuptjärnen,' he said. 'The last stretch of the drive is on old logging tracks. In the summer kids go swimming there. They like the story of Näcken.'

'The water sprite?' I said.

'People have seen him up at Djuptjärnen playing his fiddle for over three hundred years.'

'But not you?'

'No,' he said with a big grin.

'So what do you do all year, stuck out there in the middle of the forest?' Pierre asked with a slight smile.

'I buy old cars and buses, fix them up and sell them. The yard looks like a junkyard.'

'Is it a big house?' Lydia asked.

'No – it's green, though. Dad painted it one summer. Ended up a weird bright green. I don't know what he was thinking. Maybe someone gave him the paint.'

Lydia had taken out a tin of saffron crackers which she was handing out.

'They're entirely organic,' she said, gesturing to Marek to take more.

Charlotte smiled and nibbled the corner of hers.

'Did you bake them yourself?' Jussi asked with an unexpected smile, which made his heavy face look more attractive.

'I almost didn't have time,' Lydia said, shaking her head and smiling. 'I got into a bit of an argument at the playground.'

Sibel giggled loudly and ate her cracker in a couple of large mouthfuls.

'It was Kasper. When we went to the playground as usual this morning, one of the mums came over to me and said Kasper had hit her little girl in the back with a shovel.'

'Shit,' Marek whispered.

'Whatever do you do in a situation like that?' Charlotte wondered politely.

Marek took another cracker and listened to Lydia with an expression that made me wonder if he had a crush on her.

'I don't know, but I explained to the mother that I was very concerned, very upset. But she said it wasn't so bad, she thought it was probably an accident.'

'Of course,' Charlotte said. 'Children can get so boisterous when they're playing.'

'Well, I promised to have a word with Kasper and get to the bottom of it,' Lydia said.

'Good,' Jussi nodded.

'She said that Kasper seems to be a lovely boy,' Lydia said with a smile.

I sat down in my place and leafed through my notebook. I was eager to get started as soon as possible. It was Lydia's turn again.

She looked up and smiled cautiously. They all sat quietly and expectantly as I started the hypnosis. The sound of our breathing seemed unusually loud. A dark, dense silence followed our heartbeats. We sank deeper with each breath. After a while I turned towards Lydia.

'You're sinking deeper, very gently. You're really relaxed; your arms feel heavy; your legs feel heavy; your eyelids feel heavy. You're breathing slowly and are listening to my words without questioning them. You're immersed in what I'm saying, and you're completely safe. Lydia, right now you're really close to the thing you don't want to think about, the thing you never talk about, the thing you always turn away from, the thing that's always hidden in shadow.'

'Yes,' she replied with a sigh.

'You're there now,' I said.

'I'm very close.'

'Where are you now?'

'At home.'

'How old are you?'

'Thirty-seven.'

I looked at her carefully. Rippled reflections were crossing her high, smooth forehead, her neat mouth and almost unhealthily pale skin. I knew she had turned thirty-seven two weeks ago.

'What's happening? What's wrong?' I asked.

'The phone . . .'

'What about the phone?'

'It's ringing, it's ringing again. I pick it up and then put it down again right away.'

'There's nothing to worry about, Lydia.'

She looked tired, and a little scared.

'The food's going to get cold,' she said. 'I've made lightly pickled vegetables, lentil soup and fresh bread. I was planning to eat in front of the television, but it looks like that's going to be impossible . . .'

Her chin trembled, then she calmed down again.

'I wait a while, then pull the blinds up and look out at the street. There's no one there. I sit down at the kitchen table and eat some of the warm bread with butter, but I don't have an appetite. I go down to the rec room again, it's cold down there, as usual, and I sit down on the old leather sofa and shut my eyes. I need to pull myself together. I need to gather my strength.'

She fell silent, and strands of seaweed drifted between us.

'Why do you need to gather your strength?' I asked.

'So that I . . . so I can stand up and go past the lamp with the red paper shade with the Chinese writing on, and the tray of scented candles and polished stones. The floorboards that creak under the linoleum . . .'

'Is there anyone there?' I asked Lydia quietly, but regretted it at once.

'I pick up the stick and hold the bulge in the linoleum down so I can open the door, and I breathe calmly and go in and turn the light on,' she said. 'Kasper blinks in the light but stays lying down. He's peed in the bucket. He's wearing his light blue pyjamas. He's breathing quickly. I poke him with the stick through the mesh. He whimpers and moves away, then sits up in the cage. I ask if he's changed his mind and he nods eagerly. I push the plate of food towards him. Some of the cod has dried up and is now a dark colour. He crawls over and eats and it makes me happy and I'm about to say how good it is that we understand each other when he throws up on the mattress.'

Lydia's face contorted in a pained grimace.

'And there I was, thinking . . .'

Her lips were tense, the corners of her mouth turned down.

'There I was, thinking we were done, but . . .'

She shook her head.

'I just don't get it . . .'

She licked her lips.

'Do you have any idea how I feel? Do you? He says sorry. I repeat that it's Sunday tomorrow, and hit myself in the face, and scream at him to look.'

Charlotte was looking at Lydia through the water with worried eyes.

'Lydia,' I said, 'you can leave the basement now, without feeling scared or angry, you just feel calm and composed. I'm going to lift you very slowly out of this deep relaxation, up to the surface, up to clarity, and together we can talk about what you've just said, just you and me, before I bring the others out of their hypnosis.'

She let out a low, weary growl.

'Lydia, are you listening to me?'

She nodded.

'I'm going to count backwards, and when I reach one you're going to open your eyes and be completely awake and conscious. Ten, nine, eight, seven, you're slowly rising to the surface, your body feels nice and relaxed, six, five, four, and soon you're going to open your eyes, but stay sitting on your chair, three, two, one . . . now, open your eyes.'

Our eyes met. Lydia's face looked scrunched up, which was something I hadn't counted on. I still felt completely cold inside from what she had said. Sometimes the Hippocratic oath had to be weighed up against the duty to report a suspected crime, and a patient's right to confidentiality didn't apply if the safety of a third party was at risk.

'Lydia,' I said. 'You understand that I'm going to have to contact Social Services?'

'Why?'

'What you said means I have no choice.'

'In what way?'

'Don't you realise?'

Lydia's mouth grew tense.

'I haven't said anything.'

'You described how . . .'

'Shut up,' she snapped. 'You don't know me. You don't know anything about my life. You've got no right to poke your nose into what goes on in my home.'

'I suspect that your child . . .'

'Just you shut up!' she yelled, and left the room.

I had parked beside a tall hedge a hundred metres from Lydia's large wooden house on Tennisvägen in Rotebro. The social worker had agreed to my request to come with me. The police, on the other hand, had greeted my report with a degree of scepticism, but at least they had initiated a preliminary investigation.

A red Toyota drove past me and stopped outside the house. I got out of the car and went over to introduce myself to the social worker, a short, stocky woman.

Some damp flyers were sticking out of the letterbox. The low gate was open. We walked up the path towards the house. I noted that there were no toys in the unkempt yard. No sandpit, no swing hanging from the old apple tree, no bicycle with training wheels on the driveway. The blinds in all the windows were pulled down. Dead plants drooped from hanging baskets. Some uneven stone steps led up to the front door. I thought I detected movement behind the opaque, yellow window. The social worker rang the bell. We waited, but nothing happened. She yawned and looked at her watch, rang again, and then tried the door handle. The door was unlocked. She pushed it open and we peered into a small hall.

'Hello?' the social worker called. 'Lydia?'

We went inside, took our shoes off and walked through a door into a hallway with pink wallpaper and pictures of people meditating, their heads invisible against the strong backlighting. A pink phone lay on the floor beside a low table.

'Lydia?'

I opened a door and found a narrow staircase leading down to the basement.

'It's down there,' I said.

The social worker followed me down the steps to a rec room containing an old leather sofa and a brown tiled table. There was a tray holding an array of scented candles and some polished stones and pieces of glass. A dark red lampshade with Chinese characters on it hung from the ceiling.

My heart was pounding. I tried to open the door to the next room, but it caught on a bulge in the linoleum. I pressed it down with my foot and went inside, but there was no cage in there. In the middle of the floor stood an upside down bicycle with its front wheel removed. There was a set of tools and a repair kit in a blue plastic toolbox next to it. Rubber patches, glue, socket wrenches. One of the shiny wedges had been inserted beneath the rim of the tyre. Suddenly the ceiling creaked and we realised that someone was walking around the room directly overhead. Without a word we hurried up the stairs. The kitchen door was ajar. I could see slices of bread and some crumbs on the yellow linoleum floor.

'Hello?' the social worker called.

I went in, and saw that the fridge door was open. Lydia was standing in the dimly lit room, looking down at the floor. It took me a few seconds to notice the knife in her hand. A long, serrated bread-knife. Her arm was hanging by her side, the blade of the knife trembling by her thigh.

'You're not supposed to be here,' she whispered, looking up at me.

'OK,' I said, and moved backwards towards the door.

'Can we sit down and have a little talk?' the social worker asked in a neutral voice.

I opened the door to the hallway as Lydia came slowly closer.

'Erik,' she said.

When I started to close the door I saw Lydia run towards me. I rushed down the hall, but the door was locked. Lydia's footsteps were getting closer. She was making a moaning sound. I yanked open another door and stumbled into the television room. Lydia threw the door open and followed me. I knocked into an armchair as I hurried across to the terrace door, but I couldn't budge the handle. Lydia rushed at me with the knife and I took cover behind the dining table. She followed, and I kept moving around to keep my distance from her.

'It's your fault,' she said as she followed me around the table.

The social worker came running into the room. She was out of breath.

'Lydia,' she said sternly. 'You need to stop this nonsense right now.'

'It's all his fault,' Lydia said.

'What do you mean?' I asked. 'What's my fault?'

'This,' Lydia replied, and drew the knife across her throat.

She looked me in the eye and blood gushed down her apron and bare feet. Her mouth quivered. The knife fell to the floor. One of her hands fumbled for support. She sank to her knees, then slumped onto one hip and sat there like a mermaid.

Annika Lorentzon looked unhappy. Rainer Milch reached across the table and poured a glass of Perrier. His cufflink flashed, gold and royal blue.

'You realise why we wanted to talk to you as soon as possible,' Peder Mälarstedt said, adjusting his tie.

I looked inside the folder they had given me. Apparently Lydia had filed a complaint against me. She claimed that I had driven her to attempt suicide by forcing her to confess to fabricated offences. She accused me of using her as a guinea-pig, and of planting false memories in her head during deep hypnosis, and claimed that I belittled her cynically and relentlessly in front of the rest of the group until she was a broken woman.

I looked up from the document.

'This isn't a joke, is it?'

Annika looked away. Holstein's mouth was open and his face looked completely expressionless when he said:

'She's your patient, and these are serious allegations.'

'Sure, but they're obviously lies,' I said angrily. 'It's impossible to implant false memories under hypnosis. I can guide them towards hidden memories, but I can't remember for them . . . it's like a door, I lead them to the doors, but I can't open them on my own.'

'The suspicion alone could be enough to discredit your research, Erik, so I'm sure you appreciate just how serious this is,' Rainer said.

I shook my head in irritation.

'She said something about her son which I considered so serious that I felt obliged to contact Social Services. The fact that she reacted the way she did was . . .'

Ronny Johansson cut me off abruptly.

'But it says here that she doesn't even have any children.'

He tapped the folder with a long finger. I snorted and was rewarded with a strange look from Annika.

'Erik, arrogance really isn't going to do you any favours in this situation,' she said quietly.

'When someone is telling bald-faced lies about me,' I smiled angrily.

She leaned over the table.

'Erik,' she said slowly. 'She's never had any children.'

'She doesn't have children?'

'No.'

The room was silent.

I watched the bubbles rise to the surface of the mineral water.

'I don't understand, all the details matched,' I tried to explain, as calmly as I could. 'She still lives in her childhood home, I can't believe . . .'

'You might not be able to believe it,' Milch interrupted. 'But you were wrong.'

'They can't lie like that under hypnosis.'

'Maybe she wasn't hypnotised?'

'She was, I could tell. Her face changed.'

'It doesn't matter now, the damage is already done.'

'I don't know if she's got any children or not,' I went on. 'Maybe she was talking about herself. I've never seen that before, but that could have been her way of dealing with childhood memories.'

Annika interrupted me:

'That could certainly be the case, but the fact remains that your patient made a serious suicide attempt which she is blaming on you. We're suggesting that you take a leave of absence while we investigate the matter.'

She smiled thinly at me.

'I'm sure it will work out, Erik,' she said gently. 'But right now you need to stand aside until we've sorted it all out. We simply can't afford to let the press have a field day with this.'

I thought about my other patients. Charlotte, Marek, Jussi, Sibel, Pierre and Eva. I couldn't just abandon them from one day to the next, they'd feel let down, deceived.

'I can't do that,' I said in a low voice. 'I haven't done anything wrong.'

Annika patted my hand.

'It'll be OK. Lydia Evers is clearly unstable and confused, but the most important thing right now is that we do everything by the book. You take a leave of absence from the hypnotherapy project while we conduct an internal investigation into what happened. I know you're a good doctor, Erik. And, like I said, I'm sure you'll be back with your group within . . .' She shrugged her shoulders. 'Maybe within six months.'

'Six months?'

I stood up angrily.

'I've got patients that are relying on me. I can't just abandon them.'

Annika's gentle smile vanished as suddenly as a candle being blown out. Her face closed up and she sounded irritated when she said:

'Your patient has demanded an immediate stop to your activities. She has also reported you to the police. This is a big deal for us. We've put money into your research and if it turns out that the project isn't up to standard, we will be forced to take further action.'

I didn't know what to say. I felt like bursting into laughter.

'This is absurd,' was all I managed to say.

Then I turned to walk out.

'Erik,' Annika called after me. 'Don't you realise that this is a good offer?'

I stopped.

'You surely can't believe that rubbish about planted memories?'

She shrugged.

'That isn't the important thing here. What matters is that we follow procedure. Go on leave from the hypnotherapy project, see it as an opportunity for reconciliation. You can carry on with your research, you can work in peace and quiet, as long as you don't practise hypnotherapy for the duration of our investigation . . .'

'What exactly are you suggesting? I can't admit something that isn't true.'

'I'm not asking you to.'

'It sounds like it. Any request for a leave of absence will look like I'm admitting culpability.'

'Just put in your request,' she commanded.

'This is completely fucking ridiculous,' I said, and left the room.

It was late in the afternoon. The sun was glinting off the puddles left by a short rainstorm. I was running along the track around the lake, thinking about Lydia. I was still certain she had been telling the truth under hypnosis – but how? What truth had she been telling? She was probably describing a real, concrete memory, but maybe she got the timing wrong. Under hypnosis it becomes clearer than ever that the past is in no way past, I repeated to myself.

I filled my lungs with the cold, fresh early summer air and sprinted the last stretch home through the forest. When I reached our road I saw a large black car parked in front of the driveway. Two men were waiting restlessly beside it. One of them was checking his reflection in the gleaming paint as he smoked a cigarette. The other one was taking photographs of the house. They hadn't seen me yet. I slowed down and was wondering if I could just turn around when they spotted me. The man smoking dropped his cigarette and stubbed it out with his foot, and the other quickly turned his camera towards me. I was still out of breath when I reached them.

'Erik Maria Bark?' the man who had been smoking asked.

'What do you want?'

'We're from *Expressen*.'

'*Expressen*?'

'Yes, we'd like to ask you a few questions about one of your patients . . .'

I shook my head.

'I can't discuss anything of that nature.'

'Oh.'

The man looked at my red face, black running top, loose trousers and wool hat. I heard the photographer cough behind him. A bird darted through the air above us, its trajectory reflected perfectly in the gleaming car. I could see the sky growing darker above the trees. It looked like it might start raining again soon.

'We're running an interview with your patient in tomorrow's paper. She's making some serious allegations against you,' the journalist said bluntly.

I met his gaze. He had a fairly sympathetic face. Middle-aged, a little overweight.

'This is your chance to refute her claims,' he added quietly.

The windows of the house were dark. Simone was probably still at her gallery in the city centre. Benjamin was still at pre-school.

I smiled at the man, and he went on:

'Otherwise her version of the story will be printed unchallenged.'

'I wouldn't dream of discussing a patient in public,' I explained slowly, then walked past the two men towards the house, unlocked the front door and went inside. I stood in the hall until I heard them drive away.

The phone started to ring at six thirty the next morning. It was Annika.

'Erik,' she said, sounding stressed. 'Have you read the paper?'

Simone sat up in bed beside me and gave me an anxious look, and I tried to shrug nonchalantly and went out into the hallway.

'If it's about her allegations, everyone will realise that she's lying . . .'

'No,' she interrupted shrilly. 'They won't realise that. A lot of people will see her as a defenceless, weak, vulnerable person, a woman who has been victimised by a particularly manipulative and dishonest doctor. A man she trusted more than anyone, someone she confided in, who betrayed and exploited her. Because that's what it says in the paper.'

I heard her breathing heavily into the phone. She sounded hoarse and tired when she went on:

'I hope you realise this damages the entire hospital.'

'I'll write a response,' I said.

'That just won't be enough, Erik.'

She paused, then said in a monotone:

'She's going to sue.'

'She'll never win,' I snorted.

'You still don't understand how serious this is, do you?'

'What did she say?'

'I suggest you go and buy a copy of the paper. Then you need to sit down and think about how you're going to deal with this. You're scheduled to appear in front of the board at four o'clock this afternoon.'

*

When I saw my face staring out from the newsstand it felt as if my heart slowed down. It was a close-up of me in my running shirt and wool hat. My face was red, and I looked distinctly unappealing. I got off my bike on shaky legs, bought a copy of the paper and came back home. The double spread in the middle of the paper featured a photograph of Lydia, her face blacked-out, sitting curled up with a teddy bear in her arms. The article was all about how I, Erik Maria Bark, had hypnotised her and used her as a guinea-pig, and had tortured her, accusing her of monstrous crimes. According to the reporter, she had burst into tears and explained that she wasn't interested in compensation. Money could never make up for what she had been put through. She had been systematically broken down, and I'd put ideas in her head. The culmination of my harassment had been when I stormed into her home and goaded her into trying to commit suicide. She had just wanted to die, she said. It was as if she had been part of a cult where I was the leader and she had had no will of her own. Only when she was in the hospital afterwards did she dare to start questioning the way I had treated her. Now she was demanding that I never be allowed to do the same thing to anyone else.

On the next page was a picture of Marek. He agreed with Lydia, and said that my activities were potentially lethal, and that I was obsessed with fabricating sick stories which I forced them to confess to under hypnosis.

Further down the page an expert, Göran Sörensen, gave his opinion. I'd never heard of him before. But here he was, condemning my research out of hand. He compared hypnosis with séances, and insinuated that I probably drugged my patients in order to get them to do what I wanted.

I felt lightheaded. I heard the clock on the kitchen wall tick. I heard one or two cars drive past out in the road. The door opened and Simone came in. Her face drained of all colour as she read the paper.

'What's going on?' she whispered.

'I don't know,' I said, and felt that my mouth was horribly dry.

I sat there staring into space. What if my theories were wrong?

What if hypnosis didn't work on severely traumatised individuals? What if my desire to see a pattern really had affected their memories? I thought that she was describing a genuine memory, but now I was starting to feel confused.

It felt very odd walking the short distance from the main entrance to the lift up to Annika's office. None of the staff wanted to look me in the eye. When I passed people I knew and used to hang out with, they just looked stressed and conflicted, and averted their eyes as they hurried past.

When I got out, Maja slipped quickly past me, pretending not to see me. Rainer Milch was waiting in the doorway to Annika's room. He stepped aside as I walked in and said hello.

'Erik, have a seat,' Rainer said.

'Thanks, I'd rather stand,' I said curtly. I was wondering what on earth Maja Swartling had been doing with the board. Maybe she had been there to defend me. She was, after all, one of the few people who had a genuine, thorough knowledge of my research.

Annika was standing by the window at the other end of the room. I thought it both impolite and unusual of her not to greet me. Instead she just stood there with her arms wrapped around her, staring sternly out of the window.

'We gave you a chance, Erik,' Peder Mälarstedt said.

Rainer nodded.

'But you refused to see reason,' he said. 'You refused to step down voluntarily while we conducted our investigation.'

'I can change my mind,' I said quietly. 'I can . . .'

'It's too late now,' he snapped. 'We could have used that to defend ourselves the day before yesterday. Now it would just look pathetic.'

Annika opened her mouth.

'I . . .' she said in a low voice, without turning to look at me. 'I have to go on television this evening and explain how we let you get away with it.'

'But I haven't done anything wrong,' I said. 'Surely one patient making ridiculous allegations can't erase years of research, countless treatments that have always been irreproachable . . .'

'It's not one patient,' Rainer interrupted. 'There are several of them. And now we've got an expert opinion of your research . . .'

He shook his head and tailed off.

'Is it that Göran Sörensen or whatever his name is?' I asked irritably. 'I've never even heard of him, and he clearly doesn't know anything.'

'We have a source who's spent several years studying your work,' he explained, and scratched his neck. 'She says you're very ambitious, but that most of your theories are castles in the air. You've got no evidence, and you consistently ignore what's best for your patients in an attempt to prove yourself right.'

I stood there speechless.

'What's your expert's name?' I eventually asked.

They didn't answer.

'Not Maja Swartling, by any chance?'

Annika's face turned red.

'Erik,' she said, finally turning towards me. 'You're suspended, as of today. I don't want you in my hospital right now, and I never want you to hypnotise anyone here ever again.'

'What about my patients? I need to make sure . . .'

'They'll be transferred,' she snapped, cutting me off.

'It won't do them any good to have . . .'

'If that's the case, it's your fault,' she said in a raised voice.

The room fell silent. 'I see,' I said hollowly.

Just a few weeks before I had stood in that same room and been awarded more funding. Now everything was finished, in one fell swoop.

When I emerged from the main entrance a number of people approached me. A very tall, blonde woman held a microphone in front of my face.

'Hi,' she said brightly. 'Do you have any comment on the fact that another of your patients, a woman named Eva Blau, was taken into secure psychiatric care last week?'

'What are you talking about?'

I turned away, but the television cameraman followed me, the lens of the camera seeking me out. I looked at the blonde woman, saw her name badge on her chest, Stefanie von Sydow, saw her white, crocheted hat, and the hand gesturing towards the camera.

'Do you still believe that hypnosis is a good form of treatment?'

'Yes,' I replied.

'Are you going to keep doing it?'

The freshly cleaned floor of the secure psychiatric unit of Södermalm Hospital reflected the white light from the tall windows at the end of the hallway. I passed a long row of locked doors, and stopped in front of room B39.

A hard knocking sound was coming from a distant room, then weak crying, followed by silence. I stood for a few moments trying to gather my thoughts before I knocked on the door, then put the key in the lock and went in.

Eva Blau was lying on the bed with her back to me. I went over to the window and tried to let some light in. The spring in the blind was broken and it wouldn't budge. From the corner of my eye I saw Eva start to roll over. I tugged at the blind again, then lost my grip and it flew up with a hard bang.

'Sorry,' I said, 'I just wanted to let in a bit . . .'

In the sudden harsh light I saw Eva sitting there with a bitter expression on her face, looking at me through drugged eyes. My heart started to race. The tip of Eva's nose had been cut off. She was sitting hunched up with a bloody bandage around her hand, just staring at me.

'Eva, I came as soon as I heard,' I said.

She slowly beat her bound hand against her stomach. The circular wound on her nose shone red in her tormented face.

'I was trying to help all of you,' I said. 'But I'm starting to realise that I was wrong about almost everything. I thought I was on the way to making an important discovery, that I understood how hypnosis worked, but I didn't. I didn't understand anything, and I'm sorry I couldn't help you, not a single one of you.'

She rubbed the back of her hand over her nose, and blood started to trickle from the wound down across her mouth.

'Eva, why have you done this to yourself?' I asked.

‘It was you! It was all of you!’ she suddenly shrieked. ‘You’ve ruined my life, you’ve taken everything I had!’

‘I understand that you’re angry at me for . . .’

‘Shut up!’ she snapped. ‘You don’t understand anything! My life is ruined. I can wait, I can wait as long as it takes, but I’m going to get my revenge.’

Then she just screamed, with her mouth wide open, hoarse and bestial. The door flew open and Dr Andersen came in.

‘You were supposed to wait outside!’ he said in a shaky voice.

‘I got the key from the nurse, so I thought . . .’

He pulled me out into the hallway, then closed and locked the door.

‘The patient is paranoid. Hundreds of times a day she demands that we lock her door, and then lock the key in a drawer.’

‘Yes, but . . .’

‘And she keeps saying she’s not going to testify against anyone, that we can give her electric shocks, rape her, but she’s not going to talk. What have you done to your patients? She’s terrified, utterly terrified. It’s inconceivable that you just went in and . . .’

‘She’s angry with me, but she’s not scared of me,’ I interrupted, raising my voice.

‘I heard that scream,’ he said.

After my encounter with Eva at Södermalm Hospital I drove to the television news studios and asked to see Stefanie von Sydow, the journalist who had tried to get a statement from me earlier in the day. I said I was prepared to be interviewed, if they were interested. A few minutes later an assistant came down. She was a young woman with short hair and intelligent eyes.

‘Stefanie will be able to see you in ten minutes,’ she said.

‘Good.’

‘I’ll take you through to make-up.’

When I got home after the short interview, the whole house was dark. I called out, but there was no answer. Simone was sitting on the sofa upstairs in front of the television, which was switched on.

'Has something happened?' I asked. 'Where's Benjamin?'

'He's at David's,' she said expressionlessly.

'What's going on? Talk to me, Simone.'

She nodded, then asked me in an anguished voice:

'Erik, tell me the truth. Have you been having an affair?'

I could feel my heart thudding in my chest, but my voice was horribly calm when I replied:

'What are you talking about?'

'Who's Maja?'

'Maja? I don't know. Should I know who that is?'

'Have you been having an affair?' she asked, her mouth trembling.

'Simone? What's this about?' I replied, and thoughts flew through my head. 'Of course I haven't been having an affair. I'd never . . . Ah, now I understand . . . you mean Maja Swartling. Is that it? She hates me for some reason, she's already spoken to the hospital board and . . .'

'Erik,' Simone interrupted. 'One last chance. Have you been having an affair?'

'No.'

'You haven't had an affair? You swear?'

Her eyes filled with tears.

'I swear,' I whispered.

She nodded and opened a pale blue envelope and tipped out some photographs: I saw myself posing in Maja Swartling's flat, then a series of pictures of her in just her light-green panties. Her dark hair was draped across her big, white breasts. She looked happy, her cheeks were flushed. A number of the pictures were fuzzy close-ups of one breast. And in one of them she was lying with her legs wide apart.

'Simone, let me try . . .'

'I can't handle any more lies,' she said, cutting me off, then picked up the photographs and threw them at me.

The television was on. Only now did I notice it was a news broadcast. They moved on to the next item, a report on the hypnotherapy scandal. Annika Lorentzon from Karolinska

Hospital was unwilling to comment on the case while it was still under investigation, but when the reporter, who had clearly done her homework, brought up the fact that the board had only recently agreed to a significant increase in Erik Maria Bark's funding, Lorentzon became flustered.

'It was a mistake,' she said in a low voice.

'What was a mistake, in your opinion?'

'Erik Maria Bark is suspended until further notice.'

'Only until further notice?'

'He won't be hypnotising anyone else at Karolinska Hospital,' she said.

Then I saw my own face on screen, looking scared as I sat in the television studio.

'Are you going to carry on hypnotising people at other hospitals?' the journalist asked.

I shook my head almost imperceptibly.

'Erik Maria Bark, do you still believe that hypnosis is a useful form of treatment?' she asked.

'I don't know,' I said feebly.

'Are you going to continue with it?'

'No.'

'Never?'

'I am never going to hypnotise anyone again,' I replied.

'Is that a promise?' the journalist asked.

'Yes.'

74

Wednesday morning, 16 December

Erik jerks, and manages to spill coffee on his jacket and the cuff of his shirt.

Joona shoots him a curious look, then hands him a tissue from the box on top of the dashboard.

Erik looks through the window at the big, yellow wooden house, the yard, and the huge Winnie-the-Pooh with sharp teeth drawn on it.

'Is she dangerous?' Joona asks.

'Who?'

'Eva Blau?'

'Maybe,' Erik replies. 'I mean, she's certainly capable of hurting people.'

Joona turns the engine off. They unbuckle their seatbelts and open the doors.

'Don't expect too much from this,' Joona says. 'Liselott Blau may not have anything to do with Eva.'

'I know,' Erik replies faintly.

They walk up the dark slate path. Small snowflakes are swirling about in the air. It looks like a white veil, a milky haze in front of the big wooden house.

'We still need to be careful, though,' Joona says. 'This could be the haunted house.'

Erik stops in the middle of the path. The wet cuff of his shirt is already cold. He smells like stale coffee.

'The haunted house is a building in the former Yugoslavia,' Erik says. 'It's a flat in Jakobsberg, and a gym in Stocksund, a bright green house up in Dorotea, and so on.'

He can't help smiling when he sees the questioning look on Joona's face.

'The haunted house isn't a specific building, it's a descriptive term,' Erik explains. 'The hypnotherapy group called the place where the abuse or trauma had taken place the haunted house.'

'I think I understand,' Joona says. 'Where was Eva Blau's haunted house?'

'That's the whole problem,' Erik says. 'She was the only member of the group who didn't manage to find her haunted house. She never gave a description of a specific place.'

'Maybe this is it,' Joona says, pointing at the house.

They stride up the slate path. Erik feels in his pocket for the wooden box with the parrot on it. He doesn't feel well. He's still badly shaken by his memories. He rubs his forehead hard, wishes he could take a pill, any pill, but knows he needs to be clear-headed now. He needs to stop taking pills, he can't keep going the way he has been. He can't keep running away – he has to find Benjamin before it's too late.

Erik rings the doorbell and hears the heavy chime through the thick wood. He has to force himself not to throw the door open, rush inside and start calling Benjamin's name. Joona is holding his hand inside his jacket. The door is eventually opened by a young woman with glasses, red hair and a scattering of acne scars on her cheeks.

'We're looking for a Liselott Blau,' Joona says.

'That's me,' she replies warily.

Joona looks at Erik and realises that this red-headed woman isn't the person who called herself Eva Blau.

'We're actually trying to find Eva,' he says.

'Eva? What Eva? What's this about?' the woman asks.

Joona shows his police ID and asks if they can go inside. She's reluctant to let them in, so Joona asks her to put a coat on and come outside instead. A couple of minutes later they're standing on the hard, frosty grass, their breath forming white clouds as they speak.

'I live on my own,' she says.

'It's a big house.'

The woman smiles thinly:

'I'm well-off.'

'Is Eva Blau related to you?'

'I already said I don't know an Eva Blau.'

Joona shows her three pictures of Eva that he's printed out from the converted video-tape, but the red-headed woman just shakes her head.

'Take a good look,' Joona says seriously.

'Don't tell me what to do,' she snaps.

'No, but I'm asking you to . . .'

'I pay your wages,' she says. 'My taxes pay your wages.'

'Please, take another look at the pictures,' he says.

'I've never set eyes on her.'

'It's important,' Erik says.

'For you, maybe,' the woman says. 'Not for me.'

'She says her name is Eva Blau,' Joona goes on. 'Blau is a pretty unusual name in Sweden.'

Erik sees a curtain move in one of the upstairs windows. He rushes towards the house, and hears the other two call after him.

75

Wednesday morning, 16 December

Erik runs through the door and across the hallway. He looks around and sees a wide staircase, and rushes up it, taking several steps at a time.

'Benjamin?' he calls out, and stops.

The landing stretches off in both directions, with doors leading to bedrooms and bathrooms.

'Benjamin?' he calls quietly.

Somewhere a floor creaks. He hears Liselott come rushing into the house downstairs. Erik tries to figure out which window he saw the curtain move in. He hurries to the door at the end of the hallway on the right. He tries to open it, but it's locked, so he leans over and looks through the keyhole. The key is in the lock, but he thinks he can see movement reflected in the metal.

'Open the door!' he says loudly.

Liselott starts to climb the stairs.

'You're not allowed in here,' she shouts.

Erik takes a step back, and kicks the door open. The room is empty: a large, unmade bed with pink sheets, a pale pink fitted carpet, and smoke-tinted wardrobe doors. A camera on a stand is pointing at the bed. He goes over and opens the wardrobe, but there's no one there. He turns around and looks at the heavy curtains and armchair, then leans over and sees a figure huddled in the darkness under the bed: frightened eyes, thin thighs and bare feet.

'Come out,' he says sternly.

He reaches in, grabs hold of an ankle and pulls out a naked youth. The young man tries to say something. He speaks quickly and earnestly to Erik in a language that sounds like Arabic as he pulls on a pair of jeans. The bed skirt moves and another young man looks out, and says something in a harsh voice to the first, who stops talking instantly. Liselott is now standing in the doorway, and in a trembling voice keeps telling Erik to leave her friends alone.

'Are they underage?' Erik asks.

'Get out of my house,' she commands furiously.

The second young man has wrapped the sheet around himself. He takes out a cigarette and looks at Erik with a smile.

'Out!' Liselott Blau shouts.

Erik walks along the hallway and down the stairs. The woman follows him, yelling hoarsely at him to go to hell. Joona is waiting outside, holding his drawn pistol hidden close to his body. The woman stops in the doorway.

'You can't do this!' she shouts. 'It's against the law. The police need a court order to enter someone's property.'

'I'm not in the police,' Erik calls back. 'Joona, she's got two young man in there!'

'They're not underage, they're not undocumented,' she goes on.

'I hear you, and I'm sure you're right,' Joona says. 'But, on the other hand, I'm a police officer, and I just received a report of possible misconduct. That's enough to enter this property.'

He takes out his phone and calls dispatch before he asks Liselott Blau to move away from the door and walks in.

76

Wednesday afternoon, 16 December

When the local police arrive five minutes later the young men have put on some clothes. After Joona briefs his colleagues on the situation, he leaves the house and sits in the car next to Erik. He takes a piece of paper out of his pocket, and reads:

'I've got six more Blaus in the Stockholm area, three in Västerås, two in Eskilstuna and one up in Umeå.'

He puts the note away and gives Erik an encouraging smile.

'Charlotte,' Erik says quietly.

'There's no Charlotte,' Joona says, wiping the rear-view mirror.

'Charlotte Cederskiöld,' Erik says. 'She was nice to Eva. I think Eva even stayed with her for a while back then.'

'Where do you think we might find this Charlotte?'

'She lived in Stocksund ten years ago, but . . .'

Joona already has his phone out.

'Hi, Anja. Yes, thanks, same to you. Listen, I need the phone number and address of a Charlotte Cederskiöld. She lives in Stocksund, or at least she used to. Yes, thanks. OK, hang on,' he says, and writes something on the back of a receipt. 'Thanks very much.'

He flicks the indicator and pulls out onto the road again.

'Does she still live there?' Erik asks.

'No, but we got lucky anyway,' he says. 'She lives close to Rimbo.'

Erik feels his stomach clench with sudden anxiety. He doesn't know why the fact that she's moved away from Stocksund worries him.

'She lives at Husby Manor,' Joona says, and pushes a CD into the car-stereo. 'Saija Varjus, the great Finnish singer,' he says. He mutters something about it being his mother's music, then slowly turns up the volume.

He shakes his head sadly and sings along.

The mournful music fills the car. When the song comes to an end they sit in silence for a while, then Joona says, sounding almost surprised:

'I don't like Finnish music any more.'

He clears his throat a couple of times.

'I thought it was nice,' Erik says.

Joona smiles and glances at him quickly.

'Mum was there when she was crowned "Tango Queen" in Seinäjoki . . .'

As they turn off the wide, busy road onto highway 77 at Sätuna, hard sleet starts to fall. The sky off to the east is growing dark, and the farms they pass recede into the gloom.

Joona drums the dashboard. Heat streams from the vents with a hiss. Erik feels his feet start to sweat from the sudden warmth in the car.

Joona drives through a small village and onto a narrow, straight road across the frozen fields. Far in the distance is a large white house behind a high fence. They park outside the open gates and walk past the gates towards the house. A young woman in a leather jacket is raking the gravel path. She looks up at them, alarmed. A golden retriever is running around her legs.

'Charlotte,' the woman calls. 'Charlotte?'

A woman appears from around the corner of the house, dragging a black bin-bag behind her. She's wearing a pink down vest over a thick grey sweater, faded jeans and a pair of wellington boots.

Charlotte, Erik thinks. It really is Charlotte.

The slim, cool woman in elegant clothes with a neat bob is long gone. The person walking towards them looks completely different. Her hair is long and completely grey, worn in a thick braid. Her face is full of laughter-lines, and she's wearing no make-up. Erik thinks she looks more beautiful than ever. When she catches sight of him she looks astonished at first, then her face cracks into a wide smile.

'Erik!' she says, and her voice hasn't changed: deep, articulate and warm.

She lets go of the bag and takes hold of his hands.

'Is it really you? How wonderful to see you again.'

She says hello to Joona, then stands for a moment and just looks at them. A heavyset woman opens the front door and stares at them. She has a tattoo on her neck, and is wearing a bulky black down jacket.

'Do you need any help?' she yells.

'Friends of mine,' Charlotte calls back with a reassuring wave.

Charlotte smiles as the larger woman closes the door.

'I've . . . I've turned the manor into a women's refuge. There are so many rooms, so I take in women who need to get away. I let them live here. We cook together, look after the stables . . . until they feel up to managing on their own again. It's all very straightforward.'

'Sounds wonderful,' Erik says.

She nods and gestures towards the door, inviting them in.

'Charlotte, we need to get hold of Eva Blau,' Erik says. 'Do you remember her?'

'Of course I remember her. She was my first guest out here. I had the rooms in the wing, and . . .'

She stops herself.

'It's funny you should mention her,' she says, starting again. 'Eva called me only a week or so ago.'

'What did she want?'

'She was angry,' Charlotte says.

'Yes,' Erik sighs.

'Why was she angry?' Joona asks.

Charlotte takes a deep breath. Erik hears the wind blowing through the bare trees.

'She was angry at you,' she says, pointing at Erik.

He feels his skin crawl when he thinks of Eva's sharp features, her aggressive voice, piercing eyes and mutilated nose.

'You swore never to hypnotise anyone ever again, then suddenly last week you started again. It was in all the newspapers, and they were talking about it on television. So obviously a lot of people got upset.'

'I had to do it,' Erik says. 'But it was an exception, a one-off.'

She takes his hand in hers.

'You helped me,' she whispers. 'That time when I saw . . . do you remember?'

'I remember,' Erik says quietly.

Charlotte smiles at him.

'That was all it took – going inside the haunted house, looking up, and seeing the people who had hurt me.'

'I know.'

'That never would have happened without you, Erik.'

'But I . . .'

'Something inside me became whole again,' she says, putting one hand on her chest.

'Where is Eva now?' Joona asks.

Charlotte frowns.

'When she was discharged from the hospital she moved to a flat in the centre of Åkersberga, and joined the Jehovah's Witnesses. To start with we were in contact a lot. I helped her with money. She thought she was being followed, talked a lot about trying to get protection, kept saying something evil was out to get her. Eventually we lost touch.'

Charlotte stops and looks at Erik.

'You look sad,' she says.

'My son's missing. Eva is our only lead.'

Charlotte looks at him with concern.

'I sincerely hope you get him back.'

'What's Eva's name – do you know?' Erik asks.

'Her real name, you mean? She never tells anyone that. It's possible she doesn't even remember it any more.'

'OK.'

'She was calling herself Veronica when she called.'

'Veronica.'

'She took it from the Veil of Veronica.'

They hug quickly, then Erik and Joona hurry back to the car.

As they're driving back towards Stockholm, Joona makes another phone call. He asks for help finding a Veronica living in the centre of Åkersberga, and gives the address for the Kingdom Hall of the Jehovah's Witnesses.

As Erik listens to Joona, a heavy, exhausted feeling fills his head, and he feels his eyes slowly close.

'Yes, Anja, I'm writing it down,' he hears Joona say. 'Västra Banvägen . . . hang on, Stationsvägen 5, OK, thanks.'

77

Wednesday afternoon, 16 December

Erik wakes up as they're driving past a golf-course.

'We're almost there,' Joona says.

'I fell asleep,' Erik says, mostly to himself.

'Eva Blau called Charlotte the day you were in the papers,' Joona says thoughtfully.

'And the next day Benjamin was kidnapped,' Erik says.

'Because someone saw you.'

'Or because I broke my promise never to hypnotise anyone again.'

'In which case it's my fault,' Joona says.

'No, it's not.'

Erik stops, unsure of what he wants to say.

'I'm sorry,' Joona says, staring at the road.

They pass a discount store with broken windows. Joona peers in the rear-view mirror. A woman in a hijab is sweeping broken glass from the pavement.

'I don't know what happened to Eva when she was my patient,' Erik says. 'She harmed herself, and became completely paranoid, blaming me and my hypnosis for everything. I should never have let her join the group. And I should never have hypnotised anyone.'

'But you helped Charlotte,' Joona counters.

'Perhaps,' Erik says quietly.

Just beyond the roundabout they cross railway tracks, turn left at a football field, cross a river and pull up outside a big, grey block of flats.

Joona points at the glove compartment.

'Can you pass me my pistol?'

Erik opens the hatch and hands him the heavy weapon. Joona checks the chamber and magazine, then makes sure the safety is on before putting it in his pocket.

They hurry across the car park and past a playground with slides, a sandpit and a jungle gym.

Erik points towards the entrance, then looks up to see flashing Christmas lights and satellite dishes on almost every balcony.

An old woman is standing with her walker inside the locked door to the stairwell. Joona knocks and gives her a cheery wave. She looks at them and shakes her head. Joona holds his police ID up to the window, but she just shakes her head again. Erik searches through his pockets and finds the envelope of receipts he's been meaning to hand in to the expenses office. He walks over to the window, knocks and holds up the envelope. Immediately the woman walks over and presses the button to unlock the door.

'Is it the post?' she asks in an unsteady voice.

'Express delivery,' Erik says and looks at the list of names. He finds a Veronica Andersson on the first floor. The narrow staircase is covered with red graffiti and muddy children's footprints. A rancid smell is coming from the rubbish chute. They stop outside the door marked Andersson, and ring the bell.

'Ring again,' Erik says.

Joona opens the letterbox and says he has a letter from *The Watchtower* for her. Erik sees Joona's head jerk back as if he's been hit.

'What is it?'

'I don't know, but I want you to stay outside,' Joona says with an anxious glance at him.

'No,' Erik replies.

'I'm going in alone.'

A glass hits the floor and breaks behind one of the other doors on the first floor. Joona takes out a small case and pulls two thin metal objects from it. One is hooked at the end, and the other looks like a very narrow key.

As if he were reading Erik's mind, Joona mutters that it's perfectly OK to break into a flat without a warrant.

'According to the most recent legislation, you just need to have good grounds for doing so,' he says.

He's about to insert the first of the tools into the keyhole, but Erik reaches his hand out and tries the door. It isn't locked. A powerful stench billows out as the door swings open. Joona draws his weapon and gestures sharply to Erik to stay outside.

78

Wednesday afternoon, 16 December

Erik can hear his heart thudding in his chest. He can hear the blood pumping in his ears. The silence is ominous. Benjamin isn't here. The lights in the stairwell, which are on a timer, go out and darkness engulfs him. His eyes have difficulty finding fixed points to focus on.

Suddenly Joona is standing right in front of him.

'I think you're going to have to come in with me, Erik,' he says.

They go inside and Joona switches the ceiling light on. The bathroom door is wide open. The smell of decay is unbearable. Eva Blau is lying in the empty bathtub. Her face is swollen, and flies are crawling around her mouth and buzzing in the air. Her blue blouse has bunched up, and her stomach is distended and a bluish-green colour. There are deep, black cuts down both her arms. Her blouse and blonde hair are stiff with dried blood. Her skin is pale and grey, and a network of brown veins is visible across her whole body: stagnant blood has rotted inside her blood vessels. There are clusters of yellow flies' eggs at the corners of her eyes and around her nostrils and mouth. The blood has seeped across to the small bath mat, staining the fringe and one side. There's a kitchen knife in the bath next to the body.

'Is it her?' Joona asks.

'Yes. That's Eva.'

'She's been dead at least a week,' Joona says. 'Her stomach has had time to swell up considerably.'

'Oh God,' Erik says.

'She can't have taken Benjamin,' Joona concludes.

'I need to think,' Erik says.

He looks out through the window at the low red-brick building on the other side of the railway track. Eva could see the Kingdom Hall from her window. He assumes that must have made her feel safe.

79

Thursday morning, 17 December

Simone feels a drop of blood trickle from her bottom lip. She's bitten herself without noticing. Her dad, who was hit by a car, has been lying in this shady room at St Göran's Hospital for the past two days, and they still don't know how badly hurt he is. All she knows is that the impact could have killed him. She's lost Erik, she might have lost Benjamin, and now it's possible that she might be losing her dad too.

She takes her mobile phone out again just to make sure it's working, then puts it back in the outside pocket of her bag, where she'll be able to reach it quickly if, against all odds, it should start to ring.

Then she leans over her father and adjusts his blanket. He's asleep, and it's completely silent in the room. She's long marvelled that Kennet Sträng is probably the only man in the world who doesn't make any noise when he sleeps.

He has a white bandage around his head. A dark shadow spreads out from under it, a bruise that reaches across one cheek, to his swollen nose and limp mouth.

But he isn't dead, she tells herself. He's alive, he's definitely alive. And Benjamin is alive, she knows that, he must be alive.

Simone paces up and down the room. She thinks back to how she got home from Sim Shulman's flat the other day, and how she must have just spoken to her dad before the accident happened. He told her he had found Wailord and was going somewhere called 'the sea', out at Loudden.

Simone looks at her father again. He's sleeping heavily.

'Dad?'

She regrets saying it. He doesn't wake up, but an anxious look flutters across his sleeping face. Simone touches the cut on her lip tentatively. She looks at the Advent candelabra in the window, then stares down at her shoes in their blue plastic covers. She thinks back to an afternoon many years ago when she and Kennet watched her mother drive off in her little green Fiat.

Simone shivers, and realises she's getting a raging headache. She pulls her cardigan more tightly around her. She hears Kennet groan quietly.

'Daddy,' she says, as if she were a small child.

He opens his eyes. They seem clouded, not really awake. The white of one eye is red with blood.

'Dad, it's me,' Simone says. 'How are you feeling?'

His gaze floats past her. She's suddenly afraid he can't see.

'Simone?'

'I'm here, Dad.'

She sits down gently beside him and takes his hand. His eyes close again, and his eyebrows knit together as if he's in pain.

'Dad,' she asks quietly, 'how do you feel?'

He tries to reach up and pat her hand, but can't quite manage it.

'I'll soon be back on my feet again,' he wheezes. 'Don't you worry.'

The room is quiet. Simone struggles to control her thoughts. She doesn't want to put any pressure on him while he's in this state, but panic forces her to try anyway.

'Dad?' she asks quietly. 'Do you remember what we were talking about just before the accident?'

He squints at her tiredly and shakes his head.

'You said you knew where Wailord was. You were talking about the sea, do you remember? You said you were going to the sea.'

There's a flicker of recognition in Kennet's eyes and he attempts to sit up, but sinks back down again with a groan.

'Dad, tell me, I need to know where it is. Who's Wailord? Who is it?'

He opens his mouth, and his chin trembles when he says:

'A . . . child . . . it's a . . . a child . . .'

'What are you saying?'

But Kennet's eyes are closed and he doesn't seem to hear her any more. Simone goes over to the window and looks out across the hospital grounds. She can feel a draught. There's a dirty streak running down the glass. She breathes on it, and for a moment she sees the impression of someone else's face in the condensation. Someone else has stood in exactly the same place, leaning against the window.

The church on the other side of the street is dark, and the streetlights reflect off its black, arched windows. She thinks about what Benjamin wrote to Aida, about not letting Nicke go to the sea.

'Aida,' she says quietly. 'I'm going to go and talk to Aida, and this time she's going to tell me what she knows.'

80

Thursday morning, 17 December

Nicke opens the door when Simone rings the bell at Aida's flat. He looks at her curiously.

'Hello,' she says.

'I've got some new cards,' he tells her eagerly.

'That's good,' she said.

'Some of them are girl cards, but a lot of them are really strong.'

'Is your sister home?' Simone asks, patting Nicke on the arm.

'Aida! Aida!'

Nicke runs down the hall and disappears into the flat.

Simone stands and waits. Then she hears a peculiar pumping sound, followed by a clanking, and after a while she sees a thin, hunch-backed woman walking towards her. She's pulling a small cart with an oxygen tank behind her. A tube leads from the tank to the woman, pumping oxygen into her nostrils through thin, transparent plastic tubes.

The woman taps her chest with a small fist.

'Em . . . physema,' she wheezes, then her wrinkled face contracts in a hoarse, painful coughing fit.

They walk down the long, dark hallway together and into a living room full of heavy furniture. On the floor, between a stereo unit with a glass door and the low coffee table, Nicke is playing with his Pokémon cards. On the brown sofa, squeezed in between two large potted palms, sits Aida.

Simone hardly recognises her. She isn't wearing any make-up and her hair is neatly brushed and gathered in a ponytail. Her face is pretty, and she looks very young and fragile.

She reaches for a packet of cigarettes and lights one with trembling hands as Simone walks into the room.

'Hello,' Simone says. 'How are you doing?'

Aida shrugs. She looks like she's been crying. She takes a drag on the cigarette, and raises a green ashtray towards it, as if she were worried about dropping ash on the furniture.

'Sit . . . down . . .' her mother wheezes, and Simone sits down on one of the wide armchairs jostling for space with the sofa, table and potted plants.

Aida taps her cigarette in the ashtray.

'I've come from the hospital,' Simone says. 'My dad was hit by a car. He was on his way to the sea, to Wailord.'

Nicke leaps to his feet. His face is bright red.

'Wailord is angry, so angry, so angry.'

Simone turns to look at Aida, who swallows hard and then closes her eyes.

'What's this all about?' Simone asks. 'Wailord? What's going on?'

Aida stubs the cigarette out, then says in an unsteady voice: 'They've vanished.'

'Who have?'

'A gang who were being mean to us. Nicke and me. They were horrible, said they'd mark me, said they'd . . .'

She falls silent and looks at her mother, who makes a snorting sound.

'Said they'd turn Mum into a torch,' Aida says slowly.

'Little . . . bastards . . .' her mum hisses from the other end of the sofa.

'They use Pokémon names, things like Azelf, Magmortar, Lucario. They change names sometimes, so you don't know who they are.'

'How many of them are there?'

'I don't know, maybe just five,' Aida replies. 'They're just kids, the oldest one is my age, the youngest something like six. But they decided that everyone who lived here should give them something,' she continues, meeting Simone's gaze for the first time. Her eyes are amber brown, beautiful, clear, but scared. 'The little kids around here had to give them sweets, pens,' she goes on in her thin voice. 'They emptied their piggy banks so they didn't get beaten up. Some gave them things like mobile phones and Nintendos. They took my jacket, cigarettes. And Nicke . . . they just kept hitting him and taking whatever he had, they were so horrible to him.'

Her voice fades away and tears spring to her eyes.

'Have they taken Benjamin?' Simone asks bluntly.

Aida's mother waves her hand:

'That . . . boy . . . isn't . . . good . . .'

'Answer me, Aida,' Simone says, raising her voice. 'Answer me now!'

'Don't . . . shout . . . at my . . . daughter,' Aida's mother hisses.

Simone shakes her head at her and says, sharper this time:

'You're going to tell me what you know, do you hear me?'

Aida swallows hard.

'I don't know much,' she eventually says. 'Benjamin got involved, he said we shouldn't give those boys anything. Wailord went crazy, said it was war, demanded tons of money from us.'

She lights another cigarette, takes a shaky drag, carefully taps it on the ashtray, and goes on:

'When Wailord found out that Benjamin was sick, he gave the kids needles so they could scratch him . . .'

She stops speaking and shrugs her shoulders.

'What happened?' Simone says impatiently.

Aida bites her lip.

'What happened?'

'Wailord just stopped,' she whispers. 'Suddenly he was gone. I've seen the other kids, they went after Nicke the other day. Now they're following someone calling himself Ariandos, but they're really just confused and desperate now that Wailord's vanished.'

'When was this? When did Wailord disappear?'

Aida thinks for a moment.

'I think it was last Wednesday.' Three days before Benjamin disappeared, in other words.

Her mouth starts to quiver.

'Wailord's taken him,' she whispers. 'Wailord's done something terrible to him. Now he won't show himself . . .'

She starts to cry hard. Simone watches as her mother very laboriously gets up, takes the cigarette from her hand and stubs it out on the green ashtray.

'Fucking . . . monster,' the mother hisses, and Simone has no idea who she's referring to.

'Who is Wailord?' she asks again. 'You have to tell me who he is.'

'I don't know!' Aida yells. 'I don't know!'

Simone takes out the photograph she found on Benjamin's computer, of the grass, with the bushes and the brown fence in the background.

'Look at this,' she says sternly.

Aida looks at the printout, but she's closed herself off.

'What is this place?' Simone asks.

Aida shrugs and glances at her mother.

'No idea,' she says blankly.

'You were the one who sent this to Benjamin,' Simone points out angrily. 'It came from you, Aida.'

The girl looks back at her mother, who's sitting with the hissing oxygen tank by her feet.

Simone waves the paper in front of her face.

'Look at it, Aida. Look again. Why did you send this to my son?'

'It was just a joke,' she whispers.

'A joke?'

Aida nods.

'Sort of. This is where I'd like to live,' she says weakly.

'I don't believe you,' Simone declares angrily. 'Tell me the truth!'

Aida's mother gets to her feet again and gesticulates at her.

'You bitch . . . out of my house, now!'

'Why are you lying?' Simone asks, and at last Aida meets her gaze.

The girl looks incredibly sad.

'Sorry,' she whispers in a small voice. 'Sorry.'

As Simone is leaving she passes Nicke. He's standing in the dark hallway rubbing his eyes.

'I haven't got any power, I'm a worthless Pokémon.'

81

Thursday morning, 17 December

When Simone returns to Kennet's room in the hospital he's sitting up in bed. His face has a bit more colour now, and he looks like he knew she was going to walk in at that very moment.

Simone goes over, leans forward and gently presses her cheek against his.

'Do you know what I was dreaming, Simone?' he asks.

'No,' she says.

'I was dreaming about my father.'

'About Grandpa?'

'Can you imagine? He was standing in the workshop, all happy and sweaty. "My boy," he said. That's all. I can still smell the diesel . . .'

Simone swallows. There's a hard, painful lump in her throat. Kennet slowly shakes his head.

'Dad,' Simone whispers. 'Dad, do you remember what we were talking about just before your accident?'

He looks at her seriously, and it's as if a light comes on in his sharp eyes. He tries to get up, but moves too quickly and sinks back onto the bed.

'Help me, Simone,' he says impatiently. 'There's no time to lose – I can't just lie around in here.'

'Do you remember what happened, Dad?'

'I remember everything.'

He rubs his eyes, clears his throat, then holds his hands out.

'Hold onto me,' he orders, and this time, with Simone's help, he manages to sit up on the bed and swing his legs over the edge.

'I need my clothes.'

Simone hurries to the wardrobe and gets them. She kneels down and is pulling his socks on when the door opens and a young doctor comes in.

'I have to get out of here,' Kennet says before the man has a chance to say anything.

Simone stands up.

'Hello,' she says, shaking the young doctor's hand. 'My name is Simone Bark.'

'Ola Tuvefjäll,' he says, and looks rather embarrassed as he turns to Kennet, who is standing there zipping up his trousers.

'Hello,' Kennet says, tucking his shirt in. 'I'm sorry we can't stop, but we're in a bit of an emergency situation.'

'I can't force you to stay,' the doctor says calmly. 'But you need to understand that you're going to have to be extremely careful, considering how hard the blow to your head was. You may be feeling OK now, but be aware that complications could arise. It could happen a minute from now, or an hour, or even tomorrow.'

Kennet goes over to the sink and rinses his face with cold water.

'Like I said, I'm sorry,' he says, straightening up. 'But I have to go to the sea.'

The doctor looks on, disturbed, as they hurry off along the hallway. Simone tells her father about her visit to see Aida. Kennet has to lean against the wall while they wait for the lift.

'So where are we going?' Simone asks, and for once Kennet doesn't object when she gets in the driver's seat. He gets in beside her, fastens his seatbelt and scratches his head through the bandage.

'You need to tell me where we're going,' she says again when he doesn't answer. 'How do we get there?'

He looks at her strangely.

'To the sea. I need to think.'

He leans back in the seat, closes his eyes and doesn't move for a while. She starts to think that she's made a mistake. Her dad obviously isn't well, he needs to go back to hospital. Then he opens his eyes and says tersely:

'Drive out onto Sankt Eriks Street, over the bridge, then turn right onto Oden Street. Then straight on until we reach Östra station, then east along Valhallavägen, all the way to The Film House, then turn off onto Lindarängsvägen. That goes all the way to the harbour.'

'Who needs GPS?' Simone smiles as she pulls out into the heavy traffic on Sankt Eriks Street and heads towards the Västermalm shopping centre.

'I've been wondering,' Kennet says thoughtfully, then falls silent again.

'What?'

'I've been wondering if the parents have noticed anything.'

Simone glances at him as they drive past Gustav Vasa Church. She catches a glimpse of a long procession of children in white gowns. They're carrying candles as they walk in through the church door.

Kennet clears his throat:

'I wonder if the parents have realised what their children are doing.'

'Extortion, assault, violence and blackmail,' Simone says wearily. 'Mummy and Daddy's little darlings.'

She thinks about the time she went out to Tensta, to the tattoo parlour. Those boys, holding a little girl over the railing. They hadn't been scared at all. In fact, they'd threatened her. She thinks about how Benjamin tried to stop her from going up to the boy in the underground station, and realises now that he must have been one of the boys with Pokémon names.

'What's wrong with people?' she asks rhetorically.

'What happened to me wasn't an accident, Simone. I was pushed in front of a car,' Kennet says sharply. 'And I saw who did it.'

'You were pushed? Who . . .?'

'It was one of them, a child, a young girl.'

Electric Advent candles shine from the black windows of The

Film House. Simone turns off into Lindarängsvägen, crossing the ridge of slush in the middle of the road. Swollen, heavy clouds are hanging above Gärdet. It looks like a storm is about to break over the people out walking their dogs.

Loudden is a promontory just to the east of Frihamnen. In the late 1920s it was turned into an oil depot, with almost one hundred oil tanks. Today the area contains industrial buildings, water towers, a container port, underground shelters and docks.

Kennet takes out the crumpled business card he found in the child's wallet.

'Louddsvägen 18,' he says, and gestures for Simone to stop the car. She pulls over onto a tarmacked area surrounded by tall metal fencing.

'We'll walk the rest of the way,' Kennet says, unbuckling his seatbelt.

They set off between the vast, cylindrical oil tanks, whose narrow staircases spiral up the sides. Rust is creeping across the curved, welded panels and the joints and railings of the staircases.

It's raining now, just a few cold drops. They hit the metal with a heavy clang. It will soon be dusk and they won't be able to see anything. There are no streetlights anywhere, just oil tanks, loading bays, low office buildings and, nearer the water, cranes, ramps, piers and dry docks. A dirty Ford pickup is parked outside a shack attached to a large corrugated aluminium warehouse. The dark glass window of the shack has been adorned with some self-adhesive letters that have been half scraped off: *The Sea*. The smaller lettering underneath is completely gone, but its outline can still be read in the dirt: *diving club*. A heavy bar is hanging next to the door.

82

Thursday afternoon, 17 December

Kennet waits a moment, listening, then cautiously opens the door. The small office is dark. All it contains is a desk, a few folding chairs with plastic seats, and a couple of rusty oxygen tanks. On the wall is a crumpled poster showing exotic fish in emerald green water. It's obvious that the diving club is no longer here: presumably it either went bankrupt or moved.

An air-vent starts to whirr and the internal door vibrates slightly. Kennet puts his finger to his lips. They hear footsteps. They hurry across the room, open the door and find themselves looking into a large subterranean warehouse. Someone is running in the darkness. Simone tries to see what's happening. Kennet is going down a metal staircase, chasing the figure, but suddenly he cries out.

'Dad?' Simone calls.

She can't see him, but she can hear his voice. He swears loudly, then calls to her to be careful.

'They've put up barbed wire.'

Something scrapes metallically across the cement floor. Kennet has started to run again. Simone follows him, steps over the barbed wire and runs deeper into the warehouse. The air is damp and cold. It's dark, and she finds it hard to get her bearings. She can hear rapid footsteps in the distance.

The light from one of the cranes outside shines through a

dirty window. Simone spots someone standing next to a forklift. It's a boy wearing a grey cardboard mask. He's holding an iron pipe in his hand and is hunched over, shuffling his feet restlessly.

Kennet is getting close to him now, hurrying along the rows of shelving.

'Behind the forklift!' Simone calls.

The boy in the mask rushes out and throws the metal pipe at Kennet. It spins through the air and only just misses his head.

'Wait, we just want to talk to you!' Kennet shouts.

The boy opens a steel door and runs out onto the waterfront. Kennet runs after him.

Simone follows but slips and falls on the wet pier. The air reeks of rubbish. She gets up and sees her dad running along the dock. The wet sleet has made the ground slippery, and Simone comes close to sliding over the edge as she hurries after them. She runs after the two figures ahead of her, horribly aware of the steep drop beside her, where the black, half-frozen water laps against the quay.

She knows that if she slipped and fell it wouldn't take long for the ice-cold water to paralyse her. She'd sink like a rock, especially with her thick coat and boots, which would fill with water.

She's out of breath now, shaking with stress and exertion. Her back is soaked from the rain.

It looks like Kennet has lost the boy. He's doubled over, waiting for her. The bandage around his head has come loose and he's gasping for breath. His lungs are wheezing badly and a trickle of blood is running from his nose. There's a cardboard mask on the ground. The rain has started to dissolve it, and when the wind catches it, it swirls up and vanishes over the edge of the dock.

'Damn it!' Kennet says when she catches up with him.

They walk away from the water as dusk settles heavily around them. The rain is slackening, but the wind has picked up, whistling around the bulky metal-framed buildings. They walk past an oblong dry dock and Simone hears the wind singing down below. Tractor tyres hang from rusty chains along the sides. She looks down into the vast empty space, a huge pool without any water, its rough rock walls reinforced with concrete and iron mesh. Fifty metres below she can see the moulded cement floor and immense supporting struts.

A tarp flaps in the wind and light from one of the cranes flickers across the vertical walls of the dry dock. Simone spots someone sitting behind one of the concrete struts.

Kennet realises she's stopped and turns to see why. Without saying anything, she points down into the dry dock.

The huddled figure creeps back from the light.

Kennet and Simone rush towards the narrow staircase. The figure stands up and starts running towards what looks like a small door in the wall of the dry dock. Clinging onto the railing, Kennet runs down the steep steps. He almost slips but manages to keep his balance. The air smells sharply of metal, rust and rain. They hurry, keeping close to the wall, their footsteps echoing.

The floor is wet, and Simone shivers as the cold water seeps into her boots.

'Where did he go?' she calls.

Kennet hurries past the struts. He points to the place where the boy disappeared. It isn't a door, like they thought, but some sort of vent. Kennet peers through it, but can't see anything. He's out of breath, and stands up to wipe his forehead and neck.

'Out you come!' he pants. 'Enough is enough.'

They hear a rasping sound, heavy and rhythmic. Kennet starts to crawl into the vent.

'Be careful, Dad!'

There's a grinding noise, then the sluice doors start to creak. Suddenly there's a deafening roar, and Simone realises what's happening.

'He's letting the water in!' she cries.

'There's a ladder in here,' she hears Kennet shout.

Thin jets of ice-cold water are shooting into the dry dock through the tiny gap between the sluice doors. The metallic creaking continues, and the doors slide apart a little further. Water starts to gush in. Simone rushes towards the staircase and she finds herself wading through ice-cold water, knee-deep and rising. The light from the crane flickers across the rough walls.

The swirling current is strong and it pulls her backwards. She trips over one of the large metal supports and feels her foot go numb with pain. Heavy waves of black water are crashing into the dock. She's almost in tears by the time she reaches the staircase and starts to climb. After a few steps she turns around. She can't see her dad in the darkness. The water is now covering the vent in the wall. There's a creaking, shrieking sound. Her body is shaking. Her lungs are burning. Then she realises that the sound of rushing water is getting quieter. The doors close again and the flow of water stops. She's lost all sensation in the hand clinging onto the metal railing. Her clothes are heavy, straining tightly across her thighs, but she reaches the top and sees Kennet on the far side of the dry dock. He waves to her, then starts to lead a boy towards the old diving club.

Simone is soaking wet, and her hands and feet are frozen. Kennet and the boy are waiting for her by the car. The look on Kennet's face is oddly distant, and the boy is just standing there with his head bowed.

'Where's Benjamin?' Simone screams before she reaches them.

The boy says nothing. Simone grabs him by the shoulders and turns him around. She's so shocked when she sees his face that she lets out a gasp.

The boy's nose has been cut off.

It looks like someone tried to sew the wound together, very quickly, and without any medical knowledge. The look in his eyes is utterly vacant. The wind is howling, so the three of them get in the car. Simone turns the engine on to get the heater working. The windows steam up. She finds some chocolate and gives it to the boy. No one speaks, until Kennet asks:

'Where's Benjamin?'

The boy looks down at his lap. He chews the chocolate, then swallows hard.

'OK, you're going to tell us everything – understand? You've been beating up children, taking their money.'

'I don't exist. I've stopped,' he whispers.

'Why did you beat up other children?' Kennet asks.

'It just happened when we . . .'

'It just happened? Where are the others?'

'How should I know? They probably have new gangs now,' the boy says. 'I heard that Jerker does, anyway.'

'Are you Wailord?'

The boy's mouth trembles.

'I've stopped now,' he says feebly. 'I swear, I've stopped.'

'Where's Benjamin?' Simone asks in a shrill voice.

'I don't know,' he says quickly. 'I'll never hurt him again, I promise.'

'Listen to me,' Simone goes on. 'I'm his mum. I have to know.'

But she stops when the boy starts rocking back and forth, sobbing helplessly and saying over and over again:

'I promise . . . I promise . . . I promise, promise . . .'

Kennet puts his hand on Simone's arm.

'We need to take him to the hospital,' he says in a hollow voice. 'He needs help.'

83

Thursday evening, 17 December

Kennet drops Simone off at the junction of Oden Street and Sveavägen, then drives the short distance to the Astrid Lindgren Children's Hospital.

A doctor examines the boy, and decides to admit him for care and observation. He's suffering from both dehydration and malnourishment. He has infected wounds on his body, and light frostbite in his toes and fingers. The boy calling himself Wailord is actually Birk Jansson, and he lives in Husby with a foster family. Social Services are brought in, and the boy's guardians alerted. When Kennet gets up to leave, the boy starts to cry and says he doesn't want to be alone.

'Please, stay,' he whispers, covering his nose with his hand.

Kennet can feel his heart thudding like a hammer from over-exertion. His nose is still bleeding.

'I'll stay with you, Birk, but on one condition,' he says.

He sits down on a green chair next to the boy.

'You have to tell me everything you know about Benjamin and his disappearance.'

Kennet sits there, feeling increasingly dizzy, for the two hours it takes for the social worker to arrive, but all he really finds out is that someone scared Birk so badly that he stopped harassing Benjamin. He doesn't even seem to know that Benjamin is missing.

When Kennet leaves, he hears the social worker and a psychologist discussing sending the boy to Lövsta children's home in Södermanland.

In the car, Kennet calls Simone to make sure she got home safely. She tells him that she took a nap and is thinking of pouring herself a stiff glass of grappa.

'I'm going to go and talk to Aida,' Kennet says.

'Ask her about that picture with the grass and the fence – there's something about it that doesn't make sense.'

Kennet parks the car in Sundbyberg next to the hotdog stand near Aida's building. It's cold, and a few stray snowflakes drift onto the seat when he opens the car door. He sees Aida and Nicke instantly. The girl is sitting on a bench on the pavement behind the houses. She's watching her brother. Nicke is showing her something, and it looks like he lets it fall to the ground, before catching it again. Kennet stops and watches them for a little while. There's something about the way they behave towards each other that makes them seem so alone, so abandoned. It's almost six o'clock in the evening, and the city lights are reflecting off the dark lake in the distance.

Kennet feels another brief burst of dizziness, and his vision clouds for a moment. Very carefully, he crosses the slippery road and heads across the frosty grass towards the lake.

'Hello, you two,' he says.

Nicke looks up.

'It's you!' he cries, and runs over and hugs Kennet. 'Aida,' he says excitedly, 'it's him, Aida, the one who's so old!'

The girl gives Nicke a wan, worried look. The tip of her nose is red with cold.

'Benjamin?' she asks. 'Have you found him?'

'No, not yet,' Kennet says, as Nicke laughs and carries on hugging him and bouncing around.

'Aida,' he exclaims, 'he's so old they took his gun away . . .'

Kennet sits down on the bench next to Aida. They are surrounded by leafless trees.

'I came to tell you that Wailord is being taken care of.'

Aida turns towards him with a sceptical glance.

'The others have been identified,' he says. 'There were five Pokémons, weren't there? Birk Jansson has identified all of them. But he doesn't have anything to do with Benjamin's disappearance.'

Nicke, who stopped when he heard what Kennet said, is now staring at him.

'You beat Wailord?' he says.

'Yep,' Kennet says. 'He's gone.'

Nicke starts dancing around on the path. His big body is steaming in the cold air. Suddenly he stops and looks at Kennet.

'You're the strongest Pokémon, you're Pikachu! You're Pikachu!'

Nicke hugs Kennet again, even more happily, and Aida starts laughing with a look of astonishment on her face.

'What about Benjamin, though?' she asks.

'They didn't take him, Aida. They may have done a lot of horrible things, but they didn't take Benjamin.'

'It must have been them.'

'I honestly don't think it was,' Kennet says.

'But . . .'

Kennet pulls out the printout from Benjamin's computer, the photograph Aida sent him.

'Look, you have to tell me what this place is,' he says in a friendly but firm voice.

She turns pale and shakes her head.

'I promised,' she says quietly.

'Promises don't apply when lives are at stake, OK?'

But she presses her lips together and looks away. Nicke comes over and looks at the paper.

'His mum gave him that,' he says happily.

'Nicke!'

Aida looks angrily at her brother.

'But it was!' Nicke says indignantly.

'When are you going to learn to keep quiet?' Aida says.

Kennet hushes them.

'Did Simone give Benjamin this photograph? What do you mean, Nicke?'

But Nicke looks anxiously at Aida, as if he's waiting for permission before answering. She shakes her head at him. Kennet feels the bruise on his head ache, a hard, steady throb.

'Just tell me, Aida,' he says, trying to stay calm. 'I promise you, it would be wrong to keep quiet under these circumstances.'

'But the photo has nothing to do with this,' she says in an anguished voice. 'And I promised Benjamin I'd never tell anyone what happened.'

'Tell me what this is a picture of!'

Kennet hears his own voice echo between the buildings. Nicke looks frightened and sad. Aida purses her lips together even harder. Kennet forces himself to calm down. He can hear how unsteady his voice sounds when he tries to explain:

'Aida, listen to me. Benjamin is going to die if we don't find him. He's my only grandchild. I can't ignore a single possible lead.'

They stand in silence. Then Aida turns towards him, close to tears.

'It's like Nicke said,' she says in a resigned voice. She swallows hard before going on:

'His mum gave him that photograph.'

'What do you mean?'

Kennet looks at Nicke, who nods eagerly at him.

'Not Simone,' Aida says. 'His real mum.'

Kennet feels nausea rising in his throat. Suddenly his whole chest hurts, and he tries to take a few deep breaths as he hears his heart thudding hard inside him. He has time to think that he's having a heart attack before the pain subsides again.

'His real mum?' he asks.

'Yes.'

Aida pulls a pack of cigarettes out of her bag, but doesn't have time to light one before Kennet gently takes the pack away from her.

'You're not allowed to smoke,' he says.

'Why not?'

'You're not eighteen.'

She shrugs.

'Fine, I don't care,' she says.

'Good,' Kennet says, feeling incredibly thick-headed.

He searches his memory for facts about Benjamin's birth. Images flicker past: Simone's face, red from crying after a miscarriage, and then that summer when she wore that big, flowery tent of a dress, she'd been very pregnant then. And he went to see them in the maternity ward, she showed him the little bundle. 'Here he is,' she had said. 'His name's Benjamin. Son of happiness.'

Kennet rubs his eyes hard, scratches the bandage on his head, then says:

'So what's his . . . real mum's name?'

Aida looks over towards the lake.

'I don't know,' she says in a monotone. 'I swear I don't. But she told Benjamin what his real name was. She always called him Kasper. She was kind. She used to wait for him after school, and helped him with his homework, and I think she used to give him money. She was so sad that she had to give him up when he was a baby.'

Kennet holds up the photograph.

'What about this, what's this?'

Aida glances at the printout.

'That's the family grave. Benjamin's real family grave. That's where his relatives are buried.'

84

Thursday evening, 17 December

The day's few hours of natural light are already gone, and darkness has settled over the city. Advent stars are shining in almost all the windows on the other side of the street. The soft smell of grapes is rising from the grappa on the coffee table. Simone is sitting in the middle of the parquet floor looking at some sketches. After Kennet dropped her off at home, she had changed out of her wet clothes, and wrapped herself in a blanket. She fell asleep on the sofa and didn't wake up until he called. Then Sim Shulman came over.

Now she's sitting on the floor in just her underwear, drinking so much grappa that her stomach feels like it's on fire. She's laying out four sketches outlining an art installation Sim's planning for Tensta Art Gallery.

Shulman is talking to the gallery's curator on the phone. He's been pacing around the room as he talks. The floor suddenly stops creaking, and Simone realises he's stopped pacing and is looking between her thighs. She can feel him doing it. She gathers the sketches together, picks up her glass and takes a sip, pretending to ignore him. She parts her thighs slightly, and imagines him staring intently at her. He's talking more slowly now, trying to bring the call to an end. Simone lies down on her back and shuts her eyes. She waits for him, feeling a tingling heat from her crotch, a rush of blood, the slow lubrication. She still needs to feel something that can silence the anxiety in her head, the endless cycle of thoughts. Shulman has stopped talking. He comes closer, and she keeps her eyes closed and parts her legs a little more. She hears the zipper of his trousers open. She feels his hands on her hips. He rolls her over onto her stomach, pulls her up onto her knees, tugs her underwear down her thighs and enters her from behind. She isn't ready. She sees her hands in front of her, her fingers splayed across the oak floor. She looks at her fingernails, the veins on the back of her hands. She pushes back against his hard, forceful thrusts to stop herself from falling. The heavy scent of the grappa is making her feel queasy. She wants to ask Shulman to stop, to do it a different way. She'd like to start again in the bedroom, together, properly. He lets out a deep sigh and comes inside her, then pulls out and walks to the bathroom. She pulls her underwear up and remains lying on the floor. An odd lethargy threatens to overwhelm her, shut down her thoughts, hopes, happiness. She no longer cares about anything that doesn't involve Benjamin.

She doesn't get up until Shulman comes out wrapped in a towel. Her knees feel sore, but she does her best to smile as she passes him and locks the bathroom door behind her. Her vagina stings when she gets in the shower. A horrible lonely feeling wells up inside her as the warm water soaks her hair and runs down her neck, shoulders and back. She rinses herself thoroughly, then turns her head up towards the jet of warm water.

Through the roar in her ears she hears a thudding sound, and realises that someone's knocking on the bathroom door.

'Simone,' Shulman is calling. 'Your phone is ringing.'

'What?'

'Your phone!'

'Answer it,' she says, and turns the water off.

'Now there's someone at the door too,' he calls.

'I'm coming.'

She takes a fresh towel from the cupboard and dries herself. The bathroom is full of steam. Her underwear is on the damp slate floor. The mirror is misted up, and she can just make herself out as a faceless grey ghost, a figure made of clay.

'Sim? Who was it?'

He doesn't answer. Simone is about to call out to him again, but suddenly she can't bring herself to do it. She doesn't know why but all her senses are on alert. She very carefully and quietly unlocks the bathroom door and peers out. The rest of the flat is silent. Something's wrong. She wonders if Shulman left, but doesn't dare call out.

85

Thursday night, 17 December

She hears a whispered conversation that she thinks is coming from the kitchen. But who is he whispering to? She tries to shrug off her fear, but can't. Through the crack of the door Simone sees someone quickly pass the bathroom in the hallway. It isn't Shulman. It's a much smaller figure, a woman in baggy gym clothes. The woman returns from the hall and Simone doesn't have time to pull back. Their eyes meet in the narrow gap. The woman stiffens, and Simone sees her eyes open wide with fear. She quickly shakes her head at Simone, then walks towards the kitchen. Her trainers leave bloody prints on the floor. Panic fills Simone. Her heart starts to race, and she realises she has to get out of the flat. She opens the bathroom door and creeps towards the front door. She tries to move silently, but can still hear her own breathing and the gentle creak of the floor.

Someone is talking to themselves and digging noisily through the cutlery in the kitchen drawers.

Through the darkness Simone sees something large and lumpy on the floor. It takes her a few seconds to realise what she's looking at. Shulman is lying on his back next to the front door. Blood is pumping sluggishly from a wound in his neck. The dark red pool covers the floor around his body. He is staring up at the ceiling with quivering eyes, and his mouth is open and slack. Beside his hand, among the shoes on the mat, is her mobile phone. She thinks to herself that she needs to pick it up, run out of the flat and call the police. It surprises her that she didn't feel like screaming when she saw Shulman. Maybe she should say something to him, she thinks, but hears footsteps. The young woman is coming back. Her body is shaking, but she's biting her lip and trying to stay calm.

'We can't get out, the door's locked,' the woman whispers.

'But who . . .?'

'My brother,' she says, cutting Simone off.

'Why . . .?'

'He thinks he killed Erik. He didn't look, he thinks . . .'

One of the kitchen drawers hits the floor with a loud crash.

'Evelyn? What are you doing?' Josef Ek calls out. 'Are you coming back?'

'Hide!' the woman says.

'Where are the keys?' Simone asks.

'He has them in the kitchen,' she says, then hurries back to her brother.

Simone creeps along the hallway and into Benjamin's room. She's panting for breath and tries to keep her mouth closed, but then she can't get enough air. The floor keeps creaking beneath her, but Josef Ek is talking loudly in the kitchen and doesn't seem to notice. She goes over to Benjamin's computer and switches it on, and hears the fan start to whirr. She hurries out, and just manages to slip into the bathroom again when the start-up sound rings out.

She waits a few seconds, heart pounding, then leaves the bathroom, glances along the empty hallway and hurries into the kitchen. There's no one there. The floor is covered with cutlery and bloody footprints.

She can hear Josef and Evelyn moving around in Benjamin's room. Josef is swearing to himself, and she hears books being thrown on the ground.

'Look under the bed,' Evelyn says in a frightened voice.

There's a thud as the box of manga books hits the floor, and Josef snarls that there's no one there.

'Help me!' he commands.

'In the wardrobe?' she suggests quickly.

'What the hell is going on?' Josef shouts.

The door-key is on the oak table – Simone grabs it and runs as quickly as she can back to the hall.

'Wait, Josef,' she hears Evelyn cry. 'He might be in the other wardrobe.'

A glass smashes and heavy footsteps thud along the hallway.

Simone steps over Shulman's body. His fingertips are moving very slightly. She slips the long key into the high-security lock, but her hand is shaking badly.

'Josef!' Evelyn cries desperately. 'Look in the bedroom! I think he's in the bedroom!'

Simone turns the key and hears the lock click just as Josef Ek rushes into the hall. He stares at her, and a deep growl emerges from his throat. Simone fumbles with the lock, loses her grip, tries again and manages to turn it. Josef is clutching a vegetable knife in his hand. He hesitates, then starts to walk towards her with long strides. Simone's hands are shaking so badly that she can't push the handle down. The young woman runs into the hallway, and throws herself at Josef's legs, trying to hold him back, shouting at him to wait. He slashes the knife across the top of Evelyn's head without even looking. She lets out a loud moan. He keeps moving, and Evelyn loses her grip on his legs. Simone manages to get the door open and staggers out onto the landing. The towel slips off her. Josef is gaining, but stops to stare at her naked body. Behind him Simone sees Evelyn sweep her hand quickly through the pool of Shulman's blood. She smears it over her face and neck and then slumps to the floor.

'Josef, I'm bleeding,' she screams. 'Darling . . .'

She coughs and then lies on her back silently, pretending to be dead. Josef turns and sees her blood-smeared body.

'Evelyn?' he says in a frightened voice.

He goes back inside the flat, and, as he leans over her, Simone sees the knife in Evelyn's hand. It shoots up, like a dagger in some primitive trap. Evelyn stabs the blade into Josef's chest forcefully, and his body goes limp. He tilts his head, then sinks onto his side and lies still.

86

Early morning, Friday 18 December

Kennet passes two female police officers whispering to each other in the hallway of Danderyd Hospital. In the room behind them, he sees a young woman sitting on a chair, staring into space. Her face and chest is smeared with blood, and her hair looks like it's encrusted with dried blood. She's sitting with her toes turned in slightly, an unconsciously childlike gesture. He assumes that this is Evelyn Ek, sister of serial killer Josef Ek. She looks up and stares straight at him, as if she heard him say her name out loud. Her eyes reflect a peculiar mix of emotions – pain and shock, regret and triumph. Kennet looks away instinctively, feeling like he's intruding on something private. He shudders and reminds himself how lucky he is to be retired. He's glad he won't have to question Evelyn. Her experience growing up with Josef as her brother is something no one should have to carry with them through life.

A man in uniform with a grey, oblong face is standing guard outside the closed door to Simone's room. Kennet recognises him from his time on the force but has trouble remembering his name.

'Kennet,' the man says. 'You well?'

'Been better.'

'Thought as much.'

After hearing the man's voice, Kennet remembers his name – Reine – and the fact that his wife died very suddenly after the birth of their first child.

'Reine,' Kennet says. 'How did this happen?'

'Looks like she just let him in.'

'Voluntarily?'

'Not exactly.'

Then Reine tells him that Evelyn said she'd woken up in the middle of the night, went over to the front door and looked through the peephole at the police officer, Ola Jacobsson, who was asleep out on the landing. Earlier she had heard him telling his colleague he had young children at home, so she didn't want to wake him. She sat down on the sofa and looked back through the photograph album Josef had hidden among her belongings. The pictures were incomprehensible glimpses of a life that had long since vanished. She put the album back in the box and wondered if it would be possible for her to change her name and move away. She went over to the window and looked out through the blinds. She thought she could see someone standing down on the pavement. She quickly pulled her head back, waited a while, then looked out again. It was snowing heavily, and she could no longer see anyone. The streetlight hanging between the buildings was swaying in the wind. She got goose-bumps and crept over to the front door. She put her ear to the wood and listened. She felt like someone was standing right outside the door. Josef had always had a particular smell like burning chemicals, that she associated with rage. Evelyn thought she could smell it now. She was probably just imagining it, but she stayed by the door anyway, unable to bring herself to look out again.

After a while she leaned towards the door and whispered:

'Josef?'

Everything was quiet. She was about to go back to sleep when she heard him whisper from the landing:

'Open the door.'

She tried to keep her voice steady when she replied:

'OK.'

'Did you think you could get away?'

'No,' she whispered.

'You just have to do what I say.'

'I can't . . .'

'Look through the peephole,' he interrupted.

'I don't want to.'

'Do it anyway.'

Trembling, she leaned closer to the peephole. She could see most of the landing through the fisheye lens. The police officer who had fallen asleep on the stairs was still there, only now there was a dark pool of blood spreading out underneath him. His eyes were closed, but Evelyn thought he was still breathing. She could see Josef hiding at the edge of the landing. He was pressed back against the wall, but suddenly leapt up and slammed his hand against the lens. Evelyn jerked back and stumbled over the shoes on the mat.

'Open the door,' he said. 'Or I'll kill the policeman. Then I'll start knocking on doors and kill the neighbours. I'll start with the flat next to you.'

It didn't take long for Evelyn to give up hope. She felt like she was never going to get away from Josef. Hands shaking, she opened the door and let her little brother into the flat. The only thought in her head was that she'd rather die than let him kill anyone else.

Reine explains the sequence of events from what he's been told. Josef had been hiding in the terraced house, and when the police went to pick up Evelyn's personal possessions, he heard them talk about where they were taking the box.

'Jacobsson's going to make it,' he says. 'She saved him by doing what her brother asked.'

Kennet shakes his head, then says goodbye to Reine and walks away.

He knocks gently on the door to Simone's room and opens it slightly. The curtains are drawn and the lights are out. He peers into the darkness. He sees a figure that could be his daughter lying on a sofa.

'Simone?' he asks in a low voice.

'I'm here, Dad.'

'Do you want it this dark? Should I turn the light on?'

'I can't do this, Dad,' she whispers after a while. 'I can't do this.'

Kennet pads across the floor, sits down on the sofa and puts his arm around his daughter. She starts to sob.

'Once,' he whispers, stroking her back gently, 'when I drove past your nursery school in my patrol car, I saw you standing in the playground. You were facing the fence, and you were crying your eyes out, snot was streaming from your nose. You were wet and dirty, and the staff weren't doing anything to comfort you. They were standing there talking to each other, not bothered at all.'

'What did you do?' Simone whispers.

'I stopped the car and went over to you.'

She smiles to herself in the darkness.

'You stopped crying immediately, took my hand and came with me.'

He stops talking.

'Imagine if I could just take your hand and bring you home now.'

She nods, leans her head against him, then asks:

'Have you heard anything about Sim?'

He strokes her cheek and wonders if he should tell her the truth or not. Shulman had lost far too much blood. He had suffered severe brain damage. He'll never wake up from his coma.

'They don't really know yet,' he says cautiously. 'But he's in a coma and . . .'

He sighs.

'It doesn't look good, sweetheart.'

Her body is wracked with sobs.

'I can't go on, I just can't,' she weeps.

'There, now . . . I've called Erik. He's on his way.'

She nods.

'Thanks, Dad.'

He strokes her back again.

'I honestly can't do this,' Simone whispers.

'Don't cry, darling.'

She sobs louder.

'It's too much.'

At that moment the door opens and Erik switches the light on. He rushes across the floor, sits down on the other side of Simone and says:

'Thank God you're all right.'

Simone presses her face to his chest.

'Erik,' she says, her voice muffled by his coat.

He strokes her hair. He looks exhausted, but his eyes are clear and alert. She can't help thinking that he smells like home, like family.

'Erik,' Kennet says seriously. 'I need to ask you something important. You too, Simone. I spoke to Aida not long ago.'

'What did she say?' Simone asks.

Kennet takes a deep breath and says in a tired, ragged voice:

'Someone contacted Benjamin shortly before he disappeared. She told him she was his biological mother.'

Simone pulls free of Erik and looks at Kennet. She wipes her nose and asks in a voice that's high and fragile from crying:

'His real mother?'

Kennet nods.

'Aida said this woman's been giving him money and helping him with his homework.'

'That's crazy,' Simone whispers.

'She even had a different name for him.'

Erik looks at Simone, then at Kennet, and asks him to go on.

'Well,' Kennet says, 'Aida told me that this woman told him that his real name was Kasper.'

Simone sees Erik's face stiffen and feels a rush of anxiety.

'What is it, Erik?' she asks.

'Kasper?' Erik asks. 'She called him Kasper?'

'Yes,' Kennet says. 'At first Aida didn't want to say anything, apparently she'd promised Benjamin not to . . .'

He trails off. Erik's face has lost its colour, and he looks like he might faint. He stands up, takes a couple of steps backwards and almost falls over the table.

'Erik?' Simone asks.

'I don't have time to explain,' he says and hurries out of the room.

87

Friday morning, 18 December

Erik forces his way through a group of children carrying flowers, and hurries across the floor in the hospital lobby, past an old man in a wheelchair. He keeps running down the stone steps, not caring about the puddles and brown slush. He rushes across the road, and through some low bushes into the visitors' car park, key already in his hand. He gets in his car and reverses so hard that he scrapes the side of it against the bumper of the car parked next to it.

His breathing is still heavy as he turns onto the street, and calls Joona.

'It's Lydia Everson!' he says, almost shouting.

'Who?'

'Lydia Everson took Benjamin,' he says in a more controlled voice. 'I told you about her, she's the one who reported me.'

'We'll check her out,' Joona says.

'I'm on my way there.'

'Give me the address.'

'A house on Tennisvägen in Rotebro, I don't remember the number, but it's a red house, pretty big.'

'Wait for me somewhere near . . .'

'I'm heading there now.'

'Don't do anything stupid. Wait for me . . .'

Erik ends the call. He speeds up as he drives through

Norrviken, alongside the railway track and the long, thin lake. He recklessly passes a lorry near the yeast factory and feels his pulse throbbing in his temples.

He makes his way into the residential area and parks beside the same conifer hedge he parked next to ten years earlier. Now that he can see the house it's all coming back to him. He remembers that they hadn't found any indication that a child lived there, no toys in the yard, nothing to suggest that Lydia was a mother. Still, they didn't have much of a chance to take a close look around the house. They had just gone downstairs to the basement and back up, then Lydia had come at him with a knife in her hand. He remembers the look on her face as she pulled the blade across her throat, never once taking her eyes off him.

Not much has changed out here. The pizzeria has been replaced by a sushi bar, and there is a big trampoline in the yard, scattered with autumn leaves and snow. Erik leaves the key in the ignition, abandons the car and runs up the road. He slows to a fast walk as he gets closer to the house. He goes into the yard, where wet snow is lying on the tall, yellow grass. There are icicles hanging from the broken hammock. Dead plants swing in the hanging baskets. Erik tries the door, but it's locked. He checks under the doormat, and a few woodlice scurry away. His heart is racing. Erik runs his fingers along the bottom wooden rail but can't find a key. He goes around to the back of the house, picks up an edging stone from the flowerbed and throws it at the patio door. The external pane shatters, and the stone falls back down onto the grass. He picks it up again and throws it harder. The rest of the glass breaks, and Erik hurries over and opens the door. He finds himself in a bedroom where the walls are covered with pictures of angels and the Indian guru, Sai Baba.

'Benjamin?' he shouts. 'Benjamin!'

88

Friday morning, 18 December

Erik keeps calling his son's name even though he can see that the house is abandoned. Everything is dark and still, and the stale air smells like old fabric and dust. He opens the door to the basement and is met by a horrible stench, a mixture of ash, charred wood and burned rubber. He rushes down the stairs, trips and hits his shoulder on the wall but regains his balance. The lights don't work, but the narrow windows near the ceiling let in enough sunlight for him to see that the rec room has been ravaged by fire. The floor crunches under his feet. A lot of the room is black, but some of the furniture looks partially intact. The table with the tiled top is covered with soot, and the candles on the tray have melted. Erik makes his way to the door leading to the other basement room. The door is hanging off its hinges, and the inside of the room is completely burned out.

'Benjamin?' he says in a frightened voice.

Ash drifts up into his face and he blinks when his eyes start to sting. In the middle of the floor are the remains of what looks like a cage large enough to hold a person.

'Erik?' a voice calls from upstairs.

He stops and listens. The walls creak, and charred fragments of ceiling tiles fall to the floor. He can hear a dog barking in the distance.

'Erik!'

It's Joona's voice. He's already inside the house. When Erik comes up the stairs, Joona stares at him with a worried look on his face.

'What happened?'

'There's been a recent fire in the basement,' he replies.

'Nothing else?'

Erik gestures vaguely towards the basement:

'The remains of a cage.'

'I've got a K-9 unit with me.'

Joona hurries through the hall to the hallway and opens the door. He waves to the K-9 officer, a woman wearing her dark hair in a tight braid. Her black labrador sticks close to her legs. She greets Erik with a nod, and asks them to wait outside, then crouches down in front of the dog and talks to it. Joona tries to persuade Erik to leave, but gives up when he realises he's not going to succeed.

The glossy black dog moves eagerly through the house, sniffing quickly, moving on. The animal checks each room systematically. Erik stands in the hallway. He feels sick, and steps outside when he realises that he's about to throw up. Two officers are talking outside a police van. Erik walks out through the gate and along the pavement towards his car. He stops and pulls out the little wooden box with the parrot on it. He stands there holding it in his hand, then walks over to a drain at the side of the road and empties its contents through the sewer grate. His forehead is beaded with sweat, and he swallows, then lets go of the box itself and hears the splash as it hits the water.

When he gets back to the yard Joona is still standing outside the house. He meets Erik's gaze and shakes his head. Erik goes inside. The dog-handler is kneeling down, petting the labrador's neck.

'Did you go down into the basement?' Erik asks.

'Of course we did,' she replies, without looking at him.

'The inner room?'

'Yes.'

'Maybe the dog can't smell anything because of the ash.'

'Rocky can find a body underwater to a depth of sixty metres,' she says.

'What about people who are still alive?'

'If there was anything here, Rocky would have found it.'

'But you haven't checked outside yet,' Joona says behind Erik.

'I didn't know we were supposed to,' the officer says.

'You are.'

She shrugs and stands up.

'Come on, then,' she says to the labrador in her deep voice. 'Come on – should we go outside and have a look? Should we go out and look?'

Erik follows them out, down the steps and around the house. The black dog scurries through the overgrown grass, sniffs the water barrel, where an opaque layer of ice covers the surface, then goes over to the old fruit trees. The sky is dark and cloudy. Erik sees that the neighbour has turned on some colourful outdoor lights in a tree. The air is cold. The police officers are now sitting in the van. Joona sticks close to the woman and the dog, occasionally pointing at something he wants them to check. Erik follows them to the back of the house. He recognises the slope at the far end of the garden. It's the place in the picture, he thinks. The photograph Aida sent Benjamin before he went missing. Erik is breathing hard. The dog is sniffing round the compost heap, panting. It walks around it, then sniffs the low bushes and the back of the brown fence before moving on to a basket of leaves and a small herb garden. Little sticks with seed packets stuck to them indicate what's been planted in each row. The black labrador whimpers unhappily and then lies down in the middle of the little herb patch, completely flat on the wet, cultivated ground. The dog's body is shaking with excitement, and the dog-handler's face looks very sad as she praises him. Erik starts to walk towards them. Joona turns abruptly and stops him from getting any closer.

'Let go of me,' Erik yells.

'OK, just calm down,' Joona says, leading him out of the garden.

'I have to know,' Erik says in an unsteady voice.

Joona nods, and says quietly, 'The dog has indicated that there are human remains in the ground.'

Erik sinks to the ground beside a fuse box. His whole body

goes numb when he sees the police officers get out the van carrying shovels. He closes his eyes.

Erik is sitting by himself in Joona's car, looking out through the windshield. Jagged black branches stick up into the dark winter sky. His mouth is dry and his face and head ache. He gets out of the car, and steps over the plastic tape cordoning off the area. Joona is watching the uniformed officers digging. The whole herb patch has been excavated, and is now just a large, rectangular hole. On a plastic sheet alongside there's a collection of muddy rags and fragments of bone. The sound of the shovels goes on, metal against stone, then the digging stops and the police officers straighten up. Erik walks slowly closer, on heavy, reluctant legs. He sees Joona turn around with a tired face.

'What is it?' Erik whispers.

Joona walks towards him, looks him in the eye and says:

'It's not Benjamin.'

'Who is it?'

'The body's been here for at least ten years.'

'A child?'

'Maybe five years old,' Joona replies, and shudders.

'So Lydia had a son after all,' Erik says in a subdued voice.

89

Saturday morning, 19 December

Damp snow is falling, and a dog is running around in the park outside Police Headquarters. The snow is making the dog bark. It snaps at the flakes and shakes its coat. The sight of the happy animal makes Erik's heart ache. He realises that he's forgotten what normal life is like. He's forgotten what it's like not to be overwhelmed by the thought of life without Benjamin.

He feels sick, and his hands are shaking from withdrawal. He hasn't taken a single pill in almost twenty-four hours, and he hasn't slept at all.

Simone is standing in the hallway outside the interview room. She looks pale and composed. When she sees Erik approaching she walks over to him and takes his hands. He's grateful for the gesture.

'You don't have to be here,' she whispers.

'Kennet said you wanted me to come,' he replies.

She nods weakly.

'I'm just so . . .'

She trails off, then clears her throat.

'I've been angry with you,' she says calmly.

Her eyes are moist and red-rimmed.

'I know, Simone.'

'At least you've got your pills,' she says pointedly.

'Yes,' he replies.

She turns away from him and stands and stares out of the window. Erik looks at her slender frame, her arms wrapped tightly around herself. She's got goose-bumps from the cold air blowing through the vents below the windows. The door to the interview room opens and a heavyset woman in a police uniform calls them over quietly.

'Please, come in.'

She smiles gently at them. She's wearing pink lipstick.

'My name is Anja Larsson,' she tells Erik and Simone. 'I'm going to take down your statement.'

The woman holds out a neat, round hand. Her nails are long, painted red with a sparkly edge.

'Nice,' Simone says absentmindedly.

Joona is already sitting in the room. His jacket is hanging from the back of his chair. His blond hair is messy, and it looks like he hasn't washed it. He hasn't shaved either. They sit down across from him.

Simone coughs quietly and takes a sip from her glass of water. When she puts it down she nudges Erik's hand. Their eyes meet and he sees her mouth 'Sorry' at him.

Anja Larsson places the digital recorder on the table between them, presses record, checks that the red light is on, and then gives a brief account of the date, time, and who is present in the room. Then she pauses for a moment, tilts her head and says in a bright, friendly voice:

'OK, Simone, we'd like to hear, in your own words, what happened the evening before last in your flat on Luntmakar Street.'

Simone nods, looks at Erik, then lowers her gaze.

'I . . . I was at home, and . . .'

She falls silent.

'Were you on your own?' Anja Larsson asks.

Simone shakes her head.

'Sim Shulman was with me,' she says in a neutral voice.

Joona makes a note on his pad.

'Can you tell us how you think Josef and Evelyn Ek got into your flat?' Anja Larsson asks.

'I don't really know, because I was in the shower,' Simone says slowly, and her face very briefly turns bright red. The blush fades almost immediately, but leaves a vibrant glow on her cheeks.

'I was in the shower. Sim knocked on the door to say that someone was ringing the doorbell . . . No, hang on, he told me my mobile phone was ringing.'

Anja Larsson repeats:

'You were in the shower, and heard Sim Shulman tell you your mobile phone was ringing.'

'Yes,' Simone whispers. 'I told him to answer it.'

'Who was the phone call from?'

'I don't know.'

'But he took the call?'

'I think so. I'm pretty sure he did.'

'What time was that?' Joona asks.

Simone startles, as if she hadn't actually noticed him before.

'I don't know,' she replies apologetically, looking at him.

Without smiling, he asks:

'Roughly.'

Simone shrugs and says hesitantly:

'Five o'clock.'

'Not four?' Joona asks.

'What do you mean?'

'I just want to know,' he replies.

'You already know all this,' Simone says to Anja.

'So, five o'clock,' Joona says, and makes a note of the time.

'What were you doing before you took a shower?' Anja asks. 'It's often easier to remember times if you go through the whole day.'

Simone shakes her head. She looks very tired, almost dazed. She doesn't look at Erik at all. He sits in silence beside her, heart thumping.

'I didn't know,' he says, then stops himself.

She glances at him quickly. He opens his mouth again:

'I didn't know you and Shulman were . . .'

She nods.

'We were, Erik.'

He looks at her, then at the policewoman, then at Joona.

'Sorry, I interrupted,' he stammers.

With a forgiving smile, Anja turns back towards Simone.

'Please, go on. Tell us what happened. Sim Shulman told you your phone was ringing . . .'

'He went out into the hallway and . . .'

Simone stops and corrects herself again:

'No, that's not right. I heard Sim say, "Now there's someone at the door too", something like that. I finished showering, dried myself, cautiously opened the door and saw . . .'

'Why cautiously?' Joona asks.

'What?'

'Why did you open the door cautiously?'

'I don't know, I felt . . . there was something in the air that felt threatening . . . I can't explain it . . .'

'Had you heard something?'

'I don't think so.'

Simone stares ahead of her.

'Go on,' Anja says.

'I saw a girl through the crack in the door. There was a young woman standing in the hallway. She looked at me. She seemed frightened, and she told me I should hide.'

Simone frowns.

'I went into the hallway and saw Sim . . . lying on the floor . . . there was so much blood, and it was still pouring out. His eyes were fluttering and he was trying to move his hands . . .'

Simone's voice becomes indistinct and Erik can see that she's trying hard not to cry. He wishes he could comfort his wife, support her, hold her hand or give her a hug. But he doesn't know if she'd push him away or get angry if he tried.

'Shall we take a break?' Anja suggests gently.

'I . . . I . . .'

Simone gives up and lifts the water glass to her lips with trembling hands. She swallows hard and wipes her eyes.

'The front door was locked, the high-security lock,' she goes on in a steadier voice. 'The girl said he had the key in the kitchen, so I crept into Benjamin's room and turned his computer on.'

'You turned his computer on. Why?' Anja asks.

'I wanted him to think I was in there, I was hoping he'd hear the computer and rush into the bedroom.'

'Who are you talking about?'

'Josef,' she replies.

'Josef Ek?'

'Yes.'

'How did you know it was him?'

'I didn't at the time.'

'Go on,' Anja says.

'I turned the computer on, then went and hid in the bathroom. When I heard them go into Benjamin's room, I crept into the kitchen and got the key. The girl kept trying to get Josef to look in different places, to slow him down. I could hear them in there, but I think I must have bumped into the picture in the hall, because suddenly Josef was coming after me. The girl tried to stop him, she was clinging onto his legs, and . . .'

She swallows hard.

'I don't know, he managed to shake her off. And then the girl pretended she was wounded. She smeared some of Sim's blood over her neck, then lay down and pretended to be dead.'

Simone sounds like she's having trouble breathing.

'Go on, Simone,' Anja prompts gently.

Simone nods and says quietly:

'Josef saw her and went back, and when he bent down she stabbed him in the side with the knife.'

'Did you see who wounded Sim Shulman?'

'It was Josef.'

'Did you see that?'

'No.'

Silence again.

'Evelyn Ek saved my life,' Simone whispers.

'Is there anything else you'd like to add?'

'No.'

'In that case, I'd like to thank you for your cooperation, and declare that this interview is over,' the woman says, and reaches out to stop the recording.

'Hold on,' Joona says. 'Who called?'

Simone looks at him, dazed, as if she'd forgotten about him again.

'Who called you on your mobile?'

She shakes her head.

'I don't know. I don't even know what happened to my mobile, I . . .'

'Don't worry,' Joona says reassuringly. 'We'll find it.'

Anja Larsson waits a few moments, looks at them questioningly, then stops the recording.

Simone stands up and walks slowly out of the room. Erik gives Joona a curt nod and follows her.

'Wait,' he says.

She stops and turns around.

'Wait, I just want . . .'

He trails off and looks at her bare, vulnerable face, her pale, cork-coloured freckles, her wide mouth and green eyes. Without another word they embrace, tired and sad.

'It's going to be OK,' he says. 'There, there.'

He kisses her curly strawberry-blonde hair.

'I don't know any more,' she whispers.

'I'll see if they have a room where you can get some rest.'

She gently pulls away and shakes her head.

'I need to find my mobile phone,' she says seriously. 'I have to find out who called when Shulman answered.'

Joona comes out of the interview room.

'Do you have Simone's mobile phone here?' Erik asks.

Joona nods towards Anja Larsson, who's heading towards the lifts further along the corridor.

'Anja should know that,' he replies.

Erik is about to rush after her, but Joona gestures for him to wait. He takes out his phone and makes a call.

They see the woman stop and answer her phone.

'We just need to check some paperwork,' Joona says.

She turns around sullenly and they walk towards her.

'Anja was quite an athlete when she started working here,' he says. 'An incredible swimmer, the butterfly, she came eighth in the Olympic Games in . . .'

'So what paperwork do you want to check?' Anja says.

'Don't get grumpy because . . .'

'You talk so much rubbish.'

'I'm just boasting about you.'

'Yeah, yeah,' she says with a smile.

'Have you got the list of items we brought in for analysis?'

'It's not ready yet – you'll have to go down and check.'

They head back towards the lifts with her. The cables rattle as they ride down. Anja gets off at the second floor, and gives them a wave as the doors close.

Back on the ground floor, they hurry along a hallway lined with doors, corkboards and fire extinguishers. The laboratories are brightly lit, and most of the staff are wearing lab coats. Joona shakes hands with a very fat man who introduces himself as Erixon and shows them into another room. There's a collection of items lined up on a metal-topped table. Erik recognises them. Two kitchen knives with dark stains on them lie in two different metal trays. He sees a familiar towel, the hall mat, several pairs of shoes, and Simone's mobile phone in a plastic sleeve. Joona points at the phone:

'We need to look at that,' he says. 'Are you done with it?'

The fat man goes over to the list next to the objects, scans through it, then says hesitantly:

'I think so. Yes, the phone's exterior has been checked for fingerprints.'

Joona takes it out of the plastic sleeve, wipes it with a tissue, then nonchalantly passes it to Simone. She clicks through to the list of calls, mutters something, then claps her hand to her mouth and stifles a cry when she sees the screen.

'It . . . it's Benjamin,' she stammers. 'The last call came from Benjamin.'

They crowd around the phone. Benjamin's name flashes a couple of times before the battery goes dead.

'Did Shulman talk to Benjamin?' Erik asks, raising his voice.

'I don't know,' she replies weakly.

'He answered, right? That's all I'm wondering.'

'I was in the shower. I think he answered the phone before he . . .'

'Surely you can tell if the damn call was missed or . . .'

'It wasn't missed,' she says, cutting him off. 'But I don't know if Sim managed to hear or say anything before he opened the door for Josef.'

'I didn't mean to snap at you,' Erik says, struggling to remain calm. 'But we have to know if Benjamin said anything.'

Simone turns towards Joona.

'Aren't all mobile phone conversations stored these days?' she asks.

'It could take weeks to get it,' he replies.

'But . . .'

Erik puts his hand on Simone's arm and says:

'We need to talk to Shulman.'

'That's impossible, he's in a coma,' she says, getting upset.

'Come with me,' Erik says to Simone, and leaves the room.

90

Saturday afternoon, 19 December

Simone is sitting next to Erik in the car, glancing at him occasionally. The cars ahead of them form an endless column, and the streetlights flit past monotonously. The car is littered with empty water bottles, soda cans, a pizza box, newspapers, paper mugs, napkins, empty bags of crisps and sweet wrappers.

Erik is driving towards Danderyd Hospital, where Sim Shulman is lying in a coma, and he knows exactly what he's going to do when he gets there. He glances at Simone. She looks thinner, and her mouth is sad and worried. He feels almost alarmingly focused. He thinks he understands what has been happening to him and his family. He tries to explain to Simone.

'When we realised Josef couldn't have taken Benjamin, Joona told me to search my memory,' he says, breaking the silence in the car. 'And I started to look back at my past, searching for anyone who might hold a grudge against me.'

'What did you find?' Simone asks.

From the corner of his eye he can see her looking at him.

'My old hypnotherapy group . . . It was only ten years ago, but I never think about them, it was such a closed chapter of my life, and somehow I managed to block a lot of it out,' he says. 'But now that I was actively trying to remember, it was as if the group had never gone away, as if they had been waiting for me just out of sight.'

Erik sees Simone nod. He keeps on talking, trying to explain the theories he had about the group, the tensions between the patients, the balancing act he had tried to walk, and the final collapse of trust.

'When it failed, I swore I'd never hypnotise anyone again.'

'I know.'

'But I broke that promise when Joona persuaded me that it was the only way to save Evelyn Ek.'

'Do you think that's why all of this has happened to us, because you hypnotised him?'

'I don't know . . .'

Erik pauses, then says that it could have woken a dormant hatred, a hatred that might only have been constrained by his promise to give up hypnosis forever.

'Do you remember Eva Blau? She swung in and out of a psychotic state. You know she threatened me, said she was going to ruin my life?'

'I never understood why,' Simone says quietly.

'She was frightened of someone, and I thought she was being paranoid. But now I'm almost certain that she really was being threatened, by Lydia.'

'Just because you're paranoid doesn't mean they're not out to get you,' Simone says.

Erik turns off towards the scattered blue buildings of Danderyd Hospital. Rain batters the windshield.

'Maybe it was even Lydia who disfigured her face,' he says, almost to himself.

Simone jerks.

'Someone cut her face?' she asks.

'I thought she did it herself, that tends to be the pattern,' Erik says. 'I thought she'd cut the end of her nose off in a desperate attempt to feel something different, to avoid what was really causing all her pain . . .'

'Hang on,' Simone interrupts excitedly. 'Her nose was cut off?'

'The tip of it, yes.'

‘Dad and I found a boy with the end of his nose cut off. Did Dad tell you? He was terrified. Someone threatened him because he’d been bullying Benjamin.’

‘Lydia.’

‘Is she the person who kidnapped Benjamin?’

‘Yes.’

‘What does she want?’

Erik looks at her seriously.

‘You already know some of this,’ he says. ‘Lydia confessed under hypnosis that she kept her son Kasper locked in a cage in the basement, and forced him to eat rotten food.’

‘Kasper?’ Simone repeats.

‘When Kennet told me what Aida had said, about a woman calling Benjamin Kasper, I knew it was Lydia. That’s why I ran out. I went to her home in Rotebro, but there was no one there, it was abandoned.’

He drives along the rows of parked cars but there are no spaces, so he leaves the car park.

‘There’d been a fire in the basement but it had gone out,’ Erik goes on. ‘I assume it was set deliberately, but the remains of a large cage were still recognisable.’

‘But there wasn’t a cage before,’ Simone says. ‘And there was proof that she had never had a child.’

‘Joona brought a K-9 unit along, which found the remains of a child buried in the garden. They’d been there ten years.’

‘Oh, God,’ Simone whispers.

‘Yes.’

‘That was when . . .’

‘I think she killed the child in the basement when she realised she’d been found out,’ Erik says.

‘So you were right all along,’ Simone whispers.

‘Looks that way.’

‘Does she want to kill Benjamin?’

‘I don’t know . . . She probably thinks the whole thing was my fault. If I hadn’t hypnotised her, she would have been able to keep the child.’

Erik remembers Benjamin’s voice on the phone when he

called him – the way he had sounded talking about the haunted house. He must have meant Lydia's haunted house. Now they just needed to find it.

91

Saturday afternoon, 19 December

Erik parks in front of the main entrance to Danderyd Hospital, without bothering to lock the car or pay for a parking ticket. They hurry past the gloomy, snow-filled fountain and a few shivering smokers in dressing-gowns, run through the sliding doors and take the lift to the ward where Sim Shulman is being treated.

His room smells heavily like flowers. The windowsill is covered with vases of large, scented bouquets. There's a stack of cards and letters from friends and colleagues on the bedside table.

Erik looks at the man in the hospital bed, at his sunken cheeks. The regular movement of his stomach matches the sighing rhythm of the respirator. He is in a permanent vegetative state, kept alive by devices. Oxygen is being supplied through a tracheotomy in his throat. He is being fed through a gastric feeding tube, directly into his stomach.

'Simone, you're going to have to talk to him when he wakes up and . . .'

'We can't wake him up,' Simone exclaims in a shrill voice. 'He's in a coma, Erik.'

She wipes tears from her cheeks.

'We have to know what Benjamin said to . . .'

'Stop it!' she shouts, and starts to sob loudly.

A nurse looks into the room, sees Erik holding Simone's shaking frame and leaves them alone.

'I'm going to give him a zolpidem injection,' Erik whispers into her hair. 'It's a strong sedative, but it can actually awaken people from a comatose state.'

He feels her shake her head.

'What are you talking about?'

'It only works for a short period of time.'

'I don't believe you,' she says hesitantly.

'The sedative slows the overactive processes in the brain that are causing the coma.'

'Will he wake up, then? Is that really what you mean?'

'He's never going to recover fully. He's suffered severe brain damage, Simone. But this sedative might let him wake up for a few seconds.'

'What do I have to do?'

'Sometimes patients who receive this drug can say a few words, sometimes they can only look around.'

'This isn't allowed, is it?'

'I'm not going to ask for permission. I'm just going to do it, and you'll have to talk to him if he does wake up.'

'Hurry up,' she says.

Erik rushes out to get the equipment he needs. Simone sits down beside Shulman's bed and takes his hand. She looks at him. His face is calm. His swarthy, strong features look smoothed out in their current relaxed state. This ironic and sensual man has been silenced. Even the worry-line between his dark eyebrows is gone. She strokes his forehead gently, thinking that she's going to keep on exhibiting his work. A truly great artist can never die.

Erik comes back into the room. Without a word, he walks over to Shulman, then, with his back to the door, slowly pulls up the sleeve of his hospital shirt.

'Are you ready?' he asks.

'Yes,' she says. 'I'm ready.'

Erik takes out the syringe, connects it to the IV line and then slowly injects the yellowish liquid. It gradually disperses into the clear contents of the drip, and moves towards the cannula in

Shulman's arm. Erik puts the syringe back in his pocket, then unbuttons his jacket and transfers the electrodes from Shulman's chest to his own, removes the clip from his index finger and puts it on his own finger, and then positions himself where he can observe Shulman's face.

Absolutely nothing happens. Shulman's stomach rises and falls regularly and mechanically with the help of the respirator.

Erik's mouth is dry, and he feels frozen.

'Should we go?' Simone says after a while.

'Just wait,' Erik whispers.

His watch is ticking slowly. A petal falls from one of the flowers. A few raindrops hit the window. They hear a woman laughing in a distant room.

An odd wheezing sound comes from Shulman's body, like a gentle breeze through a half-open window.

Simone can feel sweat trickling from her armpits. The situation feels almost claustrophobic. All Simone wants to do is run from the room, but she can't take her eyes off Shulman's neck. She might be imagining it, but she suddenly thinks his jugular vein is pulsing faster. Erik is breathing heavily, and when he leans across Shulman he seems nervous, biting his bottom lip and glancing at his watch again. Nothing happens. The respirator wheezes mechanically. The wheels of a gurney squeak past, and then the room is quiet again. The only sound is the hum of the machines.

Suddenly there's a faint scratching sound. Simone can't understand where it's coming from. Erik has taken a couple of steps to the side. The scratching sound continues. Simone realises that it must be coming from Shulman. She leans closer, and sees that his index finger is moving on top of the tightly stretched sheet. She feels her pulse speed up and is just about to say something to Erik when Shulman opens his eyes. He's staring straight at her with a peculiar look in his eyes. His mouth stretches into a frightened grimace. Saliva dribbles down his chin.

'It's me, Sim. It's me,' she says, taking his hand in hers. 'I want to ask you a couple of important questions.'

Shulman's fingers tremble slowly. She knows he can see her,

but his eyes suddenly roll back, his mouth tenses and the veins in his temples throb visibly.

'You answered my phone when Benjamin called, do you remember?'

Erik, who has Shulman's electrodes attached to his chest, watches on the screen as his own pulse-rate increases. Shulman's feet are vibrating beneath the sheet.

'Sim, can you hear me?' she asks. 'It's Simone. Can you hear me, Sim?'

His eyes come back, but immediately slide sideways. She can hear quick footsteps in the hallway outside the door, and a woman calling something.

'You answered my phone,' she repeats.

He nods weakly.

'It was my son,' she goes on. 'It was Benjamin who called . . .'

His feet start to shake again, his eyes roll back.

'What did Benjamin say?' Simone asks.

Shulman swallows, chews slowly, and his eyelids slowly close.

'Sim? What did he say?'

He shakes his head.

'He didn't say anything?'

'Not . . .' Shulman hisses.

'What did you say?'

'Not Benja . . .' he says, almost inaudibly.

'He didn't say anything?' Simone asks again.

'Not him,' Shulman says in a thin, frightened voice.

'What?'

'Ussi?'

'What are you saying?' she asks.

'Jussi called . . .'

Shulman's mouth trembles.

'Where was he?' Erik asks. 'Ask him where Jussi was.'

'Where was he?' Simone asks. 'Do you know?'

'Home,' Shulman replies faintly.

'Was Benjamin there too?'

Shulman's head falls sideways, his mouth becomes slack and his chin sags. Simone glances nervously at Erik, she doesn't know what to do.

'Was Lydia there?' Erik asks.

Shulman looks up, then his eyes slide sideways.

'Was Lydia there?' Simone asks.

Shulman nods.

'Did Jussi say anything about . . .'

Simone stops when Shulman starts to whimper. She strokes his cheek gently and he suddenly looks her in the eye.

'What's happened?' he asks, perfectly clearly, then sinks back into his coma.

92

Saturday afternoon, 19 December

Anja walks into Joona's room and silently hands him a folder and a cup of mulled wine. He looks up at her round pink face. For once she isn't smiling.

'They've identified the child,' she says concisely, pointing at the folder.

'Thanks,' Joona says.

There are two things he hates, he thinks as he looks at the brown folder. One is being forced to give up a case, to back away from unidentified bodies, unsolved rapes, robberies, assaults and murders. And the other thing he hates is when those unsolved cases get resolved, because when old mysteries are finally cleared up, it rarely happens the way you would have liked.

Joona Linna opens the file and reads. The child's body that was found in Lydia Everson's garden was a boy. He was five years old when he was killed: a fractured skull caused by a blow from a blunt instrument was thought to be the cause of death. But there were also a number of healed and half-healed injuries to the skeleton that suggested repeated and sustained violence. Abuse, the pathologist had written, followed by a question-mark. The child had been beaten so badly that he suffered broken bones and hairline fractures. His back and arms seemed to have been subjected to beatings with a heavy object. Numerous deficiencies identified in the skeleton also suggested that he had been starved.

Joona looks out of the window for a while. He can never get used to this, and he's told himself that the day he does is the day he stops being a detective. He runs his hand through his thick hair, swallows, and reads on.

The boy has been identified. His name is Johan Samuelsson, and he was reported missing thirteen years ago. His mother, Isabella Samuelsson, said that she was in the yard with her son when the telephone rang inside the house. She didn't take him in with her, and during the twenty or thirty seconds it took her to pick up the phone, realise there was no one on the line, and hang up, her child vanished.

Johan was two years old when he went missing.

He was five years old when he was killed.

And then his remains lay buried in Lydia Everson's vegetable garden for ten years.

The smell of mulled wine from the cup is suddenly nauseating. Joona stands up and opens the window. He looks down at the inner courtyard of Police Headquarters, the jagged branches of the trees, the shiny, wet asphalt.

Lydia had the child for three years, he thinks. Three years of secrecy. Three years of abuse, starvation and fear.

'Are you OK, Joona?' Anja asks, poking her head in.

'I'll go and talk to the parents,' he says.

'I'm sure Niklasson can do it,' Anja says.

'No.'

'De Geer?'

'It's my case,' Joona says. 'I'll go . . .'

'I understand.'

'Can you look up a few addresses for me in the meantime?'

'Of course I can, sweetie,' she replies with a smile.

'Lydia Everson. I want to know where she's been for the past thirteen years.'

'Lydia Everson?' she repeats.

He feels particularly heavy-hearted as he pulls on his fur cap and winter jacket and sets off to tell Isabella and Joakim Samuelsson that their son Johan has, very sadly, been found.

Anja calls him as he's driving out of the city centre.

'That was quick,' he says, trying to sound cheery, but it doesn't really work.

'This is what I do,' Anja retorts.

He hears her take a deep breath. From the corner of his eye, he sees a flock of black birds take off from a snow-covered field. He feels like swearing loudly when he thinks about the two photographs of Johan that were in the folder. In the first he is roaring with laughter, dressed up as a policeman, his hair all over the place. And in the second: fragments of bone laid out on a metal table, all neatly labelled.

'What a fucking nightmare,' he mutters to himself.

'Watch your language!'

'Sorry, Anja, another car just . . .'

'OK, OK. But I don't like swearing.'

'No, I know,' he says wearily, unable to join in the banter.

At last Anja seems to realise that he's not in the mood, and says in a very neutral tone:

'The house where Johan Samuelsson's remains were found used to belong to Lydia Everson's parents. She grew up there, and it's always been her only registered address.'

'Does she have any family? Parents? Siblings?'

'Hang on, I'm reading . . . . doesn't look like it. No record of her father, and her mother's no longer alive. Looks like she didn't even have custody of Lydia for long.'

'No brothers or sisters?' Joona asks again.

'No,' Anja says, and he hears her shuffling papers. 'Wait a moment,' she says. 'There was one. She had a younger brother, but he seems to have died very young . . .'

'How old was Lydia when he died?'

'She was ten.'

'And she's always lived in that house?'

'No, that's not what I said,' Anja says. 'She's lived in one other place – three times, in fact.'

'Where?' Joona asks patiently.

'Ulleråker, Ulleråker psychiatric hospital.'

'Three stays.'

'That's what it says.'

'There are pieces missing,' Joona says quietly to himself.

'What did you say?'

'There are still too many missing pieces,' he replies. 'I can't make sense of it yet, and now I've got to try to explain to two parents why Lydia took their child.'

93

Saturday afternoon, 19 December

Joona turns off into the little road in Saltsjöbaden where Johan Samuelsson's parents still live. He sees their house at once, a rust-red eighteenth-century home with a hipped roof. There's a dilapidated playhouse in the yard, and beyond the rocky plot he can see the black, heavy water.

Joona rubs his face before getting out of the car. The raked gravel path is neatly edged with stones. He walks up to the door and rings the bell. Eventually he hears someone call out.

'I'll get it.'

The lock rattles and a teenage girl opens the door. She's wearing black eye-liner and has dyed her hair purple.

'Hello,' she says curiously.

'My name is Joona Linna,' he says. 'I'm from the National Crime Unit. Are your parents home?'

The girl nods and turns around, as if about to call out. But a middle-aged woman is already standing in the hallway, staring at Joona.

'Amanda,' she says in a scared voice. 'Ask him . . . ask him what he wants.'

Joona shakes his head.

'I'd rather not say standing out here on the porch. Can I come in?'

'Yes,' the mother whispers.

Joona steps inside and closes the door. He looks at the girl. Her bottom lip has started to tremble. Then he looks at her mother, Isabella Samuelsson. Her hands are clutched tightly to her chest and her face is ashen. Joona takes a deep breath, then says quietly:

'I'm so very sorry, but we've found Johan's remains.'

The mother presses a fist to her mouth and makes a whimpering sound. She leans towards the wall but slips and crumples onto the floor.

'Dad!' Amanda cries. 'Dad!'

A man comes running down the stairs. When he sees his wife sitting on the floor he slows down. It's as if all the colour fades from his face. He looks at his wife, then his daughter, and then Joona.

'Johan,' he says simply.

'I'm afraid we've found his remains,' Joona replies in a low voice.

They go and sit down in the living room. The girl holds her mother, who is sobbing with despair. The father still seems oddly calm. Joona has seen it before. There are men – and sometimes women, although that's less common – who don't seem to react, who keep on talking and asking questions, whose voices take on a particular timbre, a particular emptiness as they ask about details.

Joona knows it isn't indifference. It's a symptom of internal struggle. It's a desperate attempt to postpone the moment when the pain comes.

'How did you find him?' the mother asks between sobs. 'Where did you find him?'

'We were at the home of someone suspected of kidnapping another child,' Joona says. 'One of our dogs identified a location in the garden . . . he, Johan, has been dead for ten years, according to the pathologist.'

Joakim Samuelsson looks up.

'Ten years?'

He shakes his head.

'But,' he whispers, 'it's been thirteen years since we lost Johan.'

Joona nods, and feels utterly drained as he explains:

'We have reason to believe that the individual who took your child held him captive for three years.'

He looks down at his lap, focuses on trying to sound calm, then looks up again:

'Johan was five years old when he died.'

And the father's face crumbles. His attempt to stay calm shatters. It's a terrible sight. He stares at Joona as his face contracts and the tears start to trickle down his cheeks, into his open mouth. The air is torn by great, heaving sobs.

Joona looks around their home, at the framed pictures on the walls. He recognises the photograph that was in the folder, of two-year-old Johan in his policeman's costume. He sees a photograph of the girl's confirmation. There's a picture of the parents, laughing as they hold up a new-born baby. He really does hate this. But it's not finished yet.

'There's something I need to know,' he says, and waits a little longer, until they're in a fit state to understand what he's saying.

'I have to ask if you have ever heard of a woman by the name of Lydia Everson?'

The mother shakes her head helplessly. The father blinks a couple of times, then says quickly:

'No, never.'

Amanda whispers:

'Is it her . . . is she the person who took my brother?'

Joona looks at her sombrely.

'We think so,' he replies.

When he stands up his palms are dripping, and he can feel sweat running down his back.

'I'm sorry,' he says again. 'I really am so very sorry.'

He leaves his card on the table in front of them, along with contact numbers for a counsellor and a support group.

'Please, call me if you think of anything, or if you just want to talk.'

He starts to walk out when the father suddenly gets to his feet.

'Wait . . . I have to know. Have you caught her? Do you have her now?'

Joona clenches his jaw as he turns round and holds his hands out.

'No, we haven't caught her yet. But we're on her trail. We'll get her soon.'

Joona calls Anja as soon as he's back in his car. She answers immediately.

'Did it go OK?' she asks.

'It never goes OK,' Joona replies morosely.

Neither of them says anything for a moment.

'Did you want anything in particular?' Anja asks hesitantly.

'Yes,' Joona says.

'You know it's Saturday, right?'

'The man's lying,' Joona goes on. 'He knows Lydia. He says he's never heard of her, but he's lying.'

'How do you know he was lying?'

'His eyes. I saw it in his eyes when I asked. I'm right about this.'

'I believe you. You're always right. Aren't you?'

'Yes, I am.'

'And if anyone doesn't believe you, they have to put up with your "what did I say?" routine.'

'You know me too well.'

'Did you want anything else, other than telling me that you're right?'

'Yes. I'm going out to Ulleråker.'

'Now? You know the Christmas dinner is tonight?'

'It's tonight?'

'Joona,' Anja says reproachfully. 'It's the Christmas party, dinner at Skansen. Don't tell me you've forgotten?'

'Is it obligatory?' Joona asks.

'Yes, it is,' Anja replies sternly. 'And you're sitting next to me, aren't you?'

'As long as you don't get inappropriate after a few drinks.'

'You can handle that.'

'Can you be an angel and call Ulleråker to make sure there's someone I can talk to about Lydia when I get there? Then I'll let you do whatever you want to with me at the dinner.'

'Good God. OK, I'm calling them right now,' Anja says, and hangs up.

94

Saturday afternoon, 19 December

The lump in Joona's stomach has almost disappeared by the time he is speeding through the slush on the E4 towards Uppsala. The psychiatric hospital at Ulleråker is still in use, despite the huge cutbacks.

As usual, Anja has done a good job. When Joona walks into reception he can tell the young woman behind the desk was expecting him.

She says simply:

'Joona Linna?'

He nods and holds up his police ID.

'Dr Langfeldt will see you. One floor up, first room on the right.'

Joona thanks her and starts to climb the broad stone staircase. He can hear distant thuds and cries and the sound of a television somewhere. The air smells like cigarette smoke. There are bars on the windows. Outside the park looks like a cemetery, with dark, rain-battered bushes and slowly decaying trellises covered with vines. Joona tells himself that somewhere like this isn't really a place where people come to get better – it's a place to keep them out of the way. He reaches the next floor and looks around. To his left is a glass door leading to a long, narrow hallway. He feels like he's seen it before, and realises that it's a carbon copy of Kronoberg Prison. Rows of locked doors, metal handles, electronic locking devices. An elderly woman in a long dress stares at him intently through a glass door. Joona nods to her, then opens the door to the other hallway. It smells like strong disinfectant.

Dr Langfeldt is waiting in the doorway when Joona reaches his office.

'You're from the police?' he asks rhetorically, and holds out a broad, fleshy hand. His handshake is surprisingly soft, possibly the softest Joona has ever felt.

Dr Langfeldt's face stays expressionless as he says, gesturing slightly:

'Please, come in.'

Dr Langfeldt's office is surprisingly large. The walls are lined with heavy bookcases full of folders and files. The room contains no ornamentation, no paintings or photographs. The only picture is a child's drawing attached to the door, a stick-figure in blue and green crayon. It looks like a three-year-old drew it – a face with eyes, nose and mouth, whose arms and legs stick out from the face. The figure either lacks a body, or the head is its body, depending on how you look at it.

Dr Langfeldt goes over to his desk, which is almost completely covered in piles of paper. He moves an old-fashioned telephone from the visitor's chair and makes another reserved gesture towards Joona, who interprets it as an invitation to sit down.

The doctor looks at him thoughtfully. His face is heavy and deeply lined, and there's something lifeless about his features, almost as if his face is paralysed.

'Thanks for finding the time to see me,' Joona says. 'What with it being the weekend and . . .'

'I know what you want to talk about,' the doctor interrupts. 'You want information about Lydia Everson, one of my patients.'

Joona opens his mouth to speak, but the doctor holds up his hand to stop him.

'I presume you know that medical records are classified and you've heard of the oath of confidentiality,' Langfeldt goes on. 'Besides . . .'

'I know the law,' Joona says. 'And the crime currently under investigation is punishable by a prison sentence longer than two years, so . . .'

'Yes, yes,' Langfeldt says.

The look in the doctor's eyes isn't evasive, just lifeless.

'I could always call you in for a formal interview,' Joona says mildly. 'The prosecutor is putting together a warrant for Lydia Everson's arrest. We'll be requesting her medical records as part of the process.'

Langfeldt drums his fingers together and licks his lips.

'That's just it,' he says. 'All I want . . .'

He stops.

'I want a guarantee, that's all.'

'A guarantee?'

Langfeldt nods.

'I want my name kept out of this.'

Joona looks Langfeldt in the eye and realises that what he thought was lifelessness is actually suppressed fear.

'I can't promise that,' he says tersely.

'What if I make it a condition?'

'I'm very stubborn,' Joona says.

The doctor leans back. The corners of his mouth twitch slightly.

'What do you want to know?' he asks.

Joona leans forward and says:

'Everything.'

Joona leaves the doctor's office an hour later. He glances down the hallway, but the woman in the long dress is gone, and as he hurries down the stairs he notices that it's dark outside. The woman at the reception desk has evidently finished for the day. The building is completely silent, even though Joona knows it's home to hundreds of patients.

He shivers as he gets back in his car and drives away.

Something's bothering him. There's something he missed. He tries to identify what it is.

The doctor had pulled out a file, identical to all the others filling the shelves. He tapped the front and said:

'Here she is.'

The photograph of Lydia showed a fairly attractive woman with mid-length, reddish hair and a slightly odd smile: rage, hidden beneath an ingratiating exterior.

Lydia was only ten years old the first time she was admitted for treatment. The reason she was taken into care was that she had killed her younger brother, Kasper Everson. One Sunday she had smashed his skull with a wooden stick. She told her doctor that her mum had forced her to raise him. Kasper was Lydia's responsibility while their mother was working or sleeping, and it was her job to discipline him.

Kasper Everson was three years old when he was killed. Lydia was hospitalised, and her mother was sent to prison for neglecting her children.

'Lydia lost her family,' Joona whispers to himself.

Dr Langfeldt only treated Lydia with strong anxiety-suppressing medication, no counselling or therapy. He believed she had been acting under extreme pressure from her mother. On his recommendation, Lydia was placed in an open residential home for young offenders. When she turned eighteen she vanished from their records. She moved back to her childhood home, and lived there with a young man she had met in the residential home. Five years later she was sentenced to secure psychiatric care for repeatedly beating a child in a playground.

She came under Dr Langfeldt's care for a second time, this time as a long-term patient with conditions placed on her eventual release.

The doctor told Joona, in a tight, distant voice, that Lydia had gone to a playground and picked out a particular child, a five-year-old boy. She lured him away from the other children, and then beat him. She went to the playground several times before she was caught. The final assault had been so severe that the child's injuries were life-threatening.

'Lydia spent six years at Ulleråker,' Langfeldt explained, then smiled joylessly. 'She was an exemplary patient. Her only issue was that she was always forming alliances with other inmates. She used to create her own groups, and demanded total loyalty from them.'

She keeps creating family units, Joona thinks.

Langfeldt had closed his eyes and massaged his temples before he went on:

'After six years without incident, Lydia was allowed to leave the hospital for brief periods.'

'No incidents at all?' Joona asked.

The doctor reflected.

'There was one thing, but nothing was ever proven.'

'What happened?'

'One of the other patients had her face disfigured. She claimed she'd done it herself, but there were rumours that Lydia Everson was responsible. As I recall, it was just gossip – there wasn't any evidence.'

Langfeldt had raised his eyes, as if he wanted to move on with his story.

'Go on,' Joona said.

'Lydia was allowed to move back to her parents' home. She was still attending treatment, and she continued to do well. There was no reason at all to doubt her claims that she wanted to get better. After two years, Lydia's court-mandated treatment was almost over. She chose a form of therapy that was fashionable at the time, group therapy with . . .'

'Erik Maria Bark,' Joona filled in.

Langfeldt nodded.

'As it turned out, hypnotherapy didn't seem to do her much good,' he said drily. 'Lydia ended up attempting suicide. That was the third time she wound up in my care.'

Joona interrupts.

'Did she talk to you about her breakdown?'

Langfeldt shook his head:

'As I understood it, it was all the hypnotist's fault.'

'Are you aware that she told Erik Maria Bark that she had a son named Kasper? That she told him she had imprisoned her son?' Joona asked tersely.

Langfeldt shrugged his shoulders.

'I did hear that, but I assumed that a hypnotist could make people confess to pretty much anything.'

'So you didn't take her confession seriously?' Joona asked.

Langfeldt gave him a thin smile.

'She was a wreck. It was impossible to even have a conversation with her. I had to administer electrotherapy, and she was on serious neuroleptic medication. It took a great deal of work to put her back together at all.'

'So you didn't try to find out if there was any truth to her confession?'

'I assumed we were dealing with feelings of guilt and remorse over what she had done to her brother,' Langfeldt replied sternly.

'When did you discharge her?' Joona asked.

'Two months ago,' Langfeldt said. 'There was no doubt in my mind that she had recovered.'

When Joona got to his feet, he found himself looking at the stick-figure on the back of the door. A walking head, he suddenly thought. Just a brain, no heart.

'That's you, isn't it?' Joona said, pointing at the drawing.

Joona walked out of the office, leaving Dr Langfeldt looking thoroughly confused.

95

Saturday afternoon, 19 December

It's pitch-black at five o'clock in the afternoon. The sun went down two hours ago and the air is cold. The few streetlights are spreading a dusty glow. Joona walks through the Christmas market, where glassblowers and silversmiths are busy in their workshops. Fires are burning, horses snorting, chestnuts roasting. Some children are running around a stone maze, others are drinking hot chocolate. Music is playing, and families are dancing around a tall Christmas tree on the circular dance-floor.

Joona's phone rings and he stops in front of a stall selling sausages and reindeer meat.

'Hello, Joona here.'

'This is Erik.'

'Hi.'

'I think Lydia has taken Benjamin to Jussi's haunted house, it's somewhere outside Dorotea, in Västerbotten, up in Lapland.'

'You sure?'

'I'm almost positive,' Erik says firmly. 'There aren't any more flights tonight. You don't have to come, but I've booked three tickets for first thing tomorrow morning.'

'Good,' Joona says. 'Text me all the details you've got about this Jussi, and I'll contact the Västerbotten Police.'

As Joona walks down one of the narrow gravel paths to the restaurant, he hears children laughing behind him and shivers.

The pretty yellow restaurant is decorated with Christmas lights and fir branches. The dining room has been set with four extremely long tables laden with Christmas food. Joona spots his colleagues as soon as he arrives. They're sitting next to one of the panoramic windows offering stunning views of Nybroviken and Södermalm. Gröna Lund amusement park is on one side and the Vasa Museum is on the other.

'We're over here!' Anja calls.

She stands up and waves. Her enthusiasm is infectious, and Joona finds himself smiling. But he can't quite shake the uneasy feeling he's had since his visit with Dr Langfeldt.

He says hello and sits down next to Anja. Carlos Eliasson is sitting across from him. He's wearing a red elf's hat and nods cheerily at Joona.

'We've already done the first toast,' he says, as though letting Joona in on a secret. His usually pale skin is flushed.

Anja tries to slip her hand under Joona's arm, but he stands up and says he's going to get some food from the buffet.

As he makes his way between tables full of people talking and eating, he realises he's having trouble conjuring up a festive spirit. It's as if part of him is still sitting in Johan Samuelsson's parents' living room, or is out at the psychiatric hospital, walking up the stone steps towards the locked door leading to the long, prison-like hallway.

Joona takes a plate from the stack, stands in line for the herring, and looks over at his colleagues from a distance. Anja has squeezed her plump frame into a red angora dress. She's still wearing her winter boots. Petter is talking intensely to Carlos, and his shaved head is glinting under the chandeliers.

Joona puts three different types of pickled herring on his plate, then stops. He's looking at a woman from another party. She's wearing a tight, light-grey dress, and is being dragged over to a table laden with desserts by two girls with sharp haircuts. A man in a greyish brown suit is hurrying after them with a smaller girl in a red dress.

There are no more potatoes left in the pan, and Joona has to wait a while before a waitress brings more. There's no sign of his favourite Finnish dish, baked swede gratin. Joona carries his plate back to the table, passing some police officers who are going back for seconds. At the table, five forensics experts are holding their glasses in the air, singing a drinking song. Joona sits down and immediately feels Anja's hand on his leg. She smiles at him.

'Do you remember you said you'd let me do whatever I wanted?' she jokes, then leans forward and whispers loudly: 'I want to dance the tango with you tonight.'

Carlos hears her, and exclaims:

'Anja Larsson, you and I shall dance the tango!'

'I want to dance with Joona,' she says firmly.

Carlos tilts his head and slurs:

'I'll get in line.'

Carlos is asleep on a chair in the coatroom. Petter and his group have gone into the city to keep the party going at Café Opera. Joona and Anja have promised to make sure Carlos gets home safely. While they're waiting for the taxi they go outside into the cold air. Joona leads Anja onto the outdoor dance-floor, warning her about the thin layer of ice on the wooden surface.

They start to dance, and Joona gently hums the tune of a famous Finnish tango.

'Marry me,' Anja whispers.

Joona doesn't answer. He's thinking about Disa and her melancholy face. He thinks about their many years of friendship, and how he has been forced to disappoint her in so many ways. Anja tries to reach up and lick him on the ear, and he moves his head a little further away from her.

'Joona,' Anja sighs. 'You dance very well.'

'I know,' he whispers, swinging her round.

The air smells like wood-smoke and mulled wine. Anja is pressing against him even harder now, and it occurs to him that it's going to be difficult to get Carlos out to the car. They're going to have to start moving him shortly.

At that moment his phone rings in his pocket. Anja lets out a loud groan of disappointment as he pulls away and answers.

'Joona Linna.'

'Hello,' a nervous voice says. 'It's me, Joakim Samuelsson. You came to see us earlier . . .'

'Yes, I know who you are,' Joona says.

He thinks of how Joakim's pupils dilated when he asked about Lydia Evers.

'I was wondering if we could meet up,' Joakim says. 'There's something I'd like to tell you.'

Joona looks at the time. Nine thirty at night.

'Can we meet now?' Joakim says, adding that his wife and daughter have gone to see his in-laws.

'Sure,' Joona says. 'Can you be at Police Headquarters, the entrance on Polhems Street, in forty-five minutes?'

'Yes,' Joakim says, sounding incredibly tired.

'Sorry, sweetheart,' Joona says to Anja, who's standing in the middle of the dance-floor waiting for him. 'No more tango tonight.'

'You *should* be sorry,' she replies sullenly.

'I can't handle strong liquor,' Carlos sighs as they lead him towards the escalator.

'Just don't throw up,' Anja says brusquely. 'If you do, I want a raise.'

'Anja, Anja,' Carlos says, sounding hurt.

96

Saturday evening, 19 December

Joakim is sitting in a white Mercedes, across the street from the entrance to Police Headquarters. His face looks tired and lonely. When Joona taps on the window he jumps as if he'd been lost in thought.

'Hello,' he says, opening the door. 'Get in.'

Joona sits in the passenger seat. He waits. The car smells vaguely like dog. There's a hairy blanket spread out on the back seat.

'You know,' Joakim says, 'when I think back to the way I was when Johan was born, it's like thinking about a complete stranger. I'd had a rough childhood. I was in a home for a while, then with a foster-family. But I pulled myself together when I met Isabella. I got my engineering licence the year Johan was born. I remember, because we went on vacation to celebrate – I'd never actually been on vacation before. We went to Greece, and Johan had only just learned to walk . . .'

Joakim Samuelsson shakes his head.

'It's such a long time ago. He was a lot like me . . . the same . . .'

He trails off.

'What was it you wanted to tell me?' Joona asks after a brief silence.

Joakim rubs his eyes.

'Are you sure it was Lydia Everson who did this?' he asks in a weak voice.

Joona nods.

'I'm absolutely certain,' he says.

'OK,' Joakim Samuelsson whispers, then turns his weary, furrowed face towards Joona.

'I know her,' he says simply. 'I know her very well. We were in the same children's home.'

'Can you think of any reason she would have taken Johan?'

'Yes,' Joakim Samuelsson says, and swallows hard. 'Back then, in the home . . . Lydia was only fourteen years old. They found out she was pregnant. They got really worried, of course, and forced her to have an abortion. It was all going to be hushed up, but . . . there were complications, an infection in her womb that spread to her ovaries. She was prescribed antibiotics and eventually recovered.'

Joakim's hands are shaking.

'I moved in with Lydia after the home. We lived in her house in Rotebro, and tried to have kids. She was completely obsessed with having a baby. But nothing happened, so she got checked out by a gynaecologist. I'll never forget when she came home and told me she was sterile because of that abortion.'

'And you were the boy who got her pregnant in the children's home.'

'Yes.'

'So you owed her a child,' Joona says, almost to himself.

97

Sunday morning, 20 December, fourth Sunday of Advent

There are snow banks draped across the terminal buildings at Arlanda Airport, and more snow is falling. The runways are being ploughed constantly. Erik is standing by the big window watching suitcases roll up the conveyor belt and get loaded onto a large, brightly painted plane.

Simone walks over with coffee and a plate of saffron muffins and ginger cookies. She puts the cups down in front of Erik and then nods towards the huge window. They watch a group of flight attendants walk towards a plane. They're all wearing red elves' hats, and seem troubled by the slush beneath their feet.

In the window of the airport cafeteria a mechanical Santa Claus is moving its hips. Its batteries seem to be running down, because the movements are increasingly spasmodic and jerky. Erik meets Simone's gaze. She raises her eyebrow pointedly at the sight of Santa humping the air.

'The muffins were free,' she says. Then it occurs to her: it's the fourth Sunday of Advent.

They look at each other, not sure what to say. Suddenly Simone sits bolt upright with a look of horror on her face.

'What is it?' Erik asks.

'The medicine,' she says very quietly. 'We forgot . . . if he's there, if he's alive . . .'

'Simone, I . . .'

'Too many days have passed now . . . he won't be able to stand . . .'

'Simone, I've got it,' Erik says. 'I've brought it with me.'

She looks at him with red eyes.

'Really?'

'Kennet reminded me. He called from the hospital.'

Simone thinks back to when she drove Kennet home. She watched him get out of the car, then fall on top of a snow bank. She thought he'd slipped, but when she ran around to help him he was barely conscious. She drove him to the hospital, and they carried him inside on a stretcher. His reflexes had been weak and his pupils reacted slowly. The doctors thought it was a combination of the after-effects from his concussion and extreme over-exertion.

'How is he?' Erik asks.

'He was sleeping when I was there yesterday. They don't seem to think his condition is too serious.'

'Good,' Erik says, watching the mechanical Santa. Then, without a word, he picks up the red Christmas napkin and drapes it over him.

The napkin sways back and forth, like a ghost. Simone starts to laugh, spraying cookie crumbs on Erik's jacket.

'Sorry,' she splutters. 'It just looks so ridiculous – a horny Santa . . .'

She starts laughing again, and ends up doubled over at the table. Then she starts to cry. After a while she quietens down, blows her nose, wipes her face and goes back to drinking her coffee.

The corners of her mouth start to twitch again just as Joona Linna appears at their table.

'The Umeå Police have people on their way out there now,' he says, without bothering to say hello.

'Are you in radio contact with them?' Erik asks.

'I'm not, but they're in touch with . . .'

Joona stops talking abruptly when he sees the napkin draped over the dancing Santa Claus. A pair of brown plastic boots are sticking out from under it. Simone turns her head away, her body shaking with laughter, tears, or a combination of the two. She sounds like she's about to choke. Erik gets up quickly and starts to lead her away.

'Let go of me,' she says between convulsions.

'I just want to help you, Simone. Come on, let's go outside.'

They go out onto the balcony and stand in the cold air.

'I'm better now, thanks,' she whispers.

Erik brushes the snow from the railing and puts one of her hands on the cold metal.

'Soon everything will be better,' she says. 'Soon . . .'

She closes her eyes and her legs falter. Erik catches her.

'Simone, how are you feeling?' Erik whispers.

She peers at him.

'No one believes me when I say I'm tired.'

'I'm tired too. I believe you.'

'You've got your pills, though, haven't you?'

Erik turns away.

Simone's face crumples and Erik feels hot tears running down his cheeks. He has no internal defences any more. Everything feels very raw and open. Maybe it's because he's stopped taking the pills.

'All this time,' he goes on, his lips trembling. 'I've only had one thought in my head: he can't be dead.'

They stand there in silence, holding each other. The snow is falling heavily on them. A grey plane takes off in the distance with a thunderous roar. When Joona taps on the window they both jump. Erik opens the door and Joona comes out. He clears his throat.

'I thought you'd like to know that we've identified the body found at Lydia's house.'

'Who was it?'

'It wasn't Lydia's child . . . it was a boy who was taken from his family thirteen years ago.'

Erik nods and waits. Joona sighs deeply.

'Traces of excrement and urine indicate . . .'

He shakes his head.

'Indicate that the child lived there for quite some time, probably three years, before he was killed.'

No one speaks. The snow goes on falling softly on them. Jets roar in the distance.

'So you were right, Erik . . . Lydia did have a child in a cage, and she thought of him as her own.'

'Yes,' Erik replies almost inaudibly.

'She killed the boy when she realised what she'd said under hypnosis – what it meant, what it might lead to.'

'I honestly thought I was wrong. I'd accepted that,' Erik says flatly, staring out across the wintery airfield.

'Is that why you stopped?' Joona asks.

'Yes,' he replies.

Simone wipes her forehead with a shaky hand.

'You came to Lydia's attention again when you broke your promise. And she had Benjamin in her sights,' she says in a low voice.

'No, she must have been watching us the whole time,' Erik whispers.

'Lydia was discharged from Ulleråker two months ago,' Joona says. 'She took her time creating a relationship with Benjamin, and then she escalated – probably when she felt you broke your promise.'

Joona thinks that Lydia held Joakim Samuelsson responsible for the abortion that left her sterile, and that's why she took his son. Then Lydia felt forced to kill Johan because of Erik's hypnotherapy. That's why she took Benjamin when Erik started to practise hypnosis again.

Erik's face is sombre, hard and impassive. He opens his mouth to say that he probably saved Evelyn's life by breaking his promise, but stops when he sees a police officer walking towards them.

'We need to go,' the man says quickly. 'The plane takes off in ten minutes.'

'Have you spoken to the police up in Dorotea?' Joona asks.

'Yes, and there's been no contact with the patrol who went out to the house,' the police officer replies.

'Why not?'

'I don't know, but they say they've been trying to reach them for almost an hour.'

'What the hell? They should be sending back-up,' Joona says.

'That's what I said, but they wanted to wait.'

As they walk the short distance to the plane, Erik suddenly feels momentarily and unexpectedly relieved: he had been right all along.

He looks up at the snow. It's swirling through the air, light and heavy at the same time. Simone turns around and grabs his hand.

98

Thursday, 17 December

Benjamin is lying on the floor, listening as the curved runners of the rocking chair squeak on the shiny plastic mat as it moves slowly back and forth. His joints are hurting badly now. The wind is whistling over the tin roof. He hears the bulky spring on the porch door creak, and then heavy footsteps in the hallway. Marek stamps his boots. Benjamin raises his head, but the dog-leash pulls at his neck.

'Lie down,' Lydia says from the rocking chair.

He lowers his head to the floor, feeling the long, coarse tassels of the rug against his cheek. It smells like dust.

'It's the fourth Sunday of Advent this weekend,' Jussi says. 'We should bake some ginger cookies.'

'Sundays are for discipline, nothing more,' Lydia says, and goes on rocking.

Marek snickers at something, but stops abruptly.

'Laughing, eh?' Lydia says.

'It was nothing.'

'I want my family to be happy,' Lydia says quietly.

'We are,' Marek replies.

The floor is cold, and the walls are drafty. Benjamin is still wearing his pyjamas. He thinks back to when they first arrived here. There had been snow on the ground. Marek led him through a jumble of vehicles in front of the house: old, snow-covered buses, cars perched on bricks. He walked through the snow, his bare feet stinging. Walking between the big, snow-draped vehicles had been like walking through a trench. The lights were on inside the house, and Jussi came out onto the porch with his elk-hunting rifle over his arm, but when he caught sight of Lydia it was as if all his energy drained away. She wasn't expected, wasn't welcome, but he couldn't turn her away. All he could do was submit to her will, and do her bidding like some tame animal. He just shook his head when Marek took the rifle from him. They heard footsteps inside the house, then Annbritt came out. Jussi muttered that she was his girlfriend, and that they should let her go. When Annbritt saw the dog-leash around Benjamin's neck her face turned white and she tried to go back inside and shut the door, but Marek stopped her by sticking the barrel of the rifle through the crack in the door and asking with a smile if they could come in.

'Should we talk about Christmas food?' Annbritt asks now in an unsteady voice.

'Herring and pâté are the most important things,' Jussi says.

Lydia sighs irritably. Benjamin looks up at the gold ceiling fan. The shadows of the fan-blades look like a grey flower on the ceiling.

'The boy will have meatballs,' Jussi says.

'We'll see,' Lydia says.

Marek spits in a flowerpot and looks out at the darkness.

'I'm starting to get hungry,' he says.

'We've got plenty of elk and venison in the freezer,' Jussi says.

Marek walks around the table, pokes at the bread basket, then breaks off a piece of a breadstick and puts it in his mouth.

When Benjamin looks up Lydia jerks the leash. He coughs and lies back down again. He's hungry and tired.

'I'll need my medicine soon,' he says.

'You'll be fine,' Lydia replies.

'I need an injection once a week, and it's been more than a week since . . .'

'Shut up.'

'I'll die if I don't . . .'

Lydia jerks the leash hard, making Benjamin whimper with pain. He starts to cry, and she yanks it again to get him to be quiet.

Marek turns the television on, and there's a crackle, followed by a distant voice. A sports programme. Marek clicks through the channels but can't get a picture, so he switches it off.

'I should have brought the TV from the other house,' he says.

'There are no cable channels up here,' Jussi says.

'Why doesn't the satellite dish work?' Marek asks.

'I don't know,' Jussi replies. 'The wind can get pretty strong. It probably knocked it out of position.'

'Fix it, then.'

'Do it yourself!'

'Stop arguing,' Lydia says.

'There's nothing but crap on TV anyway,' Jussi mutters.

'I like *Let's Dance*,' Marek says.

'Can I go to the bathroom?' Benjamin asks quietly.

'You can piss outside,' Lydia says.

'OK,' he replies.

'Take him, Marek,' Lydia says.

'Jussi can do it,' he replies.

'He can go on his own,' Jussi says. 'He can't escape. It's five degrees below freezing and . . .'

'Go with him,' Lydia interrupts. 'I'll look after Annbritt while you're gone.'

Benjamin feels dizzy as he sits up. Jussi has taken the leash from Lydia. Benjamin's knees are stiff and jolts of pain run up his thighs as he starts to walk. Every step is unbearable, but he clenches his teeth to stop himself from making any noise. He doesn't want to upset Lydia.

There are diplomas hanging on the wall. The room is lit by a brass wall-lamp with a frosted glass lampshade. On the cork-coloured linoleum floor there's a plastic bag from the ICA supermarket, with the logo 'quality, care, service' on it.

'I need to take a shit,' Jussi says, dropping the leash. 'Wait on the porch when you come back in.'

Clutching his stomach, Jussi disappears into the bathroom and locks the door behind him. Benjamin looks back and sees

Annbritt's broad shoulders through the crack in the door. Marek is talking about Greek pizzas.

Lydia's green camouflage jacket is hanging on a hook in the hallway. Benjamin searches the pockets and finds the house keys, a gold wallet and his own mobile phone. His heart starts to beat faster when he sees that there's enough life left in the battery for at least one more call. He creeps over to the porch, past the pantry, and goes outside into the numbing cold. The reception is poor. He walks, barefoot, a little way along a dug-out path to the woodshed. Through the darkness he can make out the rounded, snow-covered shapes of the old buses and cars. His hands are stiff and shaking with cold. The first number he finds is his mother's mobile phone. He calls it and holds the phone to his ear. He hears it start to ring just as the door to the house opens and Jussi walks out. They look at each other. It doesn't occur to Benjamin to try to hide the phone. Perhaps he should run, but he has no idea where to go. Jussi marches towards him with long strides, his face pale and anxious.

'Are you done?' he says in a loud voice.

Jussi looks Benjamin in the eye, as if he's trying to make him understand something, then takes the phone from him and keeps on walking towards the woodshed, just as Lydia comes out of the house.

'What are you two up to?' she asks.

'I'm just getting some more wood,' Jussi calls, hiding the phone inside his jacket.

'I'm done,' Benjamin says.

Lydia lets Benjamin back into the house.

As soon as Jussi gets inside the woodshed he looks at the phone, and sees the word 'Mum' lit up on the pale blue screen. In spite of the cold he can smell wood and sap. The shed is almost pitch-black. The phone is the only source of light. Jussi holds it to his ear and right at that moment someone answers.

'Hello,' a man's voice says. 'Hello?'

'Is this Erik?' Jussi asks.

'No, this is . . .'

'My name is Jussi, can you give Erik a message? It's important. We're up here at my house, me and Lydia and Marek and . . .'

Jussi is interrupted by the person at the other end suddenly emitting a guttural scream. The line crackles and roars, someone coughs, a woman starts to cry, and then everything goes quiet. The connection's broken. Jussi looks at the phone, and is about to try calling someone else when the battery dies. The screen fades just as the door to the woodshed swings open and Lydia steps inside.

'I could see your aura through the cracks in the door. It was bright blue,' she says.

Jussi tucks the phone in his pocket, then starts to fill the wood-basket.

'Go back inside,' Lydia says. 'I can do this.'

'Thanks,' he says, and leaves the shed.

On his way back to the house he sees the ice-crystals in the snow sparkle in the light from the windows. The ground crunches beneath his boots. He hears a jerky, shuffling sound behind him, then a wheezing, panting noise that makes him think about his dog, Castro. He remembers when Castro was a puppy. He used to chase mice beneath the snow when it was still soft. Jussi is smiling to himself when the blow to the back of his head knocks him forward. He would have fallen onto his front if the axe stuck in his head wasn't holding him back. He stands there with his arms hanging by his sides. Lydia wiggles the axe to pull it loose. Jussi feels blood pouring down his neck and back. He sinks to his knees, falls forward and feels the snow on his face. He kicks his legs and rolls over onto his back to try to get up again. Jussi's field of vision is shrinking rapidly, but in his last moments of consciousness he sees Lydia raise the axe above him.

99

Sunday morning, 20 December, fourth Sunday of Advent

Benjamin is hunched up against the wall behind the television. He feels dizzy, and he's having trouble focusing on anything. But the worst thing is his thirst. He's thirstier than he's ever been in his life. It's like being suffocated, like having a throat full of open sores. His hunger doesn't feel as bad. It's completely overshadowed by the thirst and the pain in his joints. He doesn't know how many days he has spent on the floor of this house now not doing anything.

Benjamin listens to the snow on the roof. He thinks back to the way Lydia came into his life, running after him one day as he was walking home from school a couple of months before.

'You forgot this,' she called out, handing him his wool hat.

He stopped and thanked her. Then she looked at him strangely and said:

'You're Benjamin, aren't you?'

He asked her how she knew his name. Then she stroked his hair and told him that she had given birth to him.

'But I called you Kasper,' she said. 'I wanted your name to be Kasper.'

She handed him a tiny, pale blue knitted outfit.

'I made this for you when you were in my tummy,' she whispered.

He told her that his name was Benjamin Peter Bark, and that

he couldn't be her child. He felt bad for her, and he tried to speak calmly and kindly. She listened, then just shook her head wistfully.

'Ask your parents,' she said. 'Ask them if you're really their child. They won't tell you the truth. They couldn't have children. You'll be able to tell that they're lying. They're afraid of losing you, but you're not really their child. You're mine. I can tell you about your real background.'

'But I'm not adopted,' he said.

'I knew it . . . I knew they wouldn't have told you,' she said.

He thought about it, then realised that what she was saying could be true, because he'd felt different for a long time now.

Lydia smiled at him.

'I can't prove anything to you,' she said. 'You'll just have to trust your own instincts. You'll realise in time that it's true.'

They parted, but he saw her again the next day. They went to a café and talked for a long time. She told him she had been forced to give him up for adoption, but that she had never forgotten him. She had thought about him every day since he'd been taken away from her. She had missed him every minute of her life.

Benjamin told Aida everything, and they agreed that Erik and Simone shouldn't find out about this until he had had a chance to think it all through. He wanted to get to know Lydia first, wanted to think about whether he wanted her as his mother. Lydia started to contact him through Aida's email address. She sent him a photograph of the family grave.

'I want you to know who you are,' she said. 'This is where your family are buried, Kasper. One day we'll go there together, just you and me.'

Benjamin had almost started to believe her. He wanted to believe her. She was exciting. It felt odd for him to feel so special, so loved. She had given him things, little memories from her childhood, books, money and a camera. He in turn had given her drawings, things he had saved from his own childhood. She even managed to stop that kid Wailord from bullying him. One day she gave him a note that Wailord had written, swearing never to go near Benjamin and his friends again. His parents could never have managed anything like that. He started to think that his parents – people he had believed in all his life – were liars. He found himself annoyed at the way they never really spoke to him, never showed him that he meant anything to them.

He had been so incredibly stupid.

Then, a few days ago, Lydia started to talk about going to his house, being with him. She wanted his keys. He couldn't really see why she wanted them. He said he could let her in when she rang the bell. Then she got angry with him. She said she'd have to discipline him if he didn't obey her. He remembers being speechless. She explained that when he was very young she had given his parents a rod as a sign that she expected them to raise him properly. Then she just snatched his keys from his rucksack and said that she'd be the one who decided when she could visit her own child.

That was when he realised she was crazy.

The next day she was waiting for him. He walked over to her and very calmly said that he wanted his keys back and that he didn't want to see her again.

'Oh, Kasper,' she said. 'Of course you can have your keys.'

She gave them to him. He walked away, and she followed him. He stopped and asked if she'd understood that he didn't want to see her again.

Benjamin looks down at his body. He sees a big bruise that has spread across his knee. If his mum saw it she'd be in hysterics, he thinks.

Marek is standing looking out of the window, as usual. He coughs up some phlegm, then spits it on the window where he can see Jussi's body lying outside in the snow. Annbritt is sitting slumped at the table. She's doing her best not to cry, swallowing, clearing her throat and hiccoughing. When she went out and saw that Lydia had killed Jussi, she screamed until Marek pointed the rifle at her and told her he'd shoot her if she didn't stop wailing.

There's no sign of Lydia. Benjamin sits back against the wall and says in a hoarse voice:

'Marek, there's something you should know . . .'

Marek looks at Benjamin with eyes as black as peppercorns, then gets on the floor and starts doing push-ups.

'What do you want, you little shit?' he groans.

Benjamin swallows, which makes his throat sting.

'Jussi told me Lydia is going to kill you,' he lies. 'First she was going to kill him, then Annbritt, and then you.'

Marek goes on doing push-ups, then stands up with a sigh.

'Very funny.'

'It's what he said,' Benjamin says. 'She only wants me. She wants to be alone with me. It's true.'

'Really?'

'Yes, Jussi said she told him what she was going to do, that she was going to start by killing him, and now he's . . .'

'Shut up,' Marek snaps.

'Are you just going to sit and wait for your turn?' Benjamin asks. 'She doesn't care about you. She thinks we make a better family on our own, just me and her.'

'Did Jussi really say she was going to kill me?' Marek asks.

'I swear, she's going to . . .'

Marek laughs loudly and Benjamin stops speaking.

'I've already heard all the things people say to try to avoid pain,' he says with a smile. 'All the promises, all the little tricks, the deals.'

Marek turns nonchalantly towards the window again. Benjamin sighs and tries to think of something else to say when Lydia comes in. Her mouth is tight and thin, her face is very pale, and she's holding something behind her back.

'It's Sunday again,' she declares solemnly and closes her eyes.

'The fourth Sunday of Advent,' Annbritt whispers.

'I want us to relax and think about the past week,' she says slowly. 'Three days ago Jussi left us. He is no longer among the living. His soul is now in one of the seven celestial spheres. He will be torn to shreds for his treachery, through many thousands of incarnations as animals and insects.'

She pauses.

'Have you been thinking carefully?' she asks after a while.

They nod, and Lydia smiles happily.

'Kasper, come here,' she says in a subdued voice.

Benjamin tries to get up, and does his best not to grimace with pain, but Lydia still asks:

'Are you making faces at me?'

'No,' he whispers.

'We're a family, and we respect each other.'

'Yes,' he replies, with a sob in his throat.

Lydia smiles and pulls out the object she has been hiding behind her back.

100

Sunday morning, 20 December

Lydia shows Benjamin a large pair of scissors with wide blades.

'Then you won't have a problem accepting your punishment,' she says calmly as she puts the scissors down on the table without a trace of emotion in her face.

'But I'm just a kid,' Benjamin says, swaying.

'Stand still!' she roars at him. 'Why is it never enough? Why do you never, ever understand? I struggle. I do everything I possibly can to make this family good and pure. I just want it to work.'

Benjamin is crying with his head bowed, deep, hoarse sobs.

'We're a family, aren't we?'

'Yes,' he says. 'Yes, we are.'

'So why do you behave like this? Going behind our backs, betraying and deceiving us, stealing from us, saying horrible things and spoiling everything . . .? Why would you do that to me? Poking your nose where it doesn't belong, gossiping and spreading lies?'

'I don't know,' Benjamin says. 'I'm sorry.'

Lydia picks up the scissors. She's breathing heavily now, and her face is sweating. Her cheeks and neck are flushed.

'You will be punished, and then we'll all move on from this,' she says brightly.

She looks over at Annbritt and Marek.

'Annbritt,' she says. 'Come here.'

Annbritt, who has been sitting staring at the wall, walks over hesitantly. Her eyes look nervous and her chin is trembling.

'Cut his nose off,' Lydia says.

Annbritt's face turns bright red. She looks at Lydia, then at Benjamin. Then she shakes her head.

Lydia slaps her hard across the face. She grabs Annbritt's thick upper arm and drags her closer to Benjamin.

'Kasper has been sticking his nose in places it doesn't belong, so now he's going to lose it.'

Annbritt rubs her cheek, looking almost detached, then she picks up the scissors. The blades glint in front of Benjamin and he looks at the woman's nervous face, sees her eyes and mouth twitching as her hands begin to shake.

'Do it!' Lydia roars.

Annbritt holds the scissors in front of Benjamin, crying loudly now.

'I'm a haemophiliac,' Benjamin whimpers. 'I'll bleed to death if you do this! I'm a haemophiliac!'

Annbritt's hands tremble as she snaps the blades together in front of him. She drops the scissors on the floor.

'I can't,' she sobs. 'I can't do it . . . The scissors hurt my hands, I can't hold them.'

'This is a family,' Lydia says in a strict, weary voice as she leans down laboriously and picks up the scissors.

'You will obey and respect me – do you hear?'

'I just said, the scissors hurt my hands! They're too big for . . .'

'Be quiet,' Lydia interrupts, hitting her hard across the face with the handle of the scissors. Annbritt moans, leans unsteadily against the wall and holds one hand over her bleeding lips.

'Sundays are for discipline,' Lydia says, panting.

'I can't,' she pleads. 'Please . . . I can't.'

'Come on,' Lydia says impatiently.

Annbritt just shakes her head and whispers something.

'What did you say? Did you call me a cunt?'

'No, no,' Annbritt sobs, holding her hand out. 'I'll do it,' she sniffs. 'I'll cut his nose off. I'll help you. It doesn't hurt that much. It'll soon pass.'

With a look of satisfaction, Lydia hands her the scissors. Annbritt goes over to Benjamin, pats him on the head and whispers quickly:

'Don't be scared. Just run, run away as fast as you can.'

Benjamin looks at her quizzically, trying to read the look in her frightened eyes and trembling mouth. Annbritt raises the scissors, but turns towards Lydia instead and lashes out. There's no real force behind it, though, and Benjamin sees Lydia counter the blow. Marek grabs Annbritt's wrist, and pulls her arm out of the socket. Annbritt shrieks with pain. Benjamin is already out of the room by the time Lydia picks the scissors up off the floor, and sits astride Annbritt's chest. Annbritt is shaking her head side to side, trying to escape.

As Benjamin passes the porch and emerges into the freezing cold of the front steps, he can hear Annbritt screaming and coughing.

Lydia wipes the blood from her cheek, and looks around for the boy.

Benjamin walks quickly along the cleared path.

Marek grabs the rifle from the wall, but Lydia stops him.

'This is a good lesson,' she says. 'Kasper has no shoes, and he's only wearing pyjamas. He'll come running back to Mother when he's cold enough.'

'Or he'll die,' Marek says.

Benjamin is trying to ignore the pain as he runs between the rows of vehicles. He's so thirsty that he's eating snow as he runs. He can't feel his feet any more. Marek is yelling at him from inside the house. He knows he can't outrun him, he's too small and too weak. His best option is to hide in the darkness somewhere, then make his way down to the lake once things have calmed down. Maybe there'll be someone fishing through the ice.

Benjamin has to stop to catch his breath. He listens for footsteps behind him, then looks over at the dark forest and starts to move again. He's not going to get much further. His whole body is burning with pain and cold. He tumbles over and crawls under a large tarp covering a tractor, crawls beneath the next vehicle and then stands up. He realises that he's standing between two old buses. He finds an open window in one of the buses, then manages to climb up on top of the wheel and slip through the opening. In the darkness he makes his way through the bus until he finds a pile of old rugs on one of the seats, and wraps himself in them.

101

Sunday morning, 20 December, fourth Sunday of Advent

Vilhelmina Airport is a red-painted building in the middle of a white, flat plain. It's ten o'clock in the morning, but there's barely any daylight. Floodlights illuminate the concrete landing strip. After an hour and a half flight, their plane is now taxiing slowly towards the terminal.

The arrivals hall is warm and surprisingly cosy. Christmas music is playing over the loudspeakers, and the smell of coffee comes from what seems to be a combination newsstand, information desk and café. An array of handicrafts that are supposedly Sami hang outside the shop – butter knives, wooden cups, knapsacks.

Joona takes out his phone as Erik points at a taxi-minibus waiting outside the deserted exit. Joona shakes his head, and sounds increasingly irritated with whoever it is he's talking to. Erik and Simone can hear a gruff, tinny voice talking back to him. When Joona ends the call the look on his face is impossible to read. His eyes are glinting icily.

'What is it?' Erik asks.

Joona cranes his neck to look out of the window.

'The police officers who went out to the house still haven't been in touch,' he says, sounding distracted.

'That's not good,' Erik says quietly.

'I'll talk to the station.'

Simone pulls Erik aside.

'We can't just sit here waiting for them.'

'We're not going to,' Joona replies. 'We're going to get a car – it should be here by now.'

'God,' Simone sighs. 'Everything takes such a ridiculously long time.'

'Distances are different up here,' Joona says with a sharp look.

Simone shrugs. They head towards the exit, and as they pass through the door a different, drier sort of cold hits them.

Two dark-blue cars pull up in front of them, and two men dressed in orange mountain rescue outfits get out.

'Joona Linna?' one of the men asks.

Joona nods.

'We were told to provide you with a car.'

'Mountain rescue?' Erik queries anxiously. 'Where are the police?'

One of the men straightens up and explains tersely:

'There's not always much of a difference up here. Police, customs, mountain rescue – we're always helping each other out.'

The other man adds:

'And there aren't a lot of people around right now because of the holiday . . .'

They stand there in silence. Erik looks desperate now. He opens his mouth to say something, but Joona gets in first:

'Have you heard anything from the patrol who went out to the house?' he asks.

'Not since seven o'clock this morning,' one of the men replies.

'How long does it take to get there?'

'You should plan on a couple of hours if you're heading out to Sutme.'

'Two and a half,' the other adds. 'Given the time of year.'

'Which car are we taking?' Joona asks impatiently, starting to walk towards one of them.

'Whichever,' one of the men says.

'Give us the one with most petrol,' Joona says.

'I've got forty-five litres in mine,' one of the men says quickly.

'Ten more than me, then.'

'Good,' Joona says, opening the door.

They get in the warm car. Joona takes the keys, then asks Erik to tap the coordinates into the brand new GPS.

'Hang on,' Joona calls to the men when they're about to get in the other car.

They stop.

'The patrol that went out to the house this morning – were they mountain rescue as well?'

'Yes, they were.'

They head northwest towards Volgsjön, then turn right onto highway 45. According to the GPS, after ten kilometres they will turn off onto a winding road that will take them the last eighty kilometres to Klimpfjäll and Daimadalen.

They drive in silence. Once Vilhelmina is behind them and they're on the road to Sutme, they notice the sky getting brighter around them. It's an odd, soft light that seems to open up the view. They can make out the contours of the mountains and lakes around them.

'It's getting lighter,' Erik says.

'But it shouldn't get lighter for several weeks,' Simone says.

'The snow catches the light of the clouds,' Joona says.

Simone leans her forehead against the car window. They drive past a snow-covered forest interspersed with vast white areas where the trees have been felled, as well as dark lakes and bogs that spread out like huge dark fields. They pass signs bearing names like Jetneme and Trollklinten, and the Långsele River. In the darkness they can see a stunningly beautiful steep-sided lake called Mevattnet. It's bare and frozen, shimmering softly in the snowy light.

After an hour and a half of driving in a roughly northwesterly direction, the road starts to get narrower as it slopes down towards Borgasjön, a very large lake. They're close to the Norwegian border now, and the landscape rises up into tall, jagged mountains. A car coming towards them flashes its headlights at them. They pull over to the side of the road, and the other car stops and reverses back towards them.

'Mountain rescue,' Joona says when he sees it's the same sort of car as theirs.

Joona winds the window down and fresh, ice-cold air sucks the heat out of the car.

'Are you the people from Stockholm?' one of the men in the car shouts at them in a strong Finnish accent.

'Yes, we are,' Joona replies in Finnish. 'Metropolitan know-nothings.'

They laugh, and Joona reverts to Swedish.

'Are you the guys who went to the house? They couldn't reach you.'

'Radio shadow,' the man says. 'Waste of petrol. There's nothing up there.'

'Nothing? No signs of activity round the house?'

The man shakes his head.

'We went through the layers of snow.'

'You did what?' Erik asks.

'It's snowed five times since December 12th – so we looked for evidence in the five different layers.'

'Good work,' Joona says.

'That's why it took us so long.'

'So no one's been up there?' Simone asks.

The man shakes his head.

'Not since the 12th, like I said.'

'Damn,' Joona says quietly.

'Are you coming back with us, then?' the man asks.

Joona shakes his head.

'If we've come all the way from Stockholm, we're not turning back now.'

The man shrugs.

'Well, suit yourselves.'

The men wave and continue east.

They drive on in silence. Joona, Erik and Simone are thinking the same thing: that this trip could be a fatal mistake. They may have been lured in the wrong direction, into a crystalline world of snow and ice while Benjamin is being held somewhere else entirely, defenceless, without his medication. He may even be dead already.

It's noon, but this far north, deep in the forests of Västerbotten, it feels like it's the middle of the night.

102

Sunday morning, 20 December

When they reach Jussi's house, the air is icy, still and thin. They walk the last stretch across the snow. Joona draws his pistol. He's thinking about how long it's been since he saw real snow and felt the sting of dry cold in his nose.

Three small buildings are arranged in a U-shape. The snow has thrown an undulating blanket over the roofs and blown in drifts against the sides, right up to the small windows. Erik looks around. The tyre-tracks made by the mountain rescue team's car are clearly visible, as are their footprints around the buildings.

'Oh, God,' Simone whispers, hurrying forward.

'Wait,' Joona says.

'There's no one here, it's empty, we've . . .'

'It seems empty,' Joona interrupts. 'That's all we know.'

Simone waits, shivering, as Joona walks across the snow towards the buildings. He stops at one of the narrow, oblong windows, leans forwards and looks in at a wooden chest and a few rag-rugs on the floor. The chairs have been placed on top of the dining table, and the fridge has been emptied and left open.

Simone looks at Erik. He's acting strangely, walking jerkily around on the snow, then standing in the middle of the yard between the buildings and looking around. She's about to ask what's the matter when he declares in a loud, clear voice:

'This isn't the place.'

'There's no one here,' Joona says wearily.

'I mean,' Erik says, in an almost shrill voice, 'I mean that this isn't the haunted house.'

'What are you saying?'

'It's the wrong house. Jussi's haunted house is bright green. I heard him describe it. There's a pantry off the porch, a tin roof with rusty nails, a satellite dish up on the roof, and the yard is full of old cars and buses and tractors . . .'

Joona gestures with his hand:

'This is his registered address.'

'Well it's the wrong place.'

Erik takes a couple of steps towards the building again, then he looks seriously at Simone and Joona and says firmly:

'This isn't the haunted house.'

Joona curses and pulls out his mobile phone, then curses again when he remembers that there's no signal.

'Well, we're not going to find anyone to ask out here, so we'll have to drive back until we get a signal again,' he says, getting back in the car. They reverse back towards the road, and just as they're about to pull away Simone sees a dark figure between the trees. He's standing perfectly still, watching them with his arms hanging by his sides.

'Over there!' she cries. 'There's someone over there!'

103

Sunday morning, 20 December

The forest on the other side of the road is dense and dark, and the trees are sagging under the weight of the snow. Simone gets out of the car even though Joona tells her to wait. The car's headlights are reflecting off the windows of the house, and Simone tries to use the light to see between the trees. Erik catches up with her.

'I saw someone,' she whispers.

Joona draws his pistol and follows them. Simone walks quickly towards the edge of the forest. She spots the man again, a little further in the trees.

'Hello, wait!' she calls.

She runs a few steps, but stops when she sees his face. He's an old man, with a very wrinkled face. He's extremely short. He barely reaches her chest, and he's wearing a thick, stiff ski jacket and jeans. He's holding a pale green mobile phone in his hand, but slips it into his pocket.

'Sorry to disturb you,' Simone says.

He replies something that she doesn't understand, then looks down and mutters something. Erik and Joona are approaching cautiously. Joona has already tucked his pistol back inside his jacket.

'It sounds like he's speaking Finnish,' Simone says.

'Wait,' Joona says, and turns towards the man.

Erik hears Joona introduce himself, point at the car, then say Jussi's name. He's speaking Finnish, very clearly and calmly. The old man slowly nods, and takes out a packet of cigarettes. Then he leans his head back, as if he's looking or listening out for something. He shakes out a cigarette, looks at it, then asks Joona a question in a lilting, melodic voice before shaking his head sadly. He looks at Erik and Simone with a sympathetic expression on his face. When he offers them the packet of cigarettes, Erik has the presence of mind to take one, thank him, and use the proffered lighter.

The Sami breaks the filter off his cigarette and lights it. Simone hears him explain something at great length to Joona. He breaks a twig from one of the trees and starts to draw in the snow. Joona leans over, points and asks something. Then he takes a notepad from his pocket and copies the map. Simone whispers 'Thank you', then they head back towards the car. The little man turns around, points into the trees, then disappears along a path through the forest.

They walk quickly back to the car. They left the doors open and the seats are now so cold that they sting their backs and thighs.

Joona gives Erik the map he copied from the old man's drawing.

'He spoke a peculiar kind of Umeå Sami, so I didn't understand all of it. He talked about the Kroik family's land.'

'But he knew Jussi?'

'Yes. If I understood correctly Jussi has another house, a hunting cabin even further in the forest. There's supposed to be a lake ahead on the left. Then we drive to a place where three large stones have been erected in memory of the Samis' former summer grazing ground. The snowplough doesn't go any further than that, so we have to walk north from there until we see an old camper.'

Joona looks at Simone and Erik with a wry smile and adds:

'The old man said that if we go through the ice on Djuptjärnen, then we've gone too far.'

Forty minutes later they slow down and stop in front of the three standing stones. The stones shimmer in the car's headlights for a few seconds, then disappear.

Joona parks the car at the edge of the forest, then says that he should probably try to camouflage it. He cuts a few fir branches but there's no time to do more. He glances up at the starry sky, then sets off as fast as he can. The others follow him. There's a thin, hard crust on top of the deep, soft snow. They move as quietly as they can. The old man's directions are good: after a kilometre and a half they see a rusty old camper. They turn off the path, and realise that people have walked this way before. They see smoke coming from the chimney of the house below. Light seeping from the windows illuminates mint-green walls.

This is Jussi's house, Erik thinks. This is the haunted house.

The large yard is littered with snow-covered vehicles that form a bizarre labyrinth.

They move slowly towards the house, making their way through the narrow passageways between the cars, buses, tractors, ploughs and scooters.

Suddenly they see a figure dart quickly across the window of the cabin. Erik can't hold back any longer and starts to run towards the house. Simone follows him, gasping for breath. They hurry across the snow to the edge of a dug-out path. A shovel and an aluminium sled are leaning against the house. They hear a muffled scream, then quick, sporadic thuds. Someone looks out of the window. A branch snaps over by the edge of the forest, and the door of the woodshed slams shut.

104

Sunday morning, 20 December

The person at the window has vanished and all they can see is the snow swirling through the air. Suddenly the door is thrown open and Simone and Erik are dazzled by the abrupt light. Someone is shining a torch at them. They squint and shield their eyes with their hands in order to see.

'Benjamin?' Erik calls out.

The beam of light sinks to the ground and he sees that the figure standing in front of them is Lydia. She's holding a large pair of scissors in her hand. The light from the torch illuminates a shape in the snow. It's Jussi. His face is bluish-grey, covered in ice. His eyes are closed, and there's an axe sticking out of his chest. He's covered with frozen blood. Simone is standing silently beside Erik, and he can hear from her shallow, frightened breathing that she's seen the body as well. At that moment he realises that Joona isn't with them. He must have gone another way. Erik thinks: I can creep up on Lydia from behind if I manage to hold her attention long enough.

'Lydia,' Erik says. 'Good to see you again.'

She stands still, just looking at them without saying a word. The scissors glint in her hand, swinging idly. The light from the torch reflects off the grey surface of the path.

'We've come to get Benjamin,' Erik explains calmly.

'Benjamin?' Lydia says. 'Who's that?'

'He's my son,' Simone says, half-swallowing her words.

Erik tries to gesture at her to keep quiet, and maybe she sees it, because she takes a step back and attempts to control her breathing.

'I haven't seen anyone else's son. Just my own,' Lydia says slowly.

'Lydia, listen to me,' Erik says. 'If we can have Benjamin we'll just walk away and forget all about this. I promise, I'll never hypnotise anyone . . .'

'But I haven't seen him,' Lydia repeats, looking at the scissors. 'It's just me and my Kasper here.'

'Just let us give him his medication,' Erik pleads, and notices that his voice has started to shake.

Lydia is in the perfect position now, he thinks feverishly, she has her back to the house, all Joona has to do is sneak into the house from the back, then overpower her from behind.

'I want you to leave now,' she says curtly.

Erik thinks he can see someone moving along the row of vehicles off to one side of the house. A wave of relief rushes through him. A wary look appears on Lydia's face and she raises the light and shines it towards the woodshed, then across the snow.

'Kasper needs medicine,' Erik says.

Lydia lowers the torch again. Her voice is hard and cold.

'I'm his mother. I know what he needs,' she says.

'You're right, of course you're right,' Erik replies quickly. 'But if you just let us give Kasper some medicine . . . you can raise him, discipline him. It is Sunday, after all, and . . .'

Two people come around the end of the house. Joona is in front, walking stiffly. Marek is behind him, holding a hunting-rifle against his back.

Lydia smiles and steps up onto the snow from the dug-out path.

'Shoot them,' she says bluntly, then nods at Simone. 'Her first.'

'There are only two cartridges in the rifle,' Marek replies.

'Do it however you want, as long as you do it,' she says.

'Marek,' Erik says. 'They suspended me. I wish I could have helped you to . . .'

'Shut up,' he snaps.

'You'd started talking about what happened in the big house in Zenica-Doboj.'

'I can show you what happened,' Marek says, looking at Simone with calm, sparkling eyes.

'Just get on with it,' Lydia sighs, looking impatient.

'Lie down,' Marek tells Simone. 'And take your jeans off.'

She doesn't move. Marek turns the rifle on her and she backs away. Erik steps forward and Marek quickly aims at him instead.

'I'll shoot him in the stomach,' Marek says. 'Then he can watch while we're having fun.'

'Just do it,' Lydia says.

'Wait,' Simone says, and starts to unbutton her jeans.

Marek spits in the snow and takes a step towards her. He doesn't seem entirely sure what to do. He glances at Erik, and swings the gun towards him again. Simone's eyes are downcast. He aims at her with the rifle, first at her head, then at her stomach.

'Don't do this,' Erik says.

Marek lowers the rifle again and moves closer to Simone. Lydia steps back. Simone starts to pull down her jeans and underwear.

'Hold the rifle,' Marek says quietly to Lydia.

She steps forward slowly. There's a clicking sound from among the snow-covered vehicles. Then there's a loud roaring noise. It's an engine starting up. Bright lights come to life under the crust of snow, and the ground at their feet suddenly lights up, dazzling white. An engine howls and roars, and the snow starts to move, as an old bus covered in a large tarp rumbles out of the snow bank and heads straight for them.

105

Sunday morning, 20 December

When Marek turns to look at the bus, Joona moves with astonishing speed. He grabs the barrel of the rifle. Marek clings to it, but is forced to take a step forward. Joona punches him hard in the chest, and tries to kick his legs out from under him, but Marek doesn't fall. The barrel hits the top of Joona's head and slides across his scalp. Marek's fingers are so cold that he loses his grip on the weapon. It spins through the air and lands in front of Lydia. Simone rushes towards it, but Marek grabs her by the hair and jerks her back.

The bus has got caught on a small pine tree and the engine is roaring. Exhaust fumes and churned-up snow fill the air. Its front door keeps opening and closing with a pneumatic wheezing sound.

The engine revs harder again. Its wheels are spinning, making the snow-chains clank and rattle.

'Benjamin!' Simone screams. 'Benjamin!'

Benjamin's confused face is visible through the windshield. His nose is bleeding. Lydia runs towards the bus clutching Marek's rifle and Erik follows her. Lydia pushes through the door and yells something at Benjamin, then she hits him with the barrel of the gun and drags him out of the driver's seat. Erik doesn't get there in time. The bus rolls backwards, swings sharply to one side and begins to careen down the slope towards the lake. Erik yells at Lydia to stop, and rushes after them along the path that's been carved through the snow.

Marek won't let go of Simone's hair. She's screaming as she tries to pry his fingers loose. Joona moves quickly sideways, lowers his shoulder, spins his body and rams his clenched fist up from below, hitting Marek with full force in his armpit. His arm snaps back as if it were broken. Simone, suddenly free to move, scrambles away, then sees the scissors lying on the snow. Marek lashes out with his other hand, but Joona deflects the blow and puts his body weight behind his elbow as he slams it into Marek's neck, breaking his collarbone with a dull snapping sound. Marek falls to the ground screaming. Simone lunges for the scissors but Marek kicks her in the stomach. He grabs them and sweeps them back in a wide arc with his functioning arm. Simone screams when she sees Joona's face stiffen as the blades penetrate his right thigh. Blood squirts onto the snow. Joona stays on his feet. He's holding his cuffs in his hand. He uses them to punch Marek above his left ear. It's a hard blow. Marek stands absolutely still, and tries to say something as he stares straight ahead. Blood is trickling from his ear and nose. Breathing hard, Joona pushes him onto his stomach and cuffs his limp hands behind his back.

Erik is gasping for breath as he rushes after the bus in the darkness. The rear lights are shining in front of him, and the beam of the headlights is flickering across the trees ahead. There's a bang as one of the side-mirrors gets knocked off by a tree.

Erik hopes that the cold will help his son – the fact that it's below freezing might lower his body temperature just enough for Benjamin's blood to thicken slightly, maybe enough for him to survive even though he's been injured.

The ground falls away steeply behind the house. Erik stumbles on something hidden beneath the snow, but gets back up again. The bus is like a shadow in the distance, a silhouette surrounded by a fuzzy glow.

The bus brakes, but then he sees it turn and head towards the ice instead. He screams at her to stop.

One of the ropes gets caught on the jetty and pulls the tarp from the roof.

As Erik approaches the beach he can smell diesel. The bus is already twenty metres out onto the lake.

He slips down the slope, badly out of breath now, but keeps running.

Then the bus stops. Panic rises to his throat as Erik watches the rear lights tilt upwards, like someone slowly raising their eyes.

The ice is making a terrible rumbling, creaking sound. He stops at the edge and tries to see what's happening. Erik realises the ice has cracked. The bus has gone through. The wheels are spinning in reverse, but they only churn the ice up even more.

Erik snatches up the lifebelt from the stand on the beach and starts to run across the ice, his heart thudding in his chest. There are repeated creaking, splashing sounds as the ice breaks up.

Erik thinks he can see a white face in the rolling water behind the bus.

'Benjamin!' he cries.

Waves lap up onto the ice, making it slippery. He ties the line attached to the lifebelt around his waist, knotting it tightly so he doesn't let go. He throws it into the dark water, but he can't see anyone there now. The front-mounted engine is roaring. The red glow of the rear lights spreads across the icy slush and snow.

The front of the bus is sinking. The headlights disappear beneath the water. Only the roof is visible now. The engine suddenly cuts out, and the silence feels peculiar after so much noise. The ice is still creaking and hissing, and the black water bubbles.

Erik sees that both Benjamin and Lydia are still inside the bus. The floor is sloping badly, and they're trying to move towards the rear. Benjamin is clinging onto a handrail. The roof at the front is almost underwater now. Erik hurries towards the hole in the ice and leaps across to the bus. In the distance he can hear Simone shouting. Erik crawls over to the hatch in the roof, stands up and kicks it in. Splinters spray across the seats and floor. He climbs in, dangling from his arms, and manages to put his feet onto the back of one of the seats and clamber down.

Benjamin looks terrified. He's dressed in nothing but his pyjamas, blood is trickling from his nose and he has a small scratch on his cheek.

'Dad,' he yells.

Erik turns to see what he's staring at, and sees Lydia standing at the back of the bus with a fixed look on her face. She's clutching the rifle and her mouth is bleeding. The driver's seat is now underwater. The bus lurches and the floor slopes even more. Water is pouring in past the rubber seal around the door.

'We have to get out of here,' Erik cries.

Lydia just shakes her head slowly.

'Benjamin,' he says, without taking his eyes off Lydia. 'Climb up on me and out through the hatch in the roof.'

Benjamin doesn't answer, but he does as Erik says. He makes his way over to him unsteadily, climbs onto one of the seats, then up on Erik's back and shoulders. When he reaches the open hatch with his hands Lydia raises the rifle and fires. Erik feels a jolt in his shoulder so powerful that it knocks him over, but it isn't until he gets back up that he feels the pain and sees the blood running down his arm. Benjamin is dangling from the hatch. Erik goes over and, with his one good arm, helps him up. He can see Lydia raising the rifle towards him again. Benjamin is already on the roof when the gun goes off. Lydia misses. The bullet flies past Erik's hip and a large window behind him shatters. Icy water gushes into the bus. Things are happening quickly now. Erik tries to reach the hatch in the roof but the bus lurches sideways and he ends up underwater.

106

Sunday morning, 20 December

The shock from the sudden cold makes Erik pass out for a couple of seconds. When he comes to, he kicks his legs in panic, breaks the surface and fills his lungs with air. The bus is starting to sink into the black water. It rolls again, and he hits his head and finds himself underwater again. His ears are roaring, and he's enveloped by unbelievable cold. Through the windows he sees the headlights shining down into the depths of the lake. His heart is thudding in his chest. His face and head feel horribly tight. He can see Lydia under the water, she's clinging onto one of the handrails in the back row. He can see the open hatch in the roof, and the window that was shot out. He knows that the bus is sinking. He has to swim out. There's not a moment to lose. He has to fight, but his arms won't work. He's almost weightless, and he can't feel his legs. He tries to move, but has no coordination.

Erik notices that he's surrounded by a cloud of blood from the wound in his shoulder.

His eyes meet Lydia's. They hang in the cold water, looking at each other.

Lydia's hair is swaying with the currents of the water, and tiny bubbles of air are streaming from her nose like a string of pearls.

Erik needs to take a breath. His throat is tightening, but he resists his lungs' efforts to inhale. His temples are throbbing and a white light is flickering inside his head.

His body temperature is so low that he's on the verge of losing consciousness. There's a ringing tone, shrill and piercing, getting louder in his ears.

Erik thinks about Simone, and Benjamin. It feels like a dream, floating in the icy water. With remarkable clarity he realises that he is going to die, and his stomach clenches with angst.

He's lost all sense of direction, of his own body, of light and darkness. The water feels warm, almost hot now. He knows that he's going to have to open his mouth soon and just give up, let his lungs fill with water and let the end come. He feels the rope around his waist tighten. He had forgotten that he had tied the lifebelt around himself. Now it's caught on something. He's being pulled hard to one side. He can't help himself, he has no strength left. His limp body slips around a pole and then up through the hatch in the roof. The back of his head hits something, one of his shoes comes off, and then he's out in the dark water. As he is carried upwards, he watches the bus sinking into the depths without him. He can barely see Lydia inside the illuminated cage as it sinks quietly towards the bottom of the lake.

107

Thursday, 24 December

Simone, Erik and Benjamin are travelling into Stockholm beneath a dark sky. The air is heavy with rain and the city is suffused with an almost purple light. Colourful lights are hanging from Christmas trees and along the railings of balconies, and the shop windows are full of elves, tinsel, and stars.

The taxi-driver who drops them off at the Birger Jarl Hotel is wearing an elf's hat. He waves gloomily at them as he drives off, and they see that he has a plastic Santa Claus stuck to the taxi sign on the roof.

Simone looks at the lobby and the unlit windows of the hotel restaurant. It feels strange to stay in a hotel when you're only a couple of hundred metres away from home.

'But I really don't want to go back to our flat again,' she says.

'Of course not,' Erik says.

'Never again.'

'Me neither,' Benjamin says.

'What should we do?' Erik asks. 'See a film?'

'I'm hungry,' Benjamin says quietly.

Erik was hypothermic by the time the helicopter reached the hospital in Umeå. The gunshot wound wasn't serious. The half-jacketed bullet had passed straight through his left shoulder-muscle and only grazed the bone. After his operation he was put in a room with Benjamin, who had been taken in for observation and rehydration. He hadn't suffered any serious bleeding, and made a quick recovery. After just one day in the hospital he started asking when he could go home. At first Erik and Simone were reluctant to agree. They would have preferred that he stay in the hospital longer, both because of his condition, and so that he could see a counsellor to help him deal with what he had been through.

His psychologist, Kerstin Bengtsson, seemed overworked, and didn't really appear to appreciate the danger Benjamin had been in. After talking to Benjamin for forty-five minutes, she declared that the boy was doing very well under the circumstances, and that Erik and Simone should let him deal with everything at his own pace.

They wondered if she was just trying to make them feel better. They were well aware that Benjamin was going to need serious help. They could see him digging through his memories. Clearly they were difficult to process, and they were worried he would bury them.

'I know a couple of really good psychologists,' Erik said. 'I'll talk to them as soon as we get home.'

'Good.'

'How about you? How are you feeling?' Erik went on.

'I've heard of this hypnotist who . . .'

'Watch out for him.'

'I know,' Simone smiled.

'Seriously, though,' he said after a while. 'We're all going to have to find a way to deal with this.'

She nodded, then looked even more thoughtful.

'Little Benjamin,' she said gently.

Erik went and lay down in the bed next to Benjamin's again, and Simone sat down on the chair between them. They looked at their son as he lay there, pale and thin, and gazed at his face as if he'd just been born.

'So, how are you feeling?' Erik asked him gently.

Benjamin turned his face away and looked out of the window. The darkness outside turned the glass into a blurry mirror as the wind battered against it.

108

Thursday, 24 December

After Benjamin climbed onto the roof of the bus, he heard the second shot. He slipped and almost fell into the water. At that moment he saw Simone standing on the edge of the hole in the ice. She shouted to him that the bus was sinking, that he had to get across to the ice. Benjamin saw the lifebelt in the rippling black water behind the bus, and jumped. He grabbed it and put it around him, then used it to swim to the ice. Simone pulled him out of the water. She took her jacket off and wrapped it around him, hugged him and told him a helicopter was on its way.

'Dad's still down there,' Benjamin screamed.

The bus was sinking rapidly. Big air-bubbles broke the surface. Simone stood up, and watched as the fragments of ice started to settle again on the rippling water.

She slumped back onto the ice and was holding Benjamin tightly when suddenly his body jerked. He was pulled from her arms. The rope from the lifebelt ran in a taut line across the ice and down into the water. Benjamin was being dragged backwards. He fought against it, but his bare feet were sliding across the ice as he screamed. Simone grabbed him, and they slid closer to the edge together.

'It's Dad!' Benjamin yelled at Simone. 'He had the rope tied around his waist!'

Her face took on a fixed, determined look. She grabbed the

lifebelt, hooked both arms round it, and tried to dig her heels into the ice. Benjamin grimaced with pain as they kept being pulled closer to the water. The line was so taut that it was making a sawing sound as it dragged across the edge of the ice. Then the tug of war suddenly reversed: it was still heavy, but they could move backwards, away from the water. Then suddenly there was almost no resistance at all. They had pulled Erik through the hatch in the roof of the bus and now he was floating towards the surface. A few moments later, Simone was able to drag him onto the ice. He lay there on his stomach, coughing and sputtering as a red stain spread out beneath him.

When the police and ambulance arrived at Jussi's cabin, they found Joona in the snow with a makeshift tourniquet around his thigh, next to a bellowing Marek. Jussi's frozen corpse was lying there with the axe in his chest at the bottom of the porch steps. The police and mountain rescue team found another survivor inside the house: Jussi's girlfriend Annbritt, who had hidden inside the wardrobe in the bedroom. She was bleeding from a cut on her face when they found her huddled up behind the clothes like a small child. The paramedics carried her to the waiting ambulance for emergency treatment.

Two days later police divers went into the lake to recover Lydia's body. The bus was standing on its six wheels at a depth of sixty-four metres, as if it had just stopped to pick up passengers. One of the divers went in through the front door and shone his torch across the seats. The rifle was lying on the floor at the end of the aisle. It wasn't until he shone the light upwards that he found Lydia. She had drifted up and was floating with her back pressed against the roof of the bus, her arms and head hanging down. The skin of her face had already started to split and loosen. Her red hair was swaying gently in the current, her mouth looked relaxed, and her eyes were closed, as if she were asleep.

Benjamin had no idea where he had been kept for the first few days of his kidnapping. It's possible that Lydia kept him at her house, or maybe at Marek's, but he was drugged and he didn't really understand what was going on. He may have been given more injections when he started to come around. Those first days were just blank, completely missing.

He came to in the boot of the car while they were heading north. He found his mobile phone still on the cord around his neck. They had snatched him in the middle of the night, and it hadn't occurred to them that he would have his phone on him while he slept. He'd managed to call Erik, but they must have heard his voice from inside the car, and they took the phone away from him.

Then came the long, terrible days. Erik and Simone had only really managed to get him to tell them fragments of it. They knew little more than the fact that he had been forced to lie on the floor in Jussi's cabin with a dog-leash around his neck. Judging by his condition when he reached the hospital he'd had nothing to eat or drink for several days. One of his feet was frostbitten, but that would heal. He told them he managed to escape with Jussi and Annbritt's help, then said nothing for a while, before going on to explain that Jussi saved him when he tried to call home, and how Annbritt helped him run off into the snow, then Lydia cut off the end of her nose. Benjamin crept in amongst the old cars and crawled into one of the snow-covered buses through an open window. He bundled himself in a mouldy blanket, which had probably saved him from freezing to death. He fell asleep in there, and woke up several hours later when he heard his parents' voices.

'I didn't know if I was alive or not,' Benjamin whispered.

Then he heard Marek threaten them, and realised he was sitting in the driver's seat of the bus staring at the key in the ignition. Without really thinking about what he was doing he turned the key, and heard the engine sputter to life, before he drove towards where he thought Marek was standing.

Benjamin fell silent again, tears hanging from his eyelashes.

109

Thursday, 24 December

After two days in the hospital in Umeå, Benjamin was strong enough to start walking again. He went with Erik and Simone to see Joona, who was lying in the post-operative ward. His thigh had been badly damaged when Marek stabbed him with the scissors, but doctors said he should be back to normal after a few weeks' rest. A beautiful woman whose hair was in a soft braid draped over one shoulder was sitting beside him, reading out loud, when they went in. She introduced herself as Disa, a friend of Joona's for many years.

'We've got a reading group, and I have to make sure he keeps up,' Disa said in a Finnish-Swedish accent, putting the book down.

Simone saw that she was reading Virginia Woolf's *To the Lighthouse*.

'I'm renting a little flat from one of the mountain rescue guys,' Disa said with a smile.

'You'll get a police escort from Arlanda,' Joona said to Erik.

Both Simone and Erik had tried to object. They felt they needed to be alone with their son, and they didn't want to meet any more police officers for a while. When Benjamin was discharged Simone immediately organised plane tickets home, then went to get coffee. But for the first time the hospital cafeteria was closed. The cafeteria had nothing but a jug of apple juice and some crackers. She went out to try to find a café somewhere, but everything was strangely deserted. A gentle calm lay over the city. She stopped at a bus station and just stood there for a while, staring off at the snow-covered tracks. Far off in the distance she could make out the river, its shimmering black water streaked with white ice.

Only then did she start to relax. It's over, she thought. They had Benjamin back.

When they arrived at Arlanda Airport they saw Joona's police escort waiting for them next to a dozen journalists armed with cameras and microphones. Without saying a word to each other they went to a different exit and caught a taxi.

Now they're standing awkwardly outside the Birger Jarl Hotel in Stockholm. They start walking, up Tule Street to Oden Street, then stop at the junction with Sveavägen and look round. Benjamin is wearing a tracksuit from the police's lost and found that is too big for him, and a wool hat that Simone bought for him at the airport, along with a pair of knitted Lovikka mittens. The Vasastan district of Stockholm is deserted and empty. Everything seems to be closed – the underground station, bus-stops and restaurants are all still and silent.

Erik looks at his watch. Four o'clock in the afternoon. A woman is hurrying along Oden Street carrying a large bag.

'It's Christmas Eve,' Simone suddenly says. 'It's Christmas Eve today.'

Benjamin looks at her in surprise.

'That would explain why everyone's been wishing us a Merry Christmas,' Erik says with a smile.

'What are we going to do?' Benjamin wonders.

'At least one place is open,' Erik says, pointing.

'We're going to have Christmas dinner at McDonald's?' Simone asks.

It starts to rain. Thin, icy drops fall on them as they hurry towards the fast-food restaurant tucked beneath Observatorielunden. It's an ugly, low-ceilinged restaurant squeezed beneath the ochre-coloured cylinder of Stockholm Central Library. A woman in her sixties is standing behind the counter. There are no other customers.

'I'd love a glass of wine,' Simone says. 'But I don't suppose there's any chance of that.'

'A milkshake,' Erik says.

'Vanilla, strawberry or chocolate?' the woman asks sourly.

Simone is on the verge of hysteria, but forces herself not to laugh and says with hard-won seriousness:

'Strawberry. Definitely strawberry.'

'Me too,' Benjamin adds.

The woman taps their order into the till with small, angry gestures.

'Is that everything?' she asks.

'Get a bunch of things,' Simone says to Erik. 'We'll go and sit down.'

She and Benjamin head off towards the empty tables.

'Window table,' she whispers, and smiles at Benjamin.

She sits down next to her son, holds him tight and feels tears run down her cheeks.

'Are you cold?' she asks.

Benjamin doesn't answer, he just leans against her and lets her kiss him on the head.

Erik puts one tray down on the table, then goes and gets a second one before he sits down.

'Lovely,' Benjamin says, sitting up.

Erik hands him a Happy Meal toy.

'Merry Christmas,' he says.

'Thanks, Dad,' Benjamin smiles, looking at the plastic-wrapped toy.

Simone looks at her child. He's frighteningly thin. But there's something else, too, she thinks. It's as if he's still weighed down by something. He seems to be focused in on himself, she thinks, like a reflection in a dark window.

When she sees Erik reach out and pat Benjamin on the cheek she starts to cry again. She turns away, apologises, and watches a plastic bag blow up against the window from a dustbin.

'Should we try to eat something?' Erik suggests.

As Benjamin is unwrapping a large burger, Erik's mobile phone rings. He looks at the screen and sees that it's Joona.

'Merry Christmas, Joona,' he says when he answers.

'Erik,' Joona says. 'Are you back in Stockholm now?'

'We're having our Christmas dinner.'

'Do you remember I told you we were going to find your son?'

'Yes, I remember.'

'You had your doubts, though, when we . . .'

'Yes,' Erik says.

'But I knew this would turn out OK,' Joona goes on, in his usual sombre Finnish tone.

'I didn't.'

'I know, I noticed,' Joona says. 'That's why there's something I need to say to you.'

'Oh?'

'What did I say?' he says.

'What do you mean?'

'I was right, wasn't I?'

'Yes,' Erik replies.

'Merry Christmas,' Joona says, and ends the call.

Erik stares ahead of him in surprise, then turns towards Simone. He looks at her translucent skin and wide mouth. The worry-lines around her eyes have deepened recently. She smiles at him, and then they both turn to look at Benjamin.

Erik gazes at his son for a long time. His throat hurts from trying not to cry. Benjamin is eating fries with a serious look on his face, lost in thought. His eyes are blank. He's lost in his memories and the gaps between them. Erik reaches out his good arm, squeezes his son's fingers, and Benjamin looks up.

'Merry Christmas, Dad,' Benjamin says with a smile. 'Here, have some of my fries.'

'How about we take the rest of the food with us and go see Grandpa?' Erik says.

'Seriously?' Simone asks.

'How much fun is it being stuck in the hospital?'

Simone smiles at him, then calls for a taxi. Benjamin goes over to the counter to get a bag for the food.

As their taxi slowly drives past Odenplan, Erik sees his family reflected in the window, superimposed over the Christmas tree outside in the square. They glide past the tree as if they're dancing around it. It stands there tall and sturdy, with hundreds of twinkling lights reaching all the way up to the shining star.